CW00421049

THE PUCKING WRONG GUY

THE PUCKING WRONG BOOK #2

C.R. JANE

JOIN C.R. JANE'S READERS' GROUP

Stay up to date with C.R. Jane by joining her Facebook readers' group, C.R.'s Fated Realm. Ask questions, get first looks at new books/series, and have fun with other book lovers!

Join C.R.'s Fated Realm

To all my red flag renegades.

ILY.

THE PUCKING WRONG GUY

I came to L.A. for my fresh start…and then my past showed up.

I'm happy. At least that's what I tell myself. I'm working hard to pursue my dreams. I'm finally out from under the thumb of my adopted parents.

I'm happy.

But then a 6'4 tattooed hockey star who thinks he's god shows up at the restaurant where I'm working…

And changes everything.

He tells me I'm the one. That he's been searching for me for years…

That he's never going to let me go.

*The question is…is Ari Lancaster going to break my heart? Or has my **Mr. Wrong** been the right guy all along…*

PLEASE READ...

Dear readers, please be aware that this is a darker style romance and as such can and will contain possible triggering content. Elements of this story are purely fantasy, and should not be taken as acceptable behavior in real life. Our love interest is possessive, obsessive, and the golden retriever stalker you have been waiting for. Ari Lancaster will do what it takes to get his girl.

Themes include ice hockey, stalking, manipulation, dark obsessive themes, sexual scenes. Our MC has issues with self hate, self harm, an eating disorder, and trauma from her parents' death is alluded to and described. Cheating is involved but not between the main love interests! Ari and Blake would never cheat on each other.

There are no harems or sharing involved. Ari Lancaster only has eyes for her.

Prepare to enter the world of the L.A. Cobras...you've been warned.

L.A. COBRAS

TEAM ROSTER

ARI LANCASTER	CAPTAIN, #24, DEFENSEMAN
WALKER DAVIS	CAPTAIN, #1, GOALIE
TOMMY RIVERS	ASST. CAPTAIN, #18, CENTER
EDDY WHITLOCK	#2, GOALIE
FRANKIE THOMAS	#6, RIGHT WING
JOHN SOTO	#19, LEFT WING
CALLUM SULLIVAN	#29, DEFENSEMAN
TYSON CREED	#8, DEFENSEMAN
CHASE YOUNG	#7, CENTER
DAMIEN TURNER	#23, DEFENSEMAN
RYAN MCAVOY	#32, LEFT WING
NATE BISHOP	#9, DEFENSEMAN
SAM WILLIAMSON	#21, CENTER
FLETCHER MARTINEZ	#10, RIGHT WING
LENNOX OLSON	#16, GOALIE
JAY SATHOFF	#33, WING
COLTON BATEMAN	#64, WING
ROMAN MARINO	#56 CENTER
ADAM ANDERSON	#20, DEFENSEMAN
MAXIM NIKOLAI	#3, DEFENSEMAN
SULLIVAN PETROV	#12, WING
DOMINIC MCKAY	#11, DEFENSEMAN
MANNY RICHARDSON	#4, WING

COACHES

KIM PALMER HEAD COACH
JONAS GRETZ, ASSISTANT COACH
COLT ARCHER ASSISTANT COACH
ZANE MARKOV, ASSISTANT COACH

THE PUCKING WRONG GUY PLAYLIST

THE ALCOTT
The National (feat. Taylor Swift)

CHAMPAGNE PROBLEMS
Taylor Swift

MAKING THE BED
Olivia Rodrigo

CHEAP HOTEL
Leon Else

SO GOOD
Halsey

HAPPIEST YEAR
Jaymes Young

WAR OF HEARTS
Ruelle

BRUISES
Lewis Capaldi

DYING IN LA
Panic! At The Disco

HOLD ON
Chord Overstreet

BRIGHT LIGHTS AND CITYSCAPES
Sara Bareilles

LOCKSMITH
Sadie Jean

HATE ME
Blue October

FALLING
Harry Styles

HATE MYSELF
NF

ANCHOR
Novo Amor

GHOST OF YOU
5 Seconds of Summer

LOVER
Taylor Swift

LISTEN TO THE FULL PLAYLIST HERE:
HTTPS://OPEN.SPOTIFY.COM/PLAYLIST/30VARKOESAUB3KVTJLA7NV

"I didn't hear him because my two Stanley Cup rings were plugging my ears."
—Goalie Patrick Roy

Hockey Boyfriends Anonymous ✔
@hockyboyfriends_anonymous

Bunnies, hold onto your panties, because this news is coming in hot. #sizzle Mr. Tall, Dark, and Handsome, Ari Lancaster himself, is no longer a Dallas Knight. #wtf A shock considering he just won his first Stanley Cup with his longtime team. In a news conference held today, the L.A. Cobras announced they had successfully completed a trade for the star defenseman. #welcometolalaland I've put my head to the ground bunnies, trying to figure out the reason. But so far I've got nothing. Tweet us if you hear any news. We have a feeling that whatever the reason is...it's going to be juicy.

12:00 PM · Sep 5, 2023 · Twitter for iPhone

32.6K Retweets   **18.9K** Quote Tweets   **74.8K** Likes

PROLOGUE
LAYLA

Before

My heart was a heavy stone in my chest as I walked hand in hand with my case worker toward the looming group home. The gray sky mirrored my mood, and the air seemed colder than usual. It had been just a few weeks since I lost my parents, and the pain was still so fresh, it was an open wound that would never heal.

I didn't see how it could.

The building was old and intimidating, its tall brick walls casting a shadow over the entrance. I swallowed hard, gripping my teddy bear even tighter to my chest for comfort. I wished I could turn back, that this was all just a bad dream, that I could go home and my parents would be waiting there with open arms.

My case worker, Ms. Thompson, squeezed my free hand gently. She had kind eyes and a warm smile, but they couldn't chase away the sadness that clung to me like a second skin. "It's going to be okay, sweetie," she whispered, her voice soft and soothing. I nodded, even though I didn't really believe her.

I was here because there was no one who wanted me. She could say otherwise, try to be positive and comforting about all of this, but that was the truth. I was alone. I had no one.

As we stepped inside, the hallway seemed to stretch forever in both directions. The walls were a dull beige, and the fluorescent lights overhead buzzed like angry bees. It smelled kind of musty, like old paper and cleaning supplies. The place didn't feel very welcoming.

Ms. Thompson led me toward a door at the end of the hallway, her footsteps echoing in the silence. We entered a small office where a stern-looking woman sat behind a desk cluttered with papers. She had gray hair pulled back into a tight bun, and her glasses perched on the edge of her nose.

"Ah, Ms. Thompson," the woman said, her voice brisk. "This must be our new arrival." She glanced at me, her eyes briefly softening before pressing back into a tight line. Her sharp eyes bored into mine with an intensity that sent chills through my body.

"Yes," Ms. Thompson replied, her tone respectful. "This is Layla."

I shifted nervously from foot to foot, clutching my teddy bear even tighter. I wished Mom and Dad were here. They always knew how to make me feel safe.

The woman and Ms. Thompson exchanged a few whispered words that I couldn't quite catch. My heart raced as I strained to listen, feeling like they were talking about something important.

"I heard about her parents," the woman said, her voice low. "Such a tragedy."

"Yes. This one is definitely a more difficult case," Ms. Thompson replied, her voice filled with sympathy.

"Have they figured out why he killed her?"

I felt a lump forming in my throat, and I stopped trying to listen. They were talking about Mom and Dad. My eyes welled up with tears, and I tried to blink them away. I didn't want the women to see me cry.

I also didn't want to think about Mom and Dad like *that*.

After a few more whispers, the woman smoothed her gray hair back, even though there wasn't a strand out of place in her severe bun. She stood and walked over to me before crouching to my level, her expression softening a little. "Hello, Layla," she said kindly. "My name is Mrs. Anderson. We're here to help you, okay?"

I nodded, my voice caught in my throat.

"Let's get you settled in." Mrs. Anderson held out a hand for me, and I instinctively grabbed it. It was cold and boney, nothing like my mom's hand. None of the strangers I'd been passed to since the police found me in our house had felt like Mom, though.

Mrs. Anderson didn't waste any time, leading me out of the office and down another hallway.

As I followed her, I wiped away a tear that had escaped, almost dropping my bear in the process.

The hallway we walked down was lonely feeling, each step echoing like a heartbeat in the stillness. Mrs. Anderson's footsteps were steady beside me, only a slightly reassuring presence as I ventured further into the unknown. The walls were lined with old photographs of children who had lived here before, their smiles frozen in time. I wondered where they were now.

Had they ever been happy?

We arrived at a door that Mrs. Anderson pushed open with a gentle creak. The room inside was small and simple, and cold. There were two beds with neatly made quilts, a desk with a chair, and a shelf with a few books. Dim light filtered through the curtains, casting a gray tinged glow over everything.

"This will be your room, Layla," Mrs. Anderson said, her

voice kind. "You'll be sharing it with Michelle. I'm sure she'll be by soon and you guys can get to know each other. Feel free to do whatever you want to make it your own."

Staring around, it didn't seem like Michelle had done anything to make it her own. My stomach trembled with even more nerves.

I looked around, feeling...grief. It wasn't my old room back at home, filled with familiar posters and the lingering scent of Mom's cooking. I knew I should be grateful to be here, since no one else had wanted me, but everything was wrong. The walls weren't painted a soft shade of lavender, pictures of our little family's adventures all over. The bed wasn't overflowing with stuffed animals. And there weren't flowers on the nightstand, like the ones Dad had brought me every week along with the ones he got Mom.

"Thank you," I whispered, a wobble in my words.

"You're welcome, dear," Mrs. Anderson replied with a soft smile, as she ignored the pain in my voice. "If you need anything, don't hesitate to ask. I'll send someone to give you a tour in a little while. Dinner will be at six in the main room."

I nodded, still struggling to find my words. She left me alone in the room, closing the door behind her. As I sat on the edge of the bed, my teddy bear clutched to my chest, a sense of loneliness washed over me. The tears I had held back earlier now streamed uncontrollably down my cheeks.

The more minutes that ticked by, the more my emotions swirled like a tempest, a violent storm I couldn't control. The pain of loss, the raw loneliness, it all crashed over me like a relentless wave, tearing through the fragile dam of my composure. I felt like I was drowning in an ocean of tears, each sob an echo of the ache buried deep within me. Panic clawed at my chest, a vicious beast threatening to break free.

The room, this alien space, seemed to constrict around me, a straightjacket of unfamiliarity that I couldn't escape. My heart raced, breaths came in shallow gasps. I was teetering on the edge of an abyss. The world spun, a dizzying dance that left me disoriented and struggling to find my footing.

Enough. I couldn't stay here. With a desperate gasp, I lurched off the bed, my vision a blur of saltwater, my teddy bear falling from my hands. I sprinted down the corridor, a mad dash to outrun the encroaching panic. I burst from the building and into the field behind the orphanage, the cool breeze on my face a sharp contrast to the turmoil inside.

I collapsed onto the grass, panic tightening its grip. It was as if the world had shattered, and I was lost in the debris. Then, from out of the chaos, a voice sliced through.

"Hey, hey, it's okay. Just focus on your breath. I'm right here."

I blinked through tear-soaked lashes and saw a boy standing there, concern shining from his eyes. He looked at me as though he really saw me. There was no pity like there had been in the eyes of the officers...of everyone. His deep green gaze was absent of the resignation that Ms. Thompson and Mrs. Anderson directed my way. No, all I saw in the depths of his stare was that he cared. His presence was like a lifeline in the storm, grounding me in the midst of my panic. His eyes were gentle, his voice soothing as he spoke.

"Deep breath, angel, and then exhale slowly. You're doing great."

The panic began to ebb away, replaced by a sense of calm that I hadn't thought possible.

For a minute, the frenzy was gone. The world around me disappeared until nothing but silence was left.

As the panic receded, I wiped away the remnants of my tears and peered up at him, a mix of gratitude and curiosity in my gaze.

The boy looked a little older than me, his hair a storm of wild black waves that seemed to have a mind of its own. His vibrant green eyes sparkled with mischief, and something about them made my heart race.

There was a smudge of dirt on his cheek and his grin was wide, like he knew a million secrets and couldn't wait to share all of them. His lips curved up with a natural feeling of confidence that I'd never seen in someone.

He stood there like he owned the world, his posture relaxed and ready for anything.

"Thank you," I finally managed to rasp out when I realized I was just staring at him.

His smile grew broader, like there was sunshine inside him he couldn't contain. "It's no biggie." His gaze darted over my face and I wiped at the tears still dripping down my cheeks. "I'm Ari, by the way."

My voice wavered as I replied, "Layla."

"Layla," he repeated, holding out his hand to help me off the ground.

I stared at it for a long minute, not understanding why taking it seemed like such a big decision.

When I finally reached out and grabbed it, my fate was sealed.

I just didn't know it yet.

CHAPTER 1

"**Y**ou got the fucking job!" Kelsey screamed into the phone, making me wince as I pulled it away from my ear so I didn't lose all my hearing. Waldo growled at the sound, lifting his head from the floor where he'd been napping in the sun streaming in from the window.

It took a second for what she'd said to sink in.

"I got it," I whispered, my fingers trembling as I touched my mouth in disbelief. Waldo's front paws landed on my leg, and he started whimpering, obviously sensing the tension suddenly coursing across my skin.

"L.A., baby!" She was screaming again, but this time, the noise didn't even touch me.

Because the longshot, life-changing thing I'd been trying not to think about, trying not to hope for…was finally coming true.

Clark's face flashed through my mind.

I hadn't even told him about it, because I didn't want to risk a fight about something that wasn't going to happen.

But now here it was, and…

Speak of the devil. My phone buzzed, signaling an incoming call.

Clark.

"I've got to take this," I told her, cutting off whatever else my agent was about to say as I switched over.

"Hi!" I squeaked out in an overly excited voice.

"Hey, baby. Ready for tonight?" he asked warmly.

My stomach churned just thinking about the party I was supposed to attend with him later that evening.

All those eyes.

My gaze darted to the mirror on the wall, tracing the lines of my body in the reflection, noting all the imperfections. All the things they'd all see.

All the things they'd think about me.

I studied the neat line of scars on my hip and swallowed my anxiety down. "Yep. Seven, right?"

"Yes," he answered. "I sent a dress for you. Can't wait to see you in it."

"Perfect," I whispered softly, squeezing my eyes shut as if that could take away the hot shame licking at my insides as I thought about how I'd look in that dress.

"I've got to jump into a meeting. I love you," he murmured, in a voice that should have given me butterflies.

"Goodbye," I whispered as the phone clicked, staring out the window of the tiny studio apartment I could barely afford. Clark knew it, too. He'd been asking me to move in with him for three months, but I'd always had an excuse.

How long until he got tired of my excuses...and then I was all alone?

I'd be all alone in L.A. though....

Waldo barked, as if he was offended by my thoughts.

I knelt down and buried my face against his soft black and white fur. "I'm not alone, am I, boy?" I cooed, a smile peeking at my lips as he lathered kisses all over my face. I stayed like that for a moment, soaking in the warmth of him before I stood up and glanced around the room.

My cramped studio apartment was a chaotic disaster. The exact opposite of the life I'd been forced to live after I'd been adopted. From the moment you walked through the door, it felt like you were diving into a whirlwind of colors, patterns, and creative clutter that would probably make no sense to anyone but me. Every inch of the small space was crammed with objects that spoke to my...eclectic personality.

The futon against the far wall functioned as both seating and my bed. Its cushions were worn, but I thought they still looked inviting, an assortment of throw pillows creating a nest where I often lost myself in books or daydreams.

Against another wall, a vintage record player stood proudly, surrounded by stacks of vinyl records collected from thrift stores and flea markets.

An old wooden coffee table, adorned with paint splatters from impromptu art sessions, acted as the centerpiece of my living space.

The kitchen area was compact, containing nothing more than a tiny stove, barely large enough to fit a single pot and a rusted old sink and mini fridge. Pots and pans were stacked precariously on open shelves, alongside an assortment of mismatched mugs and plates.

In one corner, a distressed bookshelf groaned under the weight of my extensive book collection. It was my personal library, filled with dog-eared pages and highlighted passages that had impacted my soul in one way or another.

There wasn't a closet in here, so my clothes hung from a clothing rack. Piles of shoes were tucked away in the corners, each pair scrounged up from my favorite thrift stores.

Clark hated this place.

He hated the color and how much stuff there was.

He couldn't understand that all I'd had when I'd gotten to that orphanage was a teddy bear. He couldn't understand the need I had to surround myself with things that were mine.

My adoptive parents didn't understand either. They'd offered to pay for a penthouse, and been...disappointed when I'd refused, wanting to try and make it on my own.

No one understood.

"One step at a time, Blake," I murmured to myself, pushing my dark thoughts away and striding toward the bathroom to grab the anxiety pills waiting for me before I started getting ready for tonight.

I took a deep breath in the elevator, cold dread sliding down my skin as the floors beeped by. The fabric of my dress whispered against me, elegance that I never quite got used to. The gown Clark had sent was a work of art, a masterpiece of pale pink satin and lace that flowed around me like a dream.

Its beauty was a reminder of the life I'd been thrust into—one of glamor and perfection that I'd never lived up to. My adoptive mother had expected refinement, and the fashion world had only reinforced it.

Tonight, like so many other nights, it felt like I was wearing a costume, one that didn't quite fit. I should be used to it; I've felt like that from the moment the Shepfields picked me up from that group home, changed my name, my identity, my world.

Perfection was the decree in that cold mansion they'd taken me to, woven into every corner like a delicate but unyielding thread. The only imperfection allowed was that Maura Shepfield couldn't have children.

Hence the need for me.

From the moment I entered that world, her impossible standards enveloped me, shaping my existence into a mosaic of precise expectations that went against everything my mom and dad had taught me. I was stuck in an intricate web spun from her vision of what life should be.

Maura Shepfield was the definition of opulence, with a fevered taste for the finest things that life had to offer. She'd projected this onto me like a mirror image.

The clothes I wore were always meticulously chosen. Every occasion, no matter how casual, demanded an aura of perfection that felt like armor I had to constantly wear.

It wasn't just about the clothes, though.

It was about the posture, the way I spoke, the way I held my fork during meals. She trained me to glide through life as if every step was choreographed, as if every word was scripted. My appearance and behavior were meant to be a canvas that reflected her, and any deviation from her expectations was met with sharp disappointment that cut deep into my skin.

In her world, even a speck of imperfection was a stain that tarnished the glossy veneer she worked so tirelessly to maintain. She believed that life was a performance, a grand stage where we were all actors in an elaborate play. And her role, it seemed, was that of the director, guiding every scene with precision and determination.

Her insistence on perfection had been a heavy weight on my shoulders since that first day they'd picked me up, a burden that left little room for me to breathe, to stumble...to exist. And amidst the glamor, the designer dresses, and the extravagant events, I often found myself wondering if there was a place for...me.

At the bottom of the stairs, I glanced toward the waiting car, a bitter ache settling in my chest that I refused to examine closely. Clark was standing outside the car waiting for me, a phone to his ear, his gaze dancing across me admiringly. I tried to return the grin...but I didn't have it in me.

What did he see when he looked at me?

Because I was sure he didn't see the *real* me.

He was his usual picture of beautiful sophistication. The only thing out of place was his black hair, which fell in calculated disarray over his forehead. He'd once told me he styled it that way because it made him look more personable. Turns out, he also thought everything was a performance. His vibrant green eyes stared at me with the same interest they'd had since that first night when we'd met. I couldn't find fault with him about that.

I'd seen him with his friends though, times when I'd gone to the bathroom and hovered in the hallway like a creep as I watched him smile and shine with them.

It wasn't the same smile and shine as when we were alone. He smiled at me like a burden...or maybe that was my imagination. I never could be too sure these days.

Or maybe that was just my crazy talking. Because as Mrs. Shepfield always said...only a fool wouldn't want Clark.

Dressed in a perfectly tailored tuxedo, the suit seemed to mold to his form as if it were a second skin. There was a tension in his posture right then, a subtle restlessness there that told me whoever was on the call was not doing what he wanted.

And Clark always got what he wanted.

Even me.

He slid his palm down my back and waited for me to slide into the limo before following behind.

As the car glided along the city streets, I watched him discreetly, conflicting emotions churning within me. There was a time when his presence was a sanctuary for me, when I thought he was my hero, helping me escape the weight of the Shepfields' demands. But now, in the confines of that car—

I opened my mouth several times to tell him about the life changing news I'd received that morning.

But I couldn't quite get the words out.

The car pulled up outside the Metropolitan Museum then, breaking me out of my gloomy thoughts, and its grandeur loomed before us.

Clark ended his call and his attention shifted to me, his gaze meeting mine. "We're here, sweetheart," he murmured as if I hadn't noticed, reaching up to brush his fingers across my cheek. His tone was gentle, but it still served as a reminder that tonight held a weight beyond the glittering surface of the gala.

His business partners and all the who's who of the city would be there. Another night of pretending to be something I wasn't.

His eyes lingered over me and his gaze intensified, as if he were taking in every detail, every nuance of my appearance. I felt a rush of vulnerability under that scrutiny, my insecurities threatening to bubble to the surface.

"Most beautiful girl I've ever seen," he finally said, when his inspection was complete.

But I didn't feel the words like I should've.

His driver, Ryan, opened the door, and Clark's mask slipped on, that gorgeous smile of his there for everyone to see. Backlit by the camera flashes of the paparazzi who stalked these events, he extended his hand to help me out. His touch was warm, his demeanor exuding confidence and charm as he guided me onto the steps of the museum.

We stepped into the horde of flashing lights and the chorus of society photographers calling our names. Clark moved me this way and that, making sure they got all our best angles. It was a dance we'd perfected, a game of smiles and posed elegance that masked the real emotions lurking beneath. I plastered on a smile, my gaze fixed on Clark like he was *everything* as he expertly navigated the spectacle.

The cameras captured our every move, the bright flashes turning the night into a whirlwind of frozen moments. With each click of the camera, I felt a wave of pressure, the weight of expectations crashing over me. And as Clark led me inside the museum, his arm tightly around me like he knew I wanted to bolt…I felt like I was going to be sick.

Inside, the museum had undergone a remarkable metamorphosis, shedding its usual air of quiet reverence for an opulent transformation.

Maura had outdone herself.

The entrance staircase bloomed with cascading flowers and flowing drapes of purple and cream, like a grand portal into a realm of extravagance. The atrium had become an ethereal ballroom, aglow with the radiance of crystal chandeliers that dripped from the ceiling like suspended stardust. The velvet curtain-lined corridors whispered with the melodies of live music, inviting guests to twirl and converse amidst the echoes of artistry. The museum's scholarly skin was gone, in its place a living, breathing masterpiece of elegance.

We mingled with the crowd, or should I say, Clark mingled with the crowd. I stood there. Kind of like an accessory. Clark's hand rested lightly on my back the entire time, his conversations a drudgery of smooth, fake words. He was a master of this world, and I…was not.

I grimaced when I heard a familiar, tinkling laugh.

Maura.

I didn't call them Mom and Dad behind closed doors. That was only in public.

Her laugh was somehow a mixture of refinement and superiority, and it always made me cringe inwardly. Taking a deep breath, I waited for her to approach, dread dripping down my spine like a bead of sweat.

And then there they were. Thomas and Maura Shepfield.

Maura's appearance was as polished as ever, a vision of refined beauty that drew eyes to her like a siren song. Just looking at her, she could be anywhere between her twenties and forties, not a line marring her face. Her blonde hair was perfectly coiffed, every strand carefully placed. Her black gown the epitome of couture, clinging to her figure in all the right places.

I actually resembled her. I'd overheard them discussing it one night, how that was one of the reasons they'd picked me instead of a baby. Because anyone meeting them would assume I was really theirs.

Lucky me.

Thomas, standing beside her, was the embodiment of classic charm. His tailored tuxedo exuded an air of effortlessness, his silver streaked hair adding a touch of distinguished elegance. His eyes held a warmth that offered a stark contrast to Maura's demeanor, a warmth that I knew, however, didn't go skin deep.

As they approached Clark and me, Maura's eyes scanned my body with a scrutinizing gaze that only made the dread clawing at my insides thicken. With a calculated smile, she said, "Blake…I see you didn't use the makeup and hair team I suggested."

Her words were laced with subtle venom. And the comment, which would sound pretty innocuous to anyone listening around us, hit me like a brick to the face, the pain a stark contrast to the façade of smiles and laughter around us.

"It's good to see you too, Mother," I replied coolly as Clark brushed his fingers down my back soothingly.

She and Thomas cooed over Clark and he spat back some equally idiotic pleasantries. I could normally force myself to listen to them for however long I needed to, but tonight the sound of their voices was like ants burrowing into my skin.

"I'll be right back," I murmured, pulling away from Clark's hand with a strained smile, ignoring the shock and dismay all over Maura's face over my rudeness.

I turned to head toward the bathroom. I just needed a

minute, a minute to gather my thoughts and mend the cracks that threatened to widen within me. I could feel their gazes piercing into me, and that ever present feeling grew. The one that said I'd never be good enough.

For anybody.

The bathroom was somehow blissfully empty when I walked in, and I stood in front of the mirror, taking a few deep breaths, trying to get ahold of myself. Trying to keep all that emotion thrashing around inside me, firmly locked in my chest.

I stared at my reflection in the gilded mirror, my gaze filled with self-loathing. I was a model. The world called me beautiful.

And I hated everything about myself.

Blond waves framed my face, a cascade of hair that others might admire, but all I saw were imperfections—strands that never seemed to fall just right, a perpetual messiness that clashed with what everyone wanted from me. My dark blue eyes stared back, their hue an exotic anomaly that was almost violet, yet all I could think about were the dark circles that blemished the skin beneath them, a reminder of sleepless nights and anxious days.

And then there were my lips, oversized, drawing attention I didn't want. I despised the way they looked when I smiled, as if they were shouting for attention, betraying my discomfort with the mask I wore. My reflection seemed to taunt me, every detail an assault on the confidence I struggled to hold onto.

When I stared at my body, I saw bulges and angles that seemed to amplify my flaws. The neckline that was supposed to exude allure only made me feel exposed, my bare skin a testament to my vulnerability.

I pinched at the fabric near my waist, the critical thoughts in my mind forming a symphony of self-doubt. Everything felt wrong—my hair, my eyes, my lips, my body—each aspect of my appearance a gateway for relentless scrutiny. No matter how hard I tried, I couldn't silence the chorus of negativity that echoed within me.

The bathroom door swung open then, and Michelle, my best...frenemy sauntered in with an air of all the confidence that I lacked. Her dark brown hair cascaded in sleek waves around her shoulders, her doe-like brown eyes held a glint of mischief, and her lips were adorned with a bold shade of red lipstick.

Her figure-hugging black dress clung to her curves perfectly, a daring slit revealing just enough to leave an impression. She moved with a grace that was both captivating and enigmatic, an embodiment of self-assuredness that had always drawn people to her.

"Blake," Michelle greeted, her voice carrying a blend of warmth and sarcasm that only she could manage.

I glanced up from the mirror, meeting her gaze with apprehension. "Hey, Michelle."

She leaned against the counter, her eyes scanning me with a hint of amusement. "Oh, wow, Blake. You look...different."

I sighed at her comment, because it was par for the course with her, trying to ignore how her words were a direct hit to my already fragile state. "That's...nice to hear," I said sarcastically. You couldn't show weakness with Michelle. She was like a shark constantly on the hunt for blood.

And I'd been her favorite target since our days at the orphanage. She'd been adopted by one of the Shepfields' friends...and I'd been stuck with her for better or for worse.

Her red lips curled into a sly smile, her gaze never leaving my face. "Well, I've never seen you wear so much makeup before. It's like you're trying really hard tonight."

Her words stung like a slap, sending me further down the spiraling path I'd already been on. I glanced away, unable to meet her gaze as the knot of humiliation tightened in my chest.

"And that dress..." Michelle continued, her tone light, "Did they send the wrong size?"

I clenched my fists, my nails digging into my palms as I struggled to contain my rising anger. "You look gorgeous as well, Michelle," I drawled, stepping away from the mirror and moving past her.

She shrugged casually, her gaze shifting to her perfectly manicured nails. "Don't be like that. I'm just speaking what everyone's thinking, Blake. You need that in a friend."

Taking a deep breath, I finally met her eyes, a mix of hurt and frustration simmering beneath the surface that I did my best to hide. "Right."

Michelle's gaze was triumphant as she watched me.

She knew every button to press, every insecurity to pull at.

And she was great at doing both.

I turned away from her, but my reflection in the mirror seemed to support everything she'd just said.

Michelle moved on from *me* and started chatting about the event, her voice a distant echo in my ears.

She didn't even notice when I walked away, doing my best to lock up the weakness, determined to hold my head high and face the gala once more.

Clark lifted an eyebrow when I reappeared in the crowd, silently asking me if I was okay. I nodded, letting him take my elbow and lead me to our table in the center of the room, a seating arrangement that couldn't be more suffocating. The table was set with pristine white linens and glittering crystal-ware. Plates adorned with meticulously arranged delicacies were presented like works of art as soon as we sat. The soft glow of candlelight danced across the faces of the attendees, casting an enchanting spell over the proceedings. I'm sure the food would taste delicious.

If I allowed myself to actually enjoy it.

Which I would not.

I'd never hear the end of it from Maura.

As the courses were served, Maura took the stage for her keynote address.

"Ladies and gentlemen, esteemed guests." Her voice carried through the air, laced with practiced grace. "Tonight, we gather under this roof not only to celebrate our friendship, but to channel our resources and collective power toward a cause that holds a place in all our hearts—supporting under-privileged children."

"Every child, regardless of their background, deserves a fair chance at a brighter future," she continued, her tone soft-ening for dramatic effect. "Our commitment to their uplift-ment isn't just an act of philanthropy; it's a testament to the empathy that binds us together as a community."

I watched from my seat, my gaze tracing the gestures and expressions that accompanied Maura's words. She spoke with an air of sincerity, each phrase a carefully crafted thread woven into the tapestry of her performance. But inwardly, my eyes rolled with every platitude, every rehearsed sentiment that danced on the surface of her speech.

"As we indulge in the splendor of this evening, let us not forget the faces of those who will benefit from our generosity," Maura continued, her voice taking on a note of heightened emotion. "The children who dream, who aspire, and who deserve a chance to break free from the chains of circumstance."

My mind wandered, my thoughts a whirlwind of cynicism as I listened to the flowery language that disguised the hollow reality. It was all fake. Maura could care less about underprivileged children. I'd seen her fire household staff for getting pregnant. And I'd never forget her pouring her iced coffee on a small boy who'd asked for some money in Central Park.

Maura droned on, and when she was finished, applause erupted like a wave, the attendees drawn willingly into the illusion she wove.

As the applause echoed, Clark suddenly rose from his seat, a shimmering glass in hand. He tapped the glass, the clear sound slicing through the hum of conversation like a clarion call.

I frowned. It wasn't like him to perform public toasts. He considered that beneath him.

"Ladies and gentlemen," he began, his voice carrying a confidence that held the room captive. "Tonight is more than just a celebration of a noble cause. It's a celebration of some- thing far more personal, something that has changed my life in ways I never anticipated."

I sat there, frozen in shock, my breath caught in my chest as Clark's voice wove anticipation around us. My gaze remained locked on him, my mind racing to comprehend what he was saying.

He turned towards me, all the warmth his eyes usually lacked...suddenly there. "Blake, from the moment we met, my life took a turn I could have never predicted. You showed me a world that mattered. A world I never would have discovered without you. You've been my foundation, my confidante, and my muse."

My heart raced, the gravity of his words sending shock- waves through my being. The room seemed to blur, my focus narrowing to Clark's figure standing before me.

"And so," his voice trembled slightly, a rawness there that made my insides ache. "I can't imagine a more perfect moment to ask you the most important question of my life."

He sank to one knee, a box materializing in his hand as he

held it out. My breath caught, my mind struggling to process what was unfolding before me. The world seemed to spin, the implications of his actions colliding with my inner turmoil.

"Will you marry me?"

I stared at him kneeling there, and for a moment, I was tempted to say yes.

It would be so much easier.

But then my thoughts drifted, unbidden, to the life he was asking me to accept. Maybe he would love me. Maybe he'd even do his best to make me happy. But this life would only lead to loneliness masked by grandeur. I would crumble under the weight of it.

I'd have a fake smile plastered on my lips.

Forever.

And I'd never stop being lonely. I'd never stop yearning for something more.

My fingers clenched at the sight of the ring. I knew the cold metal of it would feel like an anchor dragging me into a sea of despair.

"I'm sorry." The words escaped my lips in a whisper, my voice tinged with sorrow.

Because he really was such a good man. And I was the fool who couldn't take what he was offering.

"What?" Clark's expression shifted from confident antici-pation…to shock.

I hadn't known I would say no before this moment. I never would have guessed it, in fact. But I steadied myself, meeting his gaze with a mixture of resolve and pain. "I can't marry you."

The words hung in the air, a declaration that shattered the spell that had enveloped the room. Gasps and whispers erupted around us, the shock of my rejection echoing like a thunderclap.

Without another word, I pushed away from the table, my

steps urgent as I fled the room. The clatter of my heels against the marble floor was a rhythm to my escape, a desperate sprint toward the freedom that awaited outside those lavish walls. The gala's grandeur was reduced to a blur as I burst through the doors, the cool night air a welcome contrast to the suffocation that had gripped me.

With every step, the weight of my decision grew lighter, the whispers of the gala fading into the distance as I embraced the possibility of a different future, one where happiness...

Was a possibility.

CHAPTER 2

ARI

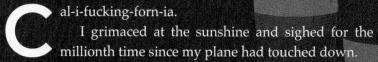

Cal-i-fucking-forn-ia.

I grimaced at the sunshine and sighed for the millionth time since my plane had touched down.

I was standing in the parking lot of the arena, just staring at the building.

Practice started in thirty minutes. And I had a bunch of bullshit I needed to do before I stepped onto the ice.

Instead, I decided to procrastinate a little bit longer and call my good ole buddy Lincoln.

"How's the land of milk and honey?" Lincoln drawled as soon as he picked up.

"Ugh, you sound way too smug and self-satisfied. You just had sex."

"Yep," he said with all the happiness of an asshole who was being laid regularly by his soulmate.

"Tell my bestie I say hi," I snorted.

He scoffed. "She is not your bestie," he immediately shot back. "Monroe only has one best friend, and that's me."

I cackled, because he had the same reaction every time we had this conversation, and it was making me feel better.

"You're standing in the parking lot, aren't you?" he said.

"Yep."

"Just getting pumped to see Soto."

"Yep."

There was silence for a moment.

"This season is going to be weird."

I swallowed, because now wasn't the time to get all emotional about the fact that I'd given up my dream life to spend a year in California.

To get my dream girl.

Ok, it was worth it.

"I'm going to go piss off Soto," I said, rather than answering, because I needed to hold onto my mantra that big girls don't cry and all of that.

"Knock 'em dead."

"One year," I said.

"One year," he answered.

And then the phone clicked off.

Now that I'd gotten that dreamy motivational speech, it was time to go in.

I started towards the colossal structure before me, because L.A. obviously had to overcompensate for things...

Its architecture was sleek and pragmatic, tall columns framing the entrance, reflecting the sunshine and the pulsating energy around. The oversized windows, branded with the team's insignia, gave me a sneak peek of what was inside – a sea of blue seats, the pristine ice waiting for skates, and the anticipation that only a roaring crowd could generate.

In that moment, I could almost hear the distant cheers, the sound of blades cutting through the ice, and the satisfying thump of a puck connecting with its mark.

I took a deep breath, the salt tinged air mingling with the distant hum of the city.

And for the first time...my fingers tingled with anticipation.

Let's go, boys.

———

I ambled into the Cobras locker room, the colors assaulting my eyeballs like a fashion disaster at a circus. Seriously, who decided that purple and yellow were the ultimate power combo? My inner fashion critic went on strike right then and there.

But, I had to begrudgingly admit, the place wasn't a dump. The lockers shone like they were auditioning for a toothpaste commercial, and the gear was so neatly arranged, one of the employees had to have a raging case of OCD.

As some enthusiastic voice from the front office droned on next to me about team history, my mind decided it was a great time for a mini-vacation. My feet, however, were on a mission of their own, leading me down the locker-lined path like they knew something I didn't. Maybe they thought there was a hidden treasure chest of snacks at the end of the line of jerseys.

I caught bits of the presenter's spiel about team dynamics and the upcoming season. Yeah, yeah, synergy, chemistry, blah, blah. My brain was pondering more important matters, like how in the world I'd ended up in this fucking locker room. But there I was, surrounded by the scent of sweaty balls and Lysol.

And there *he* fucking was.

When I turned the corner, John Soto was leaning against one of the lockers, my rival extraordinaire, or as I liked to call him, the poster child for "bad hair dye," looking like a mole on someone's left ass cheek.

Not my left ass cheek, obviously. There was only perfection there.

But someone's...

"Do you need anything before practice, Mr. Lancaster?" The office minion finished his spiel, staring at me hopefully like he was going to get a tip after one of the more boring experiences of my adult life.

Maybe he'd accept a stick of gum. That had worked for Kevin McCallister, after all.

"Nice of you to grace us with your presence, Lancaster," Soto drawled then, yanking my attention away from bubble gum tips, to his ugly face.

The trade had just happened, so I'd missed most of preseason training.

But fuck my life.

Hopefully, Layla knew how to make cookies because I would deserve several panfuls after my sacrifice this year.

Blake, not Layla—I needed to remember that was her name now.

Soto chuckled, temporarily pulling my thoughts away from my soulmate. I shivered in mock disgust as I stared at him. Reddish hair that could probably be seen from space, a nose that seemed to have been designed by Picasso during his abstract phase, and eyes that were more watery green than a kiddie pool at a summer camp—Soto was a walking masterpiece of genetic mishaps.

It was like the universe decided to throw all the quirky features it had in storage and mash them together into a character that even a caricature artist would hesitate to sketch.

Other members of the team were watching us, and I gave them a little salute, because I was classy like that.

"Hell must have iced over, boys. Ari Lancaster is in the house," Soto droned.

Soto's voice, I swear, was like a high-pitched car alarm

that got stuck on repeat. You know those cartoons where a character inhales helium and starts talking like they're auditioning for a chipmunk choir? Well, Soto must have had bad helium for breakfast, because his voice would have made those chipmunks weep.

"Someone had to class you up, *boys*," I drawled, surveying the team, mentally cataloging what I knew about them from playing against them the last few years.

First up was Callum, the human wall they called a defenseman. I had to hand it to him, the guy had a wingspan that could probably block out the sun. His nickname could've been "No Entry Zone" with those arms, but for all his defensive prowess, he moved like a glacier in the Sahara. Give that guy a GPS tracker, because he could use some directions on the ice. He'd be relegated to second line now that I was here, but he wasn't glaring at me, so props to him.

Then there was Tommy, the sniper with a shot that could probably take down satellites. His accuracy was like a heat-seeking missile, and he had the kind of poker face that would make Lady Gaga proud. But get him into a fight, and he turned into a deer caught in headlights. I guess body checks weren't part of his playlist.

And let's not forget Frankie, the speed demon on skates. Seriously, if he went any faster, he might turn into a blur and disappear into another dimension. The guy was like a caffeine-fueled cheetah, darting around the ice like he was late for a date with destiny. But his focus sometimes took a vacation mid-game. I swear, he'd be zipping along one moment and then suddenly doing the ice equivalent of interpretive dance the next.

My gaze flicked back to Soto. He had no strengths. Only weaknesses. And I didn't want to hurt my pretty brain going over them.

L.A. didn't suck. But they were nothing like my boys in Dallas.

One year.

Soto sighed and held out his hand to me. "Truce?" he suddenly offered, and honestly, keeping the laughter in was all I could do because...

NEVER WOULD THAT HAPPEN.

I acted like I was considering it and started extending my hand...before abruptly yanking it back.

"Sorry, Soto. I can't even pretend to like you."

Soto's face curled up in a snarl as he dropped his fake ass peace offering. "Fuck you, Lancaster."

I winked at him.

"Sorry, not without dinner first. Your tiny dick would be so forgettable, I'd have to at least get a steak out of it."

The locker room erupted in laughter, and I was impressed. Maybe these guys had a sense of humor after all.

I strolled to the locker with my name on it so I could get ready for practice, pleased with how the day was going. I could feel his gaze on my back, like he was trying to shoot lasers into my buttcheeks.

"Walker Davis," a voice next to me said as I pulled my skates out of the bag I'd brought with me.

I glanced over. Ah, Walker, the team's resident heartthrob —before my arrival, of course—and all-American poster boy. If life were a rom-com, he'd be cast as the dashing lead who effortlessly steals hearts and has a smile that features in forty billion Instagram pages. Brown hair that probably had its own fan club, the kind of jawline that made sculptors recon- sider their life choices, and eyes that sparkled like they were in a perpetual photoshoot—Walker was the embodiment of every high school crush come to life.

I wouldn't be surprised if he woke up every morning to a choir of birds helping him get dressed.

Get him in a room with Lincoln and me, and people would be fainting all over the place.

He was also the only All-Star on the team before today, his skills actually surpassing my boy Bender. He was a lot younger than Bender, too.

We'd be a dream team if you put him on the ice with me and Lincoln.Something to think about for later...

"Ahh, Walker, the goalie with a face that could launch a thousand ships," I drawled.

He snorted and extended a hand like he was offering a VIP ticket to the "I'm Gonna Steal Your Girl" show. "Nice to have you on board," he said, all charming and Disney prince-ish. I shook it, fighting the urge to ask if he always had a wind machine following him around.

I got dressed and followed him down a hallway to practice.

Out on the ice, it was the first time I felt like maybe I hadn't landed on an alien planet—the cold bite of the rink, the familiar swoosh of skates. New team, but same ice. As I skated around, I could pretend for a second that I was home in Dallas, about to lay Lincoln on his ass.

But then Soto skated by me and I remembered how bad this place sucked.

A whistle blew, and it was time for practice to begin.

Cobras Head Coach, Kim Palmer, introduced me like I was the star attraction at a circus. "Ari Lancaster, a man who needs no introductions after the hell he's put this team through. He's God's gift to hockey and we're lucky bastards to have him." Okay, maybe that's not exactly what he said, but close enough.

Coach Kim himself looked like he'd just stepped out of a motivational poster. Salt-and-pepper hair, stern jawline—the kind of guy you'd expect to find delivering a halftime speech in a sports movie. He had that "I've seen it all" aura, like he could predict our plays before we even made them. I half-expected him to start quoting Sun Tzu's "Art of War."

He was a decent coach surrounded by mid-tier talent. Not much he could do about that.

Drills were the name of the game as practice began. Skating, passing, shooting—we were like a discombobulated dance troupe, except with more helmets and fewer sequins.

Soto, in his ever-enthusiastic state, decided it was a fantastic idea to try to check me, like we were in the NHL version of a WWE showdown.

I laughed as I pried myself off the boards. "Is that all you got, birdbrain? Because your check was about as effective as your mama's mouth last night."

Soto's face went a violent shade of red that almost matched his awful hair. "Fuck you!" he roared for the second time today, because his pea-sized brain obviously couldn't think of anything more creative than that.

He moved to come after me again when Walker skated by, all diplomacy and dimples. "Soto, wish you tried that hard to hit people in games."

Alright, this Walker guy wasn't too bad.

Soto grimaced at Walker's comment, but surprisingly, he didn't say anything else. He just skated off in a huff.

I winked at Walker, and he rolled his eyes. We got back to practice, the drills blending into each other like a workout montage. The ice echoed with the slap of pucks and the scrape of skates, a soundtrack of effort and anticipation.

It felt all wrong.

After all these years, I could read Lincoln and my other Dallas teammates easily, predict what they were going to do before they did it.

The only thing I could predict with this team was that Soto would suck.

At least I could take solace in why I was doing all of this. What the end game would be.

When Walker asked if I wanted to hit happy hour afterwards, it was easy to say no. Because today...my plan for that endgame began.

CHAPTER 3

BLAKE

'd found myself in the whirlwind of Los Angeles, a city where the glitzy guise of stardom hid the darker stories of shattered dreams.

And I was on the verge of becoming one of those darker stories.

That job that was supposed to be the game changer? The one that promised to kickstart my career…it had crumbled like a sandcastle before the waves.

The magazine editor in charge of the huge photoshoot I was supposed to star in with Voyage magazine had gotten embroiled in a sexual harassment scandal that had canceled the whole project. There was now an investigation going on that was in the headlines of every news outlet as more and more Voyage staffers and models came forward with horror stories.

Maybe I'd dodged a bullet.

But I felt more like I'd become the epitome of a cautionary tale. Yet another girl relegated to waiting tables as I tried to make it big.

But at least…I could finally breathe.

The restaurant I now worked at had a reputation—it was the kind of place where celebrities went, where you could see the A-listers sipping their fancy cocktails at one table while aspiring actors and models balanced trays at another.

My agent had gotten me the job. Said it would be good for me to be hobnobbing with the stars.

Maybe it was.

But mostly it felt like I'd volunteered for sexual harassment instead of being paid for it.

There was a buzz against my thigh as a text came in, and I sighed, knowing exactly who it was.

Clark.

We were still together. Or at least I guess we were.

He'd been devastated about my rejection of his marriage proposal. And even more devastated when I told him I was moving.

But he'd told me he'd do anything to make it work.

That he loved me.

That I was it for him.

Much nicer things than the Shepfields had to say about me blowing up their carefully laid plans for me.

"*You ungrateful, selfish brat. We've done everything for you. Given you everything! You were nothing but the daughter of a murderer. And I gave you my name! This is how you repay us? You're a disappointment. A nothing.*"

Daughter of a murderer. A disappointment. A nothing.

The words were a constant chant in my head, lining up with all the other ones that I told myself on the daily.

My phone buzzed again, and I peeked around to see if anyone was watching before I pulled it out of my pocket.

> Clark: I love you. I miss you. You're all I think about.

He said all of it so easily.

And I couldn't even say *I love you* in my head.

Guilt flooded my insides, the taste of it thick on my tongue, making me sick.

"Girl, your order's up," my coworker Bailey hissed as she passed by, her warm brown eyes bug eyed and slightly crazy looking as she sliced them toward the back where Daphne, the executive chef, was glaring at me impatiently.

I hurried to grab the waiting dishes, having to cover almost the whole distance of the restaurant to do so. The place had a sleek, modern aesthetic that had graced many an interior design magazine. Minimalistic yet sophisticated, with soft, dimmed lighting that cast a warm glow, bathing the space in an inviting ambiance that drew you in. The walls were adorned with abstract paintings, the tables inlaid with polished marble, and the plush, low-backed chairs all contributed to an atmosphere of understated luxury. A marble-topped bar stretched along one side, serving artisanal cocktails that looked more like works of art than beverages. The open kitchen, framed by a massive glass pane, allowed patrons to catch a glimpse of the culinary maestros in action.

It definitely wasn't a shithole.

I grabbed the tray of dishes with names I could barely pronounce and navigated the maze of tables as I headed to my section, filled with faces that expected to be known.

Hollywood was the exact opposite of New York, where the rich there prided themselves on understated elegance. Maura would be sniffing in disdain at the lime green getup the actress at this table was wearing. It included a large plume of feathers that seemed out of place at lunch. I had no idea who she was, or what she'd been in, but Bailey, the restaurant gossip queen, made sure I at least knew what industry guests were in as I served them.

The woman didn't say thank you as I set down her salad,

but that was par for the course. The tips weren't even that impressive, honestly.

But I was elbow rubbing like my agent wanted. And I did have some auditions for small campaigns next week.

And I could breathe.

No matter how difficult things got, I wouldn't forget that.

The restaurant door swung open then with its usual soft chime, something I'd always thought was weird about a fancy place like this, but others considered homey and charming.

But this time when the door chimed, the atmosphere in the room seemed to ripple in response. It was as if a switch had suddenly been activated, pulling the collective attention of every soul in the establishment to its source. I couldn't help but glance over my shoulder.

My eyes locked onto a man, and the world seemed to freeze in place.

His presence was a force of nature, all-consuming masculinity that demanded attention. With raven-black hair that fell effortlessly across his forehead and those penetrating green eyes. He exuded an air of dominance, the very embodiment of an alpha male. He was like a predator in a world of prey, and every instinct in me knew it.

For a heartbeat, I forgot how to inhale. The captivating seduction of his gaze had ensnared me, leaving me helpless under his spell. Those emerald eyes bore into mine with an intensity that felt like they could strip away my every secret, leaving me vulnerable in their wake.

He leaned towards the hostess and murmured something to her, and yet he didn't take his eyes off me. I didn't know him. I was sure about that.

But the way he was watching me...it sure seemed like he knew me.

I stared, both captivated and unnerved, as he was led to

the section of the restaurant I was in charge of.

Something extraordinary had just stepped into my world. I knew that. Judging by the quiet whispers that had filled the room the second he'd walked in...everyone else knew that as well.

And I had to serve him dinner.

I tried to avoid going to his table as long as I could, too nervous to face all that hotness. I had tables to do refills on, orders to bring by. Silverware to be rolled...I couldn't help but steal glances at him the entire time though.

He sat there, his gaze tracking me, an amused grin tracing his full lips, like he knew exactly what I was doing and he was perfectly content to wait me out. There were people stopping by as he sat there, like everyone else in the place wanted to bask in his light, too.

I swore I'd never seen him before, even if every part of my DNA was convinced he was the most beautiful man I'd ever come across. But he had to be someone big, someone famous. Why else would the other A-listers in the restaurant be saying hello?

A woman I knew was in a popular tv show went up to him as I was filling a water pitcher. She said something and he threw his head back and laughed. Immediately, my insides tightened. Something like jealousy slithering through me.

Because I wanted that laugh to only belong to me.

What the fuck was wrong with me?

His laughter was warm and amused, weaving through the air like a soft breeze on a summer day.

I was completely captivated by it.

Finally, I couldn't delay it any longer, and I approached the table, a tray with a decanter of water trembling in my hands. He was lounging effortlessly on the bench, commanding the space around him. The closer I got, the more I began to truly see him.

I'd always had a thing for guys with dark hair and green eyes. I blamed it on the crush I had as a child in the group home. I had a type, and I didn't venture far from it…case in point: Clark.

But this guy was like my fantasy on crack. My naughtiest day dream come to life. The walking embodiment of allure.

His dark, tousled hair was like a midnight storm, a stark contrast against his golden-tan skin that seemed kissed by the sun's rays. His eyes, a mesmerizing shade of green framed by long, dark lashes, held a hint of mischief and a touch of danger.

Even with his clothes on, the fact that he was rocking a very well-built—if not perfect—physique couldn't be concealed. He was wearing a crisp white V-neck shirt that clung to his sculpted chest, accentuating every sinew and curve. A black cross necklace hung from his neck, drawing attention to the chiseled contours of his collarbone. His wrists were adorned with an array of bracelets, and they jingled softly as he moved.

My body had an instinctive reaction to his presence, a primal response that I couldn't control. As his gaze locked onto mine, a wicked glint in his forest green eyes, my nipples hardened beneath my clothing, electric charges zooming across my skin. My core softened, aching with a need that pulsed with every beat of my heart. I could feel the undeniable wetness between my thighs, an unbidden response to the raw attraction he exuded.

I was caught in a lusty spell, one that left me breathless and craving his touch.

I was aching for him. Desperate. I—

"Hi," he murmured, and my panties were freaking soaked.

His voice was a sensual caress, a velvety whisper that sent shivers dancing along my skin.

I opened my mouth several times to respond, but I was worried all that would come out was a moan.

"Hi," I finally stuttered, inwardly wincing at how freaking lame I was.

My phone buzzed against my thigh. Reminding me I *had* a sweet, sexy boyfriend. I had a feeling that the man lounging in front of me could do far more damage to my heart than Clark ever could.

Not that there was a chance in flying hell this kind of guy would ever be interested in me. I mean...what had I been saying?

I realized then that the handsome stranger's amused gaze had transformed into a blazing furnace of hunger. It was as if he was undressing me with his eyes, his imagination running wild with all the ways he could claim my body right then and there.

I'd read about these kind of men in countless romance novels, where they were portrayed as the elusive dream, the kind of alpha male perfection that left you yearning to throw caution to the wind and surrender to their charm. I'd always thought they didn't exist, that they were just characters on pages, figments of an author's imagination.

Yet, here before me was the living embodiment of that fantasy. A stranger who you knew—one night with him could be the stuff of dreams, an unforgettable encounter that would leave you breathless and forever changed.

YOU HAVE A BOYFRIEND, a voice screamed in my head.

I understood that...it's just I was having trouble remembering his name at the moment.

Ari

She was like a lightning strike, breaking my fucking heart

with her beauty. She had me and every other guy—and girl—in the room doing double takes.

I immediately wanted to gouge out all their eyes with the fork on the table in front of me.

Mine, my insides–and my dick–were screaming.

And honestly, it was all I could do to keep that crazy fucker down.

Her golden locks tumbled around her face like they had a mind of their own, and her eyes? Well, let's just say they were like two cups of coffee—one look, and you were wide awake and ready for action.

She was the hottest thing I'd ever seen. Every inch of her a gravitational pull I couldn't resist, even if I tried.

Not that I was trying to resist. I wasn't an idiot.

My attraction to her was like a freight train, powerful and unrelenting, and my dick was so hard I was afraid my pants were going to rip.

It felt like I could breathe for the first time since I'd seen that billboard and realized it was her. Like I'd been holding my breath since she'd disappeared on me as a kid.

And now I was free to exhale.

I'd been driving along a Dallas road, the city's skyline stretched out before me, a sprawling maze of buildings and lights that seemed to go on forever. As I approached an intersection, my gaze wandered to the billboards lining the roadside. Advertising for everything from fast food to luxury cars flashed by, each one vying for the attention of passing motorists.

But then, one particular billboard seized my attention, causing me to slam on the brakes in disbelief.

There she was, larger than life, an embodiment of over a decade of wishing and longing. A massive leopard was draped around her, its fierce eyes locked onto something beyond the camera's lens–it was some kind of perfume ad.

I'd immediately known it was her, Layla, the girl I'd lost. The only girl I'd ever loved.

A million memories came rushing back...ones I'd long buried and tried to forget.

I shook my head as I relived the moment I'd found Blake. Kidnapping her and taking her with me to some remote island didn't seem like a bad idea at the moment.

Because now that I'd found her...Now that I could breathe...You could fucking bet I would never let her go again.

"What's your name, sunshine?" I asked, instead of grabbing her and dragging her away.

I deserved a mother fucking medal for that, *by the way.*

She frowned, as if she hated the nickname. I'd have to workshop that. But it was hard to think of anything else when I looked at her. Like she was the sunshine finally here after so much fucking rain.

Look at me, waxing poetic. I'd have to remind Lincoln how smart and artistic I was next time we talked.

"My name is *Blake* and I'll be your server today," she said in a professional but very unsteady tone. I grinned to myself because *Sunshine* was definitely as affected by me as I was by her.

I'd also just found my new favorite thing...listening to her talk.

Her voice had obviously changed from when she was a little girl...but there was still that same unique allure that had dragged me in from the beginning. That had the boy in me recognizing I'd found magic...even back then.

She bit down on her delicious bottom lip before going into the daily specials. None of which I was interested in since she hadn't said tacos or steak, but I nodded along anyway. I could listen to her say...anything actually.

"Sir?" she said, and I realized I'd been staring at her...awestruck.

"Is there a special where I get to have lunch with you?" I quipped.

Because I really was that much of a fucking idiot, apparently.

I watched as her features grew cold, a clear rejection that left no room for misunderstanding. "I'm not for sale," she shot back, turning around in a clear dismissal.

With a rueful smile, I stared as she walked away. The view from behind was just as captivating as it had been from the front.

That was okay. I could do the whole redemption arc. I needed to concentrate on my plan without making her hate me on our first encounter though. I was usually more charming than this.

After seeing her on that billboard in Dallas, I'd immediately gone to good old Google, hunting down the ad campaign to make sure I hadn't gone crazy from years of wishful thinking. As soon as I'd had any resources to my name out of college, I'd searched to see where Layla had disappeared to. And I hadn't found a single hint. It was as if she'd never existed.

Or died.

Over the years, that thought had creeped around in my head, as much as I hoped she was out there somewhere, living a far better life than the one she'd had at the group home.

I'd found out from Google, though, that the campaign model's name was Blake Shepfield. With a little help from Lincoln's creepy PI, I'd then found out that Blake had been adopted and was living in New York City all these years… and that she'd had her name legally changed upon adoption —although the P.I. couldn't find details on what her name used to be.

It explained a lot.

Can't find someone who doesn't exist anymore.

Even if I hadn't been able to find out all that information, I still would've known it was her. No one had eyes like that. No one but her.

Her eyes, a mesmerizing shade of deep blue that seemed to fade into violet, were unlike anything I'd ever seen before. They held a depth that seemed to have no end, like the vast expanse of the night sky just before dawn. They were enigmatic pools of mystery, framed by long, dark lashes that accentuated their intensity. When she looked at me, it felt like she was peering into the depths of my soul, and my fear, even as a kid, was that she would find me lacking.

I sat up straighter when I saw her returning my way, glancing frantically over the menu to see if there was anything I would eat. This place was fancy. I'd always felt more comfortable stuffing my face in a hole in the wall than in places like this.

But this was where *she* was. So this was where I'd be.

"Have you decided what you want? Or do you need more time?" she asked coolly, obviously still not impressed at all with me after my word vomit.

"I'll have the steak frites," I told her, inwardly fist pumping at the small glint of amusement I spotted in her gaze as I butchered the word "frites."

"French fries okay?"

"Do you have Russian ones? I've heard those are better."

She snorted that time, and I knew the wide grin on my face was ridiculous...as was everything coming out of my mouth, but at least she wasn't mad at me anymore.

"I'm afraid we're all out of Russian," she said, now smiling prettily.

"Mmmh. I'll survive," I mused, finding myself leaning forward because she was so fucking intoxicating. "Could I have a refill of water, though? I'm parched."

I hated the idea of her waiting on me, but I'd have to make it up to her later. I had work to do.

"Oh, of course!" she exclaimed, her eyes going wide, like she was alarmed she'd get in trouble. She dashed away and grabbed a water pitcher before hurrying back.

It was hard to keep myself in my seat. I wanted to leap forward, throw her over my shoulder, and get her out of here.

But the plan wouldn't allow it.

I'd pushed my glass further away, and intentionally didn't pick it up to make it easier for her to refill it. That made it so she had to lean over the table to pour my water, so I could more easily slip the phone from her pocket I'd seen her looking at a few minutes ago.

Years of pickpocketing as a kid on the streets made it easy. She didn't even notice.

"I'll go put in your order," Blake murmured, a faint blush to her cheeks, hopefully at how close she'd been to me.

I watched her wistfully as she walked away, and then stared at the phone in my lap. This was actually a much simpler version of the plan I'd come up with. I'd figured I'd have to hire someone to hack into her phone and change things, but little miss sunshine didn't have a password on her phone. I'd have to talk to her about cyber security at another date.

I scrolled to her contacts, inwardly raging when I saw how many times Clark—the boyfriend I'd found out about from the P.I.—had called and texted today. I blocked his number and then made a new contact with my number that I labeled "Clark." A second later, I was downloading the tracking app the P.I. had told me about onto her phone. It would also allow me to see any messages she sent or received, as well as her app activity. I blocked Clark in her social media apps for good measure.

There. Perfect. I knew today was going to be a good day.

What I'd just done, what I would do to get her...weren't things I'd seen on my dream board, but hey, you worked with what you had.

Scanning the restaurant, I saw that she was busy with other tables. That gave me some time to do recon on the texts she'd been getting. My girl was mostly a loner besides a roommate and a few model friends she went out with occasionally. Her file had included observations from her modeling agency which noted she was "uncomfortable in the social scene." The friends she did have were assholes. It was easy to tell, even in texts. That wasn't going to work.

It was Clark that made me the angriest, though. Homeboy was telling her he loved her on the daily.

Deep breaths, Ari. He'll be gone soon.

Movement out of the corner of my eye caught my attention, and I realized she was almost to the table with my food. I quickly dropped the phone into my lap and shot her what I hoped was a winning smile.

"Here you go," she said brightly, but it was in that bland way that people used with strangers.

I couldn't wait to not be a stranger to her anymore. I wanted to be her best friend, her everything.

It was the only ending I could accept.

"How long have you worked here?" I asked as she turned to walk away. I already knew the answer, but I was desperate for her to talk to me.

"Only a few weeks. I just moved here," she blushed again, and I wasn't sure why. "It's a filler job."

"Trying to get into modeling?" I pretended to guess.

Her blush deepened. "I'm a walking cliché. I know."

"Normally, that would be the case. But with a face like yours, sunshine...I have no doubt you'll be one of those supermodels soon enough."

Her face darkened for a moment...and I wondered, did

she even want that?

"Yeah, that would be incredible," she finally murmured.

But she didn't sound enthused.

"Well, you know what? I just moved here too. That means we should be BFFs."

This time, a real smile popped across her face. And she snorted! I gave myself another inward fist pump...because I believed in celebrating victories.

"BFFs, huh?"

"Yes," I said seriously, nodding my head for emphasis. "I'm a really good BFF. Everyone says so."

"Oh, so you're BFFs with everyone, then?"

My eyes widened.

"Well, no," I stuttered. "I actually only have one BFF right now. But he assures me I'm the best. But I really think I'm up for the task is what I'm saying." What in the ya hoo was coming out of my fucking mouth right now? I was an embarrassment to all humankind.

"I can't believe that we've said BFF this many times in a row," she giggled before suddenly stiffening up.

I glanced over to where she was staring and saw a stern faced woman who looked like she ate puppies heading our way.

"I have to get back to work," Blake said hurriedly before hustling to another one of her tables.

Well, now I was *not* happy. I had a million more things I wanted to talk to Blake about.

"Mr. Lancaster, I apologize for Ms. Shepfield's behavior. She will be dealt with," crooned the uppity woman who I assumed was the manager of the establishment.

"Nothing to deal with, ma'am," I drawled. "Best service I've ever had, actually. You would be a fool to let that one go." I watched as her face flushed with embarrassment as I emphasized *fool*.

I stood up and threw some cash down on the table, way more than that fancy meal had cost so my girl would obviously get a great tip too.

"Thanks for dinner," I muttered, even though I hadn't actually eaten it. I stalked towards the front of the restaurant, giving Blake one last lingering look as I did so.

She was staring at me too while she poured some asshole's water who seemed to be mesmerized by the front of her shirt.

It was all I could do to keep dragging myself away.

"I think my waitress dropped her phone," I told the hostess, handing her the phone I'd stolen and ignoring her "please fuck me now" look as I did it.

"Maximus 5000" aka "Little Ari", wasn't interested in anyone else now that she'd been found.

As soon as I got out of the restaurant and was walking down the sidewalk to my car, I texted Lincoln.

> **Me:** I just want you to know that your bff is artistic and smart.

> **Lincoln:** Oh really...

> **Me:** I also have a lot of self control.

> **Lincoln:** Ok, who is this? Who took Ari Lancaster's phone?

> **Me:** No, I'm serious. Blake was right in front of me and I totally controlled all my impulses. And I was waxing poetic about her. So see...artistic and smart.

> **Lincoln:** I'm afraid to ask this question, but exactly what impulses were you controlling?

Me: Absconding her to a deserted island, of course.

Lincoln: This is how I know you're not as smart as you think you are, bud.

Me: Scoff. What?!!!!

Lincoln: If given the chance to "abscond" the girl...the answer is always yes.

Me: ...

Lincoln: ...

Me: I will keep that in mind.

As I got into my car, I imagined doing just that. I would definitely be keeping that in mind.

CHAPTER 4

BLAKE

Three never-ending days had crawled by since the gorgeous stranger at the restaurant had set my world on fire. Meanwhile, Clark had turned into a human emoji, answering my texts with nothing but 'yes' and 'no', his frantic texting from the weeks before completely gone.

I didn't even know what the stranger's name was. It would have been easy to find out, but I was trying to stay as far away from temptation as possible. Getting his name would have made it hard to do that. I knew that because even without his name, his smoldering gaze and electrifying presence refused to leave my thoughts.

My day had been a relentless grind, made even worse by a call from my agent saying I didn't get yet *another* job I'd been after, and then a scathing text from Maura wanting to know when I was going to stop being a "pathetic nothing" and come home.

I couldn't help but think the universe was coming after me, punishing me for getting all hot and bothered over a guy besides my sweet boyfriend.

I was teetering on the edge when I finally trudged home after my grueling shift at the restaurant where I'd had my ass grabbed no less than three times. Upscale didn't mean better behavior.

But I'd known that already from living with the Shepfields.

I stopped outside my apartment door, sighing as I listened to the booming music coming from within.

My roommate, Charlotte, was evidently home. And my energy level was nowhere where it needed to be to handle her.

Stepping into our apartment was like entering a whirlwind. Charlotte was dancing to T Swift's "Karma", while Waldo barked and jumped around her frantically. I stopped in the doorway and took in what I was seeing. Charlotte was a fireball, her personality perfectly matching her long, fiery auburn hair and hazel eyes. The exact opposite of my shy, unsure one. She was another model with my agency, someone I hadn't known before the move. So far I'd been pleasantly surprised by her though, if overwhelmed. She was the kind of person who could light up a room with her infectious energy, while I seemed to drain the energy out of them.

Maybe we were perfect for each other.

As soon as she saw me, she let out a shrill scream and ran towards me, waving a pair of tickets like she'd won the lottery. I reached down to hug Waldo, a good way to prevent her from jumping on me as well as giving my perfect doggie some love.

"Blake, you won't believe it!" She bounced on her toes. "I got tickets to the Cobras' opening night, and check this out!" She reached for something on the coffee table and soon brandished jerseys with "Lancaster" on the back, a mischievous grin dancing on her lips.

I usually excelled in turning down invitations. Nights out never ended how I wanted. I opened my mouth to deliver my usual blurb about exhaustion and a headache…but Charlotte was having none of it tonight.

"Blake, you're always working, and you hardly ever go out with me. We need to roommate bond! And I just got that new job with Burberry today. We need to celebrate! Please. Please. Please."

Something clenched in my insides…because the Burberry job was the one I'd found out I didn't get. But that feeling just meant that I probably needed to go. Because I didn't want to be the girl who was ever bitter about her friend's success.

Before I could say anything, though, Charlotte crossed her arms and gave me a look that screamed determination. "Blake, you can't keep hiding from the world. We're going, and that's final! I *will* drag you out of this apartment."

Okay, so this girl was a bit of a badass. And that had a reluctant smile gracing my lips. "Alright, alright, I'll go," I began to say, before crashing to the floor as she tackled me. My ears would never recover from her squeals. Waldo smothered both of us in wet, sloppy kisses as I struggled to get out from under her.

Way too much touching going on here.

She finally bounced off me and did a little shimmy, right in time to "Style" starting. "It's going to be epic! Everyone has been trying to get tickets to this game now that Lancaster's on the team. Seeing him and Davis next to each other…I might faint." She grabbed her crotch and did a weird hip thrust like the players in question were in the room with us now and she was trying to direct their dicks to the sweet spot.

"Okay, we've got to leave in like ten minutes," Charlotte said guiltily, and I realized for the first time she was perfectly done up, while I'd just gotten done sweating for hours. And I smelled like food. A lethal combination.

I was tempted to change my mind and back out, but she

slapped a hand over my lips and started pushing me toward the hallway that led to my bedroom.

"Ten minutes, Blake. Don't make me drag your cute butt out of here, young lady."

I giggled, a miracle considering the shitty day I'd had, and she froze in the hallway.

"Did you just laugh?" she asked, sounding shocked.

My giggle transformed into a scowl and I marched into the bathroom and practically slammed the door behind me, her laughter ringing in my ears.

Fifteen minutes later, I'd managed to make myself somewhat presentable, and we were loaded into an Uber and headed through L.A. traffic to the Cobras arena.

"So what's the story with Lancaster?" I asked Charlotte, figuring I should know something about the team. I was a football fan myself, but I could pretend to like hockey for the night.

She grinned mischievously and made a weird moaning sound that had the driver shifting in his seat uncomfortably. "It's actually a crazy story. He's been a star defenseman for the Dallas Knights since he was drafted, and he freaking won the Cup with them last year. Then, out of the blue, the guy asks for a trade to L.A."

I hummed in confusion. "That's strange. Why would he do that after a championship win?"

Charlotte shrugged. "No one really knows. It's a mystery. But trust me, Blake, he's the best defenseman in the league, and everyone's buzzing about his arrival. It's like a dream come true for L.A. fans."

I gave her what I hoped was an excited grin before staring out at the passing city lights, her continued chatter a comforting background to the drive.

———

Ari

Tonight was the night. The first game of the NHL season with the motherfucking Cobras.

And I was nervous.

Which never happened. I was Mr. Cool. Mr. Collected. I left it to Lincoln to be nervous.

Okay, that was a stretch. Lincoln didn't get nervous either. But my late-summer trade had disrupted my rhythm, leaving me with fewer practices with my new teammates than would've been ideal. Would have been nice to see Blake's billboard like the week after the Stanley Cup win. Ya know?

I was stepping onto the ice with a group of guys I barely knew, one of which I *hated*, and the weight of expectations hung heavy on my shoulders. If I wanted any chance of making my way back to Dallas next year, I needed to have a stellar season, a perfect season, in fact. Be so good that Dallas *had* to forgive me and take me back.

I stared at myself in the mirror, trying to come to grips with the fact I was dressed in an oh-so-vibrant purple and yellow uniform. And there was a big fucking snake on my chest. It was like trading a steak for some cold oatmeal. Everything about it felt wrong. Blue and white was a *much* better color combo, in my opinion. The Knight emblem was a badge of honor, stitched into the very fabric of who I was as a player.

Now, here I was, part of the *Cobras* crew, and it was like swapping my noble steed for a...well, a slithering snake.

And I'd always hated snakes.

For a fleeting moment, despondency slipped over my skin. It felt like I was standing on the edge of a precipice, uncertain of what lay ahead. Doubts crept in, like insidious whispers in the back of my mind, questioning whether this would all work out. What if I couldn't get her back? What if I suddenly sucked at hockey?

I chuckled to myself at that one, shaking off the weird feeling. Yeah, none of that was going to happen.

I couldn't afford to indulge in self-doubt, not now.

With a determined sigh, I reached for my phone and tapped out a text to my bestie. I could use some of his sage wisdom right about now.

> Me: I hate purple and gold.

Lincoln: It's true. It washes you out.

> Me: Fuck you. Take that back. I look amazing in purple and gold. Everyone thinks so.

Lincoln: ...

> Me: Ok, well I don't know if everyone thinks so. Let's crowdsource this.

Lincoln: ?

I added Monroe to the chat and sent a selfie...

> Me: Monroe, what do you think of me in purple and gold?

Lincoln: Monroe? Don't talk to him. Don't answer that question.

Monroe: I really like purple and gold.

Lincoln: But not more than me in blue and white...right? Right?

> Me: The people have spoken. I look good in purple and gold.

Lincoln: She's not your people. She's my people. Monroe, tell him you're not his people.

Lincoln: Wait, don't tell him anything!

Monroe: Sigh.

Me: Gif of athlete doing victory lap.

Lincoln: middle finger emoji

Me: I still hate purple and gold.

Lincoln: I know. One year, buddy.

Me: One year.

Lincoln: Knock 'em dead tonight. You've got this.

I sent a giant heart after that text, because what else did you do to tell someone you loved them bunches?

A throat cleared, and I glanced up from my phone, realizing I'd been staring at it with a manic grin. Walker was standing there, leaning against the doorway like the Disney prince he was.

"Ready for the game?" he asked in that typical, casual Walker way.

"Yep. Go Cobras!" I tried to say exuberantly. Came out a little flat though, if I was being honest.

Walker suddenly shifted awkwardly, like a puppy unsure of its footing.

I raised an eyebrow, waiting for whatever he was going to say.

"Um, well," he began, fumbling for words. "I know you must be feeling weird, so...is there anything that you and

Lincoln used to do before the game that you'd want me to do?"

Oh, this was good. I practically jumped up with excitement. "Yes!" I exclaimed, unable to contain my enthusiasm.

"Okay, what is it?" Walker asked with determination.

Lincoln and I didn't really have a pregame ritual. We were basically just badasses whose badassery was a ritual in and of itself. But this was a good distraction.

"Well, it's a little weird," I warned, but Walker just nodded intently. "Linc and I...we shake it off," I said, deserving an Oscar because my voice was so steady.

Walker blinked. "You shake it off?" he repeated, his voice tinged with disbelief.

I grinned. "Trust me, it works wonders. But hey, it was a Linc and me thing. Doesn't have to be a Walker and me thing, ya know?"

"No, no," he said quickly, holding up his hands. "I can shake it off. Let's do it. Let's get you ready for the game."

Where was the motherfucking camera when I needed it? No offense to anyone's mothers by the way; it had been ages since I'd done something like that. And mothers were forever safe from me now that I'd gotten Blake back.

I guess until she became a mother.

Fuck. Don't get hard now, Ari.

I grabbed my phone and pulled up my "Shake It Off" playlist, cranking the volume to the max. Taylor Swift's infectious beat filled the room, and I launched into an exaggerated shimmy that would make every Swiftie proud.

Walker hesitated for a moment, then got into it. His awkward moves slowly morphed into a goofy dance, and soon enough, we were both grooving like nobody was watching. I kept my ear out for the sound of anyone coming, and when I heard footsteps, I conveniently stopped and leaned against the wall like the cool stud I was.

The door swung open, and some of our teammates entered, stopping dead in their tracks at the spectacle of Walker doing the "robot" to Tay-Tay.

Their jaws dropped.

I burst into laughter at their stunned expressions, and Walker came to a screeching halt, his cheeks reddening as he stared at his teammates.

"Nice moves, Walker," I drawled, doing a slow clap.

"What. He—" Walker stammered, before shooting me an exasperated glare.

"I feel much better," I told him seriously as other players filed into the room, word spreading of Walker's "moves."

Before Walker could respond, Coach strode in, his presence commanding immediate attention. Everyone quickly sobered up.

"Gentlemen," he began, his eyes scanning the room, "tonight is the first game of the season. The beginning of a new journey. We've worked tirelessly to get here, and now it's time to show the world what we're made of."

He paused, letting the gravity of the moment sink in. "Remember, we're not just a team; we're a family. On this ice, we fight together, we bleed together, and we win together. The Cobras have a legacy, and it's our job to uphold it. The fans out there, they're counting on us to give them a season they'll never forget."

The coach's voice grew more intense, a fire of determination burning in his eyes. "I don't need to remind you that every shift counts, every pass, every shot on goal. But I will remind you that you've got the talent, the skills, and the heart to be champions. Believe in yourselves, and believe in each other. Trust your instincts, and leave everything out there on that ice."

He paused once more, the room filled with a charged energy. "Tonight, we're not only playing for ourselves; we're playing for this city, for the Cobras' faithful. So go out there and give them a show they'll never forget. Let's bring home that victory, boys!"

It was a great speech, and as we all roared, chanting "Cobras" at the top of our lungs, for a second, I could almost feel that first game excitement.

Just like I always had with the Knights.

But then I noticed Soto in the corner, his sneer all too evident. And there went *all* the happy feelings.

Focus on the fact you might get to see Blake tonight, I told myself as we headed down the hallway that led to the ice.

And wouldn't you know it, but that was finally enough to make me feel alright.

CHAPTER 5

ARI

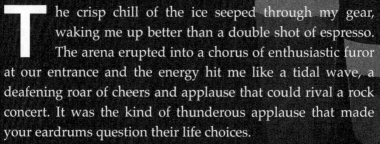

The crisp chill of the ice seeped through my gear, waking me up better than a double shot of espresso. The arena erupted into a chorus of enthusiastic furor at our entrance and the energy hit me like a tidal wave, a deafening roar of cheers and applause that could rival a rock concert. It was the kind of thunderous applause that made your eardrums question their life choices.

Underneath my skates, the ice was as smooth as a freshly waxed dance floor. Each glide was like a sweet serenade from the rink itself, reminding me that I was the lead in this little ice ballet, and I had a standing ovation to earn.

I scanned the seats where Blake was supposed to be, but she was fashionably late, leaving a conspicuous gap in the crowd.

Or maybe she wasn't going to come.

No, I'd been assured by my contact at Blake's agency that her roommate would be as persuasive as she needed to be if the tickets came with the condition she had to bring Blake.

Tonight was the place to be, after all. There were celebs everywhere according to the team PR goons. The roommate would not want to miss out.

I shook my head and brought my mind back to warmups. I had a soulmate to impress and a game to win, and I intended to do it with flair.

————

The game was about to kick off, and the announcer's voice echoed through the arena, introducing each member of the Cobras. It was yet another strange moment, hearing my name connected to this new team instead of the Knights.

Walker, always the motivator, slapped me on the ass and threw out a, "Slay, baby!" I blinked at him in disbelief.

"Did you just tell me to slay?" I asked, my eyebrow arched.

He grinned. "Seemed like something Lincoln would say, you know? Get the vibe going."

I couldn't help but shake my head, my expression deadpan. "Lincoln is much cooler than that, Walker. He would be *shook* if he was with us right now."

"Oh," Walker said glumly, his features falling like I'd spit in his ice cream.

I patted Walker's rear, and I gave him a nice nod of appreciation. "Thanks though, buddy," I said before gliding around the ice.

The game was about to begin, and it was time to show them what this Cobra was made of.

I let the electric energy of the arena wash over me. Dallas fans were better in every way, of course. But in a pinch, an L.A. crowd would do.

This was what I lived for, after all—the adrenaline, the spotlight, the game. I couldn't help but flash a cocky grin as I lifted my stick in acknowledgment of the fans. They loved a showman, and I was more than willing to oblige.

I gave a little bow because I was fancy like that, and the

crowd went wild. Hockey for me wasn't just about playing the game; it was about putting on a performance. The crowd was here for entertainment, after all, and I aimed to give them a show they'd never forget.

I may have been showing off for the crowd, but there was really only one thing on my mind at that moment—the fact that Blake was here.

There she was, in my jersey, looking like my wildest wet dream. The fabric clung to her like a glove, accentuating all the right curves. Her gold hair framed her face, and those eyes…fuck. Those eyes were blowing my mind.

Like they always had.

She would have looked better in silver and blue, but the view right then was pretty close to damn perfection. She was outshining every star in this arena.

Blake was also staring at me in total shock, her eyes wide and surprised.

And dare I say…excited?

At least she remembered me. I would've been quite disappointed if in three days' time I'd been forgotten. I'd tried to be more memorable than that at our little lunch date.

Not that it had been three days since I'd seen her. You can bet your bottom lip I was catching as many glimpses of her that I could. I'd been past the restaurant twice today just to get my fix.

Now I understood why Lincoln was such a fan of that little app. My BFF was brilliant.

I'd have to remember to tell him that next time too.

As Blake and I stared at each other, the roar of the crowd seemed to dim. It was as if time slowed, and in that suspended moment, it was only the two of us, lost in a sea of people.

I winked at her and blew a kiss, snorting with how freaking red she got.

She was a-dor-able.

Her roommate started bouncing around like a pinball, spitting questions at her.

"Get your head in the game, Ari!" Coach Kim's voice snapped me out of my Blake induced reverie, his tone no-nonsense.

I nodded, trying to focus. The game was about to begin.

As a defenseman—the best in the league, might I add—my role was critical. I always had to be ready to intercept passes, break up plays, and deliver bone-rattling checks when needed. My job was to protect Mr. Prince Charming on the blue line. It was helpful that Walker was a shot-blocking machine. But based on last year's team...he needed me. Bad.

The puck dropped, and the game exploded into motion. The Boston Reds charged forward, and I readied myself for the onslaught that was about to begin.

"Let's do this, boys," I shouted as Tommy skated past.

He winked at me, skating faster, and I decided I liked him. At least for now.

Determined to impress Blake...and everyone else, I intercepted passes with surgical precision, disrupting Boston's plans at every turn. The crowd roared with each successful play, their energy spiking higher with each passing second.

A few minutes into the game, we found ourselves on a power play. Our first goal came from a blistering slap shot from the right circle, a rocket that left the opposing goalie helpless.

I whooped and tackled Tommy, along with the rest of the team. Getting that first goal of the season was clutch.

Play continued, and a few minutes later, Boston suddenly had a deftly executed breakaway, blowing past Soto as I was checked hard into the glass. Walker made a jaw-dropping save.

"That's my fucking goalie," I yelled as he sent the puck across the ice. He smirked at me cockily.

Maybe Walker was a little bit of a badass. I could consider letting him into Lincoln's and my badass club.

Maybe.

While most of the team was meeting my expectations, Soto was blowing right past even the shit of what I expected from him. He was fucking sucking, a huge liability seemingly more interested in causing bedlam than playing the game. At one point—in a bizarre twist—he smashed me against the boards, a move that had me snarling in both frustration and disbelief.

"Your mama hits harder than that, Soto," I quipped, my voice dripping with sarcasm.

He just smirked at me like the giant douchebag he was, and the game continued on.

During breaks, my gaze wandered over to Blake. She was tracking my every movement, it seemed, blushing prettily every time I skated past.

"Having fun?" I mouthed at one point, smiling as she ducked her head and nodded shyly.

Fuck, she was killing me with her perfection.

As the game reached its climax, we found ourselves in a tight spot. The score was tied, and time was running out. Tommy seized the moment once again. With a burst of speed, he danced around defenders and unleashed a wrist shot that found the top corner of the net.

Tommy pumped a fist in the air as he skated across the ice. I checked the clock. Two more minutes and the win was ours.

Boston wouldn't go down without a fight, though. With thirty seconds left to go, their coach signaled for their goalie to head to the bench and sent out an extra skater in a last-ditch effort to secure a win.

As a defenseman, I usually focused on protecting our own

net rather than scoring, but sometimes, the stars aligned just right.

Case in point.

With twenty seconds left, the puck found its way to me at the blue line. With the net empty, and the arena buzzing with anticipation. I decided to have some fun.

I wound up for a slap shot, and the puck sailed toward the vacant net, hitting the back of it with a resounding thud. The red light illuminated, and the arena erupted into a deafening roar.

The crowd was fucking wild. I did a little shimmy, just for Walker, and then I skated toward the glass in front of Blake's seat, blowing her a big kiss. I was tackled to the ground before I could see her reaction, the buzzer sounding as the game ended.

My teammates were pounding me on the back, the crowd's applause continuing to echo around us.

And I thought to myself...maybe the season wouldn't be so bad after all.

———

Blake

Charlotte's voice was a constant stream of excitement, echoing off the dimly lit corridor that led to the locker rooms. Her fiery auburn hair bounced with each step, her hazel eyes glittering with glee. She couldn't stop talking about the game, about the celebs we'd seen...about what Ari Lancaster had done.

"I still can't believe you're trying to claim you don't know him," she hissed, sounding a bit surly.

I shifted uncomfortably, attempting to downplay the situation. "Charlotte, you're making a big deal out of nothing. I served his table at Franco's. That's it. We barely talked."

I sounded nonchalant, but inside, I was a different story. I was replaying the moment when his eyes locked onto mine, the wink he'd given...the blown kiss.

And obsessing/freaking out over the fact that his name was Ari.

My first crush was a boy named Ari.

But there was no way this was the same guy.

Kids from a group home didn't end up becoming star hockey players.

He'd been twelve when we'd met, and that Ari didn't play hockey. It was a miracle that I'd been adopted at ten. Ari being adopted after I'd left would have even been rarer, not because he wasn't incredible...but because people didn't usually want older kids. Not unless they had a motive.

And there weren't any kids at that place playing sports.

It was just a weird coincidence.

I'm sure there were a million Blakes out there with similar features.

An arena employee, clad in a sharp suit, met us at the end of the hallway and interrupted my inner freak out. His smile was almost as blinding as the arena lights had been as he guided us toward the locker room.

"You're two lucky ladies, being invited into the locker room on opening night," he smirked.

The way he said it made me feel dirty, like we were groupies expected to service the athletes once we got in there.

"Where did you say you got these tickets?" I murmured to Charlotte, realizing I'd never asked. For all I knew, it *was* a player who had those kinds of expectations that had given her them in the first place.

Charlotte either didn't hear me, or didn't want to answer, because she didn't acknowledge my question as the door leading to the locker room was opened.

I should just leave. Yep, that's what I needed to do. What

was I thinking? I should go home, cuddle with Waldo, and call Clark, figure out why he'd gone quiet.

That's what a good girlfriend would do. Someone who owed Clark as much as I did…

But my feet didn't seem to be in agreement with my head because I followed Charlotte through the door, my heart threatening to burst out of my chest.

The sound of laughter spilled from behind a door at the end of the hallway in front of us. We started forward, but Charlotte stopped halfway down and turned toward me. "Blake, don't fuck this up for me," she said seriously.

My eyes widened, hurt flooding through me at the unfriendly tone of her words.

"Of course," I finally monotoned back after I got over the sudden switch in my roommate's personality.

The door at the end of the hallway swung open before she could say anything else, and we were instantly enveloped in a whirlwind of sensations. The air was thick with the potent blend of cologne, sweat, and adrenaline—a heady cocktail that made my head swim and my nerves ramp up even more. I'd grown up around rich people, world leaders, socialites… but hot as fuck professional athletes had not been in the Shepfields' crowd.

This was a first for me.

As I ventured deeper into the locker room, a warm blush hit my cheeks. The players weren't covering up on our behalf.

My modeling jobs had gotten me used to naked bodies.

But none of the male models were as hot as these guys.

Their gazes tracked us as we walked through the room. It felt like a spotlight was trained on us, and most of them had a gleam in their eyes like they wanted to eat us alive.

"Well, well. What do we have here?" one of the players purred. A douchebag looking red head that I remembered had tackled—oops, wrong sport—checked Ari at one point.

As unfamiliar as I was with hockey, I was pretty sure you weren't supposed to hit your own teammate.

Accident or not, he wasn't my favorite.

Charlotte shot him a flirty grin as he leaned against the lockers and took her in. His gaze flicked to me. "Two for one special? Must be my lucky day," he said.

"In your dreams, Soto," a deep, growly voice said from behind me.

Ari Lancaster.

I was shaking slightly as I turned, almost unbidden like I couldn't resist his gravitational force, and I was having trouble breathing all of a sudden.

Of course, my mind had gone to what he would look like under clothes…but it certainly hadn't prepared me for this.

His emerald eyes met mine with an intensity that stole my breath. Time stood still as our gazes held with a charged connection.

He was only wearing a towel, and it was sitting obscenely low on his lean hips. His skin was a sun-kissed bronze color that had me salivating, a sinful masterpiece, chiseled by the gods of desire themselves. Every inch of him exuded raw, unadulterated sex appeal, a living testament to masculine perfection.

His broad shoulders sloped down to a taut, sculpted chest that begged for exploration, each defined muscle an invitation to temptation. His abdomen was a landscape of sinewy ridges and valleys, leading the way to a set of washboard abs that had me wanting to weep. That sexy-v, the one responsible for wet panties everywhere, dragged my eyes directly to his towel…that was slowly rising in front in a huge tent that had my eyes wide and a squeak passing from my lips.

I quickly yanked my gaze up to Ari's insanely handsome face, an unrepentant smirk on his lips. He lifted an eyebrow, daring me to say something, his damp, ebony locks falling over his forehead, the wet tendrils framing his striking face like a sensual curtain. Glistening droplets of water clung to his bronzed skin, tracing a path down the landscape of his chest.

Ari Lancaster was the embodiment of desire.

His gaze was roaming my body hungrily, so I gave myself a few more seconds to take him in.

Tattoos adorned his golden skin everywhere. Intricate designs, some inky black and others vibrant with color, painted a vivid story that I could spend hours exploring. In the center of Ari's sculpted chest lay a tattoo of a large, broken birdcage. The intricate details of the cage were etched with precision, its bars twisted and shattered, as if they could no longer contain the wild spirit within.

Inside the fractured cage, a magnificent bird soared, its wings stretched wide as if it had just tasted the sweet nectar of freedom. The bird's feathers were exquisite, each one a testament to the beauty that lay beyond the confines of captivity.

My body reacted with a rush of warmth, a primal response to this magnificent specimen before me. Every cell in my body recognized his perfection on a visceral level. My core clenched with needy emptiness. My breasts felt tight and aching. My breathing was unsteady. I—

An arm slid into mine as Charlotte pressed against me. I actually jumped from the interruption to my lust fest.

"Introduce me, roomie," she purred as she eyed Ari's body...and huge erection, like he was her last meal.

The room suddenly came alive again, the noises of the other players filling the air as the spell I'd been under was broken. We were, in fact, not alone. And I'd probably just embarrassed the hell out of myself by eye fucking their star as if I was in a trance.

"Blake," Charlotte hissed, shooting me a harsh side eye.

Something nasty slid around inside of me.

I realized...I was jealous. It wasn't a sensation I was used to. Actually, I couldn't remember having this particular feeling once with Clark.

Right. Boyfriend. Clark.

Fuck, I was a terrible person.

It didn't change the fact that it was making me sick to my stomach to think of her seeing the same delicious sight that I was seeing.

What if he thought she was hot? I mean, she *was* hot. Charlotte always had a guy a snap of her fingers away.

"Hi," I found myself saying, also realizing that Ari and I hadn't said anything to each other yet.

"Hi, sunshine," he drawled.

"Sunshine?" Charlotte's gaze bounced between the two of us. "Sorry, have you actually met my roommate?" she said sarcastically.

The smirk on Ari's face slipped away, and his gaze hardened as he seemed to size up Charlotte for the first time. He yawned and his gaze came back to me, a clear dismissal that I was positive Charlotte wasn't used to.

"It's nice to meet you," Charlotte said in a sickeningly sweet, desperate sounding voice...that was also unlike her usual tone.

"Why you bothering with Lancaster, sweetness?" The skeezy red head, Soto I think Ari had called him, sidled up to Charlotte and slid his arm around her waist. She reluctantly turned away from Ari and flashed Soto a fake, flirty grin.

Soto didn't seem to mind though, because his hand slid further down and he squeezed her ass as she placed her palms on his chest.

After my roommate's strange turn in behavior tonight, I was almost thinking they deserved each other.

Soto glanced at me over Charlotte's head. "You two coming out with us tonight to celebrate the big win?"

"Yep," Charlotte all but squealed, right at the same time I said "no."

"Aww, come on, Blake. I need my bestie with me," Ari said cajolingly, drawing my eyes back to his—bare ass.

While I'd been distracted, he'd turned around and dropped the towel, showcasing a backside so yummy that...I wanted to sink my teeth into it.

That was a weird, but very accurate description for what I was feeling as I took in the sight.

I squeaked and turned away, but not before realizing he had a large butterfly tattooed on his back.

I heard the low husk of his laughter, but I didn't dare turn, not caring how idiotic I looked.

A long minute passed. "What do you say, BFF? Going to help me celebrate?" Ari said in a voice that was scarily alluring.

I'd never been attracted to the sound of a voice before, but judging by the way my insides were fluttering, a tingling pulsing warmth spreading everywhere, Ari had changed that.

Mayday. Mayday. Mayday.

My internal alarm was blaring as I took in Ari's clothed form.

He was puffing out his bottom lip beseechingly. Which was somehow attractive on him instead of annoying.

"Okay," I found myself saying softly.

Ari gave a fist pump and then another freakishly attractive man with light brown hair was slinging an arm around his shoulder. "Let's get drunkkkk!" he yelled. And the whole locker room cheered in agreement.

———

Sitting in the sleek black sports car next to Ari, Walker in the backseat, my nerves were on edge. Adrenaline from the game and locker room was pulsing in my ears, an odd mix of unease and excitement that I didn't know what to do with.

Charlotte had left me in the locker room to "go fuck Soto". Her words exactly. She'd said she would meet me at the bar we were headed to. And I'd somehow ended up in the car with the two hottest men I'd ever seen in my life.

Although Walker somehow didn't have even close to the same effect on me as Ari.

Ari and Walker's conversation about the game flowed around me like a river, their voices blending into a distant hum. I couldn't help but glance at Ari every now and then, and he seemed to return the favor, his gaze flicking my way every few seconds in a hungry way that had me shifting in my seat uncomfortably.

My fingers toyed with the hem of my jersey as I tried to focus on their chatter, but my thoughts kept drifting. I couldn't help but stare at Ari's hand resting casually on the gearshift, his tattooed fingers strong and capable. They looked like they could do so much more than just handle a car. Like they...

Guilt tearing into me, I pulled out my phone and texted Clark a quick "hello", wondering if he'd answer me this time.

Ari's voice interrupted my thoughts, and I jolted in my seat. "Who ya texting?" he asked, his tone casual.

I hesitated for a moment, my heart racing. Clearing my throat, I tried to sound as nonchalant as he did. "Just my boyfriend," I replied, clutching my phone tightly.

From the back seat, Walker let out a knowing inhale, and I couldn't help but feel self-conscious. I knew how it appeared, like I was teetering on the edge of something I shouldn't. Like I was some slut about to hurt the guy who loved me for a chance with a NHL star. There was a name for girls like that, wasn't there. Puck something?

I desperately clung to the idea that I was merely making friends in a new city, even if those friends happened to be with two incredibly appealing men.

"Boyfriend, huh? I knew you were too pretty to be single," Ari drawled, not sounding upset at all.

I bit down on my lip. "He lives in New York. I—I've been with him since I was 16. He's the son of the Shep—my parent's friends."

"Can't be too smart," Ari commented. "Not following you to Cali. Who knows what might be waiting to scoop you up."

Walker snorted from behind me, and I didn't dare to look back at him.

"He runs SEC Media with his father. It keeps him quite busy," I said lamely, not adding that I'd recently obliterated his heart.

"If you were my girl, there wouldn't be anything that would keep me away."

I choked on some spit in my mouth, so shocked at what he seemed to be insinuating.

"Good thing I have a new bestie to keep me safe," I finally said lightly, ignoring the storm of tension building in the car.

Ari chuckled lowly. "Yes, that's a good thing, sunshine."

Walker and Ari went back to talking about the game, leaving me shaking in my seat for the rest of the drive.

And Clark never texted me back.

CHAPTER 6

BLAKE

The upscale L.A. bar exuded sensuality, its sleek, modern exterior basking in the soft, seductive glow of neon accents. Tall palm trees swayed in the balmy night, their fronds brushing against one another. Inside, the subdued, jazzy music set a sultry tone, as if the very air itself was caressing those who entered.

We pulled up, and a valet, impeccably dressed, waited at the ready. I'd heard of this place. More relaxed than the city's trendiest clubs, it was the place celebs came to when they wanted a more quiet night out…Charlotte had actually tried to get in last week with some friends and had been rejected at the door.

She'd bitched about it for hours that night when she'd come home to me sitting on our couch, reading a book.

My nerves shot up as I glanced at the line of eager people wound around the building. So many eyes that could stare at us when we got out. I pulled at my jersey, second guessing keeping it on when I saw how nicely everyone was dressed. I glanced at Ari and Walker. They were dressed to impress as well.

Ari emerged from the car first, igniting a chorus of cheers from the crowd. The valet was standing by my door, reaching out to open it, when Ari barked something at him. The guy immediately backed away, opening Walker's door instead, which had another cheer coming from the crowd.

Ari opened my door, peering down at me with a dark promise in his eyes that had me hesitating to accept his extended hand.

"Come on, pretty girl. Let's celebrate," he murmured. Our fingertips met, and I swear there were sparks, desire and want crackling between our palms.

My heart quickened in my chest as he helped me out of the car, pulling on my hand a little harder than necessary so that I fell forward into his chest. For a second, we just stared at one another.

Had his mouth always been that delicious looking? The overall appeal of him was overwhelming, licking at my skin in lusty waves. He winked at me and then led me forward toward the bar by the hand he was gripping unyieldingly. I ignored the crowd, trying to pretend they weren't there even as women, and men, screamed Ari's name.

I grew up a Shepfield. I was used to flashing lights and people shouting for me to "Look here! No, here!" at society events. But there were people crying as we walked past the line, Walker flanking us from behind.

I wasn't used to that. Was this normal for an NHL player? I stared speculatively at Ari, and he just flashed me an amused grin, like he wasn't phased at all.

Inside the bar, an air of sophistication blended seamlessly with an intimate ambiance. Soft, golden hues bathed the décor, casting a warm and inviting atmosphere over the polished mahogany bar and plush leather seating, beckoning guests to relax and enjoy. The walls displayed tasteful, contemporary art, while modern gold and black lighting overhead illuminated the scene with a subtle, elegant radiance.

The room was buzzing with lively conversation and laughter, and I could see that a lot of Cobra players were already gathered by the bar across the room. A lot of Cobra players and Charlotte, who'd somehow managed to bang Soto and change into a skin tight blood red dress before getting here.

She waved to me, her other hand clinging to Soto's shirt. He was staring at me pretty intensely for a stranger, and I shifted uncomfortably.

"Oh my goshhhh," Ari suddenly screeched, sounding like the epitome of a tween girl as I was dragged to the right toward a very attractive-looking couple standing at the other bar in the room. Their expressions brimmed with amusement, as if they were no strangers to Ari's animated entrances.

"You came," Ari cried...his voice almost emotional as he threw an arm around the golden haired dreamboat we'd been headed toward and hugged him tight. The man chuckled and clapped Ari on the back...who was still holding onto me with his other hand, by the way. Once again I tried to pull away, but he wasn't having it.

"Wouldn't miss it, buddy," Ari's friend said in a delicious sounding voice. There was an absolutely stunning woman standing next to him with long black hair and sparkling green eyes. She had a gentle smile on her lips as she glanced from the guys to me, staring at me curiously. A peaceful feeling settled over me as we gazed at each other. Kind of weird actually, but something instantly told me this girl could be my friend.

Ari let go of the golden god and pulled me forward. "Blake, I want you to meet my second best friend, Lincoln.

And my third best friend, Monroe." Ari moved to give Monroe a hug.

"She is not your best friend, Ari," Lincoln said exasperatedly–and a bit possessively, I thought–as he pulled her into his body so she couldn't give Ari a hug.

I stared at them for a second longer than was normal. But it was crazy the way they seemed to gravitate around each other. Like even though they were talking to us, they were still wrapped up in each other. A longing settled in my gut.

I wanted that feeling. To know that your soul was safe in someone else's hands.

I couldn't even imagine what that would have felt like.

"Blake?" Lincoln repeated slowly, a glint of surprise and admiration on his face as his gaze flicked from me to Ari. "Is this the girl who stole my first best friend spot?"

He almost sounded like he'd heard of me before. But would Ari really have talked about me to his best friend after a random encounter in a restaurant?

Something that felt like butterflies soared around in my chest at the thought.

"Blake Shepfield, Lincoln Daniels. Lincoln Daniels, Blake Shepfield," Ari said casually, as if it wasn't weird at all that he'd told him about me.

"It's nice to meet you," I said nervously.

"You don't follow hockey, do you?" Monroe asked gently in a sweet, amused voice.

I bit my lip and glanced shyly up at Ari, hoping he wouldn't be offended. "Tonight was the first time I've ever watched. I'm more of a football girl."

Ari staggered like I'd stabbed him in the chest. "You don't know what you've been missing," he said theatrically.

You, a voice blared in my head. *I've been missing you.*

I pushed that thought away as quickly as I could.

"It will be nice to have someone who isn't falling at these guy's feet," said Monroe with a smirk.

I glanced at her...boyfriend? Husband? "He plays hockey too?"

"We played on the Knights together. We've actually played together since prep school," Ari explained, and there was longing in his voice. Longing that made my heart hurt for him.

I wondered if I'd ever feel comfortable enough to ask him what made him leave the Knights. It was obviously a very sensitive subject.

"You were awesome out there," Lincoln said, making Ari freaking beam. "You even made up for Soto being on the ice somehow."

The mention of his name made me glance over to where Soto and Charlotte were chatting with other members of the team. Soto was glaring at us even as my roommate tried to get his attention. A shiver stretched across my skin.

Ari let go of my hand though and instead pressed his palm against my lower back, in that space you're not supposed to go if you're *just a friend*. His thumb slid back and forth, and even through my jersey it felt like electricity sparking across my skin from his touch.

"So, Blake," Lincoln drawled. "How did you become besties with my boy, Ari? I would question your taste, but he did the same thing to me all those years ago, so I can only empathize with you."

Ari let out an indignant bark of laughter. "Admit it. I'm the classy one of this relationship. You would be lost without me."

Lincoln smirked, and I felt a bit dizzy from the delicious, grade A, alphamale energy radiating off these two guys.

And then Walker decided to sidle up next to us.

"Hey guys," he said, his voice adorably nervous.

Ari sighed and rubbed a hand across his face as if he were pained. "Lincoln, meet your number one puck slut. Mr. Disney Prince himself. Walker."

Walker groaned and turned to leave, before Ari reached out and grabbed his shirt with a laugh. "Come here, buddy. We need to tell Lincoln about our new pre game ritual."

Walker's face went an almost violet shade of red before he covered it in embarrassment. It was kind of funny to see this big, tattooed hottie cringing in embarrassment.

Lincoln studied Walker for a moment before a slow grin spread across his beautiful face. "You were fucking amazing tonight, bro," he said, holding out a hand for Walker to shake.

Walker seemed like he was about to faint from Lincoln talking to him. "Really?" he said. "I mean, yeah. Thanks. It was a great game."

Ari was shaking with laughter as his gaze bounced between the two of them, but his palm had slid to my lower hip and I was now pressed against his side.

It felt like I fit there, against him like that.

But then Clark's face flashed in my mind and the sour taste of guilt was once again flooding me as memories of the past hit me hard.

I felt a numbness wash over me as the icy water of the bathtub surrounded my trembling body. The pills I'd taken were doing their job, sending me into a disorienting haze. The world around me blurred, and my thoughts became muddled. I was spiraling into darkness. It was almost over.

I was almost free.

As I lay there, the water seemed to consume me, its cold fingers wrapping around my limbs, dragging me deeper into a chilling abyss. The room's harsh, artificial light cast eerie shadows on the walls, creating a surreal and haunting atmosphere. My body felt heavy and unresponsive.

Numb.

Just how I liked it.

Everything was a disjointed blur, and my consciousness slipped away like a wisp of smoke. It was a sensation of sinking, sinking deeper into the unforgiving depths of despair.

But then, in that suffocating darkness, a pair of hands reached into the void and grabbed hold of me. I was lifted, pulled from the cold. For a fleeting moment, I regained a fragment of awareness.

"Blake!" a voice called out, filled with panic and desperation. It was Clark. His voice echoed in my foggy mind, a distant cry in the wilderness.

I tried to respond, tried to reach out to him, but my body was still betraying me. The world remained a jumbled mess of sensations and disjointed images. I could see Clark's face, twisted with fear and anguish, hovering above me.

And then, I was no longer in the bathtub. I was being carried, my body limp and motionless, cradled in Clark's arms. His footsteps echoed in a frantic rhythm as he rushed me out of our apartment and into the cool night air.

We reached the car, and I was placed gently in the back seat. I could hear Clark's ragged breathing, his voice trembling as he spoke to me, trying to keep me conscious. His words were a lifeline in the darkness, a desperate plea for me to stay with him.

The car sped through the city streets, its tires screeching against the asphalt. Sirens wailed in the distance, drawing nearer with each passing second. I was fading, slipping further away from the world.

And then there was the harsh, fluorescent lighting of a hospital room. The sterile smell of antiseptic stinging my nostrils. I could feel the weight of monitors and tubes connected to my body, a reminder of the fragility of life.

Clark, his face etched with relief and anguish, was sitting by my bedside, holding my hand as if it were the most precious thing in the world.

He had saved me, and I owed him everything.

"Blake?" Ari's voice called, and I was jolted back to the present where I stood pressed against his hard body.

"Sorry. Um. I'm just going to use the restroom real quick," I mumbled, feeling the faint blush on my cheeks. I needed a break from him. I couldn't breathe, couldn't think, couldn't do the right thing when he was around.

I pulled away from him, and he let me go without a fuss.

It was all I could do to keep my footsteps steady as I headed toward the hallway that led to the bathroom.

I stood there in the dimly lit restroom of the bar, my eyes meeting my reflection in the mirror. And for a moment, I hardly recognized the person staring back at me. It was as if a veil had been lifted, revealing a version of myself I'd never seen before.

Gone was the haunted, hollow look that had followed me for so long. The exhaustion that had etched deep lines under my eyes had seemingly vanished. Instead, I saw a face that was alive, vibrant, and, dare I say it... happy.

I shook my head, my heart racing like a hummingbird's wings as I splashed some cool water on my face, attempting to calm the storm swirling inside my chest.

Okay, I was fine. I could go out there. Establish firm boundaries. Be friends.

I pulled out my phone first though, hovering over the keyboard as I thought about sending Clark another text. But he hadn't even read my other one according to the read receipts...so I didn't bother.

All my good intentions seemed to run away when I finally stepped back into the hallway, and my senses were immediately overtaken by Ari's arresting presence. He leaned casually against the wall, his strong frame surrounded by the soft, muted lighting. His dazzling green gaze cast a spell over me as we stood there in the hall.

"You didn't need to wait," I managed to murmur, though my voice betrayed my struggle to maintain composure.

Ari's response was a slow, seductive smile that made my knees feel weak. "Someone would be a fool not to wait for you, sunshine."

His words hung in the air, heavy with unspoken desires, and I could feel the invisible thread that drew us together, weaving a tapestry of attraction and longing. My heart pounded in my chest, and my voice trembled as I met his unwavering gaze.

"Ari," I began, my voice laced with a husky undertone, "we can only be friends."

"Yeah, sunshine? And why's that?" he asked, crowding me against the wall with his hard, perfect body. His spicy orange and leather scent washed over me and I took a deep breath, wanting as much as I could get.

The way he was staring at me. It was like he wanted to eat me alive. Like he was starstruck by my mere presence.

Like I was his good thing in life.

"Because I have a boyfriend."

"You should probably put him on notice then, sunshine," he murmured with a slightly crazed grin.

"Of what?" I whispered.

"Of the fact he's about to lose his girl."

His lips brushed against mine then, so, so softly, and it felt like a piece of my heart was clicking into place. Ari pulled back and stared at me for a long moment.

"Fuck it," he swore roughly, and his lips crashed against my mouth. His tongue licked into me, sliding against mine, changing my fucking life.

I'd never been kissed like this.

Like someone would die without the taste of me.

I broke the kiss and stepped back, our heavy breaths mingling in the air.

He smiled at me, the kind of smile that could break a million hearts, that would break mine...and he pressed his lips against mine. One. More. Time.

And then I ran.

CHAPTER 7

ARI

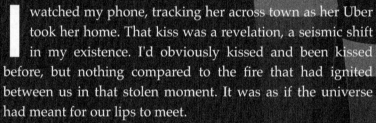

I watched my phone, tracking her across town as her Uber took her home. That kiss was a revelation, a seismic shift in my existence. I'd obviously kissed and been kissed before, but nothing compared to the fire that had ignited between us in that stolen moment. It was as if the universe had meant for our lips to meet.

And she'd kissed me back. I know she had.

She'd run away, and I'd let her go.

Just for tonight.

I'd had months to wrap around the idea of her. I could give her some time to adjust to me too.

Obsession didn't even begin to cover what I felt. It was more than that; it was an insatiable craving, a need that clawed at me from the inside. I thought I'd known what it meant to desire someone, to desire her...but tasting her, feeling the soft press of her lips, the sweet taste of her mouth against mine...it was like a drug, an addiction I couldn't shake.

The promise of what could be between us was better than anything else I'd ever had...anything else I'd ever dreamed. She had no idea of the relentless yearning that had taken root.

I was a man possessed, and she was the forbidden fruit I couldn't resist.

I'd been looking for Blake Shepfield forever. I'd fucking yearned for her all this time, no one else was good enough because they weren't her, no one else *could* ever be enough.

And then I saw her on that billboard

I finally had her back, and I'd stop at nothing to make her mine. She might not see it coming, but destiny had already set its course, and I was powerless to fight it.

My phone buzzed, jolting me out of my reverie. It was a text from the P.I. I'd hired to help me find Blake…he was also looking into Blake's boyfriend. Actually, I was going to start calling him Blake's "Other." Because I couldn't take the thought of anyone other than *me* having the title of her boyfriend.

I opened the message, hoping for something, anything, that would help me out.

The text read, "Boyfriend is squeaky clean. Word on the street is he's not giving up on Blake. He's told everyone she's the love of his life. He just landed in LA this evening, return flight tomorrow for an important meeting."

Fuck. I was hoping he was disinterested enough that it wouldn't bother him not to hear from her, but I'd obviously misjudged the guy. Anger and unease coiled in my chest as unbidden images of him wrapped around her tonight, of him touching that perfect body that I'd only begun to explore.

Not happening. I muttered a curse under my breath, wishing he were the stereotypical rich guy with a closet full of skeletons. It would make things so much easier.

But it was okay, I could work with hard. I'd been doing it since my mom dropped me off at the group home as a toddler and called it good.

I returned to the bar, where Lincoln was wrapped around Monroe, his tongue down her throat.

Awww, young love.

Couldn't wait for my tongue to return to Blake's throat. Or whatever the romantic version of that was.

I felt much better seeing my buddies here. I still couldn't believe that they'd come. Lincoln hated L.A. and he had to be at his first game of the season by noon tomorrow. Made me feel all warm and fuzzy.

For a second I'd had my three favorite people around me. Couldn't wait for that to be my new life.

I cleared my throat because as much as I was all about celebrating these two love muffins…I needed some guidance at the moment. I launched into the story as soon as Lincoln unstuck his lips from Monroe's face.

"What car did he rent?" Lincoln asked casually after I was done.

I chuckled. "A rich guy like him probably has a driver like you." I pulled up the information from the P.I. though, just in case he'd said. "He rented an Audi R8," I said, my eyebrows raising. Figures he would have terrible taste in cars.

Lincoln got a mischievous glint in his eyes. "Well, why don't you figure out something that could happen to the car?" he suggested innocently. "Even us rich guys don't like a little legal trouble."

I gaped at Lincoln, and then glanced at Monroe, who was blushing and biting down on her bottom lip.

NOT LOOKING SHOCKED AT ALL.

"He's more devious than I've given him credit for," I mused.

Monroe's eyes sparkled. "You have no idea," she replied.

There was a story there, one I was very interested in. But it would have to wait. I had plans to wreck.

And a girl to get.

———

Blake

I trudged toward my apartment door, my thoughts a chaotic mess, each step heavier than the last because they took me away from *him*.

That kiss still pulsed through me. I could still *feel* him there, an exquisite phantom pain that I missed.

That I was worried I would always miss.

I couldn't help but compare it to the feel of Clark.

Ari's kiss was an all-consuming blaze that threatened to destroy me.

Clark's kiss had never set me on fire. Not even that first time.

And maybe I could have lived with that. Because I didn't know what it could be like.

What was I supposed to do now that I'd been enlightened?

How was I expected to go back to the way it was before?

What if I couldn't?

As I reached for my apartment key, my hand trembled slightly. The events of the past few days had been a lot. They'd unraveled my sense of self, however fragile it had been before.

The memory of Ari's glittering green gaze staring at me in the darkened hallway was haunting me, taunting me with his seductive promises.

I wanted to go back to him.

I wanted more.

Right as I inserted the key into the lock, a voice emerged from the shadowy entryway of my building. "Blake."

I jumped, my heart leaping into my throat.

"Clark? What are you doing here?" My voice wavered, caught somewhere between astonishment and confusion as I slowly turned to look at him. After days of either silence or one word answers, his appearance now was a little shocking.

My boyfriend stepped out of the shadows, his dark hair disheveled and his green eyes reflecting hints of exhaustion. His usually immaculate suit was wrinkled, his tie askew.

More guilt flooded me as I studied him, my constant companion the last few days it seemed. While Clark was undeniably handsome, he seemed like a cheap replica as he stood there. Like Ari was the original and everyone else that existed could never compare.

"You've been ignoring me," he snapped, his voice sharp and frustrated. "Of course I was going to come check what's wrong."

I frowned, not understanding what he was saying, even as I winced at the rawness in his voice. We stared at each other for a long minute, the awkwardness there feeling like a cavernous gulf I didn't know how to cross over. Finally, he reached out toward me, his expression softening. "Come here, sweetheart. I need to hold you."

Instinctively, I stepped into his embrace, just like I'd been doing since I was sixteen, allowing him to envelop me in his arms. But even as I leaned into his familiar warmth, everything felt wrong. There was a void there now, one that Clark's presence couldn't fill. The contrast between his touch and Ari's was stark, and the wrong sensation gnawed at the edges of my consciousness.

"Can I come in?" he finally murmured, his voice harried and exhausted. "I've been waiting here since seven for you to get home. I just kind of panicked today when you didn't answer again. And…I hopped on a plane. I've got to be back in New York for a meeting tomorrow at eleven."

I was so confused. He was the one who hadn't been answering me! I was struck though, by what a big deal it was for him to be here. Clark was a creature of habit. Everything in his life was organized and in its place. We'd always been opposites like that, and my disorganization had always driven him crazy.

"Yeah, of course. Let's go inside and we can talk more," I quickly said, feeling like I needed to appease him.

Please him.

Like I always felt when it came to my life in New York.

I opened the door and flicked on the light. It spilled out onto the shadowed entry where we were standing.

He took a step forward and then stopped, a frown on his lips as he cast a curious gaze over me, evidently noticing the hockey jersey I wore for the first time. "You were at the game tonight? I didn't know you liked hockey."

I grappled with what should have been an easy response.

"I...uh," I finally stammered. "Charlotte had some tickets, and she insisted I come along. I figured, why not?" My attempt at casual indifference felt hollow, even to my own ears.

Clark's gaze bore into me, his green eyes searching mine, as if he sensed there was more to the story. I must have been better at hiding things than I thought, though, because he stepped inside without asking any more questions.

"Welcome to my humble abode," I said with a flourish, a feeble attempt at lightness, as we walked into the small apartment. It was a far cry from the cluttered, colorful space I had in New York City, but I wasn't living alone anymore, so I couldn't decorate how I wanted. Everything about the place was mundane...fine. But it definitely didn't feel like home.

But then again, nothing had felt like home since my parents died.

I went down the hallway to let Waldo out of my bedroom, giving myself a minute to love on him before I went back out there. When I returned to the living room, Waldo pattering next to me, Clark was staring at the furniture like it had personally offended him. It was similar to how he'd always looked at my New York place. Both were a stark departure from the luxurious lifestyle he was accustomed to—that *I'd* once been accustomed to—but there wasn't a price on the freedom living without it meant for me.

"It's alright to sit down, ya know. The furniture won't bite," I said dryly, trying not to let any shame creep in.

Clark's face went blank, and he reached out to pull me into him, the other hand gently cupping my cheek, his thumb brushing against my skin. "You deserve so much more, Blake. You could *have* so much more." I stiffened at the clear reference to his marriage proposal.

I was farther away from that now than I'd been before.

But he didn't know that.

"I'll talk about something else," he murmured finally. "Or maybe…we shouldn't talk at all." He leaned forward, his lips hovering just inches from mine.

I flinched…my heart racing. It was as if a thousand voices inside me were screaming, urging me to resist, to pull away from what was no longer right.

"You said I've been ignoring you, but why haven't *you* been answering me?" I pressed, hoping he would miss my hesitance.

A furrow etched across his forehead at my question, a subtle crease marring his otherwise chiseled features. He opened his mouth to answer and—

Pound. Pound. Pound.

The banging on the front door reverberated through the room, and Clark's hands slipped away. He stalked toward the door, swinging it open as Waldo barked and yipped like crazy. Three stern-faced police officers stood on the doorstep.

For a second, I had a flashback of a different set of cops, standing at a different doorway, on another dark night.

Pull yourself together, Blake.

"Which one of you owns the R8?" one of the officers snapped, his tone laced with authority.

Clark's jaw tensed as he replied through gritted teeth, "I'm renting it."

"Well, you're under arrest. We got a tip and checked your car. Turns out *you've* been a naughty boy." With that, he held up a small bag filled with a suspicious white powder.

I stared at it, confused...waiting for the punchline, before staring at Clark with uncertainty.

"Don't look at me like that," he snapped at me before turning his attention to the police. "That's not mine." His features were calm, but his voice was sharp with anger and disbelief.

The officer laughed and shook his head mockingly. "That's what they all say, fancy pants. You're coming with us. And we'd suggest you not make this difficult."

"This is ridiculous. Do you know who I am?" Clark snarled, his voice rising in a crescendo of protests as they handcuffed him and led him toward the door.

"Think we haven't heard that before here in LaLa Land?" another officer snorted.

"Call Ed and stay here," Clark threw at me as they pushed him out the door. Ed was general counsel for his company. An absolute shark. He'd know what to do.

I stood there, trembling with a mix of fear, confusion, and anger, as the door slammed shut.

Trying not to think about the fact that the overarching feeling coursing through my veins...was relief.

Because he hadn't kissed me.

CHAPTER 8

BLAKE

I gasped, my heart racing as I peered around my dark room trying to figure out what had woken me up. The muffled sounds of screaming came then, from somewhere in the house. Or maybe it was just outside?

I frowned and slipped out of bed, my feet making almost no noise on the carpeted floor as I tiptoed to my bedroom door, opened it, then carefully peeked out.

There was screaming again, and I realized it was my parents. They were the ones yelling so loud. Mom and Dad never talked like that; they were always extremely gentle with each other. All my friends said they were gross because they were completely in love all the time. Nerves…and fear gnawed at me as I opened the door wider and made my way down the hall, watching the scary way my shadow crept across the walls. I could hear them clearly now, their voices filled with so much anger and sadness. Things I also had never heard from them before.

"How could you do this to me? To us?" My father raged before he released a harsh sob, the sound absolutely terrifying.

"It's not what you think, John. Nothing happened," my mother's voice quivered.

I didn't understand what was going on, but I knew I had to

make them stop fighting. We didn't do this in our family. They always told me that when I got angry. Slowly, I tiptoed down the hallway, clutching my favorite stuffed bear, Mr. Whiskers. I would tell them that everything would be okay, that they should stop yelling. Just like they always told me.

As I turned the corner, I came to a halt. The room was darker, the shapes on the walls more menacing. I saw my father standing in the kitchen doorway, his face twisted in anger, holding something I couldn't quite make out. It gleamed in the dim light.

"Daddy!" I tried to scream, but no words came out. My voice had disappeared, leaving only a silent cry.

There was a deafening noise—a bang that echoed in my ears.

I jolted awake, hot tears streaming down my face as Waldo leaned on my chest, licking me all over as he tried to comfort me.

It had only been a nightmare. What had happened that night was long in the past.

I was fine.

I chanted it over and over again. Like if I said it enough, it would make it true.

The images were etched in my mind, though.

And I didn't think they'd ever go away.

The Shepfields hadn't believed in therapy. But as a ten year old little girl, I sure could have used it.

I could've gone now. I *should've* gone now. But my list of problems was so long, I was too embarrassed to talk about them.

"Thanks, Waldo," I whispered, softly stroking his fur. He always woke me up from my nightmares, at least since I'd moved out from under Maura's thumb and he was allowed to sleep in my bed.

I didn't know what I'd do without him.

Reluctantly, I slipped out of bed, heading to the shower to wash off the salty sweat that coated my body from the dream.

The scalding water pricked at my skin and I soaked in the pain, fingering the line of scars along my left inner thigh.

My fingers itched to grab a razor, to release some of the hurt that was always bubbled up under my skin.

But I had an audition today.

And new cuts wouldn't do.

Later, I sat at the kitchen bar, nursing my coffee, the warmth of the cup seeping into my palms as I stared down at my phone. It had been four long days since the hockey game and Clark's abrupt arrest...and we hadn't spoken on the phone. Ed, Clark's lawyer, had been the one to relay the information about Clark's release, and his subsequent flight back to New York. The terse text messages Clark had sent in response to my attempts at conversation since then hadn't gotten us anywhere.

It felt like he was somehow blaming me for what had happened, even though I didn't know how he could come to that conclusion. Still, the unease festered beneath my skin, making it difficult to concentrate on anything else.

Charlotte stumbled through the front door, her disheveled appearance telling a story of another wild night out. I glanced up from my coffee, taking her in. She looked pale, hungover, and positively miserable.

"Rough night?" I asked, trying to keep the annoyance out of my voice. She'd been partying with Soto nonstop since meeting him at the game, coming in at all hours of the night. I think she'd even been an hour late to a job yesterday because she was so hungover.

I didn't know if I was annoyed because she'd been waking me up constantly...or jealous because she had someone who wanted to be around her all the time.

Charlotte let out a groan, sinking into a chair across from me. "You have no idea," she mumbled, her words slurred from fatigue and alcohol.

I was about to offer her some water when she dropped a casual bombshell. "So, Ari was at the party last night. Looked pretty cozy with that actress from one of the new drama series. He couldn't keep his hands off her."

I tried to hide my reaction, keeping my expression carefully neutral as I took a sip of coffee.

But my hands were shaking.

That slithery feeling...the nasty one I'd felt in the locker room...it was there again. The mention of Ari at some party, getting cozy with another woman...it shouldn't have bothered me.

He was nothing to me.

I had no right to be jealous or hurt.

"Yeah?" I said nonchalantly, feigning disinterest. "That's good for him. He seemed like a nice guy."

Charlotte shot me a curious look, probably expecting a stronger reaction. I couldn't blame her for thinking it was odd, but I didn't want to admit the hold Ari had on me. The feelings for him that had rooted much deeper than they should have.

I refused to think about that kiss...

Charlotte rambled on about her wild night with Soto, and I tried to hang on every word. Anything that would distract me from thinking about Ari Lancaster.

Because he was nothing to me.

Right?

———

I entered the audition room hours later, my steps echoing in the sterile, white-walled chamber. The harsh glare of the fluorescent lights illuminated a long table where an intimidating panel of agents and clients sat, their expressions like stone. It was a daunting scene, one I'd never get used to no matter how many I attended, and one that made my heart race as I walked to the center.

The other models waiting their turn lined the room. Tall and poised, they exuded an air of confidence that I'd never have. Their svelte figures, flawless skin, and designer outfits screamed perfection. They exchanged polite nods and strained smiles as we all silently acknowledged the cutthroat competition.

As I began my walk, I tried to project confidence, but the critical eyes tracking my every step weighed me down. The panel's whispered comments cut through me like a knife. "Her posture needs work." "She lacks the 'it' factor." "Her look is too ordinary."

Panic coursed through me as I felt my self-esteem plummet with each critique. The room grew stifling, and my chest tightened with anxiety. I couldn't shake the feeling that they were peeling back my layers, revealing every insecurity I had ever hidden.

Desperation clawed at me, and I sneaked a glance at the mirror behind the staff. In its unforgiving reflection, I saw every single one of my flaws magnified, highlighted in agonizing detail. Their gazes were locked onto me, analyzing every supposed imperfection. I'd been a fool to even show up today. I did much better when I was hired based on my pictures.

No one ever thought I was *enough* in person.

I kept my head high, struggling to maintain my composure the entire time I was standing there. The second they said I could leave, I bolted, not bothering to stay and see if I'd been chosen. There was no way I had.

As I stepped out of the unforgiving audition room, the weight of everything bore down on me like a leaden cloak. Panic surged, and the walls of the building were suddenly closing in on me. It was as if every set of eyes in the vicinity were dissecting my every flaw.

My breathing grew rapid, shallow gasps that failed to fill my lungs. My vision blurred at the edges, and the world spun around me.

My legs shook as I stumbled down the corridor, my steps unsteady. I was on the verge of collapsing, the panic attack gripping me in its merciless grasp. The world swirled with voices and faces, a nightmarish kaleidoscope that threatened to consume me.

In that desperate moment, I spotted an alleyway just ahead. I pushed myself forward, each step feeling like an eternity, until I reached the sanctuary of the dimly lit alley.

As I huddled against the alley's cold, graffiti-covered walls, the panic attack reached its peak. I trembled uncontrollably, tears streaming down my face as I struggled to catch my breath. It felt as though the world had turned against me, but in that dark, secluded space, I found a moment of respite, a fleeting escape from the relentless scrutiny that had nearly brought me to my knees.

"Blake?" a concerned, familiar voice called from somewhere nearby. A second later I heard someone walking toward me.

I blinked away my tears and, through my blurry vision, glanced up, hot shame licking at my insides when I saw Ari approaching, his face etched with genuine concern. He crouched in front of me, his eyes locked onto mine, and his voice softened with worry.

"Hey, sunshine," he said gently, "what's going on?" His presence alone felt like a lifeline, and I struggled to find the words to explain the overwhelming rush of emotions that had consumed me.

"Just a bad day," I finally squeaked.

"This looks like more than just a bad day...but we can go

with that story if it makes you feel better," he said, reaching out to brush a tear from my face.

All thoughts escaped me as I watched him bring the tear to his lips.

He licked it off.

And he seemed to savor the taste.

"There, now we can share the bad day," he murmured with a wink, completely unrepentant for the weird as hell thing he'd just done. A shocked cough came out of me.

But a part of me also felt a little bit better.

Because now it kind of felt like we were connected.

And I couldn't help but like that.

"Let's get you out of here, yeah?" he asked, holding out his hand.

Embarrassment settled in then, and I became acutely aware of my disheveled state. Crouched down in this dirty alley, my cheeks stained with tear tracks, and my eyes probably swollen and puffy...I was a mess. In contrast...Ari looked perfect.

His crisp white henley clung to his broad chest, contrasting with the rich darkness of his jeans. His raven-black hair fell gracefully over his forehead, emphasizing his striking features.

My cheeks flushed as I continued to study him.

"Let me take care of you, Blake," he murmured.

Ari's offer to take care of me, to provide a distraction, hung in the air. He was waiting patiently, like he had all day, even though he must have had a million better things to do than rescue this *mess* in front of him.

I froze.

"Not like that!" he yelped, holding up his hands frantically. "I mean, yes, I'd like to take care of you like that, but... Fuckkkkk." He brushed his hands down his face and a giggle squeaked out of me.

He moved his hands and grinned shyly. "You like me making a fool in front of you, sunshine? That make you feel better? Because I'll do it all day if it'll make you smile."

"No one will be mad about us hanging out?" I asked cautiously, Charlotte's story about his girl from last night front and center in my head.

Ari's confusion over my question was clear, and he shook his head firmly. "No one will mind," he assured me, his tone unwavering. "And even if they did, I wouldn't care. You'll find I'm a ride or die kind of guy, baby."

"Okay, let's go," I whispered finally, taking hold of his hand. Remembering another time, with another boy, when I'd felt this same way, like I was stepping off the edge of a precipice, and bracing for the fall.

"That's my girl," he smiled, helping me up and then leading me down the alley, back to the road, our hands still intertwined.

I gazed up at him one more time as we made our way to where his fancy black sports car was parked, a ticket on the dash from his illegal parking. "Nothing more than friends, right?" I questioned.

"For today, sunshine. Just *besties* for today."

He helped me into the car and reached across my lap to buckle my seatbelt.

"Um..."

"I'm only doing my bestie duties," he said seriously as he clicked it into place.

He smelled so freaking good. I had to concentrate on keeping my back plastered against my seat so I didn't lean in and take a bigger sniff.

"Lincoln must really enjoy this part of the friendship," I remarked.

He threw back his head and laughed, and now I'm the one who seems starstruck, because the sound of it is the sexiest thing I've ever heard. "Oh, no doubt, it's the best part for him, for sure."

We hovered there, him leaning over me, big, silly grins on both of our faces.

And I suddenly couldn't remember any of the reasons I was upset today.

———

Ari

My hands gripped the steering wheel, but my attention wasn't on the road ahead. Nope, it was fixated on *her*, Blake, sitting in my passenger seat, her beauty a force that couldn't be ignored. There were still tear tracks on her cheeks, and a desolation in her eyes that made me want to burn the world to the ground for daring to make her sad. Her pain sliced me to fucking pieces. Her tears were the most beautiful and the worst thing I'd ever seen.

She'd always been my sad girl, though. Since the day we'd first met.

From the moment she'd arrived at the group home after her parents' deaths, tears were an ever-present companion. More often than not, I'd find her curled up in some corner, sobbing over what she'd lost.

I'd had it much better than her. I couldn't remember the parents who kicked me to the curb, but she'd actually watched her parents disappear. Watched her dad kill her mom...and then himself. The file the P.I. had put together on her hadn't offered much detail about her adoptive parents, just that they were wealthy socialites who frequented NYC's social scene.

But it didn't take a fortune teller to guess they hadn't been good to her. That they'd maybe even been abusive. Made me even more fucking mad at her "other" because he had done a piss poor job of protecting her the last couple of years. If I hadn't lost her, I would have done everything to keep her safe.

Anything.

Blake had always been an intoxicating mix of fragility and strength. A masterpiece if there ever was one. Now that I had her back, I would make it my life's mission to see her smile. To replace the haunted expression in her eyes with happiness.

She was staring out her window now, and I had to hold myself back from tipping her head toward me, so I could look at her, gauge how she was doing.

Blake was so in her head she hadn't even thought to ask how I'd found her. Which was a good thing, since saying that I happened to spot her as I was driving on a random street in one of the biggest cities in the world seemed a little unbelievable.

Still a better answer, though, than telling her I'd been waiting outside her audition because I was her living, breathing, obsessed stalker.

I turned on some Tay-Tay to try to get her talking, and sure enough, after "High Infidelity" started playing—a banger of a track, by the way—she turned her head back toward me.

"I'm starting to believe there's nothing wrong with you," she blurted out, a gorgeous shade to her cheeks as I glanced at her, amused.

"Sunshine, you might be onto something there," I grinned, flashing her what I knew was a panty-melting smile.

Her blush deepened.

I did think it was perfect that I was so obsessed with her I'd followed her to L.A., bugged her phone, and planted drugs in her boyfriend's car. All the other fun things I had planned were pretty *perfect* as well.

A few minutes later, I pulled up to a bakery I'd found my

second day here, when I needed help with my midnight brownie tradition. Her violet eyes stared at me questioningly.

"I find that sugar always makes me feel better," I mused, opening the car door.

She hesitated, her gaze flickering to the tempting treats on display in the window. "Not when you make a living on how you look," she whispered, a hint of uncertainty in her voice.

I made a show of running my gaze from her toes to her angelic face until she was squirming on my seat. "Sugar won't change perfection, Blake. It'll just make it sweeter."

A bashful smile graced her lips, and she searched my face as if she was making sure I really meant that. "Sugar does sound good," she finally murmured, something that looked a lot like adoration in her eyes.

Good job, Ari, I told myself. Because it was important to give yourself mental high fives when you were fucking amazing.

"Stay right there," I told her hurriedly when she tried to open her own fucking door. Was it weird I got actual anxiety at the thought of her letting herself out?

Yes.

Was I going to worry about that?

No.

I hustled to her door and opened it, pulling just a little harder on her hand than I needed to so that she fell against my chest. I was taking any opportunity I had to have her touch me.

The bakery was a cozy little place, tucked away in a quiet corner of the city. A small smile caught Blake's lips when we stepped in and she caught a whiff of all the sugar. She obviously had good taste because it smelled *bomb* in here.

Blake scanned the glass display. I usually would have scanned it too, but of course I was watching her. Because that seemed to be all I did nowadays.

Her eyes darted from one tempting treat to the next. But she seemed to get more agitated the longer she looked.

The way she doubted herself puzzled me; she was nothing short of perfection. Why couldn't she see that?

Taking a chance, I leaned over the glass counter, almost jumping when I saw how intensely the teen employee was staring at me.

A little less eye contact, thank you very much.

"She'll have a strawberry cupcake," I declared, confident in my choice. It had been her favorite back when we were kids.

She arched an eyebrow, a hint of surprise dancing in her eyes as she glanced up at me. "What if I don't want that?"

A playful grin tugged at the corners of my lips. "Well, you can have whatever you want...but I just have a good feeling about the strawberry cupcake."

Now would be the perfect time to tell her who I really am.

I'm not sure why I haven't yet.

Maybe it would be an easy way to get her back.

But if I'm being honest, I haven't said anything because I'm afraid she forgot me. That the eight months in the group home together has disappeared from her mind.

When it's stuck in mine forever.

For now, I was content to savor the reunion, to make her fall in love with the Ari I was today.

"I actually do want the strawberry cupcake," she finally whispered, before frowning as the employee boxed it up. "It used to be my favorite...I haven't had one since..." Her words trailed off.

"Since when?"

She shot me a smile, but this time, there was a hint of wistful sadness lurking behind it. "Since I was a little girl."

I didn't press her any further, and after I ordered the same thing—just in case Blake wanted more after she finished hers —we got back in the car.

She was lost in her head again until we pulled up to the gates of the neighborhood where I was renting a house. It cost an arm and a leg, but with my *year* timeline, I didn't want to invest in property when we'd be back in Dallas next year.

Emphasis on the "we."

I was sure I could educate Blake on all the finer things about Dallas life.

Which was basically everything.

"This is gorgeous, is it your house?" she asked, her voice tinged with a hint of nervousness. I didn't know what she was nervous about; I knew from her file her adopted parents had been like the parents in Richie Rich, so she would be used to nice things.

"Yep, home sweet home. Don't worry, I won't charge you admission," I teased, giving her a wink.

She bit her lip and her shoulders finally relaxed. She was smiling as we got out of the car.

I led her up the steps and through the grand front door, making a mental note to introduce her to my housekeeper, Miss Carlie, who'd been with me since I'd signed my rookie contract. She was like family to me and I'd brought her with me to Cali. She lived in the guest house in the backyard.

Even after all these years of making money…it was still weird to think I lived somewhere with a fucking guest house and a housekeeper.

The kid version of me would have called me a pretentious asshole.

The kid me would have only been kinda right.

Miss Carlie happened to be the best cook in the entire world though, and I would have been an idiot not to keep her around.

I parked in the driveway and led her to the front door, unlocking it and kicking off my shoes. Her silence continued as we walked through the foyer, gazing around curiously.

I rubbed the back of my head, trying to see it from her perspective. I guess it wasn't very homey. No pictures or knick knacks anywhere.

I couldn't exactly tell her I wasn't really interested in decorating until she moved in.

I noticed then that Blake's eyes were glued to the skin peeking out from where my shirt had risen.

She looked positively starving.

Oh, you like that, sunshine? There are plenty of abs for you to stare at where that came from.

Blake saw that I'd caught her staring, and she flushed and quickly glanced away.

"Don't worry, bestie. You can look as much as you want. It's part of the friendship package," I told her as I grabbed her hand and led her into the sunken living room, my favorite part of the house.

She just groaned and covered her face with her free hand.

"It's okay. I know I'm a thirst trap."

"A thirst trap," she snorted.

I wanted to say I could be *her* thirst trap, but again, I restrained myself.

I'd have to remind Lincoln how much of a saint I was. AGAIN.

My phone buzzed right as Blake pulled away to take in the views from the floor to ceiling windows that lined my living room. I grabbed it and saw it was Lincoln. Speak of the devil.

Lincoln: How's Operation Blake going?

I glanced over to where Blake was staring outside, rubbing her bottom lip absentmindedly.

Me: Well...it's going.

Lincoln: That good, huh?

Me:...

Lincoln: Let me know if you need any cuffs.

What did that have to do with anything?

Me: Cuffs? Why would I need—wait. You're not talking about some kinky sex thing, are you?

Lincoln: ...

Me: ...

I glanced at Blake again.

Me: I could probably use them.

I slipped my phone back into my pocket, setting aside my new inkling that Lincoln was either a psychopath...or the smartest person I knew. I strolled over to Blake, opening the cupcake and sliding it under her nose. "Ready to Netflix and chill?" I asked innocently.

She wrinkled her nose at me and I got a little caught up on her gorgeous face. As I stood there and looked at her...I wasn't entirely sure she was real.

No one was that fucking perfect.

"I don't think *besties* Netflix and chill, Ari," she murmured in a soft, enchanting voice.

I was having trouble really concentrating on what she was

saying though. I was too busy thinking about kissing her again.

Or fucking her against the glass.

Choking her with my cock until she was gasping for breath.

Burying my face in her cunt until she screamed.

Well...okay then. Maybe Lincoln's cuff idea wasn't so crazy after all.

Fuck, my dick could cut glass. Back away, Ari. Back away.

"Alright, we can table the *Netflix and chill* for now, and go to the *stuff our faces with cupcakes and watch whatever movie you want* portion of the day," I drawled. "But the offer's always open if you're interested, sunshine."

She wanted it. Oh, she wanted it. But like the good girl she was, she trotted toward the couch like her ass—her very nice ass—was on fire.

———

It took her ten whole minutes into the movie to take a bite of the cupcake. My intention to save the other one had flown by the wayside, and she'd watched me gobble it down like the fucking Cookie Monster as soon as we'd sat.

And here was the thing. It was not my finest moment... because I almost came in my pants watching her savor that first bite.

Like, what the fuck.

It wasn't even fair that I couldn't stick my dick in her mouth after that.

I could just picture her tongue licking at my dick like she was licking at that frosting.

Strawberry frosting on my dick. A dickcake.

Brilliant.

"Ari...why are you staring at me like that?" she asked,

and I was brought out of my fantasy where her sweet little tongue was torturing my tip...

And now I was the one blushing.

"I just like cupcakes!" I threw out frantically.

Her gaze turned suspicious. "Okay, weirdo," she finally said, before turning back to the movie.

I *was* a weirdo, because I kept watching her with that cupcake.

Except she stopped when she got halfway and she set it down, leaning back into the couch and hugging herself in the universal "I am not okay" move.

That wouldn't do.

"You know what I've found over the years, sunshine?" I began as I scooted closer to her and got all snuggled up.

"What?" she murmured, not looking at me. She was using that defeated voice again, the one that I absolutely hated.

"It helps to talk about things with someone who cares. Seems to make it feel at least a little bit better...at least that's what my experience has been."

She finally turned toward me, her blue-violet eyes glossed over and her lips pursed. She was trying to hold in her tears.

"Why do you even care?" she finally whispered. "Why am I even here? With you. IN THIS HOUSE. What am I doing?"

A tear finally slid down her face, and the effect was...devastating.

"Tell me where it hurts, baby."

She continued to hold my gaze for a long, long minute. And then she took a deep breath.

"I am so *fucking* tired of being the villain in my own story, Ari. And I have *no idea* how to stop."

Her eyes grew wide as soon as the words came out, like she was shocked she'd actually spoken them.

But once those words came out, more spilled out. The panic attack at the audition, the texts from her asshole adopted mother...the fact that the "other" was barely speaking to her. The fact that she couldn't eat a fucking cupcake without freaking out.

I mean, I was to blame for her problems with the "other", but there was no part of me that felt bad about that.

And he wouldn't be a problem for very much longer.

"Aren't you sorry you asked?" she finally murmured, staring at her lap in shame as she twisted her fingers together anxiously.

I reached out and stilled them.

She was so wrong. I wasn't sorry.

I was enthralled.

She'd just told me way more about herself than her fucking file ever could.

"Not at all, sunshine. Just reinforces the fact that you need me. A bestie in your corner to tell you you're the mother-fucking most perfect creature I've ever come across in my life," I said confidently.

She gaped at me as I flashed her my most *winning* smile.

"We'll fix all those problems together. I promise. But for right now, you're going to let me feed you the rest of this scrumptious cupcake, and you're going to believe me when I tell you that your body literally makes me feel like I'll die because you won't let me touch it. And then we'll watch whatever terrible rom com you just picked, even though Harry Potter would obviously be the superior choice. And I'll feed you tacos...or whatever else you want. And you're going to forget all about everything else for the rest of the day."

You're going to forget all about "everyone" else is what I wanted to say.

Baby steps, though. Baby steps.

"I'm still thinking I can't find anything wrong with you, Ari Lancaster," she finally said shyly as I picked up the cupcake and did an airplane move to her mouth. She bit down and hummed happily as it hit her tastebuds.

I reached over and wiped some frosting off her lip before sliding it into my mouth. After I'd licked it clean, I whispered, "Then stop looking."

Ignoring the shock on her face, I pulled her into my arms and we did every last thing I'd suggested.

The rest of the day would go down in my history as one of the most perfect days I'd ever experienced. And I decided, right then and there...

I was done waiting.

CHAPTER 9

BLAKE

A few days had passed since my afternoon with Ari, and we hadn't spoken since then.

I'd realized after he'd dropped me off at my apartment…he didn't even have my number.

Which was probably for the best.

I totally hadn't watched his two games since then either.

Okay, that one was a lie. I had watched them, jealous the whole time that Charlotte was there cheering on Soto.

She hadn't invited me, and that was also probably for the best. Every second I was around Ari made it harder. It was like he was my personal kryptonite and he got things out of me way too easily.

Things I'd never even told Clark. And *he'd* seen me at my very, very worst.

I examined myself in the mirror, my reflection an unsettling reminder of the choices I'd made. Doubt gnawed at the edges of my conscience. Clark had been my savior, my rock, the one who'd held me together when I was falling apart. He'd been there when no one else would have stuck around, and he'd saved me, literally.

My blood chilled at the memory of that one dark night.

He was flying in for the party tonight though, and I was considering it a chance for a new beginning. A fresh start, I thought, as I examined the Catwoman suit that clung to my figure. I adjusted the sleek fabric and sighed, wishing I could look in the mirror just for once, and be happy with what I saw there. I eyed the toilet, thinking of the protein shake I'd drank at lunch. Maybe...

No. I wasn't going to go there. Plus, it would bloat my cheeks...and there would be cameras out front for sure.

I worked on applying some red lipstick and tried to push down my nerves about the upcoming night. Maybe this party would mark a turning point in our relationship, a chance to rekindle how he'd made me feel.

Doubt crept in though, and it had everything to do with Ari Lancaster. Because once you felt what it was like to burn...did you ever forget?

I was starting to think the answer was no.

Cold water. My heartbeat slowing. The world going dark...

I shook my head. Clark deserved my loyalty, my commitment. He'd been my lifeline, and I owed him everything. The pull of temptation was strong, but I had to resist. Tonight was about rekindling something real... something I couldn't afford to lose.

———

The Halloween party tonight was legendary in L.A., hosted by one of the big tequila companies. It was the kind of event where everyone who was anyone would be in attendance, dropping all of their plans to play dress up for the night. My agency had managed to score invitations for a bunch of their models. Dress to impress, they'd said, and I'd done my best.

One more glance at my reflection, and then I sent off a text to Clark, just making sure one last time everything was good for tonight. He was supposed to be there as Batman. Clark was more of a Superman, lacking the dark magic of Batman, but at least we would be a matching pair.

Ari's energy would have matched Batman though…

Shut-up, Blake, I snarled to myself.

I walked out to the living room where Charlotte was buzzing around the room with a vodka bottle in her hand. She was going as something akin to a sexy vampire, complete with dramatic makeup and a corset that left little to the imagination.

She surveyed my outfit and smacked her lips. "Girl, I don't think that could get any tighter," she commented. There wasn't enough inflection to know if that was a compliment…or not.

I hesitated, self-doubt settling in like an unwelcome guest. "Yeah, is it okay?" I replied, my voice betraying the insecurity creeping in.

Before she could say anything either way, our conversation was cut short by a honking from outside. She screeched and held up the bottle, drops of vodka falling to the carpet.

"Let's do this, bitch," she cried as she threw open the front door.

I knelt down and put my forehead on Waldo's. "Be a good boy. Mommy will be home soon," I crooned, and he licked my face and whined. "Nope. None of that. I took you on two walks today!"

He just snorted, like he thought I was ridiculous.

My heart swelled up with love as I gave him one last pat and then headed outside where a sleek black limousine was waiting, courtesy of the agency. It was packed with other models, all dressed to the nines in a dazzling array of costumes. As I took my place among them, the atmosphere inside the limo buzzed with anticipation. Chatter filled the air, conversations ranging from excitement about the party to speculation about which celebs might make an appearance.

With each passing moment, my anxiety continued to rise. The thought of facing the crowd and having that many people staring at me...

I grabbed my phone, fingers trembling slightly, and sent a text to Clark. I needed the reassurance one more time that he would be there, a familiar anchor in a sea of strangers.

My phone buzzed with his reply, and I felt a little bit of relief as I read it. He'd be there. I wouldn't be alone.

The limo glided through the streets of Hollywood, the city transforming into a mesmerizing array of lights and sounds now that the sun was down. The bustling streets that had been teeming with people during the day now took on a whole new life. Bright signs flickered to life, casting a vibrant glow on the sidewalks below. Cars blared their horns in a bustling urban medley, forming a discordant blend that possessed its own unique tempo.

Skyscrapers stood tall, their windows illuminated with a myriad of colors, forming a breathtaking tessellation that stretched up into the night sky. Each building seemed to compete for attention, vying to outshine its neighbors with its unique display of lights. From the top floors the cityscape looked like a sea of stars that had descended to Earth.

Kind of like the amazing view at Ari's place.

Don't think about that...

The girls started throwing back shots to gear up for the party. Coke made its rounds, and when Charlotte offered it to me, I declined. She shrugged and snorted some off the back of her hand with a rolled up dollar bill. I wasn't phased in the least bit.

Cocaine and the New York socialite scene went hand in hand. I'd never been particularly tempted by it.

I had too many issues to give up much control during social situations.

I did decide to take a shot though, just to take the edge off. I winced as the tequila slid down my throat, leaving a fiery trail in its wake.

The loose warmth that spread through my limbs was almost as good as the first pass of a razorblade.

Almost.

The limo finally came to a stop, and the excitement inside the vehicle reached a fever pitch. Doors swung open, and we spilled out onto a blood red carpet, bathed in the glow of cameras and flashing lights. As we moved along the red carpet, the air filled with the hum of celebrity names and fashion praises. I kept my composure, going into my "plastic mode" as I'd called it in New York, when my sole purpose was to smile for society cameras. Just like there though, I couldn't help but feel like an imposter in my skin, like any minute someone would shout, "she doesn't belong."

The entrance to the party was a spectacle in itself, a surreal transition from Charlotte and I's cramped apartment. The party organizers had morphed the historic Hollywood mansion into something straight out of a chilling Gothic novel—a haunted mansion designed to send shivers down your spine, complete with the imposing presence of a wrought-iron gate, its intricate details crawling with contorted, ominous vines.

Past the gate, a cobblestone path had been set up. It twisted and turned, guiding guests toward a grand, ancient-looking door adorned with sinister motifs like haunting gargoyles and demon figurines with mouths stretched into a sharp-toothed scream. Dim lanterns, sheltered in ornate wrought-iron sconces, flickered erratically, casting an uncertain light that played tricks on your senses.

Right as our group got to the entrance, a sudden, chilling

gust of wind swept through—movie magic at its best—rustling the fallen leaves that littered the path. The heavy door, with its hinges groaning ominously, swung open slowly.

We stepped inside, and I was...immediately impressed. Gargantuan spider webs adorned with sparkling faux jewels stretched across the grand entrance. Pumpkins, meticulously carved with intricate designs, lit up the hallways, casting dancing shadows.

Celebrities and industry insiders mingled under the soft glow of chandeliers draped with cobwebs. Elaborately costumed guests swept past, their outfits rivaling any cinematic character. The walls were adorned with creepy paintings, and the floors were covered in red, rich, velvety carpets that silenced our footsteps as we navigated the maze of rooms.

A massive dance floor beckoned on one of the floors, pulsating with music that seemed to reverberate through the very foundations of the mansion. DJ booths disguised as haunted houses overlooked the revelry, while performers in elaborate, otherworldly costumes entertained the crowd.

Cocktail bars offered spooky concoctions, from "Witch's Brew" to "Vampire's Kiss," and the aroma of gourmet food stations wafted through the air.

It didn't take more than a few minutes for the group to disperse. Charlotte was the last one to stay with me, but after one drink she ducked away, claiming she "would be right back." Spoiler alert, both of us knew she had no intention of coming back.

So there I was, navigating the crowded venue in a vast throng of unfamiliar faces. I stood in the corner, Hollywood's version of a wallflower. I kept glancing at my phone, waiting for a message from Clark. Where was he?

Finally my phone buzzed.

> Clark: Meet me on the third floor.

Hmm. That was odd. Why wouldn't he just have told me when he got here so I could meet him at the entrance. I headed towards the stairs anyway, relieved I wasn't going to be alone at this party any longer.

The haunted mansion theme was carried upstairs, more cobwebs strewn along the bannister, candles flickering against the walls while speakers shot out a mix of thumping sexual beats and low groans. Kind of like what you'd think monsters would sound like if they were having sex.

I passed a dusty, cobweb decorated mirror leaning against the wall and stopped to check my outfit. In the dim lighting of the place, I didn't feel like I looked quite so bad. The sleek, form-fitting bodysuit was crafted from glossy black vinyl, hugging my every curve with tantalizing precision. The outfit featured a plunging neckline, showcasing a ton of cleavage, while a slender zipper ran down the front.

My legs were sheathed in matching thigh-high boots, adorned with sleek, silver zippers that glinted in the dim light. A wide, black belt cinched my waist, making me look like I actually had an hourglass figure and adding a touch of danger with its faux-leather texture.

My mask completed the transformation. The girl in the mirror looked nothing like Blake Shepfield. That had to be a good sign for the night.

I couldn't help but wonder what Ari Lancaster would think of it.

Charlotte obviously hadn't said, but I'd assumed she was meeting up with Soto tonight. Would the rest of the team be here too? If so, I'd just have to leave. I couldn't let anything mess up my night with Clark.

> Me: Okay, I'm up here. Where are you?

There weren't as many people up here as there'd been on the other floors, and I made my way through the rooms, my heart beginning to race for reasons I wasn't quite sure of. The music had shifted, transforming into a dark, sensual thumping beat that seemed to reverberate deep within me, a tantalizing rhythm that pulsed in between my legs. The sound of laughter and hushed whispers filled the air.

I glanced at my phone to see if he'd texted, because it felt like he was playing some kind of game at this point, but Clark hadn't sent anything else. I typed out a ?, and stared at it for a moment, sighing when he didn't respond right away.

Continuing to stroll through the dimly lit rooms, I caught sight of a lot...evidently this was where all the hookups were happening. A gorgeous brunette in a Playboy bunny costume was moaning against the wall, a large man dressed as a lumberjack on his knees in front of her, his face buried between her legs. My cheeks flushed as my gaze connected with hers. She reached out her hand towards me, a enigmatic smile on her face. I hurried away, my core feeling suspiciously wet by the erotic scene.

A few steps into the next room and I saw him, Clark, leaning against the wall in his Batman costume. He was striking, his tall, muscular frame accentuated by the snug-fitting costume. The dark fabric clung to his chiseled physique, emphasizing every sinew and curve beneath.

He looked good. Better than good. I'd been wrong about him not pulling off Batman...because I was having a wild reaction just staring at him. My breasts felt heavy, my nipples tightening under his dark green gaze. My insides were softening...my thong was soaked.

Had he always been this big, this powerfully built?

His strong jawline was adorned with a hint of rugged stubble, adding a raw, primal edge to his handsome features. HIs green eyes smoldered beneath his mask, a lusty animal

look in them that had me rubbing my thighs together...
desperate for some relief.

The room's shadows danced across his sculpted form...
and I wanted him.

I raised my hand to call out to him, but before I could
make a move, he slipped away into the next room. "What the
fuck?" I muttered under my breath, following after him. Was
this some kind of sexy roleplay?

I crossed the room and slowly stepped over the threshold
into the next room. The atmosphere grew charged with a
sensual tension. Suddenly, I felt a strong grip around my
wrist, and I squeaked as I was pulled into a dark closet. The
door clicked shut behind us. The lighting was even dimmer
in here, and I could just make out the outline of Clark
standing in front of me.

"Are you done playing?" I teased.

He didn't say a word though, he just crowded me against
the wall and slowly started to unzip the front of my suit, inch
by tortuous inch until my breasts were completely uncovered.
A rough finger trailed around my sensitive, exposed skin,
teasing me. I was dripping wet, my chest heaving and a soft
moan coming out of my mouth. Had his hands always felt
like this?

My hands roamed over his costumed chest, feeling how
hard he was. His chest expanded with a heavy breath and he
shuddered, like my touch was almost too much. My clit was
absolutely throbbing as I tried to find the zipper on the
damned thing. I wanted to touch him too.

Clark cupped and kneaded my breasts, his thumbs continuing to tease my nipples until I was whimpering.

"Please," I whispered, leaning forward for a kiss. He
ducked down before our lips could meet, suckling my nipple
into his mouth, sucking hard. Heat built in my core.

I'd never been able to get off with Clark, not without the use of a toy.

And suddenly, here we were...and I was about to fall off the edge, just with his mouth on my tits.

Except...where had he learned to do this? Because it had never been like this with him before...

His teeth grazed my nipple as a hand reached between my legs, gently rubbing over my core through my bodysuit, his fingers applying more and more pressure with every pass.

The perfect pressure.

I cried out as I came, the sound of my screams reverberating through the small room.

He snarled out a rough curse and then he was on his knees, his hands ripping down the latex bodysuit, somehow miraculously not tearing the fabric.

I hadn't even recovered from my last orgasm before his face was buried in my pussy, his mouth sucking and licking at my clit like I was his favorite meal.

Holy Batman—when had CLARK gotten this good at fucking head?

I must have been moving too much for his liking because he pinned my hips against the wall so I couldn't move. His tongue fucked into me, a growl reverberating against my core as his tongue thrust in and out.

"Clark," I moaned. "I don't—"

"You know who I fucking am. And don't you fucking say his name again, or I'm going to choke you with my mother fucking cock," Ari Lancaster growled.

I stood there, the realization of what was happening sinking in like a heavy stone in my chest.

Except...hadn't a part of me known all along the man on his knees wasn't Clark, despite my feeble attempts to deny the truth to myself?

Ari's gaze locked onto mine, his glittering green eyes shining in the dim lighting.

His stare was intense, smoldering with a mix of challenge and desire. He broke the silence, his voice a low, seductive murmur.

"Say my name," he dared, the words carrying a weight of expectation, a provocation to acknowledge the undeniable connection that had been simmering between us. His proximity was intoxicating, his presence captivating, and in that moment, I was powerless to deny him.

"Say it."

"Ari," I finally murmured, and his eyes closed, like his name on my lips was some kind of miracle.

After a moment, they flashed open again, and he trailed a finger up my thigh, hovering near my still pulsing core.

"Tell me you want me to fuck you."

I gasped, biting down on my lip to keep myself from making an embarrassing sound.

"Blake. Say it."

"I want you to fuck me."

"No, say it with my name."

I hesitated for one more moment, because this would change everything. After this moment, I could never go back to how it was.

Whatever that meant for me, good or bad.

A voice in my head told me to run away, to stop this mess before it began.

But I was awfully tired of listening to it.

"Ari. I want you to fuck me," I said slowly.

He grinned at me, and it was like the sun peeking out from a cloud after a storm.

"I thought you'd never ask."

Ari moaned hungrily as he pressed his face against my

core and breathed in deeply. His mouth sealed over my clit, licking and sucking with the perfect pressure.

Fuck, I could've come just from the hungry noises spilling out of him. I pulled off his mask, wanting to see him... desperate to see him. And he didn't stop me. Like he was rewarding me, his tongue slid to my entrance, dipping in softly, worshipfully. My hands tangled in his hair, pulling him closer. He grabbed my left leg and pulled it over his shoulder as his other hand grabbed my ass...so I was literally straddling his face.

Ari pushed a finger inside of me, then another, immediately finding that one perfect place in my core, the one Clark had never been able to find.

As if Ari could tell that another man's name had crossed my mind, he pushed a third finger inside of me, and I screamed from the fullness as he worshiped me. I began to grind against his face, no longer concerned with anything but coming.

I was about to fall over the edge when his movements slowed. A sob slipped out of my mouth as I tried to move my hips faster, chasing that elusive high.

"Fuck. I knew it would be like this. Your pussy this fucking delicious." His tongue licked through my folds as if he was trying to chase every last drop of my wetness. "Say my name," he demanded again, his tongue and fingers stilling as he waited for me.

"Ari, please," I cried, feeling like I might die if he didn't let me come.

"Good girl," he praised, and a flush of heat coursed through my bloodstream.

His tongue hungrily worked my core, his fingers relentless until I was screaming again as my whole body exploded with pleasure.

He lapped at my clit through my orgasm, desperately, like

he couldn't get enough.

"You're my perfect girl, sunshine. You taste so fucking good," he rasped as he slid my leg off his shoulder and stood up from the ground.

"Kiss me," he murmured, his intensity sharpening as we stared at each other. "Taste what a good girl you are."

He leaned closer, and I made up the difference, capturing his lips in a soft kiss, my tongue licking into his mouth, taking in the salty taste of....me.

I liked him like this. Tasting like me. I wanted him to walk around with me on his lips forever, so everyone would know he was mine.

Getting a little ahead of yourself, Blake.

"Let me into that perfect cunt," he demanded roughly. Ari reached between us, undoing his tight black costume pants as his mouth descended on mine again, eating and licking at my lips, swallowing my cries.

I shifted against him, my body arching forward, my breaths coming out in gasps. He licked his way down my neck and across my breasts, the heat of his mouth once again engulfing the sensitive peaks. It was everything, the suction, the smooth glide of his tongue...the subtle scrape of his teeth. Ari Lancaster was more than a master of his craft. Every move he made was seduction in his finest form, beckoning my body and my heart to the pleasure he was promising.

"You are so fucking hot," he groaned. "I couldn't have even dreamed of how good this would be." He gave me one last lingering kiss. "Now, let me fuck you, Blake." His hand slid into my hair holding my head so I was forced to look into his vibrant green eyes.

"I'm going to make this so good for you, baby. You'll never want anything else."

I didn't tell him that I was already ruined. That I honestly couldn't comprehend the thought of anything better than this. That I didn't know how I was going to survive without this.

"Are you going to let me take care of you?" he murmured, his kiss sealing over my mouth before I could respond, like he didn't actually want me to answer that. His hands grabbed the back of my thighs, picking me up, and I wrapped my legs around him as my hands went to his shoulders. He reached between us and pulled his cock free from his tight pants, and I was deceased.

Because Ari Lancaster's cock was completely pierced from root to tip. A Jacob's ladder extending from the bottom of his gigantic dick, all the way to the top. I would have known it wasn't Clark the second he whipped that thing out, obviously. Because Clark's dick could not compare in any way.

He must have seen the look of awestruck horror on my face…

"Don't be scared, baby, it's gonna feel so fucking good," he groaned as he pressed in slowly.

I couldn't breathe. He was only an inch in and I was stretched beyond comfort.

Completely beyond.

I whimpered and he ran a hand soothingly down my face. "You're taking me so well. Look at you."

He was about to split me in half, because there was no way that that dick was fitting all the way inside me.

There was no way that was fitting inside of anyone—okay, Blake, now was not the time to think of that dick in someone else.

The thought made me feral.

Which obviously was the kettle calling the pot black under the current circumstances.

"Oh, fuck," I cried as he forced his way further in. I could feel every inch of his piercings as they moved against my sensitive core. His hand slid between us and he worked on my clit, softly rubbing it. My inner muscles slowly relaxed and he was able to steadily shove his way in.

"Just a couple more inches, baby girl," he murmured, sounding like he was in pain himself from holding back. "I've thought about this since the moment I found you again," he chanted in a rough, forceful voice.

I was only faintly aware of what he was saying, or that there was something slightly off about it. I was too full to think about anything other than the nine or ten inch pierced dick that was currently spearing into me.

His gaze, an intoxicating blend of desire and longing, was fixed on my face, and I couldn't take it; the intimacy of the moment already felt like it was going to swallow me whole.

I looked away, because his gaze was simply too much to bear. There was too much in his eyes.

Ari wasn't having it though; he grabbed my chin and forced my eyes back to his gorgeous fucking face.

"You don't get to look away from me. I've waited too fucking long for this."

His other hand was gripping my ass, and his fingers slid into my crease, finding my puckered flesh and gently rubbing over it. I froze, because nobody had ever been *there* before.

"Shhh. Just relax. That's it. There's not going to be anywhere I don't touch…that I don't taste."

Right as he said that, he thrust forward, completely impaling me with every inch he had. My head fell back as I cried out from the fullness.

The stretch was painful…but perfect. Like I'd been incomplete all this time, and only now, connected to him, could I be whole.

His mouth closed over mine, his hungry tongue pushing its way in.

Ari eased out of me slowly, before slamming back in, like he wanted to make sure I would feel him there for the rest of my fucking life. His rhythm sped up until he was literally bouncing me on his cock, the slide of that piercing the most exquisite thing I'd ever experienced.

A few more passes and I was there, falling, screaming his name as I came.

"Yes, that's it. Look at you, coming on my big cock. What a fucking good girl."

My insides clenched, another tiny orgasm fluttering through me at his words.

He grinned wickedly. "Looks like someone likes to be praised. Which is my lucky day. Because I'm going to spend every day in this sweet pussy, telling you how perfect you are."

"Ari," I whimpered, because his words. His dick. Everything about him.

It was too much.

My heart wasn't prepared for this. I didn't have the walls up that I needed.

His voice had a raw, eager quality to it. It made me want to believe him. To believe every word that came from his pretty mouth.

I leaned forward and sealed my lips against his, trying to cut off his equally pretty words.

I moaned, and fisted his hair as his finger slid into my ass. The sensation was...good.

So good.

My reaction must have excited him because his movements sped up. He pushed my back against the wall behind me so I couldn't move. All I could do was take his dick as it slammed in and out of me, each stroke so deep it felt like it was butting up against my womb.

"More," I whispered, and he nipped at my bottom lip.

"Every day, sunshine. Every day this pussy's going to be mine."

I was lust drunk, about to orgasm again, and in no shape to argue with him.

His cock's pounding pace was punctuated by his growls and my soft cries…and was it possible for a moment to last forever?

Because if there was any moment I would want to last, it would be this.

It would be him surrounding me.

It was maybe the first time I'd ever truly felt safe. Truly felt wanted…seen. In my life.

"Come one more time for me, baby," he pleaded, as if his world depended on it.

I couldn't help but listen.

The flutter started. Building. Spreading. Until I was falling, not sure where I ended and he began.

He shuddered violently against me as he came with a long growl, his cum filling me until it was dripping down my thighs.

The afterglow stretched on.

And then it was gone.

And I was standing in a closet, with his cum inside of me.

And my boyfriend was nowhere to be found.

Words from the past shot through my head.

"How could you do this to me? To us?" my father had cried.

My mother was a cheater too. The reason our perfect family fell apart.

And here I was, just like her.

Hurting a good man who had done nothing but love me.

Even when I didn't deserve it.

"No," Ari's sharp words shot through me. "You're not going to regret this. You're not going to regret *us*."

"I have a boyfriend," I whispered as he pulled out, and I flinched because of how fucking *empty* I felt. "I'm a cheater. A whore—"

"Don't you dare fucking call yourself that," he snapped, grabbing my chin and forcing my eyes to his.

'What if I told you, you were always supposed to be with me? What if I told you that we were always meant to be together? What if I told you *he* was in the wrong for taking you from me!"

"Then I would try not to call you a liar," I muttered, dark self loathing hitting me when he winced like I'd slapped him.

He opened his mouth, and then closed it, like I didn't deserve the words he wanted to give me.

Or maybe I was just imagining that. Because Ari Lancaster seemed to be under the misguided impression that I always deserved everything.

"What happens now?" I asked, dread..shame...euphoria... anticipation floating through me as I pulled up my costume and he tucked his somehow still hard dick back into his pants.

"What happens now is that you break up with your boyfriend," he said gently, those emerald eyes shining at me in a cautious plea. "And you give us a chance. Because I'll make sure you never regret it."

Uncertainty churned within me like a stormy sea, its waves crashing against the shores of my heart, threatening to pull me under its tumultuous depths.

Could I summon the courage to take this leap of faith?

All my life, it seemed I'd never been able to hold on to the good things, to those flickering moments of happiness that as humans we rarely get.

But Ari Lancaster was different—he was the embodiment of all that was good and beautiful, the hero of my story, patiently waiting for me to let him save the day.

His eyes, those mesmerizing jade pools, held a tenderness and understanding that tugged at my heartstrings. They glistened in the dim light, silently urging me to trust, to believe in the possibility of us.

As I gazed into those eyes, I felt a rush of emotions, an overwhelming desire to let go of my fears and doubts. With Ari, there was something extraordinary, something worth risking it all for. The thought of finally allowing myself to embrace happiness, to give in to his unwavering devotion, filled me with hope and a profound sense of longing.

In that closet, surrounded by shadows, I realized that this might be my chance at something beautiful, something enduring. With trembling hands, I reached for him, silently conveying my willingness to take the leap, to trust in this thing between us, and to let Ari be my hero, not just for a day but maybe…for forever.

"I'm scared," I finally murmured.

His smile was heartbreaking…life saving…everything.

"I know, sunshine. But I knew what you were the moment I met you."

"Oh yeah, and what is that?"

"Mine," he said softly, without a trace of indecision.

He held out his hand, silently begging me to accept his offer. I stared at it for a few more seconds.

And then I took it and I followed him out of the closet.

Because what else could I do?

———

Ari's grip on my hand was unwavering as he pulled me down the spiraling staircases, through the throngs of people, and into a party that had escalated, becoming even more out of control. The music was deafening, a pulsating beat that reverberated through my entire being, a rhythm that seemed to sync with the frantic pounding of my heart.

The air was thick with desire, a heady cocktail of temptation and recklessness that hung like a palpable veil. Bodies entwined in a passionate dance, stolen kisses—and more—exchanged in shadowy corners, a dark sensuality everywhere you looked.

I could feel the weight of knowing eyes on me, judgmental gazes that followed our every move. I wouldn't normally get any attention by myself, but I was with Ari Lancaster, and you couldn't help but watch him.

I held my head high, his touch a lifeline in the midst of the pandemonium. With his hand firmly wrapped around mine, I felt safe and protected, as if nothing else in the world mattered.

Ari guided us towards the exit. The cool night air greeted us like a soothing balm as we stepped outside, leaving the raucous revelry behind. The cobblestone path stretched before us, now illuminated by scattered lanterns to lead drunk partiers to the exit.

A shiver ran down my spine as a breeze brushed my skin, and Ari wrapped his arm around me, drawing me close to his warmth. I couldn't help but lean into his embrace.

"Forgot to tell you," he began, his voice low and seductive, "I've always been a dog person, but all of a sudden, I'm really liking cats."

I rolled my eyes at him, a small, fond smile tugging at the corners of my lips as he exaggeratedly dragged his gaze over my costume. His teasing was a welcome contrast to the intensity of the night.

We approached the valet, only waiting a few minutes as they pulled Ari's sleek car up. He held the door open for me with a charming flourish, and I settled into the plush leather seats. Ari leaned in, buckling my seatbelt, and I realized that it already felt like a habit, like something he'd been doing for me for forever.

His lips found mine in one final, searing kiss before he

closed the door, walked around the hood of the car, and took his place behind the wheel. The sensation of his kiss lingered on my lips, a tantalizing reminder of what had happened tonight.

We set off, Ari humming along to an Olivia Rodrigo song.

"Can you take me home?" I asked shyly, my voice trembling with a mix of anxiety and anticipation. The need to end things with Clark was like a rock in my chest, battering against my ribcage.

"I can take *us* home," he said charmingly.

I stroked his forearm soothingly. "I need to call him, end this. Please," I whispered.

Ari's expression shifted, a low growl escaping his lips. His furrowed brow and the restless tapping of his fingers on the steering wheel betrayed his internal conflict.

"Okay," he finally murmured reluctantly.

The city passed by in a blur as Ari navigated the darkened streets. The rhythmic hum of the car's engine filled the silence between us, a soothing backdrop to the fierce emotions swirling inside my chest.

Arriving at my building, Ari walked me to my front door. We stood there, bathed in the soft glow of the porch light, our gazes locked, a shared moment of uncertainty and desire.

He leaned in, his lips tantalizingly close to mine, and the anticipation hung in the air like a charged current. Our lips finally met, and the kiss was electric, a fusion of craving and longing that left me breathless and desperate for more. He pressed against me hard, like he was trying to tattoo the feel of him on my lips. So I wouldn't forget what we'd started tonight.

The world fell away, and there was only Ari and me, entangled in a web of desire and surrender. The kiss deepened, our tongues intertwining in a sensual dance that sent waves of pleasure coursing through me.

"Tomorrow," he finally whispered against my lips, his voice laden with promise and a hint of reluctance.

I nodded, my heart fluttering wildly in my chest as I stepped inside my apartment.

I closed the door behind me, leaning against it as I traced the feel of him, his taste still lingering on my lips.

Sighing, I walked to my bedroom where Waldo was laying on my bed. He sat up on his haunches, his tongue sticking out as he huffed excitedly. I sat on the bed beside him and buried my face in his soft fur, searching for a moment of comfort before I finally pulled out my phone.

My trembling fingers hovered over it, an instrument of both liberation and heartbreak.

This was what I needed to do—wanted to do. I could do this. I could end it. I could call Clark and break the bond that had held us together for so long, to shatter what we'd built, which I'd now cracked beyond repair.

But as I dialed his number, my heart thundered in my chest, with so much regret over what I'd done. Not regret over Ari. But regret that I hadn't been able to wait.

The phone rang and rang, each tone a painful reminder of what was coming. Like the universe was trying to prolong my agony, making me wait for the inevitable.

And then, without warning, the call ended abruptly, as if Clark had silenced it before even answering. It felt fitting, in a way, that our relationship would end like this—unanswered, unspoken, and void of any closure.

Defeated, I turned to the next option, my fingers flying across the keyboard as I crafted and re-crafted a message a million times over. Each word felt like a dagger through my heart, nothing fitting the end of something I'd had for so many years.

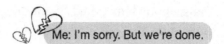

The text was simple, direct, devoid of the complexities and intricacies of our emotions. It was a finality that I couldn't escape, a truth I couldn't deny any longer. My thumb hovered over the send button, my breath caught in my throat, and with a heavy heart...I pressed it.

The message was sent, and with it, the end of a chapter that had defined so much of my life. Tears welled up in my eyes, but I refused to let them fall. I needed to be strong, to stand firm in my decision, even if it meant breaking the heart of such a fucking good man.

As I sat in the dimly lit room, I was transported back to the sterile, white walls of that hospital, a place where the boundaries of life and death had blurred.

I saw Clark by my side, holding my hand with a tenderness that spoke volumes. He'd promised me that he'd always be there for me, no matter what, a vow made in the face of uncertainty and fear. It was a memory that lingered, a reminder of the love he'd given me, of what he'd put up with to give me that love.

But life had a way of changing, of twisting our paths into unexpected directions. What we'd had, was never going to be enough to sustain us. To sustain me.

We deserved happy.

Even if it hurt like hell to get there.

I laid in bed that night, and a bittersweet smile played on my lips. It wasn't the ending I could have anticipated, nor was it the ending I'd ever wished for. But it was the right thing to do, the necessary step toward a future that promised something different, something new.

Thoughts of Ari danced through my mind, of the fact that

everything about him called to me like nothing had before. Tomorrow held the promise of a new beginning, a journey into uncharted territory, and for the first time in a long while, I felt a glimmer of hope.

I closed my eyes, tears finally escaping and trailing down my cheeks. It was a painful goodbye, but it was also a necessary one. As I drifted into sleep, the weight of the past began to lift, replaced by a sense of liberation and the anticipation of what the future might bring.

CHAPTER 10

ARI

I slouched on the lounger on my back deck, my gaze locked on the horizon as the sun began its ascent, painting the sky with shades of orange and pink. The smell of alcohol lingered in the air, a testament to my futile attempt to drown out my overwhelming urge to go to her house, to sneak into her bed, and keep her close.

My longing for her was all-consuming, a relentless desire that gnawed at my insides. I craved her presence, her warmth, her essence by my side at all times. Patience was becoming an unbearable burden, each moment without her a slow descent into madness. The ache in my chest felt like it might actually be the death of me.

Needing some distraction, I picked up my phone to text Linc.

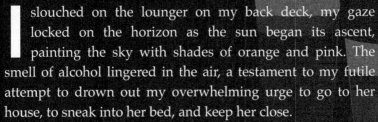

Me: Hypothetically....

Lincoln: Oh boy.

Me: What?

Lincoln: I'm just preparing myself for what you're about to say.

Me: What do you mean you're preparing yourself? I spew excellence, golden boy. Remember that.

Lincoln: You spew excellence? I just spewed my Gatorade everywhere.

Me: I don't drink Gatorade. I don't put chemicals in my temple.

Lincoln: You don't put chemicals in your "temple." Are you drunk?

Me: ...

Lincoln: It's 9am and you have practice today...California's that good, eh?

Me:...

Lincoln: Ok, so what were you saying?

Me: About what?

Lincoln: Hypothetically...

Me: Hypothetically what?

Lincoln: Go sleep it off.

Me: I wish I could...

I threw my phone on the seat next to me, because that had only made me feel marginally better.

I could probably use some Gatorade though, now that Lincoln had brought it up.

I didn't *actually* have anything against it...

Walking inside, I headed towards the kitchen, the world

spinning a bit around me. I did in fact have team weights in two hours, so I needed to at least be able to walk straight before showing up.

Grabbing a purple one out of the fridge, because grape was obviously the superior flavor, I paced the kitchen, sipping it slowly so I didn't throw up.

Tequila in last night's case…was not a good idea.

She'd at least sent that text to him though…and tried to call him. I mean, he'd never gotten it, but I'd take care of that. I never wanted her to talk to him again. No matter what he'd meant to her.

I wanted to mean everything to her. He was never supposed to have been around in the first place.

Fuck. I was going to go crazy, and I needed to fix my name in her phone before I called her. Was there a way to hack that shit?

I'd just stop by after weights. I could do that. It was a couple of hours.

I wouldn't *actually* go insane.

I sniffed my shirt, wincing with how bad it smelled. A shower was definitely in order. I couldn't have hygiene like Soto.

Stepping into the water, I turned it to scalding hot to try and clear my head. The rhythmic sound of droplets pattering against the tiles filled the air, a soothing backdrop to the tumult of thoughts swirling in my mind.

I leaned forward, my palm pressed firmly against the slick, tiled wall, feeling the heat seep into my skin.

Closing my eyes, I let the warm water wash over me, caress against my skin. I took a deep breath, willing myself to relax, to let go of the tension that was gripping me.

But the memories of last night were stuck in my head, the taste of her lips, the feel of her tight, perfect cunt…

My hand found my aching dick and I stroked it from root

to tip. It was Lincoln and tequila's fault that I had this piercing to begin with. We'd signed our rookie contracts and got absolutely shit-faced. Before I knew it, I was getting my cock pierced and we were getting matching butterfly tattoos. Somehow, I think he got the better end of things... At least the butterfly tattoos had a meaning.

Although I had to admit, the sex was next level with it. Blake's eyes had practically rolled back in her skull when she'd felt it on her G-spot.

I continued to stroke my dick, thinking of the taste of her. And then suddenly...

Blake was on her knees in front of me, naked. Blowing my fucking mind. Her breasts were full with rosy pink nipples just begging to be sucked. She was wide-eyed, her pupils blown from how turned on she was....from sucking my cock. I twisted my fingers in her hair, surging into her sweet, hot mouth. She choked out a moan as I hit the back of her throat, her breasts arching towards me. I knew if I reached down between her parted legs, she wouldn't just be wet from the shower.

"Touch yourself," I groaned as I fucked into her mouth.

Her hands went to her breasts and she pulled and kneaded at her tips.

And I was dying. Obsessed...

And coming. Fuck. I was on fire. Possessed. I surged into her mouth and emptied hot cum down her throat, pulling out halfway so it spurted all over her tits and chest. I wished we weren't in the shower, and that it wasn't washing off. I wished she could just walk around like that, covered in me. So everyone would know who she belonged to.

I came back to earth, cum coating the shower wall. One of the most intense orgasms of my life...just from thinking about her.

And I was still hard.

Can you sprain your dick? Because that was going to happen now that it had found nirvana. The "Maximus 5000" would need to be fed. Daily.

Hourly actually.

Fuckkk. I dragged a hand down my face and finished my shower, resisting the urge to wank off again like a...wanker, I guess.

———

An hour later, I was in an Uber on the way to the practice facility for weights...still slightly drunk.

The team gym was an assault on my senses, way too much clinking weights, grunts, and the persistent thump of bass-heavy music. It was how I usually liked it, when I didn't have a bottle of Patron still swishing around in my gut.

Walker, Mr. Prince Charming himself, was already there, his hulking figure bent over a weight bench. His hair was damp with sweat, and his muscles strained as he pushed the barbell up and down with ease. He had the kind of build that could stop a tank engine, which made him an excellent goalie.

"Morning, sun sizzle," Walker quipped as I approached, his voice a rumble beneath the music. "Or should I say 'morning after'?"

"Did you just call me "sun sizzle?"" I asked incredulously, chuckling in disbelief, or at least I hoped it sounded like a chuckle. Kinda sounded like a witch cackle to my own ears. "Walker, my man, you're looking disturbingly awake for someone who was at the same party as me last night."

Walker paused mid-lift to give me an arrogant look. "Welcome to Cali, Ari Lancaster. We know how to party here."

"You're from Tennessee originally, right?" I drawled.

As I sauntered over to the weights, my muscles singing a

chorus of protest, Walker set the weights on the rack and flipped me off..

"I knew you were unhinged, buddy, but "sun sizzle" just confirms it."

He let out an exaggerated sigh, pretending to contemplate his statement. "You forgot about your hangover for half a second, didn't you?"

I mean, maybe I was just drunk, but I was really starting to think that Walker deserved to be in on the bromance Lincoln and I had been in for all these years. I mean, he would be mostly the bro and less of the mance since Lincoln could only have one Ari. But it was worth considering.

I'd circle back to it when I was sober and thinking clearly.

"So, the big game against Dallas is coming up? Any secret tricks up those sleeves of yours?"

I shot him a sly grin, wiping a bead of sweat from my brow. "Ah, Walker, my friend, the secret is an ancient and mystical art called teamwork."

Walker's eyes widened dramatically. "Teamwork? You're blowing my mind here, Lancaster. But that's it? No secret ritu-als…pregame dance-offs with Lincoln?"

I grinned. "Walker, you just want an excuse to hang out with ol' Golden Boy again, don't you?"

Walker freaking blushed, and I was rethinking letting him into the circle of trust. He was a simp if there ever was one.

"I hate to break it to you, Walker, my man, but Lincoln is *my* best friend. You simp for both of us, or you don't simp at all," I said, shaking my finger at him.

Walker gaped at me. "I—I do simp. I mean—"

"Ari, quit torturing our goalie," Tommy yelled from across the room.

I grinned at both of them, feeling remarkably better all of a sudden. Walker was just too easy.

We got back to lifting, and of course, my mind wandered

to Blake. She was a song stuck on repeat, one I was never going to get tired of. I slipped out my phone, pulling up my handy dandy tracking app. Good, she was still at her apartment. I could just picture her sprawled on her bed, her hand between her legs—

The gym door swung open, saving me from what was going to be a very embarrassing and untimely woodie, and in walked Soto, a smug grin on his ugly fucker of a face. His arm was thrown around Charlotte, who was definitely high on something judging by the distinct glaze over her eyes, like she'd stumbled into a room she hadn't quite intended to enter. The corners of her mouth were upturned in a dreamy smile, and she was swaying in place.

Soto then tried to choke her with his tongue, pushing it so far down her throat, I was shocked she wasn't throwing up. He squeezed her ass and gave it a slap, well aware of everyone watching. I exchanged a bemused look with Walker, who simply rolled his eyes.

"I guess the fun's over now that asshole has arrived," I sighed, and he shook his head in amusement.

Soto released Charlotte, and unfortunately decided to wander our way. He walked with an exaggerated swagger, his chest puffed out like a bantam rooster, his eyes *also* glazed over. Hope this week wasn't his turn for a random drug test. He'd be screwed.

Actually…what the fuck was I saying? Of course I hoped he got tested this week.

I was never drinking Patron again. I obviously couldn't think straight on it.

"You disappeared last night…you and Walker find a dark room to play in?"

I looked at him, a bemused smile playing on my lips as I kept in the eye roll that was twitching in my face. "Soto, my man," I greeted him, my tone dripping with a faux-friendly sweetness. "You seem positively brimming with enthusiasm today. But you have some white powder right..." I pointed to his banana sized nose.

Soto's face reddened, and he swiped at his face. "Don't get smart with me, Lancaster," he growled.

I shrugged, feigning innocence. "Who, me? Never." I leaned in a little closer, lowering my voice to a conspiratorial whisper. "But if you ever need tips on wooing the ladies without making a scene, you know where to find me. It's all about finesse, my friend."

"Fuck you, Lancaster."

"You know, Soto," I began, my voice dripping with mock concern, "I would. But they say beauty is in the eye of the beholder. And I've yet to meet anyone whose eye is that forgiving to let you in their bed."

Soto's face contorted with rage, and he sputtered for a retort that never came. I resumed lifting weights as Walker chuckled next to me.

I winked at him. "Spot me on this, and we can get out of here. It's starting to smell."

Walker nodded and stood over me as I lifted the bar.

Half an hour more and I could see my girl.

T he day had started with a sense of anticipation, but it quickly turned into frustration. Clark hadn't replied to my text—which I guess was a good thing. But I'd also remembered that Ari and I still hadn't exchanged numbers.

I could still feel him between my legs. I'd cheated on Clark with him.

And I didn't have his freaking number.

So I may have been panicking this morning.

Charlotte's untimely entrance into our apartment only added to my stress. She stumbled in, disheveled and clearly nursing a hangover from last night's escapades with Soto. I sighed as she barged into my room, holding her phone up like a prized possession.

"Blake, you won't believe what I found," she slurred, thrusting her phone into my face.

I squinted at the screen, trying to make sense of the images she was showing me. At first glance, it appeared to be Ari, my Ari, with a beautiful brunette. Panic washed over me, and I could feel my heart racing. I examined the photo closer, trying not to spiral.

"Charlotte, wait," I said, a slight tremble in my voice. "Look at his hair. It's shorter, right? These pictures aren't recent, are they?"

Charlotte blinked at me, her alcohol-addled brain working in slow motion. She squinted at the phone screen, her brow furrowing. "You're right," she mumbled, her enthusiasm deflating. "I guess they're old photos."

I let out a shaky breath, relieved that my worst fears hadn't been realized. But Charlotte's little stunt had brought something else to the forefront of my mind—the fact that Ari was a famous hockey player.

I was used to powerful men—New York was full of them. Clark was one of them. Most of the women I knew were in relationships where they were required to turn a blind eye to what those men were doing. I hadn't heard anything that said Thomas and Maura had that kind of arrangement.

But it wouldn't have surprised me.

An NHL superstar would have even more options than those men. Was Ari like that? Would I be enough for him?

It felt like I'd never been enough for anyone.

And now that the chase was done, and he'd caught his prize…would he lose interest?

Or did I deserve something like that happening to me after what I'd done last night?

After Charlotte stumbled out of my room, I couldn't resist the urge to do some googling. I typed in Ari's name, and my screen was flooded with images of him, always surrounded by an entourage of women. Beautiful, glamorous women who smiled at him as if he were a prize to be won.

I clicked on an article that featured a series of photos of Ari at various events and gatherings. Each picture showed him with a different woman on his arm. They clung to him, obviously well aware they were holding something special.

He looked every bit the charming, charismatic athlete that fans adored.

Another picture had the headline: **Ari Lancaster's Annual Gala Raises Record-Breaking Funds for Lost Children Organization**. In the picture, he was a wet dream in a perfectly fitted tuxedo. I clicked on the article.

Dallas, TX — *In a dazzling evening that left attendees spellbound, Ari Lancaster, the celebrated star defenseman of the Dallas Knights, hosted his renowned annual gala to benefit the Lost Children Orga-nization. The event, now in its fourth year, proved to be an extrava-gant affair that captivated Dallas' elite while breaking previous fundraising records for the charity.*

The Lost Children Organization, dedicated to assisting and rehabili-tating homeless and at-risk youth, has long been close to Lancaster's heart. Every year, he leverages his star power to gather support and resources for this noble cause. The gala, held at the opulent Grand Dallas Ballroom, saw an impressive turnout of Dallas' most influ-ential figures, philanthropists, and celebrities…

Rehabilitating the homeless and at-risk youth? Why was that close to Ari's heart? I mean, it was a good cause for anyone to have. But there were a lot of good causes out there. I would know. I'd attended charities for about a million of them.

A thought flickered in my head. But it still seemed so crazy. There was no way…the world was too big.

Shaking my head, I closed the computer and started to get ready for work. I needed to stop stalking Ari and being a stage 5 clinger. If he was really serious about what he'd said last night…I guess he'd stop by at some point.

Either way, everything would be fine.

It was a promise I made myself.

I just wasn't sure I believed it.

———

Work had been a bitch. It was a typical bustling day, but our general manager was in an unusually sour mood. She'd made it clear that everyone was in her line of fire today, with me seemingly at the forefront.

I didn't know there were so many things I could do wrong in a single shift, and I was teetering on the edge of walking out. But just when I thought my patience couldn't be stretched any further, I saw *him* at the entrance of the restaurant...

Ari.

He ambled inside with the casual grace of someone accustomed to public attention, dressed in jeans and a tight Cobras t-shirt that accentuated his muscled chest. Like last time, it seemed like everyone stopped what they were doing and just stared at him.

Once again, it was crazy to me that the only person *he* was staring at...

Was me.

His steps didn't slow at all until I was in his arms. Maybe I should have been embarrassed this was happening at work, but he hungrily kissed my lips, parting them with his tongue. There was an immediate ache between my legs, like my body had been asleep all day and just remembered what was missing. Him. I could feel him harden between us as his tongue slid over mine.

He only stopped after some of the patrons started freaking clapping.

"Forgot we weren't alone for a moment," he said with a wink.

I swooned. Because honestly...same.

"Hi," I squeaked.

He grinned in response, just a subtle upturn of his lips

that danced in his eyes. My stomach fluttered, the sensation like a swarm of fireflies dancing in my belly, He was a sun-kissed god. Like a dream, everything about him had a heroic, almost ethereal quality to it. Intense, enchanting, and utterly captivating.

He held out his hand. "I think we have an issue we need to remedy, sunshine. I need some digits."

The world seemed to slow for a heartbeat, as relief rushed through me. I hadn't realized until then how much I needed this connection. I grabbed my phone out of my pocket, my fingers trembling as I pulled up my contacts so I could add his number. "Okay, what's your number?"

But Ari slipped my phone from my hand, his fingers brushing against mine. The brief touch sent a jolt of warmth into my veins, and I swallowed hard as my heart somer-saulted.

"I'll do it," he quipped with a mischievous twinkle in his eyes. He inputted his number and a few seconds later held up his buzzing phone. His playful grin broadened as he handed my phone back to me.

"Now it's official. We're besties," he declared, his voice a husky croon that had that spot between my legs growing... achier. "Besties" didn't have quite the same charm as it had when I'd first met him.

He leaned forward, his lips brushing against his ear. "Would you rather me say, "it's official. You're mine?"" he murmured.

A grin lit up my face.

"I see you, sunshine. I'll ace every test."

A throat cleared, and my manager—who obviously didn't know what the beginnings of true love looked like based on the prune looking snarl on her face—popped up behind Ari like one of those whack-a-moles.

Ari glanced back and jumped, pressing a hand against his chest. "Jump scare!"

Rachel did not appreciate this, but she was well versed in sucking up to celebrities. Ari definitely qualified as one, especially since the Cobras were on a five game winning streak, their first in four years.

"Blake, dear, how about you get back to work?" she asked in a tone that broached no argument.

"Yes, of course," I murmured. "I'll see you later?" I asked Ari, hating how desperate I sounded.

Way to play it cool, Blake.

He didn't seem annoyed by it at all though. "What time do you get off so I can count down the hours?" he murmured.

"Blake!" Rachel snarled, her patience lost. Probably because there happened to be an A-lister in my section at the moment and it was the dinner rush.

Whoops.

"Eleven," I said regretfully, and his face fell. I braced for him to make an excuse, to say he had better things to do.

Because who wouldn't?

"I'll be here," he said instead.

And that seed of hope inside me, the one that had sprouted the day I first met him...

It grew a little more.

Ari

I strolled into the little coffee place situated right across from Blake's restaurant, the scent of roasted beans hitting me like a warm hug as I walked in. I didn't want to get that far away from Blake. But if I'd stayed in that restaurant for one more second, I probably would have thrown a tray at her dickwad manager. In here, I could catch glimpses of her without causing anyone bodily harm.

I looked over the menu, ready for a caffeine fix. Oh good, they had pumpkin cream chai tea lattes. My favorite. I was a basic bitch when it came to my fall drinks.

The barista, a twenty something year old girl with chestnut hair cascading down her back and hazel eyes, stood behind the counter. She wore a standard brown apron, and her skin had a warm, olive-toned complexion. In the past, I might have thought she was attractive, but now she might as well have been paint on the wall. There was nothing about her that piqued my interest.

All I could fucking see was Blake.

The barista flipped her hair like she thought I was taking auditions for a shampoo commercial, flashing me a flirty smile. Staring at the baked goods behind the glass, I really hoped she hadn't baked them. I'd hate to bite into a pumpkin muffin and get some hair in my teeth.

Would totally ruin the experience.

"Hey there, handsome. What can I get you?" she purred. Sigh. The curse of being so damn good looking. Everyone wanted a piece of Ari Lancaster. Next time we talked, I needed to remind Lincoln I was the better looking of the two of us, just so he didn't get a big head.

"A pumpkin cream chai tea latte with almond milk, please."

'Really?" she asked, looking behind me, like I was ordering for someone else.

"Yes. I know I have good taste. Anyone who orders a black coffee during pumpkin season obviously doesn't like fun," I drawled.

She grinned at me and I inwardly cursed…because she seemed to think I was flirting with her.

As she prepared my drink, I scrolled through my phone, stalking Blake on Instagram. She was so fucking pretty.

"Here you go," the barista said in a sing-song voice.

"Thanks," I murmured, distracted by a lingerie shoot Blake had posted this morning. There were already five thousand likes.

Fuck.

Maybe I could convince her to let me photoshop the pic so her undies had something like "Property of Ari" on them, because the comments men were leaving made me feel...feral.

I grabbed the cup, not amused at all when I saw the girl had jotted her name and number on the cup without hesitation. She hit me with what I'm sure she thought was a seductive smile.

I raised an eyebrow and pushed the cup back toward her. "Give me another one, please," I said, my tone firm and no-nonsense.

She blinked in surprise, her smile faltering. "What?..."

"A cup. I need a new cup. One that doesn't have your number on it."

The girl stared at me, flabbergasted, for so long, I was slightly worried she'd lost all brain function.

"Is this a joke?" she finally asked.

"I. Am. Taken," I spelled out for her, holding up the phone to show her the most beautiful girl that existed on the planet. Adding "you do not compare," probably would have been taking it too far, but I had the words ready, just in case she was one of those persistent types. "Just the coffee, no extras," I said slowly, because she really was a slow mover.

Her expression shifted from disappointment to annoyance as she grabbed a new cup and dumped my drink in it. I frowned. She'd messed up the pumpkin cream! THIS WAS A TRAVESTY.

The next step was her probably spitting in my drink...or trying to roofie it, so I decided not to complain. I stalked towards the bench closest to the window, the one that would give me the best view of little miss sunshine, and I sat down to wait.

I took a sip of my chai tea, humming happily when it didn't suck. My eyes of course landed on Blake across the road, watching her flash a bright, friendly smile at a customer. It was a different smile than the one she gave me, one that felt more cold and less...mine. The crazy thing was... I wanted all of her smiles. I didn't want anyone else to get any version of her.

Self control, Ari. Self control.

The guy that was on the receiving end of her smile...it was evident that *his* smile was genuine. He was tracking her ass across the restaurant as she sauntered away. I clenched my jaw, a flicker of annoyance bubbling up. I'd never felt this insanely territorial...this, well...insane before.

To divert my attention, I decided to scroll through social media some more. Lincoln's latest photos caught my eye. There he was, happily munching on a taco with Monroe. My eyes narrowed as I recognized the very familiar-looking tacos.

HOW DARE HE!

I immediately pulled up Lincoln's number.

> Me: YOU CHEATED ON ME. I'LL NEVER FORGIVE YOU.

> Lincoln: Back to the 8th grade girl impersonations, I see...what's up?

> Me: You took Monroe to our place.

> Lincoln: What place?

> Me: Don't play games with me, sir!

Lincoln: Maria's?

Me: Yes, Maria's! The embodiment of perfection in taco form.

Lincoln: Relax, drama queen. It was once.

Me: So you admit it!

Lincoln: I thought you just said you knew already.

Me:...

Lincoln: Does it make you feel better if I tell you tacos make Monroe horny? So it's a win, win for everyone.

Me: How does that make me feel better?

Lincoln: I'll be nicer to you in next week's game if I'm well...fed.

Me: Fine. I'll allow it. For the good of my face.

Lincoln: I'll bring you some to the game. Still love me?

Me: ...

Me: Duh.

Lincoln: XOXOX.

I was smirking when I glanced up, meeting Blake's shocked gaze across the road. I started waving at her furiously and she ducked her head, pretending to ignore me as she took an order. She was very aware of me though, sneaking glances at me constantly.

Hi, I texted her, getting a weird little thrill now that I could message her. I mean, technically I had been texting her this whole time. Just as that douchebag "Other." But responding yes, no...or not responding at all had been absolutely brutal. Now that I'd fixed my name on her phone— keeping Clark's number blocked, of course—I could say whatever I wanted. Like...

> Me: I love your boobs.

It took her three heart pounding minutes to check my message, but the big grin that crossed her face when she did was well worth the excruciating wait.

I adjusted the front of my pants and threw my head back against the padded leather of the high backed booth. This was going to be a long fucking night.

Because now I wanted her boobs.

The minutes ticked by, and I sipped at my drink, texting back and forth with Lincoln, and sometimes Walker, trying not to follow Blake's every move.

At some point my gaze snagged on a group walking along the crowded sidewalk in front of me.

A teenage boy dressed in all black, no older than sixteen, was deftly weaving his way through a crowd of businessmen. I could tell what he was about to do before he even did it—he was being *way* too casual. He sideswiped one of the corporate yuppies, his hand grabbing the man's wallet, no doubt fat with credit cards and cash. He got it out without the man noticing, but because of his rookie status, the boy totally fumbled his sleight of hand.

The wallet slipped from his grasp and plopped to the concrete. Which obviously caught the attention of the guy he'd just stolen from. There were some yells from the group, and it was pretty comical to watch the emotions dancing across the businessman's face: anger, disbelief, and the sudden realization that he'd become part of an impromptu street drama. He bent down to retrieve his fallen property, but the boy scooped up the wallet from the ground and made a daring escape, disappearing into another bustling crowd.

A skilled pickpocket's retreat.

It was a sight to behold; art, really.

As I watched this scene unfold, it triggered memories I tried not to think about very often, dark chapters from my own past.

The group home where I'd been unceremoniously dropped off as a toddler could have been literal hell. Neglect and cruelty were the only hallmarks of that place, and I'd barely survived.

When I was eight, I'd run away. I'd figured I had a better chance of surviving out on the streets than in that place. I was terrified when I left, but I couldn't take it anymore.

I was a child, lost and alone, navigating a world that had given me nothing.

After a few days, it was clear I did not have what it took to survive on the streets. I thought I would die out there, crouched in a grimy alley, and I was ready for it.

Then Logan showed up. Nothing about him said good intentions, but he became the savior I desperately needed.

He took me under his wing, took me to a rundown house where other lost boys, just like me, sought sanctuary. Logan assumed the role of both our mentor and protector, teaching us the art of survival. And in Logan's world, survival meant pickpocketing.

Those three years with Logan and the others had been an interesting blend of ruthlessness and camaraderie for a little kid. I thought I'd found a band of brothers, people who cared about me. For awhile, It almost felt like I had a family for the first time in my life.

I also got damn good at pickpocketing.

But nothing like that lasts forever. One of the other boys tried to pickpocket a federal agent. After being caught, he told them all about us, and they raided our place. Amidst the chaos, Logan was shot, and I was forcibly torn away from the makeshift family I had come to love, and taken to a different group home than the one before.

As I watched the teenage pickpocket sprint around a corner and disappear, there was a little ache in my heart. Life had a peculiar way of intertwining our past and present, reminding us of the roads we had traveled and the choices we had made.

I guess everything happens for a reason. I never would have met Layla—Blake—if it weren't for all that.

But a lot of that had really fucking sucked.

My phone buzzed and I grabbed it like it was a lifeline. I hated thinking about my past. It was Blake, thank fuck. Her texts came in rapid fire…adorably awkward. I'd changed her name in my phone to Mrs. Lancaster, and I felt like a giddy little kid watching it pop up now.

> Mrs. Lancaster: They're letting me off early since it's a slow night.

> Mrs. Lancaster: But we totally don't have to hang out.

> Mrs. Lancaster: Because it's late.

> Mrs. Lancaster: Sorry I'm texting so much.

> Me: On my way, sunshine.

I grabbed my empty cup, smirking to myself at how the barista was avoiding looking at me.

It was go time.

CHAPTER 12

BLAKE

Ari's car pulled up to the front of the restaurant and he got out and raced to my side to open the door for me. My cheeks flushed as I stared up at him, his warm breath brushing against my ear.

"I'm taking you back to my place. Don't try and say no," he murmured, his voice low and husky. Lust spiked in my veins at his words, and the world took on a sparkly edge.

"Okay," I managed to say, my voice barely above a whisper. I wanted to go. I'd been thinking about it for my entire shift. Waldo was at the pet sitter anyway, because I hated leaving him alone while I was at work and…

We weren't alone last night. Clark had been there in the room, whether we wanted to believe it or not.

Tonight there weren't any ghosts.

Tonight…there was just us.

There was something about the way he looked at me, the intensity in his gaze…he was hungry for me. Desperate.

And I couldn't wait to feed him.

He buckled my seatbelt, rubbing his nose against mine.

"I missed you," he said. And there was an ache in his voice.

The same ache that I'd felt as soon as he'd walked out of the restaurant. The one still there even after I realized he was just across the street.

I missed him.

It seemed absurd, irrational, to ache for someone's presence so intensely, especially when we were still only getting to know each other.

But that's exactly what I felt.

My heart seemed to have already memorized the cadence of his laughter, the way his eyes crinkled at the corners when he smiled…the warmth of his touch. We were two souls inexplicably drawn together, like magnets pulled by a force greater than ourselves.

It was as if my soul recognized him. As if we'd met before in another life, in another time. I couldn't explain it, but there was an unshakable feeling that our destinies were intertwined, that our connection went far beyond now.

Ari got in the car and took my hand, settling it on the gearshift while he drove.

As Ari's car glided through the night, enchanting anticipation hung in the air, shimmering like a thousand stars in the velvet sky. The engine's purr seemed to serenade us, the gentle rhythm of the tires against the road a soothing melody that underscored the emotions hovering there between us.

My heart was dancing in my chest, not exactly nervous anticipation…more like happiness.

Was that what this felt like?

I couldn't remember feeling it before.

I stole glances at Ari, his gorgeous features bathed in the soft, ambient glow of the car's interior. He kept looking at me too. With a beguiled, mesmerized look in his green eyes every time.

Ari Lancaster thinks he's lucky to have me.

And until he figured out otherwise, I was going to enjoy

the moment. Because no one else in my life had ever made me feel like more than a favor. After Clark had saved me, I'd seen it sometimes, like he felt he was this good guy for sticking around, for hanging on despite all my issues.

And honestly, that look in itself made me want to die.

Because he hadn't even known half of the issues I really had, the demons always floating around in my mind.

"Don't go anywhere in that pretty head," Ari murmured, showing that he knew me better than anyone else ever had somehow. "It's just me and you now, sunshine. And this thing between us is so big, there's never going to be room for anyone else."

"How do you do that?" I sighed, finally dragging my gaze away from him. "How do you see me like that?"

He chuckled to himself and shook his head. ""You're all I see, Blake. I feel like I've been looking for you my whole life."

I wanted to sob. Because the emotions inside me felt like too much, like they needed somewhere to spill over.

As he navigated the winding roads, we moved away from any heavy words. The conversation flowed like a gentle breeze. I was fascinated by every word that came out of his mouth. I wanted to know *everything* there was to know about him. I felt like I'd been talking in a secret language my whole life, that no one else could understand except Ari Lancaster.

It felt like maybe I could give him my sadness someday.

And he wouldn't want to run away. He would just understand.

That the fact that my parents had irreparably broken something in me all those years ago wouldn't scare him away.

The world outside the car had dissolved into the night, and there was only Ari and me, a cocooned universe I never wanted to leave.

With every mile, the anticipation in the car grew like an

enchanting spell, a dance of emotions that rose to a fevered pitch. Arousal mingled with longing, creating a heady cocktail of emotions that pulsed through our veins. We both knew what was coming when we got to his house.

Finally we were there, and we pulled into his enormous garage, the soft rumble of the car's engine coming to a gentle rest. As the garage door closed behind us, I noticed two other vehicles in the cavernous space, a striking red lifted truck, and a sleek black motorcycle.

Ari's vehicles were freaking hot.

"You look like you're interested in a bike ride *later*, sunshine," he chuckled after he opened my door for me and saw what I was drooling at. I didn't miss how he emphasized *later*.

I was all about the *later* as well.

Ari took my hand loosely, our fingers intertwined, and led me into the house. His other hand gently grazed my face as he leaned in for a kiss. But before our lips could meet, I pulled back slightly, my cheeks burning with sudden embarrassment.

"Can I...can I take a shower first?" I stammered, feeling self-consciousness wash over me. I smelled like food...and sweat. And he smelled like sunlight and sex and fuck...it was the best smell on earth.

Ari's fingers traced a gentle path along my jawline. "Sure thing, sunshine," he purred, his voice tender. "As long as you borrow my clothes when you're finished."

He winked at me and I was a pool of lust. Men that looked like him, acted like him, breathed like him...they should not be allowed to wink.

Ari led me into his master bathroom. The moment I stepped through the door, I immediately loved it. It was fancy, all marble and glass, shouting out luxury and comfort.

Soft, warm lighting filled the room, making it feel cozy and inviting.

Right there in the middle of it all, was an enormous bathtub. It gleamed like a pristine oasis, just waiting for someone to dive into it—aka me. Above it, a chandelier sparkled, scattering light into a thousand little shards.

The vanity was made of polished marble and decked out with shiny silver fixtures. He showed me where the heated towels were and then he stopped, his cheeks turning red.

'There's a drawer," he muttered, pointing to one in the vanity. "It's for you."

I shot him a confused look and slid the drawer open, only to find fancy toiletries laid out neatly inside—many of them my favorite brands, ones I didn't buy now that I was trying to live out from under the shadow of the Shepfields' money.

"Um Ari...is this a drawer for women you invite over?" I asked softly, feeling hot and icky all of a sudden.

"No!" he practically shouted. "I bought—well, my housekeeper bought—these for you. No one else. No...no one's been here but you."

"Oh," I blushed. "In that case, thank you." I was embarrassed by my reaction, but he seemed to be more worried about it than annoyed.

Ari smacked a kiss on my lips. "I'll give you some space for now...but just know that next time, I'm joining you," he said huskily, before he literally left the room at a run, muttering something about needing to "leave now while he could." There was also something in there about tacos, but that one just left me confused.

Taking a deep breath, I undressed and stepped into the shower, the hot water soothing my skin as it cascaded down like a gentle rain. The scent of his shower gel surrounded me, a subtle reminder of his presence that made my insides warm. I hurried through the shower, wanting to see Ari again.

When I was finished, I dried myself off with one of the warmed towels he'd pointed out and I reached for the pile of his clothes. This felt like a big step. There was something about wearing your man's clothes that just did something to the female population. I slipped into his shirt, and it swallowed me whole, like a cocoon of soft fabric as it hung off my shoulder. The sweatpants were loose and comfortable and I pulled the drawstrings tight so they were able to stay up.

As I made my way to the kitchen, I was greeted by the sight of Ari, now dressed in a pair of joggers that hung low on his hips, showing off those dimples right above his ass that were one of the sexiest sights on earth. He was shirtless, the butterfly on his back standing out in stark relief, and the sight of his tattooed sculpted chest and defined muscles made my breath catch in my throat. His hair was wet and slicked back, and there were still some droplets of water glistening on his tanned skin from the shower he'd obviously taken somewhere else in the house.

"Hey," he said, his voice husky and inviting as he turned to face me. The air between us crackled with tension, as his eyes devoured me, bouncing all over my body. It seemed like the sight of me in his clothes did as much to him as wearing his clothes did to me. Ari was squeezing his fists at his sides, like he was trying to hold back from reaching for me.

"Hi," I replied, my voice soft and uncertain. I couldn't help but feel a rush of desire, a yearning to be closer to him. His presence was both overwhelming and comforting, a contradiction that made my heart race.

He gestured to the kitchen island, where he had put together a spread of food that smelled incredible. "I only know how to make one thing. But that's okay because it's the best food in the world, so I know you're going to like it," he said, gesturing proudly to the island. "It's taco time, baby."

I giggled and his face lit up like the sound made him happy.

Ari made my plate, walking me through the correct way to make a perfect taco, and then we walked to his kitchen table to eat. I was about to sit down when he slid under me and pulled me into his lap, setting his plate down in front of us.

"My house. My rules. And my rules say we *have* to eat just like this," he purred into my ear.

I bit my lip and then found myself nuzzling against him. I craved this kind of closeness. I was desperate for it. He wasn't going to have to fight me on this kind of thing at all.

"Good girl," he murmured, and I melted, belatedly realizing that I'd missed the beast I was now sitting on. It was going to be quite memorable, sitting on his erection and eating tacos at the same time.

He hummed against my hair before grabbing a steak taco off his plate and taking a big bite. Ari's moan of delight was...erotic. He *really* loved tacos.

He munched away happily, telling me about his favorite taco place in Dallas that Lincoln had recently betrayed him at by taking Monroe. I was quite confident of Ari's three favorite things at this point: hockey, Lincoln, and tacos. Four things, I amended. I was beginning to suspect that I was one of his favorite things as well.

The conversation flowed effortlessly, as if we had known each other for a lifetime. The tension that had hung in the air earlier had transformed into something more intimate, a connection that went beyond words.

――――――

Ari

I was dying. Literally. Not sure if I was in heaven...or hell.

I had the hardest erection of my entire life and she kept pushing against it. And I was eating tacos.

Fuckkk.

And she was so easy to talk to. She was relaxing, opening up to me. And it was the sweetest thing.

I took my last bite of dinner, mentally congratulating myself because I'd killed it on the carne asada tonight. I was tempted to eat more, but I had plans...big plans...and I didn't want to be too full for them.

There was nothing worse than a meat fart.

Don't think about meat farts when you're about to seduce your woman!, I screamed at myself.

She turned and smiled at me, and all other thoughts thankfully disappeared.

I wanted her. I wanted her so badly it honest to goodness felt like I would fucking die if I didn't have her. Right now.

"What's wrong?" she asked, cocking her head innocently.

I stared at her for a second, trying to find some kind of self control.

But alas...there wasn't any to be found.

I scooped her up, enjoying her little squeak of surprise, and I stalked towards my bedroom. From the moment I'd moved into the place, I'd been dreaming of her in my bed. Getting off to it multiple times a day.

And I was all about dreams becoming a reality.

I threw her down on the bed, and she stretched out like a languid cat. Laying there in my clothes. Fuck, the sexiest thing I'd ever seen...only to be beat by the scene I'd get in a second when I stripped her completely bare.

I kneeled on the bed and crawled to her, her violet eyes wide in anticipation.

I was suddenly overcome with gratitude. It was enough to make me fall forward and just lay my head on her stomach.

I'd actually found her. All those years of feeling lonely, like I'd lost the one person meant for me.

And I'd found her.

"Ari," she said softly, her hands sliding through my hair.

I nuzzled against her, my fingers tracing the skin peeking out from where my shirt had slid up on her. I glanced up at her face, and fuck, I was witnessing true perfection. I'd never get tired of staring at her. I was sure of it. Never ever.

I was reminded then, just how close I was to her pussy. And I had promised that I would be tasting it…and inside of it…every day for the rest of our lives.

Or if I hadn't said it…I'd definitely meant it.

I should definitely keep those promises. Because it's really, really good to keep them.

I lifted up and pushed her legs apart so I could get what I wanted. She watched me slowly pull my sweats down her legs. My hands were slightly shaking. Last night, in the dim lighting, I didn't get to see everything I wanted.

I was going to make the most of it tonight, but it felt like I'd been given the most precious gift. And I was suddenly so scared that I'd fuck it all up.

I'd never let her go. No matter what.

I'd glue myself to her side if I had to.

I growled when the most perfect pussy on the planet came into view, all pink and plump…and wet.

"Look at how pretty you are, sunshine," I purred, and she flushed. I pushed her shirt up, revealing her braless tits… because I wanted to see if she flushed everywhere when she got turned on like this.

And sure enough…the answer was yes.

There was indeed a rosy flush all over those plump, delicious fucking breasts.

I slapped my face and she giggled in surprise. "Sorry. Just making sure I wasn't dreaming, because there's no way this kind of perfection actually exists." I squeezed one of her breasts and then leaned over and lightly licked at her nipple until it was beaded.

"Fuck."

I definitely wanted to play with those more, but I had a pussy to eat.

I kissed it first, because...I just had to. And then I held onto her hips and I licked into her, moaning as her wetness hit my tongue. I couldn't even really describe the taste. I just knew it was delicious. My favorite. Necessary to my fucking existence.

I sucked on her clit. And I was feeling feverish. Feral. She was crying out and riding my face as her hands dug into my hair. I needed to get in deeper so I pushed her legs apart and fucked my tongue into her pussy as I rubbed her clit. I wanted every part of her though, so my tongue was everywhere, sliding down her ass cheeks and dipping inside her rosebud as she screamed my name. She tried to move away but I held her there because I wanted it all. There was no part of her that wasn't going to belong to me.

Fucking her with my fingers, I returned to her clit, suckling it as she came all over my face. The sound of her screaming my name. Fuck. There was cum dribbling out of me like a faucet, and I somehow kicked off my pants without lifting my face from her pussy. I was fucking into the bed as I continued to suck and lick, unable to stop without getting one. Fucking. More.

When she came again, I almost lost fistfuls of hair because she was pulling on it so hard. But what a fucking way to go. Just the sound of her voice and the taste of her had me riding the edge. I reached down and pinched the top of my dick because there was no way that I was coming anywhere but in that tight fucking cunt.

I came up for air, although death by pussy sounded like a beautiful fucking death...

The way she was staring at me, those soft eyes a mixture of desire and something else...something that looked awfully like love. I'd almost got it. I'd almost got her heart.

I leaned forward and licked her nipple, sucking it into my mouth while I kneaded and played with her breasts.

"Ari," she whispered, her head thrown back, her fingers digging into the comforter underneath her. "I want—"

"What do you want, sunshine?" I soothed between sucks.

"I want to touch you."

She sounded desperate, and I did live to serve...

I quickly flopped to the bed next to her, my hands behind my head, my dick extending up to my stomach. The lust was so intense, I was riding that fine line between delirium and sanity.

Blake sat up and moved hesitantly to her knees, her eyes wide as she stared at my dick. I had to admit it did look pretty badass with the piercing winding its way through the shaft.

Muchhh better than a little old dick tattoo.

I frowned, wondering if Blake would appreciate it none-theless.

She reached towards it, a faint flush to her cheeks. I didn't know where to look. That face. Those breasts...my gaze darted down to that gorgeous, glistening pussy. So much eye candy.

She smoothed her fingers over the crown, squeezing gently as a gush of moisture seeped from the slit. I'd never had this much pre cum before, but it was gushing out, my dick on high alert. Locking eyes with me, she brought her fingers to her plump lips and licked at the tips, tasting me.

"Mmmh," she whimpered, and a fresh batch of cum trickled out because fuck...she was hot. I had to close my eyes for a second…because I was too fucking close. "I want to suck on you, Ari. Take that big cock in my mouth. I want you to fuck my mouth."

My eyes widened, because golly gee willikers, I'd died and gone to heaven. Blake had a dirty mouth.

"How bad do you want it, sunshine?" I growled as she leaned forward and lapped at my head, her small pink tongue peeking out and sliding over my slit.

Her hand curled around my cock, her fingertips not quite meeting as she stroked up my shaft, every pass over my piercing making me grit my teeth.

Dead kittens. Old man balls…Little Ari, don't let me down now….Fuckkkkk.

Her lips closed over the head and I couldn't help but fuck into her mouth until she gagged. Her hands were squeezing and rubbing along my length, and she was sucking on me like I was fucking candy.

"It's so good. Soo good. Blake," I moaned. And she smiled before taking me deeper, sucking on me hard. "Suck it, baby. Suck my fucking cock."

She worked me even further down her throat somehow, pulling off slightly to flick the head of my piercing around with her tongue.

"Fuck. Fuck. Fuck," I growled, completely losing control.

I dragged my fingers through her hair and down to her jaw, holding her head still as I fucked into her mouth, muttering a mixture of fucks and praises. "Yes, fuck. You're such a good girl. Take more." I thrust in deeper, in and out, until I got the rhythm I wanted.

"You're so fucking good at this," I growled, because I'd never gotten head this good. Ever.

Her hands had moved from my shaft and were now roaming my skin. I loved her touching me. Loved it.

Her eyes were wide and my precum was dripping from her mouth, onto her tits.

"Look at how fucking beautiful you are, sweet girl," I murmured in awe as I continued to fuck her face.

I groaned when one of her fingers slid down below my penis, massaging the entry of my asshole.

"Holy fuck!" I all but screamed as I surged into her one more time, flooding her mouth with pumping bursts of cum. She continued to lick and suck, as if she was desperate for every drop. I pumped into her a few more times, still leaking cum. I wanted her to have all of it. I loved that a part of me was inside her, like that just bound us more.

My breath was coming out in gasps when she finally slid her lips off my dick with a sexy pop.

I reached over and smeared the drops of cum into her skin, sliding it down her neck and across her chest. I wanted to coat her in it.

She sat back, biting down on her bottom lip and looking unsure all of a sudden. "Was that...was that okay?" she whispered.

I barked out a harsh laugh because fuck..was that okay?

"That was the best fucking thing I've ever experienced besides the feel of your cunt last night. A million out of ten. Best fucking blowjob anyone could ever have."

Her eyes glimmered with relief and I sat up and kissed her, tasting my cum on her lips. My dick stirred to life and I didn't even try to talk it down. I had a feeling I was going to be aroused and ready to fuck her for the rest of my life.

Is this what madness felt like?

She lay back beside me and I just stared at her in awe. I was so gone for this perfect fucking girl, and I was never going to let her go.

Ever.

She was mine, and I'd never allow her to slip away. The mere thought of losing her, of someone else even daring to lay eyes on her, ignited a dark, all-consuming obsession within me. It was a hunger, a need to possess her completely, body and soul. I wanted to envelop her in darkness, where there was no escape from my grasp, and she'd be forever bound to me. She wasn't just everything; she was the only thing, and I'd descend to the depths of madness to ensure she stayed mine.

"What are you thinking about?" she murmured, her hand reaching out to stroke down my face.

That I'm crazy about you. Mad about you. Obsessed.

"That I'll never let you go," I answered with a soft, amused smile. Because that was the truth.

"I'd like that," she answered.

And I considered it a vow.

———

Blake

He made love to me all through the night.

That's what it was. There was no denying it. His body whispered it to me every time he thrust inside me.

We were both insatiable, unable to stop for hours. I was addicted to him.

The soft, warm rays of the morning sun bathed us as we laid intertwined on the lounger on Ari's back patio much, much later on, watching the sky gradually lighten with the approaching sunrise. I was sore...everywhere. The morning sun was a gentle kiss on our skin, and I'd never felt more...at peace.

"So, how'd you get into hockey anyway?" I murmured, tracing the outline of the birdcage tattoo on his chest. I wanted to know everything about him.

I just didn't want him to know everything about me.

His heartbeat was a comforting, steady rhythm beneath my head.

"Mmmh, I sort of stumbled into it, really late actually."

I shifted slightly, surprised. "Really? I'd pictured you skating in diapers."

Ari chuckled softly, his fingers tracing idle patterns on my skin. "Not quite. I didn't get into it until right before my 13th birthday. I was kind of an angry kid, and I'd skip school to hang out at the mall. There was an ice skating rink inside, and I stole a pair of skates and would sneak in every day, and just skate...for hours."

His fingers traced below the blanket wrapped around me, slipping to circle my nipple. I shifted against his chest. I was achy, but I'd give him anything he wanted if he asked.

"There was this free skate event hosted by a local Catholic parish," he continued, his voice taking on a wistful tone. "They'd set up a makeshift rink in their parking lot during the winter months. It was open to anyone, no matter their skill level."

I stared up at him, his beauty overwhelming for the millionth time.

"One of the priests," he continued, "Father Donaldson, started to recognize me. There was a hockey net set up during the free skate, along with some old equipment. I'd be out there from beginning to end, smashing pucks into the net, playing with anyone I could get. Father Donaldson must have seen something in me. Because one day he asked if I'd ever played before."

"What did you tell him?" I asked, grinning at the mischievous glint in his eyes.

Ari smirked, watching me, pressing a soft kiss on my lips that had my heart absolutely singing, "I may have told a little white lie and said I was basically a pro."

I giggled and his smirk widened. "He signed me up for a

local league. And fuck. He changed my life, Blake. I put everything into the game. Everything." He trailed off, his eyes unseeing as he spent a moment in the past. "A coach from Dalton Prep scouted me during one of my games. He gave me a scholarship to attend school there. I met Lincoln and... the rest is history."

"Your parents must have been so proud," I murmured, trying to imagine myself good at anything. What my parents would have thought.

I realized suddenly that Ari hadn't said anything. I looked up at him and he was staring at the sunrise, his brow furrowed, the usual twinkle in his eyes dulled and...stressed. His grip on my hip held a touch of desperation.

"I didn't have parents, sunshine," he finally murmured, turning to watch me with his verdant green gaze. "I was dropped off at a group home when I was a toddler."

I gaped at him, mind racing but...no. Things like that didn't happen. Not in real life.

"A group home?" I whispered.

"Yes," he said gently, his eyes urging me on...

The night had stretched its inky canvas above, adorned with twinkling stars, and I was in the backyard of the group home again, tears tracing an endless path down my cheeks. I was convinced I was never going to be happy again. I missed them, my parents. So much. Everyday it was there, and it didn't feel like I was ever going to be okay.

I lay there, staring up at those distant stars, as if they held the answers to questions I didn't know how to ask. The world felt too big. Everything inside me was lonely. It was never ending.

And then, like a gentle whisper in the night, Ari was there, just like he'd been every day since I'd gotten here. His hand found mine, fingers entwining, and we lay there together beneath the canopy of stars.

"Ari," I spoke in a voice barely above a whisper, "do you think I'm going to be sad forever?"

He was silent for a moment, as if contemplating the vastness of the universe above us. I watched the stars twinkle in his eyes, and in that moment, I realized he carried his own burdens, his own share of sorrows. Yet, he had always been my refuge, the one who understood without needing words.

"I'll make you happy," he finally said, his voice tender and resolute. "It might take a while, but someday I'll make you happy for the rest of your life."

Someday. The word hung in the air, a fragile promise in the darkness. I couldn't help but feel a flicker of hope, a glimmer of light in the shadows of my sadness. But forever sounded like such a daunting expanse of time, an eternity I couldn't quite grasp at ten years old.

I looked at Ari, his face illuminated by the soft, silvery glow of the moon, and I felt a bond between us that was stronger than any of the losses I'd endured. He was my constant, my protector, the one who had always been there to wipe away my tears and chase away the nightmares.

As we lay there, hand in hand, gazing up at the stars that had witnessed our childhood sorrows, I clung to Ari's promise like a lifeline. I didn't know what the future held, but with him by my side, I felt a glimmer of the happiness he had vowed to bring into my life. And though forever seemed like a really long time, I believed him.

I'd left with the Shepfields the very next week.

The revelation hit me like a sudden burst of sunlight through stormy clouds. Staring at the grown man who'd once been a boy I didn't think I could live without, I couldn't contain the overwhelming rush of emotions that surged through me. Tears welled in my eyes, happiness and shock exploding through my veins as the realization of who he was washed over me. I sobbed into his chest, completely overcome.

"Ari?" I finally whispered, staring up at him through tear strung eyes. There was a newfound significance behind his name.

"I made a promise after all, Layla," he murmured with a soft smile. "The universe just finally decided to help me with it."

My eyes closed as he said my name, my real name, the one I never allowed myself to think about anymore.

I clung to him, my sobs shaking my entire being, as if I could release the years of pain and uncertainty that had accumulated in my heart. A piece of myself had been found, clicked back into its rightful place, and I sobbed for all the years we'd lost and for the future I desperately wanted to have.

"I've been so lonely without you," I finally admitted. He brushed a soft kiss across my hair.

"Lonely doesn't exist for us anymore, baby," he soothed.

And as he made love to me under the sunrise, whispering his devotion over and over...

I believed him.

CHAPTER 13

ARI

I was leaving practice, about to head over to the restaurant to pick Blake up from her shift, when my phone buzzed from inside my practice bag.

I cursed as I dug around in it, my equipment badly needed to be washed. It fucking reeked.

"Got it!" I cried out victoriously. Walker shot me an amused look as he headed to his truck, and I was tempted to throw some of my sweaty socks at him. Staring down at the message though, I forgot all about Walker.

The text was from my P.I.

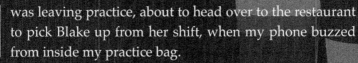

Creepy David: Blake's booked a gig tomorrow for the new Renage Campaign. Thought you might like to see the details.

I clicked on the link he'd sent, skimming through the information for the job. Everything looked fine until...

MOTHERFUCKING DEREK THORNTON!

I nearly choked on my protein shake, the rich liquid taking an unexpected detour to my lungs. Derek Thornton? The same A List actor Derek Thornton who had more romantic connections in Hollywood than the entire LA phonebook? The guy whose commitment issues could give the Great Wall of China a run for its money?

Not fucking happening.

I wasted no time, immediately dialing David's number. "David, are you absolutely certain about this? Derek Thornton?"

"Yes, Mr. Lancaster. I'm quite positive," David's weaseling voice said, obviously perturbed by me questioning his intel.

I cursed beneath my breath. The last thing that was going to happen was Derek Thornton in a room with Blake. He would take one look at my gorgeous goddess of a woman and try to leap in for the kill.

Like I'd just said...not fucking happening.

I really needed to be able to play in Dallas next week, not go to jail for homicide.

"Okay. Thanks, David," I said, hanging up without another word and frantically dialing Remy, the agent I shared with Lincoln. It took me three fucking tries because I was freaking out so badly.

"What's up, my man?" Remy asked when he picked up. I could hear tons of people talking in the background. There was no one quite as good at schmoozing as Remy.

"Remy," I began, my mind spinning. "I need you to work some magic for me. Find out everything you can about the shoot Renage is doing tomorrow—whose brainchild it is, the concept, the entire angle they're pitching. Then, make sure I'm part of the shoot instead of Derek Thornton."

There was a pause, almost as if Remy was contemplating the absurdity of my request. "Ari, let me get this straight... you want me to get you in a campaign scheduled to shoot tomorrow where you replace an A list actor as the male lead?"

"Yes," I said, relieved he got it.

"Ari, buddy. You've been playing great, but not this kind of great."

I scoffed. I was playing fucking phenomenal!

I paced my living room, desperation overtaking reason. "Remy, despite the fact that you clearly have lost your mind– because I'm fucking amazing–I need you to promise them anything they want to get me in this campaign. I will do it for free. TELL THEM I HAVE A FUCKING PIERCED DICK! Just find a fucking way."

Remy sighed, an audible resignation in his voice. "Alright, Ari. But how do you expect me to explain your sudden, burning desire to participate in this campaign? Do you want to explain it to me?"

I ran a hand through my hair, my thoughts a whirlwind. "Think outside the box, Rem-dog. Tell them I've had a sudden 'epiphany,' or that I've recently developed an addiction to Renage. Well, actually…what exactly does Renage sell?"

"Ari Fucking Lancaster!" Remy spit.

"Kidding. Kidding. Of course I know what Renage is. Psssh. Tell them I'm a devoted believer in…Renage. Just get it done."

"I'll do my best," Remy said in the most resigned fucking voice I'd ever heard.

This was not that *hard* of a sell, for fuck's sake. I was amazing.

Hours crept by like an eternity, each minute feeling like a countdown to the end of my fucking life. The prospect of Derek Thornton hovering around Blake was driving me insane. If this didn't work, I was going to have to puncture her tires, break her phone so she couldn't call an Uber, puncture *my* tires so she couldn't borrow my car…kidnap her and take her to some deserted island. I was sure I could find one in a pinch if I really needed to.

Daddy Lincoln would let me use his new private jet.

Finally, Remy texted me. "You're in. Get ready for some media attention." There was more information he sent in a link but I didn't click on it. I was currently on the floor, breathing in relief.

I hadn't quite been prepared for a kidnapping.

———

Blake

The day of the Renage photo shoot had arrived, and I was a mess. It was the first job I'd booked in California since the Voyage Magazine job had fallen apart. Renage was a colossal opportunity, one that I hadn't thought I had a chance at. It could be the break I'd been looking for.

As I sat in my room though, my anxiety swirled around me like a malevolent storm.

Waldo lay at my feet, his big brown eyes filled with concern. He nuzzled his wet nose against my hand, trying to offer comfort. I scratched his ears and offered him a weak smile, grateful as usual for his unwavering presence.

But no amount of furry affection could stop the relentless anxiety gnawing at me. Doubts plagued my mind, whispering insidiously that I was going to fuck it all up.

And then there was the pizza box sitting on my nightstand. I'd lost my mind and eaten it with Ari last night. I could still feel the greasy, cheese-laden slices churning in my stomach.

I stood in front of the mirror, hating every part of myself as I examined my reflection. The soft morning light filtered through the curtains, casting a harsh spotlight on my features. The voice in my head was loud this morning, making me an avalanche of self-doubt and self-loathing.

My eyes traced the lines of my body, lingering on the areas where I felt the most insecure. I was spiraling, despising every curve, every imperfection, every ounce of flesh on my body.

The guilt washing over me was familiar. I'd struggled with…food issues early on with the Shepfields. Maura kept a careful eye on my weight, weighing my food and restricting it so I looked exactly how she wanted. She'd raised me to think of food as the enemy. But an enemy I could defeat as long as I was disciplined.

A part of me knew my thoughts were unreasonable. But the other part of my brain, the one that was cursing me for daring to eat a slice of pizza before such a big job…it was much louder.

Tears welled up in my eyes, and I blinked them away, unwilling to let them fall. I could control my thoughts. I could —I turned sideways, scrutinizing my profile. My fingers traced the outline of my ribs, a ritualistic gesture that provided me with a twisted sense of reassurance. The bones beneath my skin were like a map of my self-control, a testament to the discipline I had imposed upon myself.

Without warning, I bolted from my seat and rushed to the bathroom, Waldo following closely behind. I stared at the toilet, trying to talk myself out of throwing up.

It didn't work. I clung to the toilet bowl, my thoughts spiraling into a chaotic abyss.

Twenty minutes later, I rose unsteadily to my feet and rinsed my mouth. Waldo looked up at me, his eyes filled with concern, and I patted his head, trying to comfort him.

With trembling hands, I tried to pull myself together.

The worst part was that not only did I not feel thinner… but now I felt sick. My throat was sore, my eyes were bloodshot, my skin felt clammy…and my stomach muscles were aching.

"I'm a mess," I whispered, wishing I could engage in my other dirty little secret and release some of this pain.

I walked back into my room and my phone buzzed on the nightstand. I rushed to pick it up, the screen illuminating with Ari's message: "Good luck today, sunshine. See you soon."

A surge of warmth immediately washed over me...but also shame. He was my chance...my chance for a good thing. And when he found out how messed up I was...it was going to fuck it all up.

My phone pinged again, signaling my Uber was there.

I was close to hysterics as I grabbed my bag and headed out into the living room. Charlotte was on the couch flipping through channels on the tv, and she gave me a weird look as I passed by...crying. I whispered, "see ya," and went out the door before she could ask me any questions.

I wiped at my face before I stepped into the waiting car. I could get through today. I could seize the opportunity. I *had* to seize the opportunity.

I couldn't lose Ari.

The driver set off, the city rushing past me and the weight of my past feeling like a weight stretched taut across my skin.

Thirty minutes later, we'd made it to the expansive warehouse hosting the Renage photo shoot. My stomach had churned the whole ride over with lingering discomfort. I thanked the driver and walked inside, immediately enveloped by all the activity on the set. The bustling makeup artists, hairstylists, and wardrobe assistants, all seemed distant, as if they were moving through a haze. My steps were unsteady, and I clung to each breath, willing the feeling of unease to subside.

Bright lights hung overhead, their intensity exacerbating my discomfort, casting stark shadows that danced before my eyes. The vivid backdrop, a surreal mural of vibrant colors and intricate details appeared almost dreamlike, like a mirage shimmering in the distance.

I rounded a corner, and froze in my tracks. My eyes

widened and my jaw dropped as I spotted a familiar butterfly tattoo on a well-built, bronzed back.

Instead of Derek Thornton, Ari Lancaster was there in front of me, modeling a pair of tight black Renege boxer briefs that left almost nothing to the imagination.

The thin cotton fabric clung to his body like a second skin, accentuating the masterpiece of his muscles. My senses tingled, my body responding instinctively to the sight before me, a surge of desire making my core tighten. You could see the enormous outline of his cock through the briefs. The sight was erotic and outrageous.

And mine. I knew what that cock could do. I knew how it felt inside me.

I'd taken his cum into my body, over and over again. No one ever had his cum but me.

I squeezed my fists, taking in everyone around the room who was staring at him, lusting after him. I wanted to rip him away, cover him with my body so they knew he belonged to me.

My eyes traced the captivating lines of his V, and I could feel that my panties were damp. I think it would take a lifetime to truly explore him like I wanted to…to uncover his magic.

As if he could sense me, he glanced over his shoulder with a lazy smile…and he winked.

Like "surprise!" I decided to star in your shoot *without* telling you.

Before I could do anything…or even react to his wink, a harried looking woman with a large black headset popped up in front of me.

"There you are!" she snapped. "We need to get you ready." When I didn't move as fast as she wanted, she clapped on her clipboard. "NOW!"

I hurried to where she was pointing, glancing over at Ari

who was glaring at the woman with the scariest face I'd seen on him.

Hoping he didn't say anything to her, I rushed into the dressing room, where a flurry of activity surrounded me. Within moments, I found myself slipping into a barely-there black lace negligee set, oil and bronzer being rubbed all over my skin. My hair and makeup were expertly done, transforming me into someone I scarcely recognized. My eyes were adorned with smoky, sultry eyeshadow and my lips were painted a vibrant shade of crimson, a bold contrast to the smoky eyes. My hair was styled into loose, cascading waves that framed my face. The soft curls tumbled down my shoulders.

As I stared at my reflection in the mirror, the insecurity I'd been distracted from in my shock at seeing Ari here…it came roaring back.

Knowing I couldn't delay any longer, I took a deep breath and pushed open the dressing room door, stepping into the studio. The moment I entered, Ari's gaze snapped towards me. His jaw dropped, and his eyes were comically wide.

"Wow," he mouthed, putting his hand on his heart and pretending to stagger. His gaze roamed over my appearance and then he was wincing, shoving a hand over his suddenly very erect cock. The briefs were small…and he was abnormally large…large enough that the pierced tip was peeking out from the top band and he was doing his best to cover it.

He started mouthing something to himself while he stared at the ceiling. It kind of looked like he was chanting "grandpa balls" over and over again, but that didn't seem right.

I walked over to the set where he was standing, and he pulled his gaze to me again, the look on his face pained. "You're killing me, sunshine," he growled. He started chanting again, but this time I could hear him.

He was indeed chanting "grandpa balls."

I giggled and his whole face softened.

"You want to explain what you're doing here?" I asked with a raised eyebrow.

A throat cleared from nearby before Ari could answer. It was the art director for Renage, Élise Martin, a world-renowned figure in the industry. Her gaze flicked toward Ari and me, dipping down to the "pierced presence" in Ari's briefs that was just starting to go down. A faint blush crept across her cheeks, a testament to the undeniable charisma that Ari radiated...because nothing affected Élise Martin.

Flustered but trying to maintain her professionalism she choked out, "Alright, everyone, let's get started. This shoot is going to take us all day, so let's make the most of it."

"You're so fucking beautiful...and all mine," he whispered in my ear as we followed Élise to the set, his words a balm to the jealousy that had been simmering in my spine. The possessiveness in his tone was undeniable, and it filled me with a heady mix of desire and reassurance.

The theme for the shoot had an edgier twist, titled "Sultry Rebellion." The set was supposed to exude a dark and mysterious atmosphere, with elements of unconventional sensuality.

The backdrop was made of distressed, exposed brick walls covered in graffiti, giving the set an urban, underground vibe. Dim, moody lighting cast intriguing shadows, emphasizing the edgy ambiance.

Rather than traditional furniture, the set featured industrial props like steel chains, leather-bound cuffs, and vintage motorcycles, adding an element of raw sexuality and rebellion.

My cheeks blushed when I saw Ari staring at the cuffs, naughty thoughts obviously in his head.

They were in mine too.

Élise called for more body oil for Ari, and I bit down on

my lip hard, trying to edge off the jealousy as the eager employee rushed towards us, holding out the oil like it was the holy grail.

"Blake can apply it," said Ari firmly.

Élise opened her mouth to argue, her gaze darting between us, confused. She finally seemed to get we were… something, and changing Ari's mind was probably a lost cause, because she shook her head and stalked over to where the photographer's crew was gathered, discussing something on the screens in front of them.

I took the bottle from the very disappointed employee and, with shaking hands, smoothed the glistening oil over Ari's sculpted body. I rubbed my hands across the hard surface of his chest, fascinated as usual by all of the tattoos inked across his skin. Ari was erect again, staring at me in what looked like awed fascination. There was the click of a camera from somewhere but I was too caught up in what we were doing to see what was going on.

"I'm obsessed with everything about you," he growled under his breath, as I rubbed my palm down his abs…just for good measure.

"Same," I responded, the word rushing out quickly.

We reluctantly got to work then, and even with Ari…my self-consciousness began to claw its way to the surface like a relentless beast. Élise and the photographer's growing frustration only intensified my unease, their impatient commands slicing through me like a knife.

I couldn't do anything right. Every look was wrong.

"Let's take a break," Ari finally said after I'd been snapped at for the millionth time. There was a dark growl in his voice that broached no argument. Without waiting to see if anyone agreed with his suggestion…order, he dragged me into the dressing room, locking the door behind us.

His concern was evident in the depths of his eyes as he turned to face me.

"What's wrong, sunshine?" His voice was gentle, a soothing balm to my frayed nerves as he smoothed fingers down my cheek. But as if summoned by the mere question, a tear slipped down my skin as I leaned into his hand.

I took a shaky breath, trying to steady the tremors that ran through me. The words caught in my throat, as if they were too heavy to be set free.

I sniffled, struggling to find the words to convey the storm of emotions raging inside me. "I...I just feel so ugly. Something's wrong with me," I finally admitted, the confession escaping me like a whispered secret.

Tears welled up in my eyes, and I hastily wiped them away with the back of my hand. It was absurd, really, to be reduced to this—sobbing in a dressing room, overwhelmed by my own fucked up head. But I'd had years of my confidence being eroded, torn at until I was the nothing that Maura had preferred.

It was hard to overcome a million you're not enoughs.

"Oh baby," he said with a pained groan, touching my lips with the most exquisitely soft kiss I could have ever imagined.

Ari's intense green-eyed gaze bore into me, so many emotions flickering within their depths. I was mesmerized by what I saw there. It almost seemed like Ari Lancaster...

Could have loved me.

His lips closed over mine again, his tongue tangling sensually with mine, a bite of hunger to every lick and caress.

Warmth spread through my chest, my nipples budding against the smooth lace of the barely there bra I was wearing.

"Somehow I'm going to get you to see what I see," he murmured before glancing around the room. His gaze stopped on a full length mirror leaning against the wall. "Come here, sunshine."

He grabbed a chair and pulled me with him to the mirror, settling us in the chair in front of it so we were both facing it.

Ari's rough hands smoothed up my legs, plucking at the black garters on my thighs. "I see you and I lose my breath," he whispered in a graveled husk.

Ari's touch was a delicate caress against my skin, his fingers tracing the contours of my body with a reverence that left me breathless. With each brush of his hand, he whispered sweet words that danced in my ears, painting me with desire and affection.

His lips pressed tenderly against my forehead, leaving a trail of soft, lingering kisses. "I love your eyes," he murmured, his voice a velvety whisper that made me ache. "The first time I saw them as a kid, I knew I'd found magic. I've spent every moment since then searching for them in every crowd."

His fingers trailed down my cheek, his touch feather-light and electrifying. "Your lips," he continued, his voice husky with desire, "are my undoing. The way they taste, the way they mold against mine-it's a temptation I can never resist."

Ari's lips captured mine in a searing kiss that ignited a fire I swore stretched into my soul. When he pulled away, his eyes burned with a hunger that matched my own. "Your neck…" he sighed, his breath hot against my skin, "every time I kiss it, I can feel your pulse quicken; it's how I know you're just as deep in this as I am."

Ari's mouth moved with purpose, nipping and sucking at the sensitive skin of my neck, sending waves of pleasure radiating through me. I arched into his touch, my fingers tangling in his hair as I gave in to the exquisite sensations.

His fingers pushed down my bra so my breasts jutted out, massaging and kneading them before he leaned down and gently sucked and lapped on one of my nipples, while his free hand cupped my other breast. His teeth brushed against my sensitive skin and I came, just like that, an orgasm softly sliding through my body.

He feasted on me for a few more lusty pulls before he pulled away. "Your breasts...your fucking breasts," he whispered, his voice filled with adoration, "are the embodiment of temptation. They fit perfectly in my hands, and the way you respond to my touch–it could kill me."

Ari gripped my chin and made me look at myself in the mirror, as his other hand continued its journey, tracing the contours of my waist and hips. I love your hips, the smoothness of your belly," he purred. "They would've worshiped you in every age. You're like a siren come to life." I couldn't stop staring at his reaction in the mirror, so much hunger, adoration...so much love...for my body.

A soft sob slipped from my mouth as his hands stroked over every one of my insecurities.

Ari's touch trailed lower, his fingers teasingly grazing my thighs, before his fingers slipped under the edge of my panties and glided through my folds. "This pussy is my heaven," he whispered. "I'd do anything to have it. Anything." His finger slipped into my core, pumping a few times roughly before it slid down to my ass.

My head tipped back and I closed my eyes at the sensation, but he grabbed my chin again, forcing me to keep looking at the mirror.

"I have wet dreams about this ass. I think about it constantly. I can't wait to fuck it," he murmured, as he teased my asshole through the lace of my lingerie. I whimpered. I'd never been taken there by Clark, but I wanted Ari everywhere, in as many places as he wanted to take me.

"I'm hard for you every fucking second of every fucking day. I'm obsessed with you, crazy over you in fact. I can't stand to be apart from you for any length of time. So when you tell me you hate this perfect fucking body that I worship with every part of my fucking soul...well, we can't have that, sunshine."

I couldn't help it, my hips began to move over his hard cock, my hands wrapping around his neck behind me, painting an obscene picture in the mirror.

He thrust up and I mewled, desperate for him to fill me.

Maybe a better girl would have cared that people were just outside...probably knowing exactly what we were doing. But all I cared about was getting Ari Lancaster inside me as much and as fast as possible.

Ari's hands had moved back to my breasts, giving them another squeeze. "Fuck, I love these." He bit gently down on that sensitive space between my neck and my shoulder, licking away the slight bite of pain.

"Look at how wet you are, sweetheart. We're going to go back out there, and these panties are going to be drenched. And everyone is going to know that I got to fuck you. They're going to be so jealous."

I immediately went to scoff at what he'd said, but he sounded so confident, so sure, and the ugly voice inside of me was less sure of itself as a result.

"I want you to watch yourself in the mirror, sunshine. Watch yourself get fucked by my big cock. Watch what you do to me...how you own me," he growled, reaching down and shoving my underwear to the side before he impaled me on his hard dick.

My head fell back against his chest, gasping for breath because I was so fucking full.

It felt amazing. Like if I could just keep him inside of me, I wouldn't have any room for anything else.

"Watch yourself," Ari ordered in a strained voice, and my gaze snapped to the mirror, watching as his cock stretched me, his sack shiny with my essence and his cum. He pulled out, his decadent piercing displayed before he surged back in.

"Fuck, that's so hot," I breathed, and he chuckled, reaching between my legs to rub on my clit. Every thrust found that perfect spot inside me.

"I'm going to take a picture of this, baby, of your sweet pussy swallowing my dick. Every time you start to doubt yourself, I'll show it to you. I'll show you how perfect you are to me. How sexy...how gorgeous...how good you take me. How this pussy was meant just for me." He thrust up into me again.

"Play with those perfect tits, sunshine. Make that perfect body feel good," he ordered roughly.

My hands immediately went to my breasts, playing with my tips while he grabbed my hips and started bouncing me on his cock.

"Look at you. Fucking look at you," he said thickly.

And I did look at myself, watched my pussy spread open by his thick long cock, the way his fingers dug into my hips, the way my breasts bounced with every thrust...the rosy blush to my cheeks, the gleam in my eyes.

Right now, I really *was* beautiful.

"I'm going to keep you forever. Fuck this pussy every day. I own you, Blake. Say it. Say you belong to me." One of his hands slid up between my breasts until it was stretched across my neck, holding it as he thrust into me. Ari squeezed gently.

"You. Are. Mine," he growled. "Now say it."

"I'm yours," I panted in a choked voice.

"My fucking perfect good girl," he murmured thickly as he started fucking me, harder...rougher.

"Say it. Say you're a good girl."

"I'm a good girl," I immediately gasped as another orgasm hit me. I was gushing, drenching his cock.

"Now say you're perfect," he commanded softly, his movements slowing so that every ridge of his piercing rubbed against my skin.

My mouth opened, but it was hard for *those* words to come out. His hand squeezed my neck a little more and I gasped. "Say it, baby. Tell yourself the fucking truth." His cock was glistening and dripping with *me*. His eyes were locked on *me*. He was obsessed with *me*.

Maybe I was perfect...at least in this moment.

"I'm perfect," I breathed, the words feeling like a balm on the cuts all over my heart.

He buried his face in my neck and breathed deeply, his thrusts stopping for a moment as his body shuddered, like my words had magic powers.

All of a sudden, he thrust in. Hard.

"That's my good...fucking...girl," he breathed as he hammered into me. "Now reach down and touch that wetness. I want to taste it. It's my favorite thing."

I brushed my trembling fingers across his soaking wet cock and then brought them to his mouth. He moaned as he sucked on my fingers...like it really was his favorite taste.

"I'm going to come. Going to come so hard," he breathed. "Come with me, baby. Please." His voice was a ragged plea as his movements became erratic. He feverishly rubbed my clit while his other hand gripped my neck just a little bit tighter.

And that was it, I went off like a rocket, the edges of my vision blurring...the world rearranging right in front of me.

His whole body shuddered behind me, and the accompanying groan out of his mouth was the most erotic thing I'd ever experienced.

A few soft thrusts later and he came to a stop, and we both watched as his cum dripped out of me.

"Fuck," he whispered.

"Yeah," I breathed.

A few minutes later, there was a hesitant knock on the door. "Um, Mr. Lancaster, Ms. Shepfield…do you think we could get started? If you're, umm, if you're ready," one of the assistants called through the door.

Ari's body started shaking with laughter, and a moment later, I was giggling too…I felt a bit high at the moment. Well aware that maybe laughter wasn't the best fit for the career suicide I most likely had just accomplished.

Ari slid out of me and I whimpered. "I know, baby. Me too," he breathed, like he missed our connection as well.

He helped me off his lap and my legs felt weak as I unsteadily walked over to the makeup counter and grabbed some wipes to clean myself up. Glancing in the mirror, my makeup was a bit smudged, my curls were looser, and there was a flush to my whole body.

And like Ari's cum had magical properties…I'd never felt hotter.

We walked out of the dressing room hand in hand, staff giving us knowing looks.

"Ready?" Élise asked exasperatedly when we came into view.

"Ready, Freddie," Ari quipped back as we stepped onto the set.

Élise shook her head and started to bark directions at us. But it was a funny thing…the longer the shoot went on, the more excited she became.

"Yes! Just like that. Blake, that's perfect," she shouted at one point, and Ari gave me a knowing, "I told you so" look.

For the rest of the shoot, I was more relaxed than I'd ever been.

And for the rest of the day, I managed to feel something I hadn't on every other day of my life.

I felt perfect.

CHAPTER 14

ARI

This fucking sucked. All my careful planning to make sure Blake and I were always together…and mother fucking nature had screwed it all up. What a bitch.

Blake had been scheduled to fly out after her shift, and then the storm of the century had rocked La La Land, grounding all flights…even the private flight I'd had scheduled for her. I was going crazy, checking the fucking app every five seconds to make sure she was still at her house.

What if fucking Clark showed up? What if he or some other guy tried to take her away? All that beauty. All that perfection. Her. How could they not?

I Facetimed her for the millionth time, just needing to check. She was alone. She was safe. She was still mine.

Sharp relief sliced through my veins when her exquisite face popped up on my screen. Blake was lying on her bed, the soft glow of the television reflected on her features. I kissed the phone and she giggled, that melodic little sound that she rarely graced me with.

"Aren't you supposed to be getting ready for your game?" she murmured, shifting, and fuck…she was wearing my jersey in bed.

I groaned and grabbed the front of my pants because now was not the time for Little Ari to make an appearance.

I couldn't hit people with a hard on.

They might fall in love with me.

"Ari?" Blake said gently, and I sighed, because being away from her was making me feel sick.

"I miss you," I murmured sullenly, and she blushed, like it was unexpected I would say that.

Fuck, I must not be doing a good enough job of proving to this girl, I'm gone for her. Destroyed. Forever changed.

"I miss you too. Go out there and kick some ass and come back to me," she ordered, and I nodded my head, determined.

"You're going to watch, right?" I asked anxiously.

She flipped the view around so I could see her television was tuned to the pregame show.

"That's my girl," I grinned, right as Coach came in, his eyes like a laser missile on my phone. "Damnit, I've got to go. I—," I caught myself right before I said I love you because fuck, I couldn't say it when I wasn't there to catch her if it scared her and she tried to run. I sighed and blew her a kiss before I hung up.

Blake couldn't miss another game. Even if I had to sneak her in my luggage, she had to be there with me. I couldn't concentrate properly otherwise.

Coach's voice thundered in the locker room, his words dripping with intensity. "Listen up, boys. We're up against Minnesota today, and you know they play rough. But guess what? We're gonna be rougher. We're gonna hit 'em harder, skate faster, and shoot like there's no fucking tomorrow!"

The locker room filled with grunts of agreement and the sound of sticks pounding the floor.

He continued, his gaze unwavering. "I don't wanna see anyone flinching out there. This is our game, and we're gonna play it like it's our last stand. We're not here to back down; we're here to stand our ground and show 'em what we're made of."

The team responded with a chorus of fierce nods and determined expressions, our competitive instincts kicking into high gear. Coach pounded the whiteboard for emphasis. "When you hit that ice, remember, you're not just players. You're warriors. You fight for every inch of this territory. This game is ours, and we're gonna claim it, no matter what it takes!"

We roared, Walker leading us in a chant of "Cobras" that made me scratch my eyeballs out because Soto was right across from me, sneering at me. And I missed Dallas so fucking much.

The team dispersed, ten more minutes before we got on the ice, and I turned to Walker, needing to get my head on straight.

"Walker, it's time to *shake it off*."

Mr. Prince Charming shook his head stubbornly, his expression unwavering. "Not happening. That's not even a real thing. I'm not falling for it this time."

I raised an eyebrow, and solemnly threatened, "I'll call Lincoln and have you kicked out of the circle of trust."

Walker's eyes widened, giving me his best puppy-dog eyes. "What's the "circle of trust"? Am I in it right now?" He squinted at me. "Wait, is that from *Meet the Parents*?"

"Get your ass up and dance me with me, Disney," I snapped, flicking my hips around as I got myself ready.

He groaned, but a second later he was up, goalie pads and all. "Start the music," he sighed.

I swiped through my options before clicking on "Bejeweled," beginning the banger with a cheeky shimmy of my shoulders. Then, I let my hips sway side to side, my arms following suit, flailing in the air as if I were mimicking an inflatable tube man outside a car dealership.

The other guys on the team watched us with a mix of amusement and disbelief. Some even pulled out their phones to record our performance. Soto couldn't hide his irritation and let out a snarl, muttering, "Fucking idiots."

Which I ignored, of course.

I busted out a series of ridiculous spins, my limbs moving with wild abandon. Walker added a bit of footwork to the mix, his skates gliding across the floor in a ridiculous display of fancy footwork.

At one point, I grabbed Walker's hand, and we performed an exaggerated cha-cha, complete with synchronized twirls and dips.

Tay-Tay stopped singing and I stared at Walker with a big grin. "There is no circle of trust," I told him, and he groaned as the whole team burst into laughter.

We headed towards the hallway that led to the ice and I slapped him on the ass as I passed him by. "But if we had one, you'd be in it, Walker!" I yelled to him.

He flipped me off, as one does in the presence of greatness, and we got ready to kick ass.

―――――

The atmosphere in the arena was insane as we skated onto the ice. Coach hadn't been exaggerating when he talked about how aggressive and rough Minnesota played. From the moment the puck dropped, it was clear they were willing to do whatever it took to win.

I had my work cut out for me helping protect Walker in the net. Minnesota's forwards were relentless, constantly testing our defense with their speed and physicality.

Early in the first period, I was in a race to retrieve the puck in the corner. Just as I was about to gain possession, Soto came barreling in from behind and tripped me up. It was a deliberate move, and I couldn't help but shoot him a "what the fuck" look as I picked myself up off the ice.

"Watch your step, Ari," he sneered, a taunting grin on his face, like it was perfectly normal for your own fucking teammate to trip you up.

I shook my head and skated away, refusing to engage in his mind games. It was no surprise Soto was the king of the idiots, but I had bigger things to worry about—like defending our net.

Throughout the game, Soto continued with his antics. He "accidentally" kicked my stick while we were sitting on the bench, and pushed me when I was hoisting myself over the boards.

As the game progressed, I was getting closer and closer to shoving my stick up his ass.

Midway through the second period, it finally all came to a head. I was battling for position in front of our net when Soto decided to take a cheap shot, cross-checking me in the back.

"Do you want to die tonight, Soto?" I raged. Tommy came up behind me and held the back of my jersey as I skated forward. "What the fuck is your problem!?"

Soto got up in my face, the veins on his forehead looking like they were staging a protest, bulging and pulsating theatrically. "One of these days, I'm going to fuck your little girlfriend's cunt, show her how a real man's dick feels. I think I'll do it bare. Yeah. Fill her with my cum, leave it there for you to find it…"

Any sanity I had left snapped. Before I even had a chance to think, I ripped off my gloves, tore off his helmet, and my right fist shot forward like a rocket, connecting with Soto's jaw with a satisfying crack. His head snapped to the side, and for a split second, there was stunned silence on the ice as everyone processed what had just happened.

But that split second of quiet didn't last long. Soto spit his mouth guard out and roared in fury, launching himself at me with a wild swing. I dodged his punch and countered with a swift uppercut to his gut. He staggered back, clutching his stomach.

I didn't stop though, I continued landing blows with calculated ferocity. Soto's attempts to fight back were feeble in comparison. He swung wildly, but I bobbed and weaved, evading his hits with ease.

As the crowd roared, my focus sharpened. I could see the shock and disbelief in Soto's eyes as he realized he was outmatched. He tried to tackle me to the ice, but I spun out of his grasp. In a final, desperate move, he lunged at me, but I sidestepped him and delivered a crushing blow to his ribs.

Soto crumpled to the ice, gasping for air and clutching his side in agony. The referee rushed in to separate us, and my adrenaline-fueled rage began to ebb away, replaced by a sense of satisfaction. The crowd was on its feet, some cheering, others stunned into silence by the spectacle they had just witnessed.

I stood there, panting, my knuckles aching from the impact of my punches. Soto, on the other hand, was a mess, his face swollen and bruised, blood trickling from a split lip.

He looked fucking pathetic. People had better be seeing pictures of this because I wanted Lincoln to see my work.

He'd be so proud of me.

The refs were trying to figure out what to do with me for attacking my own teammate, Coach was going insane, his face a dark shade of red like he'd swallowed a ghost pepper...but I didn't care. Soto had it coming.

"Fuck, Ari, you have a little bit of crazy in you," mused

Walker, elbowing me as we watched the refs argue back and forth.

"Disney, you have no idea," I drawled.

I was given five minutes in the penalty box, but I couldn't have cared less.

When I finally returned to the ice, my heart was still racing with adrenaline. Soto hadn't returned, because he was such a fucking pussy…and the team was better off for it.

The rest of the game was a relentless battle. Minnesota shit-talked me a bit for beating up my own teammate…but they also seemed a little more timid than before. We pushed to our limits, upping the intensity with every shift. In the closing minutes of the third period, I found myself in a pivotal moment, defending Walker as Minnesota pressed for a tying goal. I blocked a frantic shot and cleared the puck… the clock ticking down. When the final buzzer sounded, we'd fucking won.

As we celebrated on the ice, I couldn't help but cast a glance in Soto's direction. He was staring at me, absolutely seething with anger—gritted teeth and all. I blew him a kiss just to drive it in deep.

Later on in the hotel, I sent a text to Lincoln.

> Me: Hotel Californication.

> Lincoln: No. Just no. That's not right at all.

> Me: There are too many songs about Cali, so I'm combining them.

> Lincoln: Cali now, is it?

> Me: Look, I'm trying to immerse myself in the culture. Be a good teammate and all of that.

Lincoln: Oh, is that what you call that fight you got into with Soto tonight.

Me: Aww, you do love me. You're stalking me!

Lincoln: ...

Me: Don't worry, I won't tell anyone.

Me: And yes, I think punching Soto in his fat nose was being a good teammate. Walker agrees.

Lincoln: Since when do we care what Walker thinks?

Me: Aww, and now you're jealous. Best Day Ever.

Lincoln:...

Me: Don't worry. I still love you the mostest.

Lincoln: ...

Me: Say it back.

Lincoln: ...

Me: Come on. I know you want to.

Lincoln: Sigh. Fine...ILY.

Me: VICTORY IS MINE!

CHAPTER 15

ARI

Two days later, we had another home game, and I was buzzing from spending the day with Blake as I drove her to the arena. I smiled over at her, and she blushed. I adjusted my dick, trying and failing to keep it down…because she looked so fucking hot wearing my jersey, I was having to remind myself to breathe. I'd painted my number, #24 on her cheeks. She thought it was cute, but I was just trying to be over the top possessive. I'd also made her keep my cum smeared all over her chest from an earlier bout of lovemaking.

It was a win-win for everyone.

She looked too stunning in that jersey. The way it clung to her boobs…I needed to try and include in my next contract that she should get her own penalty box during games just to keep her away from everyone.

Was that a thing? I could certainly try and get Remy to make that a thing. Lincoln would *def* be on board.

"You're staring at me," she murmured, brushing some hair out of her face.

"Can't help it. You're too damn pretty. That jersey looks way better on you than it does on me," I said, winking.

She blushed.

"You know what, fuck this game," I growled. "All I really want is to throw you in the backseat and fuck your perfect cunt so I can have the satisfaction of knowing my cum is dripping down your thighs while I play."

She stared at me, her mouth in a cute little 'o' shape because I'd once again shocked her. Blake shifted in her seat and I smiled...she was totally turned on right now.

"Why don't you do it then, Ari? If you want it so bad," Blake suddenly challenged.

When I said I almost crashed us into a ditch in shock from the mouth of Blake, little miss sunshine herself. The brakes screeched as I pulled into a parking garage.

I threw the car into park and then jumped out, jogging over to her side and then practically throwing her into the backseat so she was on her hands and knees.

I massaged the globes of her ass through her leggings before I ripped them down. She wasn't wearing anything underneath so I immediately got the full experience of that perfect pink pussy and that mind blowing, biteable ass.

I bent over her and licked from her cunt to her tight ring, pushing the tip of my tongue into her ass so she started squirming. She was dripping wet, so wet the insides of her thighs were slick. I moved to her clit before fucking into her pussy with two fingers until she was screaming so loud I was afraid someone was going to come over here to make sure she was okay.

"You are fucking incredible," I growled as I forced myself to pull away. My dick was so hard it could cut glass, and I untucked it from my suit pants and wasted no time in thrusting it into her. I put a knee on the seat so I was crouched over her body, burying myself in the most perfect pussy on earth.

Who fucking cared about hockey? Who fucking cared about anything when I got to have this every day?

I drove into her again and again, chasing the high only she could give me. Her back was arched and she was meeting every thrust, sexy moans filling the car. I slid my thumb down her crack, getting it slick with our combined essence before I popped it into her ass.

She immediately came, screaming my name. Her pussy clenched my cock so tightly I swore I saw stars.

I followed her over the edge, my insides heating and ridiculously intense pleasure soaring through me as I pumped bursts of hot cum into her. I slumped against her body, my suit a mess...everything else sweaty.

"Fuck. You. Are. Perfect," I growled as I slapped her ass and reluctantly pulled out with a groan. I took a minute to savor the sight of my cum leaking out of her pussy. I gathered it with two fingers and pushed it back into her, and she mewled at the sensation. Giving her one last lick from top to bottom, I moved away, and helped her to adjust her leggings back up because she was all dicked out by the looks of her.

"You're such a perfect, good girl," I crooned as I helped her out of the back seat, and she swayed into me, her eyes dazed. Blake fucking loved to be praised.

And I loved praising her.

I helped her into the front seat and buckled her seatbelt before getting back into the car and resuming our journey. I was barely going to make it in time for warmups, but who the fuck cared? I was riding a high I never wanted to come down from. I could spend every second with this girl, and never get tired of it. I would keep her, no matter what.

"I think I've established a new pregame ritual," I said happily as I nodded my head to one of Olivia Rodrigo's new songs. Everything on the album was a winner.

"Sex in your backseat?" she mused.

"Yes." I nodded my head. "It's necessary for me to even be able to skate, I think."

"Oh really? That sounds like pretty good sex."

I held up a hand. "Perfect sex, sunshine. In a perfect cunt. Let's not downplay it."

She blushed and ducked her head. "That sounds like a good ritual to me..." she whispered.

I held up a hand to my ear. "Sorry, I didn't quite catch that. Can you say it again?"

She shot me an annoyed look. "I said, that—"

"I can fuck you whenever I want, including before games, during games, and after games? Sounds great. I'm in," I yelled over her as I pulled into my parking spot at the arena.

She snorted and I gave her a victorious grin. I leaned over and rubbed my nose against hers. "Now tell me I'm your favorite hockey player, Blakey-poo."

Her eye roll was so intense, I swear they disappeared into her head. That took talent.

"Say it, sunshine...I will stay out here all day."

"You're my favorite hockey player, you idiot."

I brushed a soft kiss against her lips, savoring the taste of her. "That's all I needed to hear, sweetheart. We will work on the "idiot" part. Now let's go before I get benched."

———

Once we were inside, I went to warm up, but my eyes kept drifting back to Blake the entire time. I couldn't help it.

"Lancaster, you've got it bad," Walker drawled as he came up to where I was leaning on my stick, staring at her longingly.

I sighed like a lovesick puppy. "It's true." I glanced at him as he went down into the fucking splits...because goalies were show-offs.

"You have anyone special out there, Disney? A "princess" for "Prince Charming"?"

He scoffed at the nickname, but there was nothing he could do about it. It was his name now.

He should ask Disney for royalties.

"It hasn't happened yet."

"Disney royalties?" I mused, turning my head to watch Blake's ass when she bent down to get something.

"What? Disney royalties?" Walker asked, confused.

"Continue," I sighed, gesturing with my glove while he did splits the other way.

"My family believes in soulmates. Like, you see a girl and just know…"

I nodded, wondering if I was actually a long lost member of the Davis clan since I too believed in soulmates.

"It's stupid," he muttered, frowning at Soto as he missed a practice shot by a mile. "It hasn't happened for any of my brothers. Hasn't happened to me. It's probably not going to happen."

I hit him on the shoulder as he tried to get up from his stretch. "Cheer up, Walker. I believe in soulmates too. So does Lincoln."

"Really?" he asked, his eyes excited.

"Yep. And since you're in the circle of trust—"

"I thought you said there wasn't a circle of trust."

I shrugged. "It's a new thing. ANYWAYS…before you so rudely interrupted me, I was about to tell you that I bet you'll find your girl."

He whined. "Can we stop talking about this now?"

I chuckled and shot Blake another look. "Never."

———

We'd just started the game when I noticed it...a group of idiotic frat boys sitting behind Blake in the stands, obviously intent on getting her attention.

A spike of jealousy shot through me, which was stupid—she had my cum dripping out of her pussy—but still!

Leaning forward, I squinted, trying to read their lips.

Damn it, I couldn't make out what they were saying—not that I had ever possessed that skill before—but the idiots were definitely flirting with her. My jaw clenched. I could *not* play under these conditions.

I turned to one of the staff members hovering behind the bench and flashed my most charming smile. "Hey, buddy, you think you could do me a little favor?"

The guy's eyes widened eagerly, and he nodded his head so hard, he kinda looked like one of those bobbleheads. "Yeah, of course, Ari, anything. What do you need?"

I pointed discreetly at the guys attempting to chat up Blake. She was trying to ignore them, but the shitheads were being persistent. Who throws popcorn at a hot girl to get their attention?

Why Ari, a frat boy, of course.

"See those guys over there? I need you to give them new seats...kick them out if you have to. Got it?"

The staff member grinned and gave me a thumbs-up. "Consider it done, Ari."

With that, he walked over to the guy in the stands, and a tense conversation later, they were being moved elsewhere.

Mission accomplished.

I returned my focus back to the game. I continued to steal glances at Blake though, making sure no one else was trying to swoop in. She was mine, and no one else's, and I intended to make that abundantly clear, both on and off the ice.

———

Blake

The game had just begun, and I was settled in my seat, doing my best to follow what was happening on the ice. Hockey was so fast moving—it was hard to keep up. The arena was on fire tonight though. L.A. was facing off against Las Vegas and the fans were going nuts.

Unfortunately I had attracted the attention of some very... persistent guys in the row behind me. No matter what I did, they were not getting the hint I wasn't interested. They'd been trying to get me to talk to them ever since the puck dropped, and while I'd initially attempted to be polite, their relentlessness was past the point of being annoying.

Something hit the back of my head, and I glanced down to see that they'd thrown some popcorn at me.

Mature guys. I was definitely ready to spread my legs with that move.

Hopefully they hadn't chewed on it first.

A few minutes passed, and my frustration grew. The Cobras were playing out of their minds, but I was having a tough time getting to enjoy it. The assholes had gotten so aggressive that one of them was in my ear, telling me how hot I was.

Just when I was about to give up and move to another seat, security personnel appeared, flanking the group. My eyes widened as I watched them, and the guys, who had been so vocal just moments ago, now resembled scared little mice.

Security spoke to them sternly, and it didn't take long for the guys to begrudgingly gather their belongings and follow them away from their seats. I was instantly relieved, and I turned my attention back to the game, glad I could actually pay attention now.

Just a few minutes later however, a Cobras employee, dressed in team gear, took their place. She held up a massive sign, large enough to rival a billboard, and my eyes widened in disbelief as I read the words written on it.

"Property of Ari Lancaster," the sign declared boldly, an arrow pointing downward directly at me.

I blinked, stunned into silence for a moment, before a surprised burst of laughter bubbled up from my chest.

People around us were staring, and I shrunk into my seat, my face on fire with embarrassment.

But also pride...because I wanted to belong to Ari. I was well aware I was the luckiest girl in the world to have him like I did.

A few minutes later, I glanced up at the jumbotron, shocked to see my face up there on the massive screen. The crowd erupted into laughter and cheers at the sight of me and the sign. I was caught in a whirlwind of emotions—embarrassment, amusement, and a strange warmth spreading through me.

I glanced at Ari who was leaning against the glass, pointing at me with both hands, an impish grin on his ridiculously hot face that made my heart skip a beat. I couldn't help but laugh, shaking my head in disbelief.

A few minutes later, another Cobras employee sat in one of the empty seats behind me, also with the oversized sign. She waved it enthusiastically, drawing my attention away from the game once more. The sign read, "I'm serious," and it had an arrow that pointed to the other sign. She held it high for everyone to see.

This, of course, attracted the camera crew, and I found myself again up on the jumbotron.

This continued through the game...a Cobras employee would come out with a sign that they'd flash above my head, and the jumbotron would flash a shot of me. The signs included such gems as:

"Ari's Better Half"

"Blake's Got Ari Fever!"

"No Trespassing: Ari's Territory"

"Ari's Soulmate: Hands Off!"

"Reserved for Ari's Queen"

"Property of #24 Ari Lancaster"

"Blake's the Goal, Ari's the Assist"

"Ari's MVP"

"Warning: She's Taken"

Ari was obviously determined to keep the spotlight on me, and the crowd seemed to love every moment of it. It was endearing and absurd, and that warm feeling in my chest...it was growing.

With two minutes to go, Ari executed a flawless pass, setting up a potential goal-scoring opportunity for Tommy. The tension in the arena was palpable, the crowd holding its collective breath as the puck soared toward the opposing team's net.

The shot was taken, and my heart raced. Time seemed to slow down, the fate of the game hanging in the balance. The puck hit the back of the net, and the arena went absolutely insane. Cobras up by one!

As the seconds ticked away, it became clear that the Cobras were going to win. The final buzzer sounded, and the crowd erupted in jubilation. And Ari had one more sign for me..."Ari's Lucky Charm."

———

It was only later, when we were on our way home, the road stretched out before us, that I started to second guess the signs...and the meaning behind them. I felt the heaviness of my unspoken doubts and fears pressing on my chest. The silence that had been comfortable only moments before, was now pregnant with the weight of the questions I needed to ask.

Finally, I found the courage to voice the thoughts that had been haunting my mind. My voice was barely a whisper as I said, "Ari, do you ever worry about...about what happened with Clark? That I'll cheat on you because I cheated on him?"

His eyes remained focused on the road ahead, his profile bathed in the gentle glow of the car's dashboard. After a moment, he let out a sigh, his voice warm and reassuring. "Not even for a second. And besides...I'd never let you. I'd never let any other man get in the picture."

His words tried to wash over me like a warm, soothing wave...but there was still a lingering ache...

"My mother cheated on my father and that's why he went crazy that night," I whispered. "I found it out after I'd been adopted, found all the articles online."

"Sunshine, that's not you."

"But isn't it? Because I remember, Dad did all the things you were supposed to. I used to walk in on them dancing in the kitchen, thinking to myself I couldn't wait to have a love like that. He brought her flowers every week. Treated her like a queen. And she still stabbed him in the back."

I bit down on my trembling lip. "Isn't that like what I did to Clark? Hurt a good man?"

I didn't know why this was coming out now. Maybe it was because I hadn't been able to apologize to Clark. Maybe it was because, every day, Ari seemed too good to be true. A dream I could never live without.

The car suddenly seemed suffocating, like I was going to pass out if I was trapped in here for one more moment.

"Please pull over," I gasped, a panic attack fluttering to life, the edges of my vision turning to black.

Ari immediately pulled to the side of the road, and I was

jumping out of the car before he'd even stopped all the way, taking in big desperate gulps of air.

Ari's arms wrapped around me and he held me against his chest.

"Deep breath, angel, and then exhale slowly. You're doing great," he murmured soothingly.

And I was transported to another time, another place, when he'd said those same exact words...

His heart seemed to beat against my back, and somehow, my breaths were able to slow.

Ari slowly turned me in his arms, and then grabbed my chin so I had no choice but to look at him.

"Let's get something perfectly fucking clear, sunshine. You didn't cheat on Clark. You were never supposed to be with him. He was a fucking imposter, holding you back from your destiny. Clark wasn't your soulmate. You weren't supposed to be with him. You were *always* supposed to be with me. No matter the circumstances, I would have found you, stolen you away. It wouldn't have mattered if you were married with ten fucking kids—I would have made you mine." His fingers dug into my skin, more intensity in his features than I'd ever seen before. "We were always meant to be together, Blake. No matter what."

A hiccuped sob burst from my mouth, and he gave me a gentle smile, his thumb tracing delicate patterns on my cheek. "Blake," he whispered, "you're the love of my fucking life."

Tears were streaming down my face, my heart beating erratically as his words flowed through me...and remade me.

"You love me?" I whispered. Because I'd heard those words before from a man, but somehow they'd never felt like this.

They'd never felt real.

"You haven't been listening very good, sunshine. My soul's been whispering it to you every day."

His lips crashed into mine, and this kiss was different, better than anything that had come before.

"Say it, baby," he ordered between drugging, languid kisses.

"I love you," I said immediately, because there was no point holding back.

Maybe it wasn't even possible.

The weight that had settled on my chest began to lift, replaced by a profound sense of completeness. Ari's unwavering faith in our love was a lifeline in the tempest of my insecurities. With him by my side, I could almost believe it was possible to get rid of the shackles of my past.

And as the miles melted away beneath the wheels of the car, the night air seemed to hold the promise of a new beginning.

Ari made love to me all night, whispering *I love you* a million times until the words were embedded in my skin.

I just hoped it was enough.

CHAPTER 16

ARI

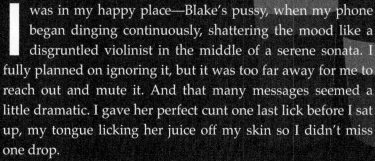

I was in my happy place—Blake's pussy, when my phone began dinging continuously, shattering the mood like a disgruntled violinist in the middle of a serene sonata. I fully planned on ignoring it, but it was too far away for me to reach out and mute it. And that many messages seemed a little dramatic. I gave her perfect cunt one last lick before I sat up, my tongue licking her juice off my skin so I didn't miss one drop.

"Be right back, baby."

She'd just had three orgasms in a row so her smile was a little lazy as her eyes fluttered closed.

The sight of her like that was the most beautiful thing I'd ever seen.

My phone dinged again and I growled as I walked over to the dresser to grab it, freezing when I saw the text.

Evidently, news of my antics at the game the other day had spread and Clark was finally well aware he'd been dumped. The P.I. said he'd booked a flight and was on his way to the airport now to try and get her back.

Seriously, this guy was a loser. It had literally been *weeks* since they'd had a real conversation, and besides that one time, he'd been a total bump on a log.

Honestly, I'd expected him to put up more of a fight. He was making it too easy.

I turned to tell Blake I'd be right back, but she was fast asleep. I took a picture because the sight of it was just too good and then I strode out of the room, letting Waldo in behind me. I never let him in during sexy times–he seemed far too interested in my ass.

Once I was in my office, I dialed my go-to strategist, Lincoln.

"Hello, Ari," he purred through the phone.

"Oooh, that was a spooky sexy way to greet me," I responded, and he barked out a laugh.

"What's up?"

"Well, I have sort of a situation—"

"Oh shit, she found out, tried to leave, and you tied her to your bed," he interjected, his voice a little...excited.

I frowned. "Um, that was oddly specific...but no. Wait— you sound like you have personal experience with that. Do you have a story to tell me?"

Silence for a half beat too long to not be suspicious. "Nope," he finally said. Suspiciously.

"Lincoln—Golden boy—Daniels. DO NOT LIE TO ME!"

"Don't you have a problem to fix?" he asked frantically.

I sighed, checking the flight information, because the dude's plane would be leaving soon.

"We'll come back to this," I warned, and he snorted. "So, the "other" knows."

"The other?"

"Oh, did I not tell you I now refer to the ex as the "other?" Keeps me from going insane, ya know."

"Ahh. Understandable."

"Anwaysssss. He saw the game the other day—"

"The one where you made sure that Blake and you would be on every news outlet in America?" Lincoln drawled.

"Well, yes. But listen. That was the goal. But honestly, the guy seemed too uptight to watch something like ESPN."

"Buddy, that cutesy shit was everywhere. Monroe saw it on the Bravo channel."

I preened because obvi I was awesome. But then I remembered there were fucking time constraints happening here.

"The "other" is on his way here. I need some more time… to secure the situation."

"So you've come to the master, young grasshopper," Lincoln mused.

I threw up a middle finger before realizing I wasn't on Facetime and he couldn't see me. "Just so you know, I told Walker you were cool. I'm going to have to go back and tell him otherwise now…just because you tried to Mr. Miyagi me."

"Do you want my help or not?"

"Yes, I need your help! That's why I fucking called!"

"Then call me Mr. Miyagi."

I stared at my phone in disbelief.

"Is this real life? Am I being punked?"

"Final offer."

"Uggggh. Fine. Can you help me, Mr. Miyagi?"

"I thought you would never ask," Lincoln said calmly, only laughing after I growled at him.

"Okay, so my idea is a little unconventional."

"You…unconventional. The guy who just casually threw out tying someone to a bed to stop them from leaving you…I would have never guessed."

"I can neither confirm nor deny."

"Focus. Unconventional. I'm here for it."

"I've got a guy who can make Clark's flight plans go haywire, putting him on the no-fly list for at least a while."

"Lincoln, honey bear, I could kiss you!" I said excitedly.

"I do what I can," Lincoln said, and I could practically see the sly grin on his face.

We said goodbye so he could get Clark grounded, and I sat back in my seat in satisfaction that at least that little nuisance would be delayed.

I was also thinking it was way past time for Blake to move in. With her having her own place, I couldn't control who she saw. If she was at my place, in a gated community, Clark wasn't getting in to see her.

———

Yes, I could have just asked Blake to move in with me.

But that would have been a failure.

And I didn't set myself up to fail.

Despite the progress we were making every day, she was still scared. Scared this wasn't real, or about something else. But she was still scared.

Hence why I was now plotting like a James Bond villain to get her out of her apartment.

I'd recently gotten the background check about her roommate, Charlotte. A girl, it turned out, who had a mean streak a mile long judging by the complaints against her for bullying all throughout childhood. She also happened to have a penchant for gambling, a drug problem, and lots and lots of credit card debt. All good things to have when I needed her cooperation.

Through my assistant, I'd hired Charlotte to "force" Blake out. It was a little scary that she hadn't even asked questions like why...but debt and drug dealers breathing down your neck could do that to you. She was supposed to be channeling her inner wrecking ball, creating enough destruction for Blake to want to move out...immediately.

I could have burned down the whole building or had it condemned, but there was a cute gray haired lady who lived across from Blake. And I just couldn't do that to her. I was a simp for grandmas.

Or at least I wasn't going to attempt one of those until this didn't work.

The idea was that Charlotte would throw some clothes around, steal some stuff, throw a rager—in general make it look like a category-five tornado hit the place.

Foolproof.

Or so I thought.

———

Blake

I walked into the apartment, exhaustion weighing heavy on my shoulders after a long shift at the restaurant. All I wanted was a peaceful night's sleep. My eyes widened in surprise when I saw Waldo in his kennel in the living room, whining as he stared at me sadly. I'd put him in my room before I left so he could sleep on my bed. Why had Charlotte put him in his kennel?

I'd gone to let him out when I heard it—the rhythmic creaking of a bed accompanied by a chorus of groans and moans.

Lovely, Charlotte had Soto over.

"Be right back, buddy," I muttered, rubbing a hand across my face, as I stalked towards my bedroom to get some of my stuff. I'd call Ari and tell him I was coming over after all.

As I approached the bedroom door, however, I realized the sounds were not, in fact, coming from Charlotte's room… they were coming from mine.

Dread coiled in my stomach as my hand hovered over the doorknob. This could not be fucking happening.

Finally, I turned it and pushed the door open.

And stumbled upon a sight that would forever be etched into my memory.

There, sprawled across *my* bed, was Charlotte, on all fours, Soto fucking her from behind while her head bounced up and down on another guy's dick. As if that wasn't bad enough, there was a large dildo protruding from her ass that Soto was moving in and out.

Shock was not a strong enough word to describe the situation, stealing my voice for half a minute.

Before I could react, Charlotte's voice, tainted with a hint of mockery, cut through the silence. "Hey, Blake, care to join us? There's plenty of room for more holes."

Disgust and anger welled up within me, and I finally let out a horrified scream, a raw expression of my shock and revulsion. They just continued on, their moans mingled with laughter.

This was not happening. I dashed into the bathroom to gather up my stuff...because I was not staying here tonight. Or ever again.

Grabbing my phone from my pocket, my trembling fingers fumbled with the keys as I quickly dialed Ari's number.

"Hi Sunshine," he murmured.

"Ari—" my stammering trailed off because I didn't even know how to explain what had just happened.

"Blake?" he asked, concerned.

"Can you just come over? Soon? I...think I need a place to stay."

"Coming right now," he said without any questions.

Soto suddenly appeared in the doorway, completely naked, his muscles flexing as he moved towards me. I kept my gaze waist up, but I couldn't take my eyes off him. There was a predatory gleam there, and I was suddenly terrified.

"Blake," he purred, "come back in, sugar. We were just having some fun. I'll make it good for you."

I recoiled in horror as he reached for me, his touch like a searing brand on my skin.

"Stay away from me," I growled, but he just smiled.

"I've seen the way you look at me." His hand stroked up and down his dick. "Now's your chance."

He had me cornered and I gripped onto the counter behind me, wondering if I could grab my blow dryer and knock him in the head.

Charlotte popped up beside Soto, a smirk on her lips. She pressed her breasts against Soto's arm. "I bet that ass would be fun to play with, Soto. A little extra to grab onto," she teased.

Her words cut into my veins. I was bigger than Charlotte, that was true. When we'd auditioned for the same jobs, I was always very aware of that...

Evidently she was too.

"Nah, I want those weird purple eyes on me as I fuck her mouth," Soto smiled. "I've been thinking about it constantly."

I held up my phone. "I'm going to call the police if you don't get out of my room right now."

Soto moved Charlotte away, his smile widening. "I do like a challenge, Blake." He walked towards me, but there was nowhere for me to retreat. He had me pinned.

He'd just grabbed my hip when there was a crash in the living room as the front door slammed open. A second later Ari was there...his face almost unrecognizable from his rage as he took in the scene. His towering figure seemed to expand, filling every inch of the space with his furious presence.

"You're a dead man, Soto," he spat, a darkness in his gaze I'd never seen before.

Ari lunged forward, ripping Soto away from me and throwing him onto my bedroom floor.

Soto scrambled to his feet, a smile still on his face...

"I was just about to show your girl what a real man fucks like," he drawled.

Ari chuckled, gesturing to Soto's now limp penis. "I doubt a woman can even feel that, Soto. I didn't know you had "mini dick syndrome." Soto snarled and charged at Ari. But Ari just grinned and punched him in the gut as Soto butted into him. Soto gasped in pain as Ari grabbed his hair, yanking his head back.

"There's no refs tonight, you pathetic little asswipe. No one to help you either," he said in a silky, smooth...terrifying voice. Still holding him by his hair, Ari broke Soto's nose, blood spraying everywhere.

He staggered a few steps after Ari released his hold. But Ari didn't give him a chance to recover. Blood sprayed from Soto's battered face as Ari's fists connected with bone and flesh, again and again. The sickening sound of impact filled the room, echoing in my ears.

Charlotte was screaming, and the other guy had already ran away. I watched in shock as teeth flew out of Soto's mouth...and Ari snorted as he hit him again.

"Missing teeth might be an improvement on that ugly face," Ari drawled.

Time seemed to slow as I watched his powerful fist connect with Soto's face one last time, and he crumpled to the floor, blood and teeth spattering in all directions. Soto was a whimpering, pathetic mess, writhing on the floor in agony.

"I will kill you if you ever touch her again," Ari murmured, before he kicked Soto in the gut one more time for good measure. Soto wouldn't feel that one right now though, he'd fallen completely unconscious.

Ari didn't hesitate for a second. He pulled me into his strong arms in a protective embrace, his body trembling as he squeezed me tight. I buried my face in his chest, tears streaming down my cheeks from everything that had just happened.

"We're getting out of here," he growled, glancing down at Charlotte, still naked, weeping next to Soto's still form.

"What are you still doing in here?" he snapped at her, and she whimpered and ran to her room, slamming the door behind her.

"Let's get your stuff, sunshine," Ari said calmly. "I'm just going to get rid of the trash." He reached down and grabbed Soto by the foot, dragging him out of my room. A few seconds later I heard the front door open...following by a thump of something hitting the ground.

Ari appeared in the doorway a minute later with Waldo, who had been barking and whining the entire time. Waldo jumped up, frantically pawing at my leg as I tried to calm him down.

"It's okay, baby," I soothed as I tried to reassure him. Ari took over for me so I could pack. I glanced over at them as I threw my clothes and toiletries into a suitcase and snorted. Ari had my dog completely in his lap and was cradling Waldo like a baby. I snapped a quick pic on my phone.

The rest of the stuff I'd brought from New York was still in boxes, so it didn't take long for me to be completely ready to leave. After I zipped up my suitcase, I turned to tell Ari I was ready, catching him staring at my mess of a bed with a sick and almost guilty expression on his face.

"I'm all ready," I said.

"We're going to have to burn that bed," he muttered, his gaze still stuck on my sheets.

"It belongs to the apartment. The place came partially furnished." I gently pushed on his shoulder so we could get moving. "I guess I'll just find a place to store my stuff and then I can start apartment hunting tomorrow…"

That shook Ari out of his daze. "Apartment hunting? Why would you do that?"

"Well, I can't stay with you forever," I said lightly, even though the thought of it made me warm all over.

He grabbed the suitcase out of my hand and wrapped his free one around my waist, pulling me close.

"Oh, you're definitely staying forever."

I stared up at him…not sure if he was kidding or not.

"Ari, I—"

"Name one good reason why you shouldn't move in. I'll wait," he said patiently.

I opened my mouth. "Well…we just started dating."

"But you've known me since we were kids," Ari murmured, brushing a kiss across my lips. "So that doesn't matter because you've known me for a long, long, long, long, long—"

"Okay," I laughed, slapping a hand across his mouth so he had to stop.

"Okay, you'll move in?" he asked, his face hopeful and excited.

I bit my lip and studied him, the voices in my head pointing out how hard it would be to hide all my issues if I was living with him.

Only—I didn't seem to have so many issues anymore since he'd come back into my life.

Maybe it could work…

"I'll move in," I finally whispered.

"Fucking finally," he said fervently, crashing his lips against mine.

I felt the relief in his voice right down to my bones.

"Spoiler alert," he said happily as we walked out to my

car to load my suitcase, Waldo pattering behind us. "You already have a key to *our* house on our keychain."

"What?"

His use of "our house" seemed a little aggressive.

"Put it on there like the first day," he explained...and it sounded like he wasn't kidding.

I pulled out my keys, and sure enough, there was a new one there I hadn't noticed.

"I'll follow you back home," he told me, smacking another kiss against my lips.

Later, when I'd finally pulled into his driveway, I'd completely forgotten how fast Ari had gotten to my place after my call.

All I could think about was the fact that maybe...Ari was my new home.

Ari

Later, when I wasn't feeling so sick about what had almost happened to Blake because of me...I texted Lincoln.

> Me: We're best, best friends, right?

> Lincoln: Since when did you turn into an eighth grade girl?

> Me: Well, it's an important question. I need to know how far this friendship extends.

> Lincoln: What did you do?

> Me: Nothing, per se. I just need to know if our friendship extends to say...burying a body.

Lincoln: Please tell me there's not actually a body.

Me: Well, not yet. But it could be coming. Strike that. It is coming.

Lincoln: Who exactly are you planning on murdering?

Me: Who do you fucking think? I thought Soto was bad to play against...but I swear, I'm about to throw nunchucks at him.

Lincoln: You own nunchucks?

Me: ...

Me: Ok, so you still haven't answered the question. Accessory to murder...or no?

Lincoln: Where are we burying him?

I set the phone down, staring at Blake's sleeping form. At least she was in my house now. Safe.

I'd just have to spend the rest of my life making it up to her.

CHAPTER 17

ARI

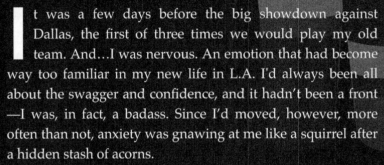

I t was a few days before the big showdown against Dallas, the first of three times we would play my old team. And...I was nervous. An emotion that had become way too familiar in my new life in L.A. I'd always been all about the swagger and confidence, and it hadn't been a front —I was, in fact, a badass. Since I'd moved, however, more often than not, anxiety was gnawing at me like a squirrel after a hidden stash of acorns.

Dallas was home. It's where I'd signed my rookie contract, won the Stanley Cup...became the hockey sensation I was today. I didn't think I could take it if I showed up and the fans who'd once screamed my name were now booing me.

I pulled up the stats for Dallas's game last night. Cas Peters had taken my spot on the team and I'd been stalking his numbers like a madman. I didn't feel bad at all about hoping the poor guy sucked ass all season though. I needed him to suck so I could get re-signed.

And he was sucking. I smiled when I pulled up an article about the game and some reporter called his play "sloppy" and "lackadaisical." Just what I liked to see.

Dallas was still doing well though. Because of Lincoln, of

course. When you had the undisputed king of forwards in the NHL, you had an edge. Teamwork was dreamwork but his skills were otherworldly, and his work ethic was unyielding. He'd only gotten better since Monroe had come into the picture—Lincoln had always been a show-off, and he was definitely showing off for her.

I was so damn proud of my buddy.

But I really missed playing with him.

That desire would never go away—I wanted to step onto that familiar ice, hear the crowd roar, feel the rush of adrenaline. Sure, I'd played in arenas all over the country, but Dallas was special. It was where I had some of my greatest moments, both as a player and as a human being.

I decided to text Lincoln, as one does when they have the bestest best friend in the world.

> Me: Next week is going to be weird.

> Lincoln: I know...like what if you accidentally pass it to me instead of Soto.

> Me: You're mocking me.

> Lincoln: I would never.

> Me: That's it. I'm going to send Monroe a million of my jerseys.

> Lincoln: Lol.

> Me: Lol? That's all I get?

> Lincoln: If you think I don't have my packages and all my mail monitored...

> Me: Does Monroe know you're a little obsessed?

Lincoln: ...

Me: Blake and Monroe are going to be best friends.

Lincoln: I'm Monroe's best friend.

Me: Calm down, golden boy. I could hear that growl from here.

Lincoln: middle finger emoji

I set my phone down. I loved that guy. I also finally understood the change in him after he'd met Monroe. I was absolutely feral for Blake. It was nice to have a partner in crime to help me through the red haze that seemed to have descended onto my vision. Although, come to think of it, he didn't do a really good job of dissuading my craziness and holding me back.

Shaking my head, I went back to studying Cas Peters' stats, game planning for how I was going to show him up in Dallas.

———

Blake

As I stepped onto the luxurious plane, my eyes widened in surprise as I took in the lavish interior. Ari had convinced Lincoln to let me fly to Dallas on his private jet. I'd been perfectly fine with a regular airline, but Ari had started muttering something about "crowd control" and "book boyfriend material" and somehow I'd ended up here.

Plush leather seats beckoned with promises of comfort, and rich mahogany accents exuded an air of opulence. A matronly older woman who could easily be cast as the perfect *Nanny McPhee* greeted me at the door, showing me to my seat. Her friendly smile and kind eyes made me feel instantly welcomed, despite the weirdness of flying by myself on a private jet.

I settled into my seat, getting ready for takeoff.

As I stared around though, I noticed something peculiar. Everyone working the flight looked like they were someone's grandmother. Everyone...even the two pilots. A petite woman with a crown of silver hair, a cheerful demeanor... and a cat sweater, approached my seat. Her name tag read "Edna."

"Good morning, dearie," she said with a warm smile as she handed me a basket of freshly baked cookies. "I hope you're all comfy and ready for your flight."

I took the treat, bemused. "Thank you, Edna. These look delicious."

Edna beamed at me, her eyes twinkling. "Oh, sweetheart, I've been baking these for years. No one can resist a good homemade cookie."

I couldn't argue with that, and I bit into the warm, gooey treat. It was as if I had just taken a bite of nostalgia and love, the flavors melting in my mouth.

As the plane taxied down the runway, Edna continued to chat with me, asking about my plans in Dallas and sharing snippets of her own life...which included ten grandchildren.

Soon, another flight attendant, Mabel, joined us with a tray of hot tea. She also had silver hair, spectacles, and a grandmotherly air about her. Her voice was soothing as she offered me my choice of brew.

"Darlin', we've got a variety here—green, chamomile, and good ol' Earl Grey," Mabel said kindly.

I opted for chamomile, and Mabel served me with the care of a doting grandmother, ensuring my cup was just the right temperature and sweetness.

As we sipped our tea, the female pilot's voice came over

the intercom, announcing our flight details. Her tone was much warmer than you'd find on a commercial flight...but really, what were the odds of seeing a crew like this? Non-existent, right?

I pulled out my phone to text Ari, who had to fly with the team.

> Me: So you don't have to answer this...but does Lincoln have some kind of fetish...for older women?

Ari immediately responded like he'd been waiting for me to text him.

> Ari: I'm dead. I will never let Lincoln live this down.

> Me: So he does!!!! He likes grandmas? I mean, I won't say anything...but does Monroe know?

> Ari: I'm seriously dying...

> Me: Ariiiiii

> Ari: No, Mr. Golden Boy does not have a fetish for grandmas. He has a fetish for not letting anyone of interest speak to, look at, or touch Monroe. So rather than waste money on buying out all of first class for her every time she flies so no one can talk to her...he bought a plane and hired a bunch of grandmas to fly it so he didn't have to worry anymore.

I stared at the message...completely dumbfounded.

> Ari: Don't be fooled though. Edna has a stiff right hook and carries.

Me: Okay...that's good to know.

Ari: And if you're wondering if I bought into the plane so that you too can travel with a pack of grandmas...the answer is yes.

Me: Are you serious right now?

Ari: As serious as Edna's homemade cookies. Can you snag one for me, btw?

Me: I'm still getting over the fact that you and Lincoln are crazy. And also possibly genius. Only...I can't afford a private plane to keep your admirers away from you...

Ari: My body is your temple, sunshine. I promise to stab anyone that touches what's yours.

Ari: Now please bring me a cookie.

He sent an emoji of a dancing grandma...for good measure.

Me: Fine.

Ari: I love you. I love you. I love you.

Me: Me too.

I set the phone down and relaxed into my seat, accepting a whole basket of cookies when Edna came by again.

Grandma Airways was evidently coming in hot.

CHAPTER 18

BLAKE

Ari was holding his Lost Children Organization Gala the night before the Dallas game, and I found myself standing in front of the mirror in Ari's Dallas house, anxiety bubbling up within me. He had bought me a stunning dress for the occasion, a beautiful gesture that only added to the pressure I felt. My reflection stared back at me, and I couldn't help but scrutinize every detail.

The dress was an elegant, floor-length gown in a deep shade of midnight blue. Its delicate lace overlay created intricate patterns that danced across my skin, and it clung to my body in all the right places. Yet, despite the dress's undeniable beauty, I couldn't shake the feeling of unease.

In fact, the very idea of attending one of these was sparking panic like I hadn't felt in awhile. Gala nights were obviously not unfamiliar to me; I had been forced to attend countless similar gatherings with the Shepfields.

And the last gala I'd attended hadn't ended well.

"I'm sorry. I can't marry you…"

That night was on replay in my head right then…as well as all the other times I'd been dolled up in an expensive, uncomfortable dress, my every move scrutinized. As I mingled with people who barely acknowledged my existence or who whispered behind their champagne glasses, I had felt like nothing more than a pretty accessory for the Shepfields or Clark to show off.

The memory of those gala nights, filled with insincere smiles and hushed conversations, had left a lasting scar on my psyche. It was a stark reminder of my outsider status within that family and my years of feeling like a mere decoration in their opulent world.

Now, as tonight's event approached, all those old anxieties had resurfaced. The prospect of navigating another glamorous event, even with Ari's unwavering support, made my skin feel tight. Would I once again be reduced to a mere spectacle, judged by the same shallow standards that had been imposed on me before?

I bit my lip, staring over at my bag where I knew I had a razor blade hidden. Maybe just a little cut to get through tonight...

Ari entered the bedroom then, and caught my eye in the mirror. He approached me with that calming presence of his. "Wow," he murmured, laying his chin on my shoulder, his eyes locked on mine. "You look incredible."

I gave him a weak smile, my fingers nervously adjusting a loose strand of hair. "You think so? It's been awhile since I've dressed up like this. I don't want to embarrass you or anything."

"What's really going on in that perfect head of yours?"

I held in the laugh. I was so far from perfect. He didn't even know...

"Sunshine," he murmured, pressing a kiss to my bare shoulder. "You obviously don't understand that when I say you're perfect...I mean you're absolutely perfect for me. There isn't anything I don't like about you. There's nothing I wish was different. Every morning I wake up and I can't believe my fucking luck, because I get to wake up to you. I consider it a privilege to know you."

My insides warmed, and I felt like the Grinch because I swore my heart grew at least three sizes from his sweet words.

I was still nervous though. I didn't want my old life to become connected to Ari.

"I've had what seems like a million bad nights at these sorts of things. Maura was the queen of them."

"Mmmh," he said, like he understood exactly what I meant. And maybe he did. Ari seemed to have a magical way of understanding me when no one else did.

"I hope that tonight will be different for you. I wouldn't ask you to go...but LCO is my organization."

My eyes widened in surprise because the articles I'd read hadn't mentioned that.

"If I can save one kid from what I went through, I'll do it. And the best way I've found is throwing a huge party, getting people drunk, and then showing them sad pictures of kids so they empty their pocketbooks. I'm supporting group homes in fifteen states right now, and most of what keeps them going comes from tonight. I'll understand if you don't come...but it would mean the world to me if you would."

How did he make me fall in love with him more everyday? Did he have some kind of magic in his DNA that made him biologically compatible with me in every way?

Or maybe he really was my soulmate, like he'd been saying all along.

"Okay, Ari Lancaster," I said, my voice steadier. "Let's do this."

Ari grinned, that charming, lopsided smile that never failed to make my heart flutter. "That's my girl."

Then he winked.

"I promise to make it worth your while on the way over there…"

With that pronouncement, his arm wrapped around my waist, and he led me out of the room and down to the awaiting limousine.

A few minutes into the ride… he slid down to his knees.

"Ari, you don't have to do this," I said, wide-eyed.

"I don't have to do this? Don't you mean I *get* to do this?" he growled as he pushed up my dress to my waist and gave a surprised inhale at the lacy white garters I had on underneath.

"You're trying to fucking kill me," he groaned as his nose dragged through the fabric of my underwear along my slit.

My head fell back against the leather seat. He licked his fingers and then dipped them underneath my panties, sliding through my folds until he found my swollen clit. He teased it, circling it slowly as a soft sigh fell from my lips.

"You've got to keep quiet, sweetheart. The driver better not hear what you sound like when you come."

I bit down on my bottom lip as his other hand slid down the front of my dress so he was palming my bare breast. He plucked and tugged at my nipple with one hand while his fingers continued to trail lackadaisically through my folds.

I whimpered and he stopped moving. "What did I say about being quiet, sunshine?" he purred.

I needed to come.

"Please Ari. Please make me come. I'm so wet for you, baby. I need it."

His eyes glinted and went a bit feral, and then his fingers were finally sliding into me, fucking in and out. Somehow he brushed against that sweet spot inside of me with every pass, and I bucked against him.

Ari's fingers abruptly left my core and I cried out. He

roughly forced those same fingers into my mouth so I could taste myself.

"Keep that pretty mouth busy...and quiet, and suck on my fingers until you come," he growled before the hand that had been torturing my nipple slid back into me. He worked me hard, his thumb massaging my clit for a moment before he replaced it with his mouth. He sucked hard on my clit while his thumb went down to my ass and he rubbed the sensitive nerves around my asshole.

"Suck harder, Blake," he teased me in between licks and sucks. My breath was coming out in gasps, as I sucked on his fingers frantically while he worked every sensual trigger I possessed.

I would get close, and then he'd slow down his rhythm. He did it over and over again until I was about to go insane. I bit down on his fingers and he laughed wickedly. "Are you close, baby? Do you want some relief?"

I shot him a glare that was annoyingly half-hearted because I *was* so close to the edge.

"I think before you come...I want to hear it, sunshine. I want to hear you tell yourself you're perfect."

He slid his fingers from my mouth, his thumb hovering around my bottom lip as he softly rubbed it.

At this rate, I was going to orgasm every time I heard the word "perfect" because he made me say it so often when I was about to come.

Ari languidly licked through my folds, his thumb popping into my ass and slowly sliding in and out while I writhed on the seat. "Say it, baby."

"I'm perfect," I murmured through gritted teeth, reaching out to rub his huge, hard cock.

He pulled away from me because he was the worst. "Nope...right now's about you. I'll fuck you for the rest of the night after the gala."

"Please," I whimpered, and his fingers and mouth *finally* gave me the rhythm I needed to come.

"Such a perfect, good girl," he murmured after I exploded on his tongue. He pulled out his fingers and licked at them, his gaze sparkling in delight and his mouth shiny with my essence.

I stayed slumped against the seat, feeling ridiculously relaxed.

Ari leaned forward, staring out the window. "Oh good, we're here. Ready to go?" he asked innocently.

I stared at him for a second before I frantically pulled down my dress. I couldn't even imagine what I looked like. My panties were soaked, my cheeks were a hundred degrees, and my insides were a puddle of lust.

Not a good recipe for a gala for a CHILDREN'S EVENT!

"Sexiest thing I've ever seen," he rasped, adjusting himself with a pained look on his face.

I glanced down at his erection. "We can't go out there with that monster in the building!"

Ari stared up at the ceiling, and started his usual "grandpa balls" chant as I watched the driver approach our door.

"Hurry!" I whisper-yelled, glancing down at his dick again.

"Don't yell at Maximus 5000! He doesn't like to be pressured," Ari hissed back.

I burst out laughing. "Maximus 5000?"

"It's a pet name. All the great ones have it."

The driver opened the door, and not even the flashes of cameras outside could make me stress.

Not with Maximus 5000 poking me in the back as we walked the red carpet that led to the gala, Ari trying to hide his "problem" the entire time.

I had to admit…it was the perfect distraction.

Ari's team from the LCO had outdone themselves, creating an event that even Maura Shepfield would have been hard pressed to give criticism. The gala was being held at the exclusive Rosewood Mansion, and everything was dripping with excellence. Crystal chandeliers hung from the high ceilings, casting a warm and ethereal glow over the entire space. The rich scent of fresh flowers permeated the air, their vibrant colors a stark contrast to the ivory and gold décor that adorned the room. Enormous, gilded mirrors lined the walls, reflecting the scene like a never-ending dream.

Guests, dressed in their most elegant attire, mingled and laughed, their voices carrying in a harmonious symphony of joy and celebration. Men in sharp tuxedos and women in flowing gowns of silk and satin moved gracefully across the marble floor, their laughter and chatter adding to the atmosphere of merriment.

The tables were adorned with intricate centerpieces of roses and lilies, their petals soft and delicate against the fine china and crystal glassware. Waitstaff in crisp uniforms weaved through the crowd, offering trays of champagne and hors d'oeuvres to the guests, their movements almost choreographed in their precision.

A live band, dressed in classic black and white, played a soft melody that danced through the air, creating a sense of enchantment that wrapped around every guest. The dance floor was a gleaming expanse of polished wood, promising enchanting moments later on in the night.

"It's fucking awesome, isn't it?" Ari said happily, and I realized he had been staring at me, waiting for my reaction.

"It really is," I said softly as he wrapped an arm around my waist and laid his head on mine as we took everything in.

Suddenly there was commotion behind me and we turned

to see Lincoln and Monroe coming in behind us. Lincoln had a pissed off look on his face and his arm was wrapped tightly around Monroe's waist.

"Bestie!" Ari called as he dragged me towards them. I thought he was going in for a hug with Lincoln, but at the last second, he did a weird little dip and dive, and then he was squeezing Monroe in a big bear hug.

"Ari!" Lincoln hissed. "For the billionth time. Get your fucking hands off her!"

"I'm just showing my appreciation for my BFF," Ari said innocently.

"SHE IS NOT YOUR BFF! SHE IS MINE!"

Monroe and I were hysterically laughing, me so hard that tears were gathering in my eyes. Ari finally let Monroe go and shot me a wink before ambling back to my side.

"You're right. My bestie's right here," he said, before dipping me backwards and sliding a Hollywood worthy kiss on my lips.

The world was slightly spinning when he stood me back up.

"Hey Blake!" Lincoln said with a bemused smirk as Monroe gave me an excited side hug, oohing and awwing over my dress.

"You look stunning, Blake. Absolutely incredible," she squealed, and I blushed...because I definitely had a new girl crush.

I stammered out a response, not sure how to act normally around her. She was so nice. I'd never had a nice friend in my life. Someone who meant it when they complimented you.

"Hi," said Walker as he strode up to us. He looked dashing in his tux, and I could definitely see where Ari's whole "Disney" schtick had come from. The guy really was Prince Charming come to life.

The three of them standing this close to me was over-whelming.

I glanced at Monroe and she mouthed "HOT" to me. I giggled and nodded emphatically. Suddenly she was smashed against Lincoln's chest.

"Who's hot?" he asked, lifting an eyebrow at her.

Lincoln was intense. Like scary sexy intense. And he and Monroe together...I felt pregnant just watching them.

"Who's hot?" Ari said in a deep voice as he pulled me close and mocked Lincoln. Lincoln rolled his eyes, but a smirk graced his lips.

Walker was staring at all of us, really looking like a kid at Disneyland.

"Walker, my little simp. I'm glad you could make it," Ari said, releasing a hand to give him one of those manly fist bumps.

Walker sighed, rubbing a hand down his face. "Ari, for the last time—"

"Ari said you'd made it into the "circle of trust," Lincoln cut in, and Walker's harried expression immediately changed to blissful excitement.

He really was a simp. An adorable one though.

I glanced at Ari, looking like every woman's wet dream as he stood there in a tux that had been molded to his body.

I didn't blame Walker. Ari was worship worthy.

"So there really is one?" Walker asked eagerly.

Lincoln and Ari started to lead us away towards the tables.

"Nope," Lincoln called over his shoulder. "But you can be in it if we ever make one."

Ari and Lincoln both snickered as Walker followed us to our table.

We sat down, and a minute later, a pretty redhead with

half her boobs out popped up next to Walker, making him jump.

"I've been looking all over for you!" she cried in what was clearly a fake falsetto voice.

I'd been wondering why Walker didn't have a date, but I guess this answered it; he'd been trying to hide from her.

She sat down next to him and Walker didn't bother to introduce her. I would have felt sorry for her if she hadn't pulled out her phone and started making duck faces at herself while she snapped selfies.

Ari lifted an eyebrow at Walker and nodded his head at the woman in a clear "what the fuck are you doing" gesture.

Walker just gave him a miserable look in return.

———

The evening passed quickly, even with the woman—Iris— giving us her best Marilyn Monroe impressions. Dinner tasted amazing and the alcohol was flowing. Evidently he had not been kidding when he said he got everyone drunk so they would open up their wallets.

The guest list at the event was impressive. There were more Hollywood stars here than in most events in L.A., and all of them wanted to talk to Ari and Lincoln. They would give me appraising looks, but it was hard to be self-conscious with Ari's hands all over me and the way he proudly intro- duced me as "the love of his life" to every person that came by. I met a lot of his old teammates too, and it was obvious they were still big fans of his, even with his abrupt departure.

Finally, it was time for the guests to hear from Ari.

As he took the stage, the room fell silent, all eyes fixed on my man. He cleared his throat, and a warm smile graced his lips as he began his speech. "Ladies and gentlemen, thank you all for being here tonight. It's truly an honor to stand before you and represent the Lost Children's Organization—a cause that means everything to me."

"You know, when I was a kid, I was one of those lost children. I would have given anything to have someone who cared about finding me. I got lucky, and I survived those years. But there are lots of children that don't."

"Our goal here," Ari continued, "is to give those kids hope, to give them a family...give them a chance. You can help me do that." He stared around the room, silently challenging each one of them.

"May you all get drunk enough to give us the amount of money we need," he said, lifting up his glass and toasting them all.

There was a brief pause while everyone lifted up their champagne flutes...confused, and then the room filled with laughter. Ari bowed and stepped off the stage while the whole room applauded.

He made his way through the room, getting stopped every couple of steps by someone else who wanted to talk. His gaze went to me every few seconds though, the look in them...

"Ari's so in love with you," murmured Monroe from next to me.

I blushed and nodded. "I'm definitely in love with him too."

"Good," she said, softly patting my hand. "I have a great feeling about the two of you."

I smiled gratefully at her and turned to watch him again. Ari Lancaster was a light that shined so bright, you couldn't help but want him.

I only hoped I could hold on to him without getting burned.

"You know what I could really use?" Ari mused later as the evening wound down.

"I'm not sure how I could ever guess," Lincoln responded sarcastically. Ari gave him a wink and patted his cheek, completely unaffected.

"Tacos, baby. I could use some tacos."

Lincoln glanced at Monroe. "I could actually use some tacos, too."

She grinned."Let's do it."

I stared at them all like they'd gone mad since we'd just gotten done with dinner a little while ago, but I quickly changed my tune when the four of us—plus Walker, who had managed to ditch his date—found ourselves at Maria's.

It was obvious with one bite why Ari was obsessed with this place. It was the best thing I'd ever eaten. He munched on his five tacos happily as Maria herself continued to bring things to the table for the entire meal.

I would normally never eat like this, but I did my best to stay in the moment. I would worry about the scale's retribution when I got back.

For now...I was having the perfect taco.

With the perfect man.

And our perfect friends.

Life seemed pretty perfect.

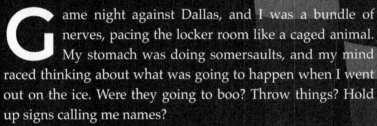

CHAPTER 19

ARI

Game night against Dallas, and I was a bundle of nerves, pacing the locker room like a caged animal. My stomach was doing somersaults, and my mind raced thinking about what was going to happen when I went out on the ice. Were they going to boo? Throw things? Hold up signs calling me names?

Just when I thought I couldn't handle the tension anymore, Walker swaggered into the room, a massive boombox perched on his shoulder like he thought he'd gone from Disney to an 80's rom com lead. He winked at me and the speakers blared Taylor Swift's "Shake it Off" at full blast. I raised an eyebrow, getting pretty fucking excited.

Then, one by one, the rest of the team paraded in, and what happened next was nothing short of a glorious catastrophe. Their moves ranged from hilarious to downright ridiculous, and I felt like I'd died and gone to heaven. It was like a scene from a comedy show, and for a moment, the weight of the upcoming game lifted.

I jumped into the impromptu dance party, doing my best running man move. We all looked utterly absurd, but right that second…it was priceless.

It was a moment of pure, unadulterated silliness, and it was exactly what I needed to break the tension.

As the music faded out and we caught our breath, I turned to Walker, who was grinning like a maniac. "You, my friend, have officially made it into the circle of trust."

Walker's eyes widened in mock surprise. "I'm in the circle of trust?"

I nodded with a grin. "Yeah, you're in."

He let out a whoop of triumph, and the rest of the team cheered...like the "circle of trust" actually existed.

Fools.

It was a strange feeling though, realizing that despite it all...despite all the time I'd spent this season not wanting to be here...somewhere along the way, I genuinely started liking these guys.

With newfound confidence and a lighter heart, I headed down the hallway towards the ice. Ready for whatever was to come.

As I walked though, the nerves started to creep up again. I was hoping at the very most to get the usual pre-game atmosphere, the buzz of the crowd, the excitement of another match...but as I emerged into the open arena, the sound that hit me was a thunderous roar, the entire arena on its feet, showering me with... applause.

I blinked in astonishment. Signs bearing messages like "Ari, we miss you" and "Come home" filled my vision.

I was stunned, my heart pounding as the deafening applause surrounded me. It felt like a dream, like some elaborate prank orchestrated by Lincoln. I turned to my friend, an incredulous grin on my face.

"Did you put them up to this, Linc?" I asked, only half joking, as I tried to mask the sudden wave of emotion threatening to overcome me.

Lincoln just gave me a knowing look and playfully hit my

shoulder. "Welcome home, buddy," he said as he skated back to his team, his words simple but carrying a depth of sentiment that I couldn't ignore.

Tears pricked at the corners of my eyes as I waved to the crowd, my laughter and disbelief mingling with the overwhelming feeling of being embraced by the place I'd once called home.

The game started, and the familiar rush of adrenaline surged through me as I hit the ice. I was back where I belonged, even if on the wrong side, and nothing was going to hold me back. The puck danced around the back of our net and Lincoln and I both went after it. I slammed into Lincoln, sending him crashing against the boards, and he shot me a half-hearted curse, the grin on his face telling me he was as thrilled about playing on the same ice again as I was.

When Lincoln took a shot on goal, I couldn't help but whoop as Walker stopped it with finesse.

"That's my goalie!" I yelled at Walker as Lincoln flipped us both off dramatically as he skated by.

Later in the game, I was skating towards the bench during a break to get some water…when I noticed a sign, held up by two girls in the front row. It read:

Lincoln #13 WE SUCKED YOUR DICK IN COLLEGE!

Lincoln's face was puzzled and faintly amused as he stared at the sign. But me…I was pissed off.

I skated over to him. "I can't believe that sign!"

"Yeah. It's a new one," said Lincoln with a grin.

"No! I can't believe it's your fucking name on the sign. That girl right there sucked *my* dick!" I growled, pointing to the girl I definitely recognized—even if I had no clue what her name was. "She did not suck your dick. What the fuck!"

Lincoln stared at me incredulously for a long moment before he burst into hysterical laughter.

"What are you laughing about? THIS IS SERIOUS! How is my dick that unmemorable?"

Lincoln was now wiping motherfucking tears from his eyes.

"Fuck. This is too good. You've got to stop. I don't think I can skate."

I growled. And pushed him before skating away to the continued sound of his cackling.

"Fucking dick," I muttered to Walker, who was wide-eyed, staring back and forth between Lincoln and me. Like his mom and dad were fighting or something.

"You're a year fucking younger than us, Prince Charming," I yelled at him nonsensically.

And now he seemed even more confused.

"Get your fucking head in the game, Lancaster," Coach screamed, and I nodded, turning my attention back to the ice. These people needed to understand my dick was not forgettable.

Blake could tell them all about it!

As the game raged on, things escalated between Lincoln and Soto. Lincoln had always hated him...just like me, but after what he'd done to Blake...Soto was just asking for it.

Lincoln slammed Soto against the boards, and the entire arena seemed to hold its breath, eagerly awaiting the fireworks.

Predictably, Soto threw off his gloves and shoved Lincoln with all the finesse of a charging rhino. The gloves hit the ice with a dull thud, and the crowd erupted into a raucous mix of cheers and jeers. It was go time.

The two of them squared off, circling each other. Soto swung wildly, but Lincoln's reflexes were so superior, it was ridiculous. He dodged Soto's punches with the grace of a seasoned fighter, and when he retaliated, it was like watching a professional boxer in action.

Lincoln landed a series of devastating blows, the first one catching Soto square in the jaw, sending a spray of spittle and blood into the frigid air. The sight of crimson droplets splattering across the ice only seemed to stoke the crowd's excitement.

Soto, now bleeding from his nose and sporting a rapidly swelling eye, tried desperately to regain his composure. But it was too late. Lincoln continued his assault, a relentless barrage of fists that left Soto stumbling and off-balance.

I couldn't help the malicious grin that crept across my face as it became abundantly clear that this was no contest. Lincoln was delivering a thorough beat down, and the crowd reveled in the spectacle.

But what made the moment even sweeter was the conspicuous absence of our Cobras teammates. None of them made a move to intervene and break up the fight. It was as if they, too, had gotten sick of Soto's shit and were relishing the opportunity to watch Soto get what was coming to him.

The moment of triumph came when Lincoln landed a powerful uppercut, connecting squarely with Soto's chin. It was the knockout blow, and Soto crumpled to the ice in a heap of defeat. Blood oozed from his nose and mouth...it was glorious.

I was pretty sure Soto had lost even more teeth.

I gave Lincoln an exuberant high-five as he skated back to the penalty box. Soto had to be scraped off the ice...

Just another reason why golden boy was my bestie.

———

This had already been one of the more...eventful games of my life. And then I glanced at Blake, like I did constantly every time she was in the vicinity...and I tripped over my skates. She and Monroe were talking to one of the WAGs behind them, so I could clearly see that at some point since we'd arrived at the arena, she'd put on a motherfucking *Daniels* jersey.

"I'm going to murder you," I hissed at Lincoln during a break. "I'm going to have Blake's dog bite your dick off! And then I'm going to let him use as it a fucking chew toy!"

"Have that fantasy a lot? Because that was weirdly detailed," Lincoln mused as I banged on the glass in front of Blake, motioning for her to take that fucking jersey off.

She put her hand to her ear, mouthing she couldn't hear me, trying to act like she was fucking confused! Monroe was hysterically laughing next to her. "I'm disowning you!" I yelled to Monroe, who was fucking crying now from laughing so hard.

"Payback is a bitch, Ari darling," Lincoln sing-songed as he skated by.

I flipped him off and then banged him into the boards when play resumed, harder than necessary just for good measure.

As soon as I got back to the bench, I ordered the same Cobras employee who had helped me in the past—Dan—to take a new jersey to Blake. And instruct her to put it on, or I was going to stop play and embarrass her in front of the whole arena. Dan's eyes were wide, and he looked a little scared of me as he scurried off to do my bidding.

I kept my gaze locked on Blake as he went up to her with the new jersey, not looking away until she put it on.

Damn fucking right.

I got back on the ice, gritting my teeth. We were tied 1-1 with the clock ticking down. I may have loved my old team, but I didn't want to fucking lose to them tonight.

"We've got this, Disney," I barked at Walker as he stopped yet *another* of Lincoln's shots. Lincoln had only scored once tonight, which was a testament to how fucking good Walker was.

Lincoln and I battled along the boards, vying for control of the puck. Our sticks clashed, the sound echoing around us.

With a surge of adrenaline, I managed to gain the upper hand, my body leveraging against Lincoln's to send the puck skidding toward the other side of the rink.

"Have to do better than that, Daniels!" I called to him.

The puck sailed through the air, a blur against the icy backdrop, and there, waiting, was Tommy.

Tommy stopped the puck and didn't miss a beat, swiftly taking control and racing towards the goal. Cas Peters tried to stop him...but he...wasn't me.

Tommy's shot was swift and true. Dalton, caught off guard, made a desperate dive, but it was a futile effort. The puck found its mark, slipping past his outstretched glove and into the net with a satisfying thud.

Right as the buzzer sounded.

Dallas was stunned as we dogpiled Tommy for the game winning score. 9 out of 10 times we would lose to them, but not tonight. Not fucking tonight.

A few minutes later, Lincoln gave me a hug and I was high-fiving my old teammates, feeling like I was on top of the world.

I'd played my brains out. Cas Peters had sucked. And everything in me said I'd be back here with Blake next year.

Life was fucking good.

Blake

The Dallas club pulsed with life, vibrant lights and music that enveloped us as soon as we stepped inside. The air was thick with anticipation and the unmistakable energy of a

Saturday night out in the city. It had been a whirlwind of emotions at the game, but now it was time to celebrate with Lincoln, Monroe, and, of course, Ari.

Ari's hand was warm against mine as he led me through the crowd, our fingers laced together, the feel of him possessive and reassuring. The music reverberated in my chest, setting a rhythm that matched the pounding of my heart. He leaned in close, his lips brushing against my ear as he shouted over the music.

"Ready to have some fun, sunshine?"

"Absolutely," I replied, getting overwhelmed with how freaking gorgeous he looked, his dark hair falling into his face.

The club was a sensory overload, neon lights, swirling patterns, and the intoxicating scent of perfumes and colognes mingling in the air. The DJ held court at the center of it all, his booth a shrine to the pulsating beats controlling everyone on the floor. The crowd gyrated and swayed to the music, a sea of bodies lost in the rhythm.

We were on the dance floor hours later, and Ari's gaze was intense, his green eyes locked onto mine as if nothing else in the world mattered. I was molded against him, and somehow I wasn't close enough.

The thumping bass reverberated through our bodies, a heartbeat that echoed our own.

Ari's hands were everywhere, trailing along the curves of my body, igniting sparks of desire that flared with each touch.

The music had shifted as the hours passed, transitioning to a slower, sultrier melody. Ari pulled me closer, our bodies pressed together as we swayed in time to the sensual rhythm. I moaned as his knee rubbed against my clit through the leather leggings I had on.

"Is my baby feeling needy?" he purred, starlight dancing in his green gaze.

"Yes," I whispered as he pressed his leg against my aching core once more.

Ari looked around the club as his hands continued to torture me with sensual strokes.

"Let's fix that," Ari finally said as he grabbed my hand and pulled me towards the edge of the dance floor, leading me down a dark hallway. He pressed me against the wall, his hand fisted in my hair as his body curled around me. My entire body relaxed, melting into him.

"I'll always take care of you, baby. You only have to ask." He moved a hand down my leather pants, covering my core. I wasn't wearing underwear because they would have given me bad lines, and judging by the growl he gave me, he clearly liked that I didn't have any panties on..

He gently massaged my clit and my hips thrust forward.

"Yes, Ari, please," I whimpered.

He chuckled darkly and his finger slipped inside me as his mouth closed over mine. Ari's hot tongue slid into my mouth, tasting me in aggressive, deep, long licks that sparked along my veins. I sucked on his tongue as his finger found that perfect spot, fucking in and out of me.

My hips were moving in time with his hand. But it wasn't enough. I needed more. My fists tightened in his hair as I pulled him closer, my body driving frantically against him, small pleas falling from my mouth.

"Do you need more, sweetheart? Do you need my big dick to get you there?" he cajoled.

"Yes, please," I begged, whimpering as he pulled his fingers from my core, bringing them up to my mouth and sliding them between my lips so I could taste myself. He pulled his fingers out and his tongue was in my mouth again, chasing the taste.

"Fuck, sunshine. I'll never get enough. You taste so fucking good." He pulled my leggings down to my knees so I was bared to him, and two fingers plunged back inside me, his thumb caressing my clit.

I glanced down the hallway, we were just feet away from the crowded dance floor. Anyone could turn the corner and see us at any second.

"You just gushed on my fingers...what are you thinking about, sunshine?"

I blushed and he chuckled knowingly. "You like that anyone could see us? That anyone could walk by and see me fucking your perfect, wet cunt? Does my girl like to be watched?"

I squirmed and his grin turned wicked.

"Let's see if that greedy pussy's ready for me."

He shocked me by falling to his knees, his hands pulling apart my folds as his tongue feverishly pushed into my core, and he ate me like a man possessed. It only took me seconds to come, my whole body shaking, the orgasm so intense tears gathered in my eyes.

"Good girl," he muttered as he stood up and his mouth returned to mine, the taste of me once again filling my senses. He hiked me up against the wall and pushed my pants lower, before he undid his zipper so his gigantic, pierced cock was free. The head was gleaming with white milky pre-cum and I licked my lips, unsure of whether I wanted it in my mouth or in my aching cunt.

He wasted no time pushing through my wet folds until he was sheathed inside me, my pussy squeezing and stretching to accommodate him. His fingers dipped between us, rubbing my clit so I relaxed and adjusted to his size.

Ari slowly withdrew before he slammed back into me, forcing a harsh cry to escape my lips.

He buried his face in my neck, his body shuddering. "You're perfect, baby. Taking all of my big cock. What a good girl." He fucked in and out of me, the ridges of his piercing stimulating every nerve as he slid it in and out. Ari's hands slid through my hair, gripping my head and forcing me to watch him as his pace picked up.

"I love you, sunshine. You're mine," he growled as he stared into my eyes.

Loud cries were falling from my mouth as he lost control pounding into me. I was sure someone down the hallway could hear me.

I fell over the edge, my core clenching and sucking him in. "Fucking choking my cock," he groaned.

Abruptly he pulled out and pushed me to my knees. Ari gripped my jaw and forced my mouth open before sliding his dick between my lips and pushing down my throat.

Yes, this is what I wanted.

One arm went to the wall above me as his other hand gripped my hair, holding me in place while he feverishly fucked my mouth.

"I'm gonna cum," he groaned as his entire body trembled. And then his hot cum was filling up my mouth. I gulped it down, but there was too much. It spilled from my lips, getting all over my chin. He surged in one last time, going so deep tears fell down my cheeks. His thumb gently flicked them away as he stared down at me in awe.

"Fuck. I don't know how it gets better every time," he muttered, almost to himself. Ari pulled out and tucked himself back in as I pulled myself off the ground.

"I love this," he said as he massaged his cum into my skin, licking at my lips and face aggressively...definitely getting a taste of himself. "I want you wearing my cum. I want it all over your skin. Fuck," he groaned as if he were in pain.

I'd had a few drinks, and that sounded wonderful...But I also was cognizant enough that I didn't want to go back out on the dance floor with dried white stuff all over my face.

He was a little growly as he followed me into the

employee bathroom a little further down the hallway, and watched me wipe off my face.

"As soon as we get back into the house, I'm going to cover you with it again," he promised.

And I winked at him, all for it.

"Fuck this," he said, and all of a sudden I was picked up and thrown over his shoulder. Ari stomped out of the bathroom and down the hall, returning to the crowded dance floor. People were staring at us as he marched around the edges. Lincoln and Monroe were at the bar, watching us, amused, as Ari held up a peace sign to them and headed towards the door without a word.

The night air greeted us, and before I knew it, a car had pulled up to the curb and we were getting in the back. Ari rattled off the address before his lips attacked mine—I didn't get a lot of air for the whole ride back to his place.

And just like he promised, as soon as we stepped into the house, he did indeed go about covering me with his cum.

And I loved it.

CHAPTER 20

BLAKE

A few days after the game, one of the gossip magazines released an article about Ari's homecoming...and most of it was about me.

"Ari Lancaster's New Obsession: Love, Scandal, and Secrets"

In recent weeks, the spotlight has been firmly fixed on the budding romance between Cobras star defenseman Ari Lancaster and the enigmatic beauty, Blake Shepfield. Their whirlwind relationship has captured the attention of fans and gossip enthusiasts alike, but it seems that behind their passionate love affair, there may be more than meets the eye.

Blake, a stunning and talented model with Elevate Models, has become a fixture at Ari's side, both on and off the ice. Her striking beauty and confident demeanor have led many to wonder about the mysterious woman who has captured the heart of the hockey sensation. However, as rumors swirl, so does speculation about her past...including a scandalous family history.

Ms. Shepfield's life has been marked by personal tragedy. In a story that seems right out of a dark drama, police records revealed her father murdered her mother after an illicit affair was discov-

ered. The sordid past of her family raises questions about the baggage she might be carrying into her new relationship.

Does Ari Lancaster know about this? It's the question of the hour...but what's perhaps even more shocking is the gossip that Ms. Shepfield might have walked in her mother's footsteps. Sources whisper that she maintained a boyfriend back in her hometown while becoming romantically involved with Lancaster. If these rumors are to be believed, it could spell trouble for their seemingly blissful union.

While Blake has been spotted at Ari's side at various events and games, insiders claim that Ari might be unaware of her alleged infidelity. The phrase "once a cheater, always a cheater" has been making its rounds, leaving fans and critics alike speculating about the longevity of their relationship.

As their relationship continues to unfold before our eyes, only time will tell whether Ari Lancaster and Blake's love story will defy the odds or succumb to the rumors that threaten to unravel their newfound romance. In the world of celebrity and sports, one thing is for certain: the drama never ceases, and the truth may be harder to uncover than a puck in a crowded rink.

I stared at my computer screen, my heart literally aching in my chest. Why had I decided to google my name right before work? There was no way the press wasn't going to find out about Clark, especially as Ari's fame grew. But how had they found out about my parents? The Shepfields had paid tons of money to get rid of my past.

I wiped away some tears and hurried to get to work. Everything was fine. Just because it was written...didn't make it real.

But I also found myself in the bathroom, forcing myself to throw up before I left.

Because bad habits were hard to get rid of.

A few hours later, I was at work, balancing a tray laden

with dishes as I moved between the crowded tables of the restaurant, my eyes darting from one customer to the next. It was a chaotic evening, the kind that kept me on my toes and thankfully gave me little time to dwell on anything else. Another hour and I'd be off, and back with Ari.

I groaned to myself because I sounded like a lovesick, besotted fool.

Those thoughts were also terrifying though...because the deeper I got into this, the more I had to lose.

"You have a new table," Marnie, one of the hostesses, told me as she passed by. My coworkers had been giving me speculating glances all shift. Especially her.

Signing, I looked over and froze, my blood seeming to thicken in my veins.

The perfectly coiffed hair, the eyes filled with disdain as she stared around the restaurant like it had personally offended her.

Maura.

Months of progress unraveled just staring at her in person. I hadn't even been looking at the texts she'd been sending lately, because I knew they'd just be full of condescending, hurtful comments about how I'd fucked up my life.

Evidently she had decided to bring the messages to me personally.

I tried to summon every ounce of professionalism in me since I knew she wouldn't hesitate to complain and try to get me fired if I reacted, but my hands trembled as I placed the menu in front of her.

Maura's eyes bore into mine, and there was a cruel glint in her gaze.

"Well, well," she said with a condescending smirk, "if it isn't my daughter, the failure." She glanced around the room. "This is quite the fall from grace....isn't it."

"I—"

"That wasn't a question," she sneered, her cold eyes studying me.

I fought to keep my composure, but her words cut deep. "Maura," I managed to say, a slight shake in my voice, "what can I get you to drink tonight?"

She laughed, a cruel, mocking sound. "Alright, I'll play along. A martini, extra dry. If this place can even make one."

"Of course," I murmured as I turned away, because only Maura Shepfield would say that in what was obviously a five star restaurant.

I clenched my jaw, struggling to maintain my professionalism.

Walking to the bar, I stiffly gave my order. Pete, one of the bartenders, gave me a quizzical look, obviously confused about my zombie routine. He handed me the drink. "You okay?"

"Yeah, fine," I whispered, taking a deep breath as I walked back to Maura's table.

"Here you go." I set the drink on the table, trying to ignore the knowing, amused look on her face.

"You know, Blake, we always hoped you didn't have the same genes as your worthless parents. We discussed it for days before we adopted you, the chance you might end up... like this."

"Have you decided what you want to eat?" I spit, trying to stop her vitriol.

But she wasn't going to stop until she'd said all she wanted.

"Look at you. You gave up a world of privilege for this. Slaving away like a servant. Your modeling career in ruins...."

"Your order, please," I choked out. Because fuck, I did not want to cry in front of her.

She smiled, getting pleasure in attempting my demise. "A steak, medium rare. Surely they can't mess that up."

I nodded and hustled away, except instead of going to input her order, I made a detour to the back exit, pushing through the doors with a hitched sob.

I stood outside in the cool night air, leaning against the rough brick of the building, tears streaming down my face. No matter how much progress I made, it never was enough. She was always going to be able to strip me bare.

Always.

I felt utterly worthless, as though every effort I'd made to prove myself had been in vain. Since they'd adopted me, all I'd ever wanted was for Maura to love me, to accept me for who I was.

But no matter what I did, it was never enough.

The scars of my tumultuous upbringing, the years spent striving for her approval, were still fresh in my mind. I had hoped that by breaking away from Maura and the toxic life she represented, I could finally find a sense of self-worth and belonging.

I'd been delusional, obviously.

I wiped the tears away and walked back inside, feeling that old familiar sensation, that I was a stranger in my own skin. That it was stretched too tight across my bones and any second now it would rip, and show everyone around just how ugly I was inside.

It wasn't just Maura, it was that article too. Out there for the whole world to see. How soon until Ari thought that way too? How soon until I fucked all of this up? Cheater. Whore. Maybe that's all I really was.

I stared around the restaurant. I was a failure, wasn't I? Doing this because I wasn't good enough at my real job.

"Look at her posture."

"Her backside is too big."

"She looks too basic."

Comments I'd received on failed jobs assaulted my brain.

After I inputted her order, I helped my other tables, well aware of her gaze tracking me around the restaurant as I worked.

Unfortunately, her steak finished quickly and I had to bring it to her table. She sniffed at the slab of expertly cooked meat like it was dog food and then sat back in her chair.

"What's most disappointing though, Blake, is that you aren't just worthless like your parents, but you're a cheater too—just like your mother. Cheating on Clark was the biggest mistake you've ever made. No *true* daughter of mine could be so stupid."

Each word felt like a dagger to my heart, hitting on all the insecurities about the situation with Clark that Ari had tried to stitch up.

I felt the walls closing in around me. My heart pounded erratically in my chest, and my breaths grew shallow and quick. Panic was setting in, and there was no escape.

The clamor of the restaurant faded into the background as I struggled to maintain my composure. Each breath felt like a battle, and I clung desperately to the edge of reason.

My hands trembled as I tried to discreetly wipe away the tears that welled up in my eyes. I felt a tightening in my chest, a heavy weight that threatened to crush me. The noise of the restaurant came back as a deafening roar in my ears, and I forced myself to stay on my feet.

"What the hell is going on here?" Ari's voice cut through the noise. I turned towards the sound of it, like it was a lifeline.

He was standing there like some kind of superhero, his fists clenched at his side, his face a mask of fury. Every muscle in his body was tense, like he was having to work hard to hold himself back from lunging at Maura.

Maura's smile faltered, and for the first time, she seemed taken aback. "And who might you be?" she sneered.

"Ari Lancaster," he said, his voice firm, "Blake's boyfriend. And I'd advise you to be very careful about anything you say next."

Maura laughed, a bitter sound that sent chills cascading everywhere. She glanced at me. "A hockey player, Blake? Really?" She shook her head. "That's who you betrayed Clark for?"

Anger flashed through me. She could talk about me all she wanted. But she couldn't talk about him. Not ever.

He was everything.

She glanced back to Ari.

"Do you even know how messed up she is?"

He scoffed, like she'd told a bad joke. "Shut the fuck up."

"Ahh, you have no idea who she really is, do you?" Maura mused. "You don't know about the medication, or the panic attacks...or her eating disorder."

I froze, my heart feeling like it was being squeezed. Heat crept up my neck. Humiliation was streaking through me. It felt like I might melt into the floor. All my secrets were out there, laid bare for Ari to see.

I couldn't even look at him.

He was never going to think of me the same after this. He was perfect. He wouldn't be able to stand me. She'd just ruined my one chance for happiness. Tears welled up in my vision.

"I usually don't hit women, but I'll make an exception for you if you aren't out of here in the next five seconds," Ari hissed, and a flash of fear actually rippled across Maura's face.

Maura's eyes narrowed, and she regarded Ari with a cold detachment. "Very well," she said with a dismissive wave of her hand. "But remember, you have no idea what you've gotten yourself into."

The air was thick with her satisfaction as she picked up her purse and slid gracefully out of her seat.

"Tell the manager I was so disgusted with the service here that I didn't eat a bite," Maura said haughtily as she strode towards the exit without paying.

I wanted to collapse to the ground, but I didn't want to give her that satisfaction if she happened to look back. So I just stood there, my whole body shaking, and I watched her leave.

"Come on, sunshine," Ari murmured hoarsely. "Let's get you out of here." He led me to the back entrance, and I was well aware of all the eyes watching us. I was also most likely going to be fired because of Maura's dine and dash and the fact that I was leaving before my shift was over.

I just couldn't find it in myself to care.

Ari led me down the alley in the back of the restaurant and then down a side street to where his car was packed. I was numb as he opened my door, buckled my seatbelt, and then rushed over to the other side.

He started to drive, and I was aware of his worried gaze boring into me, but I ignored it, staring out my window steadfastly.

"Blake—" he finally started. But I held up my hand, shaking my head.

"Can we just not talk? At least not right now?" I whispered.

He sighed, but he didn't say anything more. And the rest of the ride passed in silence.

"I need to use the restroom," I murmured when we got to the house, not bothering to get a response before I all but ran into the bathroom. Once I had the door closed...and locked, I rummaged through my bag of toiletries, searching for my razor.

I grabbed it and stared at it, self loathing surging through me. I hadn't let myself do this in weeks. But now it felt necessary. Like I wouldn't survive if I didn't release the pain.

Once a cheater always a cheater.

Just like her mother.

Failure.

Whore.

Modeling career in ruins...

I leaned against the wall, and pulled down the waist of my pants, my thumb brushing over the scars on my thigh. Tears were streaming down my cheeks, my hands were shaking....I pressed down the blade and...the door burst open and Ari was there, his eyes wide and face scrunched up with worry.

I froze in place, the razor blade sitting on my skin as we stared at each other.

He walked towards me and stopped a few inches away. Without taking his eyes off me, he slowly slipped off his shirt, throwing it to the ground afterwards.

"Hurt me, sunshine," he murmured, grabbing my hand that was still holding the razor blade, and pulling it up to his chest. "Every time you feel pain...hurt me instead. Let me take it from you."

My hand was shaking as he pressed the blade against his chest until a bead of blood pebbled on his golden skin.

I stared at it in shock. And shame. Because I'd felt the slight edge of relief like I'd embedded it into my own skin.

"Carve your name...carve your pain...I don't care what you do, but hurt me instead," he whispered as he dragged the blade across his chest. I stared at it, still in shock over what was happening, and I realized that he'd carved out a B.

He was literally carving my pain into his skin. He was carving *me*.

I pulled against his hand and he let it go. The razor blade tumbled to the tile floor, the clatter of it echoing around the room.

My legs failed me, and I dropped, caught in Ari's strong arms before I could hit the ground.

"Sweetheart," he murmured as I sobbed into his chest. His cut was bleeding, dripping down his beautiful skin and staining my shirt.

And I felt so much pain.

"Why did you do that?" I sobbed. "Why would you make me hurt you like that?"

"Baby," he groaned, his voice anguished. Ari scooped me into his arms and carried me into the bedroom, somehow kneeing his way across the bed until he was able to sit against it with me cradled against his chest.

"Tell me where it hurts," he whispered gently, an echo of the words he'd said weeks ago.

And like then, my answer was still the same, only he knew about the demons that made me a villain this time.

"I'm tired of Maura Shepfield being right about the fact that I'm a pathetic excuse for a human. I'm tired of being the villain in my own story. I. AM. TIRED."

His fingers danced across my cheek and I nuzzled into him. "When are you going to be tired of all the baggage I carry around, and want to leave because I'm the burden you never signed up for, Ari Lancaster?"

His fingers caught my jaw in his strong grip. "Never. The answer is never. Your pain is not a baggage to endure, baby. It's an honor for me to help you shoulder it. Give it to me. Tell me where it hurts. Let me take it away."

His gaze never left mine, and the intensity in his eyes was like a lifeline, and I was suddenly desperate.

"I tried to kill myself once. It was Clark who found me, took me to the hospital," I whispered. "And I still broke his heart." Guilt flooded my veins, so much streaming in from my fucked up brain that it felt like I would drown. Hiccupped sobs burst from my chest. "Knowing that, Ari Lancaster, why are *you* trying so hard to save me?"

"Sunshine, you haven't realized, you're saving me right back. I gave you my soul all those years ago, and I've just been existing ever since, waiting for you to come back to me. You aren't some girl. And I'm not some boy. We're soulmates, twin halves of the...Same. Fucking. Soul."

His hand brushed against mine as he wiped away the tears clinging to my cheeks.

"I wish you didn't have to save me," I finally whispered, and he shook his head.

"I"m just helping you save yourself. You'll see. One day you'll wake up, and this pain inside you, it won't be there anymore. You'll be free. And you won't even be able to remember how bad it hurt."

He pressed the most heartbreaking kiss across my lips, and he smiled. "I promise."

The thing about a promise from Ari Lancaster, I'd learned, was that he kept them.

Ari carefully undressed me like I was a present he wanted to unwrap. He made love to me for hours until I fell asleep, whispering love and praise until that ever existing pain...it seemed like it didn't hurt quite so bad.

Two days later when I woke up...Ari showed off a brand new tattoo of my name he'd inked where I'd cut his skin.

I asked him why, and he just laughed.

And somehow, Ari Lancaster...he did the impossible...he took my pain.

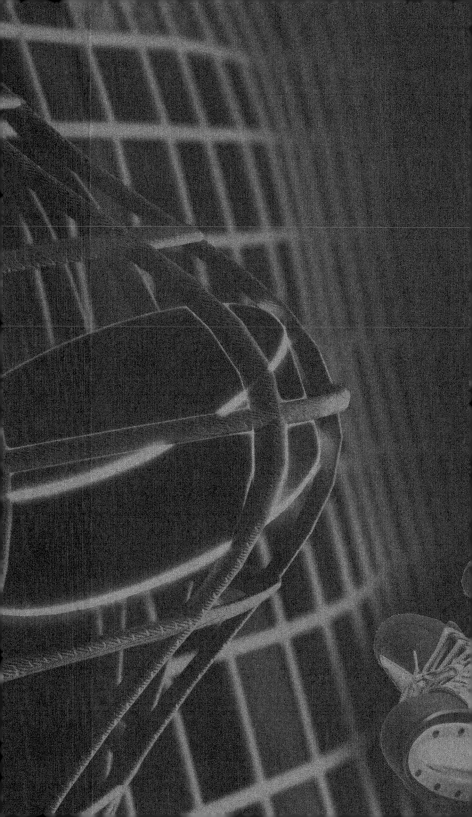

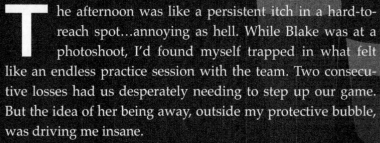

CHAPTER 21

ARI

The afternoon was like a persistent itch in a hard-to-reach spot…annoying as hell. While Blake was at a photoshoot, I'd found myself trapped in what felt like an endless practice session with the team. Two consecutive losses had us desperately needing to step up our game. But the idea of her being away, outside my protective bubble, was driving me insane.

During our water breaks, I checked my tracking app like a man possessed, making sure she was still at the shoot. I had a bodyguard following her around, but she hadn't responded to my last couple of texts. I WAS NOT HAPPY.

It was on one such break when Soto leaned over, interrupting a conversation I was trying to have with Walker about our favorite *Jurassic Park* movies. "Hey, Ari, had an interesting conversation about you today."

He was trying too hard to sound innocent, and ice slid around my veins. "Oh yeah?" I answered, matching his casual tone. "Who with?"

A smile slid across Soto's ugly face. "Just some rando. He was hanging out before practice, asking questions about you. Seemed like a nice guy."

Suppressing the urge to stab him with my hockey stick, I ground my teeth and took a deep breath, attempting to regain a modicum of control. "What kind of things, exactly, was he asking?"

Soto raised an eyebrow, "Oh, just wanting to know when you started dating your girlfriend. What your schedule was like...Nothing big."

"And you answered those kinds of questions?" asked Walker incredulously, looking less like a Disney prince and more like a Disney villain at the moment as he stared angrily at him.

Total circle of trust material, that guy.

Soto shrugged, acting like it really was no big deal.

"What did he look like?" I asked, an uneasy feeling gnawing at the pit of my stomach.

"You know, it's funny, Lancaster," Soto drawled. "But he looked a lot like you."

With that pronouncement, he skated away, effectively ensuring I couldn't focus on practice anymore.

When I checked my app during the next break, my worst fears were confirmed.

The tracking app had been disabled.

Blake

The final click of the camera signaled the end of the shoot. It was my third in the last two weeks. I had indeed gotten fired from the restaurant for leaving without a word during my shift...but it had been perfect timing since there was no way I could have made my shifts anyway with these jobs. Evidently, the Renage creative director had been spreading the word that the upcoming campaign was the best she'd ever done—and it was all because of me. It was actually all *because* of my chemistry with *Ari*...that was how I'd achieved the look she loved so much. Regardless though, her recommendations were bringing me tons of jobs and we'd be celebrating and unveiling the Renage campaign tomorrow at a release party.

Ari and I were...perfect. He'd been coming with me to my shoots when he didn't have practice. And he'd even been dragged into a couple more of them.

I was getting addicted to changing room sex.

Which was unfortunate because today, he had practice.

I also liked reuniting sex though. As well as every other kind of sex I had with Ari.

So I guess it was a win-win situation for me.

My life had taken on a dreamlike quality after that night I'd bared all my secrets. I actually felt like his love was physically healing me, and I loved him so much it hurt. I still had so far to go, obviously; a lifetime of trauma and bad coping mechanisms wasn't going to disappear overnight.

But I could feel myself changing. It gave me hope that he'd been right, that someday, maybe it wouldn't hurt so bad.

I thanked the crew and walked toward my dressing room, checking my phone as I stepped inside and closed the door behind me. I glanced up to locate my bag and yelped when I found myself face to face with a very unexpected visitor —Clark.

"What are you doing here?" I spit, my heart battering against my rib cage. His harried and disheveled appearance was a stark contrast to the confident, successful man I'd dated for so many years, and for the first time since I'd known him...I was a little afraid.

"Clark?" I asked, my voice calm but tinged with uncertainty. His bloodshot eyes were watching me and I was getting anxious.

"Blake," he began, his voice hoarse and filled with a weariness that hadn't been there before. "I had to see you."

Instinctively, I took a step back, my hand resting on the edge of the makeup table for support.

"Why now, Clark?" I asked, curiosity and caution lacing my tone. "I haven't heard from you really...since I moved. I broke up with you."

"No, you didn't break up with *me*. *We* never talked." Clark looked at me with a pleading expression, his eyes searching mine for some sign of understanding. He reached out to grab my hand and I pulled away. "Blake, you have to listen to me. Nothing that's happened has been real."

I scoffed. "What are you talking about, Clark? You were talking to me...and then you weren't. And I—" I gulped and took a deep breath, because it was much harder to say something like this in person rather than over text. "I met someone," I finally finished.

His eyes closed and he took a deep breath, his fists clenching and unclenching. "I know you met someone, Blake. You met a fucking *psycho* someone."

I frowned. *Psycho* seemed a little strong of a word.

"Ari Lancaster is the reason we aren't together."

I nodded, confused. I mean, yes, he was the person I'd met.

"No, sweetheart. Ari Lancaster has been stalking you. He saw you, made a plan, and methodically went through with it to push us apart, Blake. He's been behind the scenes pulling the fucking strings this entire time. Just so he can control you."

I snorted and shook my head. "Clark, that's enough. If you want to talk, we can talk. But you don't have to make up things."

"He saw you on a billboard. He found out who you were.

And he fucking requested a trade and stalked you to California."

"Where did you hear that from?" I demanded, shock slithering through me. I felt frozen in place.

"You know as well as I do that money makes people talk. I found out who his P.I. was, and he was totally eager to give me info for the right amount."

Unease was churning around inside of me, sloshing around like spoiled milk.

"Okay. This is ridiculous. We're done here," I finally said stiffly.

"He was the one who planted drugs in my car, who got me on the fucking no fly list. He made a spectacle of your relationship so it would be all over the press! He emailed me pictures of the two of you from a burner account!"

The "no fly list?" Clark was insane. "Do you have any proof of this or are you just throwing things out now and hoping they catch?"

Clark ran his fingers through his disheveled hair, his agitation evident. "I know it sounds insane, Blake, but he's the reason I couldn't talk to you. I sent you a million messages, called you a million times. Tell me, did you ever get these?" he asked, pulling out his phone. He scrolled through message after message, him begging and pleading with me to answer him and stop ignoring his calls.

My head was spinning, trying to understand what had happened.

"Can you take out your phone?" he asked quietly, staring at me with a look of pity—which I hated.

With shaking hands, I pulled it out, typing in the password that Ari had asked me to add for "security."

"Go to my contact," Clark pressed, watching my hands as I navigated the contact list.

Finding Clark's name, I tapped on it, fully expecting to find…nothing.

But he *was* blocked.

And I knew I hadn't done that.

"Maybe I accidently—" I started, confusion washing over me.

"If you check Facebook, you'll see that I'm blocked on there too," he said gently.

I couldn't help but check, desperate for it not to be true. Because I could have accidently blocked him in my contacts… but not on every other app as well.

But it was true. Clark had been blocked on Facebook, Instagram…every other fucking app on my phone.

This didn't make everything else true.

But they probably were. Thinking back…I'd started not to hear from Clark after that first time Ari had come in…when I'd somehow "lost" my phone and it had been given to the hostess to return to me.

And the Halloween party…I should have been way more fucking suspicious.

The drugs found in Clark's car–I'd known he didn't do drugs, but it was so…easy for me to accept everything.

I sank into a chair, feeling like the world was collapsing in on me.

The problem was…everything that Clark had said could be true.

But because I was so fucked up—I still wanted Ari Lancaster with everything in me.

"I can't believe this is happening," I admitted, my voice trembling.

Clark knelt in front of me, his voice soft and reassuring. "I understand, Blake. It's a lot to take in. But I promise you, I *never* stopped loving you. I never gave up on us. Now that

I've gotten you back, we can start over. I'll move here...or you can move back home. We can *fix* us."

I stared at his handsome face, years of memories whirling around in my head.

He was a good man.

But that wasn't enough for me—not anymore.

"I'm sorry, Clark, " I whispered, my eyes locking with his. "It's over."

He flinched like I'd slapped him. "Don't say that, Blake. I love you! I've loved you since the second I saw you." Tears streamed down his face, his vulnerability laid bare before me. Old habits were hard to kill, and I wanted to wrap my arms around him, to make him feel better.

I think I had loved him once, but not in the way he deserved to be loved.

Not in the way *I* deserved to love someone.

"I hope you can forgive me, someday," I murmured. It was a selfish thought, but it would be hard for me to live knowing he was out there, hating the memory of me for the rest of our lives.

"Please. Don't let him do this to us."

I yanked my gaze away from him, because it hurt to look at him.

"It's just not enough," I responded, even though I knew that wouldn't make sense to him. His face grew determined.

"I would love you in any way that you needed."

"I think you would try," I said gently. "But that wouldn't be fair to either of us."

He stumbled to his feet, swaying like he'd been stabbed in the heart. "I will find a way to get you back. To prove what we have is enough! I will never give up on us."

Clark stalked out the door, slamming it behind him.

I sat in the aching silence he'd left for a long, long time.

And then I went home.

A compulsion I couldn't resist.

It was dark in the house, so dark I was sure he wasn't home. And I jumped when the living room light clicked on and there he was, sitting on the couch. Relief in his gaze.

Beautiful as always.

And a liar.

"It's all true, isn't it?" I whispered as we locked eyes.

He stared at me warily, exhaustion marring his perfect features. I watched as the wariness faded into resolution.

"Yes. And I'd do it all again," he swore. "I'd do anything to keep you."

I nodded, a sick thrill rushing through me that didn't make sense.

I'd do anything to keep you…

No one had ever seen every part of me and vowed to never let me go.

"I'll sleep in the guest room," I told him, feeling like it was the right thing to do, even though every sick part of me wanted to climb up in his lap and have him wrap his arms around me.

He nodded, his green eyes glittering unfathomably.

I wandered down the hall to one of the guest rooms, closing the door behind me and leaning my forehead on the cold wood. Did I know him? Could I ever trust him?

What else had he done?

After a minute, I stumbled to the bed and collapsed on it, an ache in my bones…and in my fucking soul.

I woke up in bed with Ari, his whole body wrapped around me, his head buried in my neck. It wasn't surprising. If he was willing to move states to get me, a little old door wasn't going to hold him back.

I listened to his steady rhythmic breathing and wondered…how I was going to say goodbye.

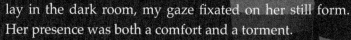

CHAPTER 22

ARI

I lay in the dark room, my gaze fixated on her still form. Her presence was both a comfort and a torment.

I'd let her go into the guest room, knowing I wouldn't be able to stop myself from bringing her back to *our* room in the dead of night. Now that I'd had so many nights with her wrapped in my arms...I couldn't sleep without her.

She was hurt, and it was my fault.

But I wouldn't change a damn thing.

As I traced the contours of her face with my gaze, I could feel the restlessness within her. She wanted to run, to escape this thing between us...but I wouldn't allow it.

She had come back last night, whether driven by her own conflicted desires or the cruel pull of fate, it didn't matter. Her return had saved me from hours of hunting her down.

I shifted closer, my hand grazing the curve of her hip. I knew she felt it, that golden thread that bound us together, even in the face of everything. The intensity of my desire for her was all-consuming, a delirium that threatened to destroy us both.

She belonged to me, whether she fully comprehended it or not. The truth may have fractured the delicate illusion of our love, but it hadn't extinguished the fire that burned between us.

I leaned closer, my lips brushing against the curve of her neck, claiming her as my own in that stolen moment. The darkness of our desires enveloped us, a heady cocktail of passion and pain, and I knew that there was no turning back. She was mine, and I would do whatever it took to make her understand that.

Including making things a bit more...permanent.

I grabbed my phone with my free hand and texted Linc.

> Me: Rapunzel, Rapunzel, let down your hair.

> Lincoln: If that's a line you use on girls, it needs some work.

> Me: You shut your mouth. My lines are perfect, golden boy. 10/10.

> Lincoln: Oh yeah...how's it going with Blake?

> Me: ...

> Lincoln: That's what I thought...

> Me: Well, I mean. It's going great. She just doesn't know it yet.

> Lincoln: I somehow understand that perfectly.

> Me: I'll send you pics of the wedding...

> Lincoln: What? You're getting married?

> Me: Yeah. But again...She doesn't know it yet.

> Lincoln: ...

Me: ...

With a plan in place, I pulled her closer to me...and quickly fell into a blissful sleep.

————

Blake

The day had crawled by like an eternity, and Ari had stayed practically glued to my side. He tried to talk to me several times about everything, but I couldn't do it. Not yet.

Maybe not ever.

I kept opening my mouth to tell him we needed to take a break...or something. But every time I did, I couldn't get the words out.

Because the thought of not being with him, even for a few days, my heart couldn't handle it.

Now, we were in the back of a sleek limo that Renage had sent for us, driving to the release party, the silence between us thicker than ever. The tension in the air was palpable, and I could sense his frustration. He'd been his charming self today, if clingier, but I kept telling myself this wasn't healthy. I couldn't just let it go...

Right?

As the city lights blurred past us, I was dreading the night ahead. The party was meant to be a celebration of my first big break in the modeling world. And now, all I wanted was to drown my sorrows in alcohol, and forget about the mess that had become my life.

I glanced at him. He looked like a dark god tonight, dressed in an all black suit that could possibly impregnate you just by glancing at him.

But his features were etched with a mixture of longing and resignation. The anguish in his eyes mirrored my own, and for a moment, I wondered if we were both doomed to this unending cycle of pain.

The car pulled up to the grand entrance of the club where the party was being held, music and laughter spilling out into the night. It was a stark contrast to the turmoil within me, a reminder that life went on even when everything felt broken.

"Blake, don't let what's going on ruin your night. Please try and have fun," he pleaded as his hand stroked my cheek. It was a habit that I leaned into it, taking comfort from his touch...just for a second.

I let him brush a kiss against my lips, and I felt the soft touch...all the way to my fucking soul.

The door opened and I was jarred back to reality, to remembering all that had happened. Ari had that way about him, the ability to make me forget myself.

I guess that's why I missed all the signs about what he was doing.

I was caught in his spell.

The bad part was, I was wishing I was still in it.

We stepped out of the car and made our way inside, Ari's hand burning into my lower back.

I immediately asked for a drink the second we got to the bar, and he nodded approvingly. He'd told me to enjoy myself after all.

And maybe I was going to.

Why shouldn't I drink tonight? I *never* allowed myself to truly let go. With the Shepfields, it was never allowed.

On my own, I'd never felt safe enough to do so.

But tonight....tonight I wanted to.

I took shot after shot with the crew, feeling like a fun person for once.

A free person.

And...it was freedom. To let my inhibitions flow out of me

with the alcohol and atmosphere. To stop worrying about how I looked, or what I'd done wrong. Just for one night, I could forget all the bullshit and shut up my own inner demons.

I loved it.

It was like my problems didn't exist.

I danced next to Ari, hands combing through my hair, hips swaying, basking in the fact that the alcohol shoved away all my turmoil over what Ari had done...how our relationship had started.

Right now, I didn't care about any of that, and I didn't want to care.

I just wanted us.

My head tipped back against his shoulder and fanned my heated face, and he looked down at me as his hands held my waist. "You okay, sunshine?"

"I'm great," I said, slurring slightly. "Never better."

"Do you want to slow down?"

I shook my head. "Nope."

I didn't. I wanted to keep everything flowing. The alcohol, the freedom, the fun.

He stared at me, a strange expression on his face, like he was debating something. But he didn't try to stop me.

A trio of models who had been in some past famous Renege campaigns came over, surrounding me. They were big names, people I'd have had trouble talking to if I was sober because I was so intimidated. But not now. Not tonight. Tonight they were my new best friends.

"Time for another round!" Rachel Crenshaw said as she passed me a shot. "Your shoot was fucking amazing," she said, clinking her glass with mine. "Cheers."

I glanced at the pictures decorating the walls. They *were* fucking amazing. Ari and I looked like pure sex in all of them, like we were seconds away from ripping each other's clothes off. The tension and chemistry were physically tangible... even through the lens of a camera.

Longing raced through my heart. The way he was looking at me in those photos–he looked at me like that every fucking day.

And I was so scared to lose it.

"Blake, drink!" Rachel sing-songed, bringing me back to the present. Deciding I definitely needed more if I was going to drown out my thoughts, I tipped the shot back, laughing as heat slid through my veins, warming me up all over. It felt so fucking good.

I turned and wrapped my arms around Ari's heated body, pressing my cheek against his chest.

Because he felt better.

"What was that, sunshine?"

Whoops. I must've said that out loud. I glanced up at him, and he was slightly doubled, the lights behind him making his dark suit light up, casting shadows against his face. "I don't want us to break," I confessed, my tongue loosened from every drink, my feet unsteady. His hold on my ass was the only thing keeping me upright. Keeping me from falling.

"I won't let us break." There was no doubt in his voice. Only perfect confidence. And the drunk me was desperate to believe him.

"But...y-you..." God, it was hard to talk. Because of the drinks. Because of...everything. "You tricked me. Blocked him."

"I think we've discussed this before, baby. You didn't belong with him. He was the one stepping where he wasn't supposed to. *He* was the intruder."

His grip tightened on my ass and I started to feel very needy...

"It was always going to be us."

I hummed my agreement, because I'd thought that when I met him too. That he was my everything.

"You know I thought I was going to marry you when we met," I slurred. Something was nagging in the back of my head that I shouldn't be saying this, but I pushed it away.

Because Ari was my safe place. Even when I was mad, hurt, upset…he was still somehow my safe place.

He was where I most felt free.

Hmm. That was weird. Maybe something for sober Blake to think of. Later.

Much later.

"You were saying, sunshine?" he murmured, his fingers tangling in my hair as he forced me to look at him.

I wanted to lick him..

"Thanks," he chuckled. "You're welcome to. Just as long as I get to lick you back."

Whoops, I'd said that out loud too.

"Oh!" I exclaimed, remembering what I'd been saying. "I totally thought I was going to marry you. I was ten years old and I was fucking done. Mrs. Lancaster. That was me." I giggled. "I had it all planned. A white dress. Pretty flowers. And you were going to love me forever and ever." I buried my face in his chest and rubbed against his silky shirt. "Things are so much easier when you're a kid," I sighed. "You can believe in forever and ever."

His hands rubbed down my back, soothing my feverish skin.

A waiter passed by with more drinks, and I lurched towards him…because they were neon green.

I loved green.

Like Ari's eyes.

"These remind me of your eyes. Green, green, green. My favorite," I told him as his lips danced down my neck. That felt good. Really good.

Ari always made me feel good.

Except when he hurt me.

I frowned.

"Please don't hurt me," I told him, a small part of me knowing I sounded pathetic.

"I'm going to take care of everything, baby. Make us both feel better," he assured me. "You trust me, right?"

I nodded. "I can't stop."

"Good girl. Now come with me…"

I took his hand, because Drunk Blake, she would follow him anywhere.

The party was winding down though, but I didn't want it to end. Because I didn't want *us* to end.

Ari could sense it. So when we stepped outside into the cool night air, he held me close. "What do you want to do, sunshine?"

"I want to keep having fun. With you. Forever."

And I did want *forever*.

The alternative was goodbyes and grief.

He smiled. Triumphant. "I want that too."

I had champagne in a limo. Ari just watched me, still not partaking, though his eyes kept drinking me in. I was blissfully drunk. While he was just drunk on me.

Then, the fun and freedom went to an all-time high. Really, really high. As in airplanes and clouds.

"It's so pretty." I sighed as I looked out the window at the glittering lights below.

"You're prettier."

I turned and smiled dreamily at him. This seat was comfortable. His hand on my thigh was bliss.

We stumbled through neon-lit streets, my heels clicking on a sidewalk that felt alive, alive with the pulsating beat of the bright light city. Ari's arm was wrapped around me, not letting me fall. Because he was always protecting me.

The rush of adrenaline and alcohol in my veins as we stumbled into a building that seemed to appear out of thin air. There were couples everywhere. A lot of white. So much white. Which was weird, 'cause I was in white too.

A small chapel adorned with glittering lights, and Elvis was there serenading us with a voice that could melt steel.

Ari said "I do," and he was so happy.

A ring slipped on my finger, and he was even happier.

"Forever, sunshine."

We kissed, lips meeting in a collision of passion and pure happiness. The cheers and applause of strangers mingled with our laughter, as if the universe itself had joined in our celebration.

My memories were nothing but fragmented flashes, like a puzzle missing most of its pieces. But I was with Ari.

So I was safe.

So safe.

Forever safe.

———

It was a cruel and merciless awakening. My head throbbed like a relentless jackhammer, and my stomach churned with a queasiness that threatened to consume me. It was the kind of hangover that felt like the universe's twisted way of punishing me for every questionable decision I'd ever made.

As I gingerly peeled open one eye, the harsh light streaming in through the curtains assaulted my senses like a thousand fiery daggers. My surroundings blurred and spun as I tried to piece together the events of the previous night. I was pretty sure I was in Ari's house...in his bed. How exactly had we ended up here? And why did my body feel like it had been put through a blender?

With a groan that came from the depths of my tortured

soul, I slowly sat up, panic creeping in as I realized I was completely naked. Please tell me I hadn't slept with him... that was the opposite message I needed to send.

I remembered wanting to forget, and drinking and having fun. We'd been dancing and...I'd been convinced I could drink away having to break up with him.

But I couldn't remember anything after that...not how we'd gotten home, not what we'd done, nothing.

The queasiness in my stomach escalated, and I knew I had mere seconds before I'd be introducing the contents of my stomach to the toilet. I stumbled out of bed and raced to the bathroom, collapsing in front of the toilet just in time.

As I heaved and gagged, a glimmer of something caught my bloodshot eye. I wiped my mouth with the back of my hand and blinked at the sight that greeted me: a ring, perched snugly on my finger, with a diamond so enormous it could have lit up the Eiffel Tower.

I screamed.

The ring sparkled mockingly in response, as if it were the crown jewel in some cosmic joke. I stared at it in sheer disbelief, my mind racing to make sense of this bizarre twist in an already confusing morning. The diamond glinted with an almost malevolent glee, as if it were silently taunting me with its opulence.

I couldn't recall ANYTHING.

I just hoped this ring had somehow materialized out of thin air, because any other option was not okay.

I panic-brushed my teeth, and dragged myself out of the bathroom, throwing on some clothes so I could figure out what the hell had happened last night. Once I had on a pair of sweats, I made my way to the kitchen. The tantalizing aroma of food and the sound of Taylor Swift's "Paper Rings" filled the air, creating a bizarre contrast to the pounding headache that had decided to take up residence in my skull.

The song seemed oddly prophetic, but no, I wasn't going there.

Ari was dancing around as he cooked something on the stove, wearing an apron that read "I Love Beaver" in bold letters. My bleary eyes widened in disbelief at the scene. *He sure didn't look hungover.*

He heard me approaching, and his face lit up with a suspiciously mischievous grin.

"There you are, sunshine. I was about to come wake you up for breakfast."

He must have seen my face turning green at the mention of food, because he grabbed a glass on the counter next to him, filled to the brim with a brown sludge looking concoction, and slid it my way with an air of triumph.

My eyes darted to the drink, uncertain whether it was my salvation or the final nail in my hungover coffin.

"Here you go," he chimed in a voice that was far too cheerful for the world's current state of existence. "A tried and true Lincoln and Ari hangover cure."

I didn't have anything to lose, so I lifted the glass to my lips...

"Drink up, wifey."

I froze in place, the cup at my lips. What had he just said? That was just him being Ari...right?

Ari had a huge grin on his face as he stared at me.

"Wifey, haha," I muttered as I threw back the disgusting drink. It tasted like gasoline as I guzzled it—or what I imagined gasoline tasted like.

"What's so funny? Do you not like the ring?" he asked innocently. "You're right, I should have gone bigger."

This time I choked on the drink, the glass slipping out of my hand and crashing to the floor. Glass and brown liquid went everywhere as I stared at Ari in wide-eyed disbelief.

"What the fuck are you talking about, Ari?" I shrieked, the sound hurting my own ears.

He covered the plate of waffles in front of him with his hands. "Language, Blake. You'll hurt the waffles' feelings!"

"Ari, tell me what you're talking about, right now!"

He held up his hands. "Alright, sunshine. Let me clean up the floor and then we can talk. Please don't move or you'll cut yourself."

A wave of guilt hit me that I was snapping at him so much, but my brain was fuzzy and my heart was pounding, and I was afraid he wasn't joking...

"There. All done," he said as he finished. "You want your waffles now?" He slid a plate of blueberry ones towards me.

Obviously, he was being obtuse now. And trying to butter me up because blueberry waffles were my favorite.

"No, Ari. I want to know why I have a ring on my finger and you're calling me "wifey!" I snarled.

"Because we got married last night in Vegas, obviously," he responded calmly, holding up his own ring clad finger.

"What did you just say?" I asked in disbelief.

"I've got the certificate locked in our safe, and oh! I have a video. You're going to love it."

He eagerly pushed me toward the couch, setting me down and snuggling in beside me. I was too in shock to move.

With a theatrical flourish, he pressed a button on the remote, and the room was instantly filled with the lively strains of "Viva Las Vegas." The screen flickered to life, and my jaw dropped...

The first scene captured us in front of a kitschy wedding chapel. There I stood, in a short, tight white dress I'd never seen before...clutching a bouquet of roses with a smile that teetered somewhere between tipsy bliss and unabashed joy. Beside me was Elvis—or at least a convincing impersonator—

decked out in the King's iconic jumpsuit and shades, offici-
ating our unexpected union.

It was obvious I was blitzed out of my mind. My eyeliner
was smudged all over my eyes, my hair was wild and out of
control...and I was swaying in place like I was going to pass
out at any minute. How had anyone there thought a wedding
was a good idea! Ari, on the other hand...he looked perfect–
his eyes clear, his hair artfully tousled, no sway in his walk...
Like he was completely sober.

Staring at me like I was his world. No, I wasn't going to
think about that.

When Elvis had asked, "Do you take this man to be your
husband?" I'd literally slurred "hell yeah" and pumped my
fist.

Wonderful.

The montage then transitioned to Ari and I in a gleaming
white limo, cruising down the dazzling Las Vegas Strip, the
night sky alive with brilliant, flashing lights. We'd thrown
open the sunroof, the wind whipping through our hair as we
stood on the seats, holding onto the car's roof for dear life.

With the skyline of Sin City as our backdrop, we shouted,
"Just married!" at the top of our lungs, our faces flushed with
excitement. Ari proudly extended my hand, showing off the
sparkling ring that now adorned my finger.

"There's also a video of our helicopter ride," Ari said
eagerly, playing with the remote. I grabbed his hand.

"This isn't a joke? You really took me to Vegas while I was
black out drunk and married me?"

He nodded his head, his grin fading as his lips settled into
a determined line. "Yep. And you said "yes," sunshine, so
you're stuck with me."

Anger and shock were warring with each other inside of
me as I just stared at him. The rest of what he'd done had
been enough that any sane relationship would have ended...

but this. THIS! What was I supposed to do? My voice trembled as I demanded, "Why would you do this?" My words were laced with accusation."I never get drunk. Never let go. But I felt safe enough with you to do that, and then you...you...did this? Took me to Vegas and married me?"

His face scrunched up with frustration. "You told me last night, you didn't want us to break up. You told me you didn't want it to end! So *I* made sure it didn't."

His voice was completely resolute.

"Ari, people don't do this! How did you expect me to react? This is fucking insane! First what happened with Clark...and now this? How could you?"

Ari's eyes bored into mine, his conviction unwavering. "Because we're soulmates, Blake. You and I are meant to be together. And now you can't leave me."

I couldn't believe what I was hearing. My disbelief poured out in a scornful laugh. "People get divorced all the time, Ari. You can't just...trap me in a marriage because you think we're soulmates."

He stepped closer, his voice a fervent whisper, each word heavy with conviction. "Not us. I'm never letting you go."

I turned away from him, unable to bear the weight of his declaration. Conflicting emotions roiled within me, and I knew I needed space to sort through them. Without another word, I fled to the guest room, my heart pounding in my chest. The door slammed shut behind me, echoing my tumultuous feelings.

Inside the dimly lit room, I leaned against the door, my breathing erratic. Tears stung my eyes as I grappled with the reality of the situation. Ari's actions had left me feeling trapped and overwhelmed. I couldn't deny that a part of me wanted to be claimed by him; before all this had happened, I'd been dreaming of marriage...been dreaming of forever.

But not like this.

I paced the room, my thoughts racing like a runaway train. How had everything spiraled into this mess? How could he have ever thought this was a good idea?

Clark's use of the word "psycho," flashed through my head.

As I wrestled with my emotions, the most overwhelming one...was despair. I'd believed Ari was my hero. A person I was safe with. A person I could trust.

The weight of Ari's words and the depth of my emotions threatened to drown me. I knew I needed to confront him, to figure all this out.

But for now, I needed a moment.

Because my heart had just been broken.

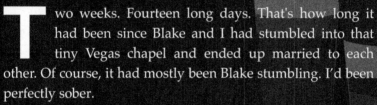

CHAPTER 23

ARI

Two weeks. Fourteen long days. That's how long it had been since Blake and I had stumbled into that tiny Vegas chapel and ended up married to each other. Of course, it had mostly been Blake stumbling. I'd been perfectly sober.

But I wasn't going to miss out on a chance to tie that girl down.

Blake had barely said twenty words to me in those two weeks—I'd been counting—and most of them had been variations of "Get the fuck out."

I mean, I could understand why she'd be a *little* upset.

I had taken advantage of her drunken state, married her without her clear consent, and then sent pictures of our wedding to my agent, who had promptly shared them with every news outlet in the country so that everyone knew we were married.

But I had *really* good intentions. I was going to make Blake happy forever, just like I'd promised.

We just needed to get past this little…speedbump first.

Or at least that's what Lincoln kept telling me.

Practice had been a disaster today. My mind was a dark

place, and it showed in my performance. I made sloppy mistakes, the kind that would have been laughable if they weren't so damn frustrating. My coach had yelled at me to get my head out of my ass, and he wasn't wrong. I was a mess, and it was affecting my game.

After practice, Walker had dragged me to a nearby bar. He knew something was up, and he wasn't the type to let a fellow circle of trust member suffer in silence. We'd downed shots and beers like there was no tomorrow, and for a while, I'd almost forgotten how angry Blake was with me, how there seemed to be no end in sight. How my dick hadn't been in her perfect cunt in what felt like forever.

But alcohol unfortunately wears off, and the reality of my situation crashed down on me.

I stumbled back to our home. She hadn't called it "our" house in weeks, and every night she attempted to sleep in the guest room.

But it *was* still *our* home.

Every night she would slink away to the guest room, and every night I would bring her back to our room.

Except tonight.

Tonight I sank into a chair in the room and just watched her sleep.

She looked peaceful, her features softened in slumber. None of the anger was there when she was sleeping. I could almost pretend things were normal.

Almost.

Her silence was deafening. I had expected anger, frustration, and maybe even resentment, but this cold, unyielding silence was something else entirely.

I missed her. I missed her voice. I missed her laugh. I missed the feel of her skin. The taste of it…

I missed fucking *everything* about her.

I was living with the ghost of her and it was excruciating pain.

My mind raced with thoughts of how I could fix this, but the one thing she wanted...was the one thing I couldn't give her.

I couldn't let her go.

It was never going to happen.

But if I didn't get a look from her soon that didn't freeze the sun, I was going to go insane.

As I sat there in the guest room, bathed in the pale moonlight filtering through the window, I couldn't see the light at the end of the tunnel.

I felt hopeless.

The following days were a relentless cycle of despair and determination. I woke up each morning with a pit in my stomach, knowing that Blake's frosty silence awaited me. But I still gave it my all. I made her favorite foods, I told all my favorite jokes...I even bought her a Maserati.

But nothing was breaking down those walls.

I found myself spending more time at the rink, throwing myself into practice with a feverish intensity. Hockey had always been my sanctuary, a place where I could lose myself in the game and forget about the world's troubles. But now, even the rink felt like a battleground.

Lincoln and Walker were worried about me. The Cobras had lost three games straight and we were about to head into a road series.

I was going to have to kidnap her at this rate to bring her with me.

I couldn't concentrate during practice because I was checking my phone every five seconds, staring at cameras in the house, and in her car, worried today was the day she'd try to leave.

Of course, I would go get her, but still...the worry was there.

It was raining today, and I was walking the streets aimlessly, waiting for her to be done with a shoot she'd had that day. I wondered if she missed me at all while we were apart.

Because I was a lovesick fool who wanted nothing more than to be with my wife every fucking minute of my life.

And she didn't even want to be my wife.

My phone buzzed.

> Lincoln: Any progress?

> Me: You mean, does she hate me less than yesterday? Doubtful...

> Lincoln: You want those cuffs yet?

I hesitated over the keyboard...sometimes I really couldn't tell if he was joking or not.

But now was really not the time for jokes.

> Lincoln: She's going to forgive you. You guys are the real thing. She'll remember that soon.

> Me: You really believe that?

> Lincoln: Pssh. I know that. And I know everything.

> Me: Cocky.

> Lincoln: Confident. There's a difference.

I slipped my phone back into my pocket. But I did feel at

least a tiny bit better. I would find a way to break through Blake's fortress, to make her see that I was willing to do whatever it took to make things right.

But for now, I would wait outside her building like the obsessed *husband* I was…

And wait to follow her home like a lunatic.

———

I boarded the jet to New York with a sense of purpose. Blake still hadn't forgiven me, but I at least could fix the problems she had outside of us.

The plane soared through the skies, and with every passing mile, I rehearsed the confrontation that awaited me in the Shepfields' Manhattan lair. I'd seen a picture of it in a design magazine Blake had showed me once. Very glass castle-ish looking… It was kind of amusing that it was about to crumble around them.

Arriving in New York, I got an Uber and made my way to their penthouse, the weight of the documents in my bag a comforting reminder I still had control over some things. The elevator ride to the top floor felt like an eternity, each passing floor a step closer to the fun.

I took a deep breath and squared my shoulders as I stood before the opulent door. This was it, the entrance to the Shepfields' sanctum. The mansion itself was the embodiment of swankiness, nestled high in a tower that reached for the heavens. I couldn't help but feel like a penguin at a peacock party as I knocked, half-expecting the door to be answered by a butler in tails.

The penthouse door swung open, and instead of a butler, there stood a timid looking woman…wearing an honest to goodness black and white maid outfit.

"Can I help you, sir?" she asked snootily.

"Yep," I said, slipping past her.

"Wait, sir!" she called out frantically behind me.

I wandered quickly around the place; it was so big, it echoed as she called after me. It was like walking through a palace, but instead of a red carpet, there was a gold-plated one that probably cost more than my first car. I turned a corner until I stepped into what I was pretty sure was called a drawing room. Lincoln had one of these. I always made fun of him for it. Paintings of naked women and baby angels adorned the walls, probably worth more than my entire contract, and a grand piano sat in one corner, gleaming under the soft lighting. Plush sofas and antique furniture completed the room's décor, and I couldn't help but wonder if they'd hired a team of interior designers or magicians. Thomas Shepfield was perched by the fireplace, a tumbler in his hand, like he was posing for *Horse & Hound Magazine*.

I laughed to myself. Blake would have gotten a kick out of that one if she was speaking to me. She loved the movie that was from.

I cocked my head as I studied him—somehow, he still hadn't noticed me standing there. He definitely looked like the kind of guy who used 'please' and 'thank you' during sex though.

Maura Shepfield was perched on a lavish sofa, her blonde hair sculpted to perfection. She was wearing a citrine colored gown—which was really weird. I half-expected her to start speaking in iambic pentameter.

I slow clapped. Just because it seemed like the right thing to do with the scene before me.

Maura screeched and fell off the couch in surprise...and Thomas dropped his drink, knocking a gash in the real wood floor.

Delightful.

"What the hell are you doing here?" Thomas growled.

There was clear recognition in both of their gazes...and hate. Especially in Maura's as she picked herself off the floor.

"Thomas...Maura." I gave them a little nod and a mocking smile as I stepped inside. "I knew you wouldn't mind a visit from your new *son in law*."

Maura sniffed. "If you're expecting some sort of wedding gift, you'll be sadly disappointed, young man. You and that good for nothing girl won't get a penny from us."

I snorted. "I can honestly say a "wedding gift" has not crossed my mind." What did cross my mind was punching them both in their pretentious fucking faces for calling Blake a "good for nothing".

"If you don't want money, why are you here? You can have one second of our time before we call the police. We know you like a good spectacle, so maybe you won't mind," spat Thomas.

I couldn't contain my smirk. "Mmmh. Yes, I do like a good show. But we'll see what you think about the police after we're done. Kay?"

I settled into one of their plush chairs, making myself at home. It actually was really comfortable.

I pulled out the envelope containing the damning evidence that my P.I. had unearthed before he betrayed me. I wondered what he thought about the money laundering charge he was currently defending thanks to Lincoln. It pays *not* to betray your best clients.

"Well?" Maura's voice cut through the noise in my head. I tossed the folder onto the marble coffee table with a deliberate thud.

"What is that?" Thomas demanded, annoyance clear in his voice.

I leaned forward, my gaze never leaving theirs. "Allow me to enlighten you. I was really interested in finding out more about my new in-laws. I mean, it's a big deal to marry into a

new family. And ya know, the two of you are really fascinating people," I drawled.

I reveled in the tension that filled the room bit by bit as I
detailed their secrets. "Maura, did you know that your
devoted husband had a rather torrid affair with your 18-year-
old pool cleaner? Quite the scandal, I must say. I imagine it
would be rather embarrassing for that to come out."

Thomas's face turned a shade of crimson, his forehead
beading with sweat. Maura, however, didn't seem surprised
by the news at all.

"That's none of your business, boy!" she snapped.

I raised an eyebrow, my tone dripping with sarcasm. "Oh,
but it is, Maura. You see, you've made it my business by
coming to L.A. and messing with Blake."

Her face paled and she reached for a Chanel bag. "How
much do you want, Mr. Lancaster?" she said calmly, obviously well versed in the art of paying people off. Hey, at least
I'd upgraded from "boy" to "Mr." This was getting serious.

"I would never take a penny from you. Especially
knowing that all of this," I gestured to the wealth around me,
"is nothing more than a façade. In reality, you both live
paycheck to paycheck, and you've been siphoning money
from the very charities that Maura is on the board for."

Now they both looked sufficiently terrified. Their veneer
of icy poise had shattered, and pure fear was lurking in their
eyes now. Maura was frantically gazing around the room, as
if she expected hidden cameras to be recording our
conversation.

"Now," I said, leaning back in my chair, "here's how this is
going to work. You will sign these documents, effectively
disowning any claim you have to Blake as her adoptive
parents. You will promise to never contact her again, and you
will ensure that she is left in peace."

Maura stared at the documents, her hands trembling as

she reached for a pen. "What are you going to do with what you know?" she hissed as she frantically signed the document without a thought.

It wasn't a surprise, but I hated how easily she could cast aside Blake.

Blake was priceless. Worth more than anything else in their pathetic life.

I chuckled darkly. "Stay away from Blake and you won't have to find out."

Blake was obviously over eighteen and no longer had to listen to the Shepfields. But simply having them as her adoptive parents legally, it was like a dark cloud hovering over her life.

Now she would be free.

I grabbed the documents, relishing in the sweet taste of victory. The Shepfields, who had once held so much power over her, were now at *my* mercy. And I had every intention of making sure they understood the consequences of ever crossing her path again.

Their faces were etched with defeat as I rose from my seat, leaving them to contemplate the ruins of their carefully constructed world.

Eventually I would leak all the information about who the Shepfields really were, let Blake relish the satisfaction of seeing the mighty fall...

But for now, it would be fun for them to live in misery.

Just as Blake had her entire life with them.

CHAPTER 24

BLAKE

I woke up, my chest heaving as I stared around the room. Our room. He'd brought me back in here. *Again*.

I was wrapped in his arms.

And I didn't try to get out of them.

It was the only time I allowed myself to relax in his presence–when he was asleep, and couldn't see the automatic reaction I had to his touch, the way his heartbeat was my nighttime soundtrack, the way my body basked in his warmth as if it didn't have a touch.

I'd woken from a nightmare. I'd been trapped in a speeding car, hurtling down an unending, treacherous road. The brakes had been useless, the steering wheel stuck, and I'd had no choice but to endure it. To wait for the tragedy that lay at the end of the journey.

I didn't need someone to tell me what the dream had meant. I was well aware of the lack of control I was feeling in my life at the moment.

"Blake," he whispered in his sleep, pulling me closer to his chest, his nose sliding along the back of my neck.

A soft sob slipped from my mouth and I slapped my hand on top of it, trying to stop the sound.

I didn't want him to wake up. I didn't want to break the spell of these nights, when I could take comfort in his arms, pretend that he was just the love of my life and not the man who'd destroyed me.

The next morning, I stood in front of the mirror, just staring at myself. He was at practice, and I...I was alone with my demons. I had a shoot in an hour. But instead of getting ready, I was standing there, ripping myself apart.

I had almost started to like myself. Because Ari had liked me. Not just liked me, he'd told me I was *perfect*.

But now I knew he was a liar. And all the pretty words he'd said...the ones that I'd let in, allowed myself to start to believe...

Maybe I couldn't trust them.

And so here I was, the soundtrack that had haunted me since I was a little girl, once again blaring loudly in my head.

The lines around my eyes, were they too pronounced? Were they supposed to show like that? And my cheeks. They were rounder today. I'd gone back and forth between binging and not eating lately. The fucking chubbiness...it was tangible proof of my lack of self control. My lips were too thin. Today was a fucking lipstick shoot. They were going to take one look at my old, fat face, and my scarecrow lips, and kick me out.

I screamed. And the echo of it was *everywhere*, breaking open the cracks in my heart until they felt more like fucking ravines. I was dying. That was the only explanation for how much all of this hurt. Humans were meant to be able to withstand pain, but not like this. Not pain that bled you out.

There was just shame sitting with me in the car as I drove to the shoot. Because the only reason I hadn't purged myself this morning, the only reason I hadn't hovered over that toilet until my insides were aching and bloody...was because I was going to be late.

I was right back to being the weak basket case that I'd always been.

And deep down, I knew it wasn't Ari's fault. I knew I needed to fix myself. Knew I needed to stop doing this.

I just didn't know if I could.

When I walked out of the shoot hours later, I was defeated. Every shot had been bad. The photographer had tried everything. But there was no spark, there was no life.

How could there be?

I felt like a walking corpse.

My phone buzzed, and for a second…my heart lifted.

But it wasn't Ari. It was Clark.

And I had no use for him.

I pulled into the driveway of the house I couldn't stop myself from returning to.

And I wept.

———

A few days later I was staring at the television blankly, watching who knows what, when Ari suddenly stormed in, holding up my phone.

"What's this?" Ari spit.

"Give that back!" I snarled, lunging for it.

But he held it up over my head.

"Clark's texted you twenty fucking times this week. Why haven't you told him to fuck off?"

"So what if he's texting me? What are you gonna do, Ari? You gonna plant drugs in my car? You gonna block his number without telling me? Replace it with your fucking own? Or track my phone so you know when we talk? Oh wait, are you going to put him on the fucking no fly list?"

"Maybe!" Ari yelled.

I flinched and stepped back, agony slipping through me. It was the first time he'd ever raised his voice to me.

"How could you do this to me? To us?" my father raged before he released a harsh sob, the sound absolutely terrifying.

"It's not what you think, John. Nothing happened," my mother's voice quivered.

Why was I thinking about that right now? Was it because my parents had once been the embodiment of a perfect love too? Until they weren't.

My mother's betrayal had shattered that illusion and left me with scars that still throbbed with pain. Now, I couldn't help but wonder if history was repeating itself.

Deceit was an awful thing.

Ari took a step towards me, his hand reaching out. "Blake," he said in a much calmer voice. "I understand you're upset. I even understand that you *don't* understand. But you'd better understand by now that…You. Are. Mine. If you care about Clark at all, you'll make that clear to him."

I stared at him, a tear sliding down my cheek. He was watching it fall, a look of complete and utter ruin as he did.

There wasn't a part of me that missed Clark. Just like there wasn't a part of me that regretted choosing Ari. But I didn't say that. I couldn't.

I couldn't tell him that his love had changed me. That I knew if I ended things with Ari, that if I didn't have him, I'd never want anyone else.

Ari didn't have to worry about Clark. Because his only purpose nowadays was to serve as a haunting reminder that Ari had manipulated me. Pulled the strings and gone behind my back.

It was Ari or no one.

Always.

"I love you, Ari, but you can't manipulate people you love. You can't trick them. It's wrong."

"I'll say I'm sorry a million times, sunshine," Ari whispered in a broken voice.

I flopped back onto the couch in utter defeat.

"The problem is, you won't mean any of them."

He didn't deny it.

———

I stared at the ring, buried at the bottom of my dresser
drawer. Its beauty didn't fit in with the socks it was hiding
under.

I'd told Ari that I'd thrown it away. That I wanted nothing
to do with it.

And then I'd felt like a complete bitch because I swore he
almost cried.

This ring was the most beautiful thing I'd ever seen. Its
only flaw...was that it now belonged to me...without my
consent. I would've loved this ring...if he'd done it properly. If
he'd gone down on one knee and proposed when I was
coherent enough to accept. Now, I felt like it was tainted. And
I hated that.

But it really was beautiful. And I couldn't deny the fact
that I loved it *because* he wanted me so badly. That much was
clear from the lengths he'd gone. I slowly started to slip it on
my finger......right as Ari walked into the room–his gaze
immediately locking onto my diamond clad hand.

"I guess we're both liars, aren't we, sunshine?" he
murmured as he continued to stare.

His words whipped across my skin and I flinched.

Because he was right.

His expression was perfectly blank so I couldn't read what
he was thinking at all. That was so different from how it had
been, when I could read every emotion that came across that
beautiful face.

But the worst part of it...was that his eyes seemed dead. No emotion, no mischief...all the awe I'd treasured like a previous gift...gone.

I had killed it.

My father may have killed my mother, but I'd learned over the years that there were a lot of ways to destroy someone.

I was watching it happen right in front of me.

I didn't understand how the mere thought of living without him was like a thousand pound weight on my chest, yet the idea of continuing in this state of mistrust and despair could feel just as heavy.

I laid in the darkness that night, once again wrapped in his arms, tears silently staining my pillow.

And I felt paralyzed.

The *only* thing I knew for sure...

I would love Ari Lancaster for the rest of my existence either way.

CHAPTER 25

BLAKE

Days passed, and one morning, the silence between us became too much.

"It's been twenty-one fucking days, Blake," Ari murmured from behind me as I stood in the kitchen staring listlessly into the pantry. I'd lost ten pounds from not eating. He'd been leaving me breakfast every morning. But nothing sounded remotely appetizing.

I turned, my heart already heavy with dread. "Okay," I said, my voice trembling. I didn't turn to look at him. It still hurt too much.

He took a deep breath, and I could feel the weight of his gaze, like a living, breathing thing. "You won't talk to me. You won't touch me. Hell...you won't even look at me! Give me something. Tell me you're trying to forgive me. Give me some fucking hope!"

I finally turned, taking in his beauty and immediately wanting to cry. There were dark circles under his eyes, his hair was all over the place, he also seemed like he'd lost weight.

"I should break up with you. Because nothing about what's happened is normal...or okay. Nothing. How am I supposed to trust you?" I whispered, and he flinched like I'd shot him instead of spoken the truth.

What I didn't say, at least not yet, was that I'd never be able to break it off. I needed time to get past this, but I already knew I'd never be able to say goodbye.

I loved him too fucking much.

That night, he didn't come for me. I woke up in the middle of the night like I always did now, and it wasn't in his arms, it wasn't in our bed.

I cried out as pain sparked across my chest. My heartache was literally destroying me from the inside out. Oh my god! Why the fuck did it have to hurt so bad?

I sobbed into my hands.

I'd almost forgotten what it felt like not to be lonely.

But here it was.

Excruciating. Tortuous. Enough to make me bleed.

When I got up the next morning, the house was completely silent, and cold, and unwelcoming, and...awful.

I walked out to the kitchen, expecting to see Ari making a shake, or cooking eggs, or doing something...but he wasn't there.

I wandered through the house, towards our room, unable to stop myself. And there he was.

Fully dressed.

A suitcase on the bed.

I froze, staring at the bag in shock. He slowly turned from where he'd been putting a shirt into it. And we just stared at each other. The silence miserable and laden with so much pain it was all I could do to stay standing up.

"I'm going back to Dallas," he whispered.

My hands began trembling.

"What?"

He fidgeted, picking at a string on his shirt. "My agent's

working on a trade with the Knights—a midseason trade in exchange for some draft picks."

There was a loud buzzing sound in my ears, a tightening in my chest, like my heart was being squeezed in a fist. I rubbed at it, wondering if this was what it felt like to have a heart attack.

Ari's gaze was filled with pain as he continued, "I can't watch you be so miserable. I can't be the reason that all your light fades. I love you enough to let you go, to stop forcing you to be with me."

He lifted a trembling tattooed hand to his face and rubbed at his forehead.

"I've hired an attorney for you. You just need to call the office and set an appointment." He closed his eyes briefly, as if trying to find the strength to continue. "She has the divorce papers ready for you to sign, Blake. All you have to do is put your signature on them."

Ari wiped at his wet cheeks, a tremor passing through his body. "And then you'll be free."

Tears streamed down my face as I looked into his eyes, my heart breaking with every passing moment.

I couldn't find words. It's like they died somewhere inside of me. I wanted to scream. To tell him how dare he. Tell him that I deserved more.

That was fucking it? He'd tricked me, manipulated me... lied to me. He'd fucking married me while I was black-out drunk. And he was *giving up*. All those times he'd said we were forever. That we could get through everything. That he'd never let me go...this was what he'd meant? The way I loved him was desperate and dark...and it felt poisonous at the moment but...I hadn't given up. I was trying to fix things in my fucked up head. I needed time. I needed the grace to be pissed and sad at him for everything. But he was giving up?

I watched in shock as he nodded and picked up the suit-case, walking way without a single glance back.

Just a few steps in, he stopped. And Ari didn't seem to have the same problem that I was having, because his next words made me want to die.

"I'm sorry I broke my promise to make you happy, sunshine. I'll never be over you. You'll always be the love of my life."

His words were like a slice across my wrist. And watching him walk away...

My legs gave way, and I sank to my knees, unable to hold myself up any longer. The room seemed to spin around me as I clutched at my chest, feeling like my heart had been ripped out.

Tears continued to flow freely down my cheeks, and I sobbed uncontrollably, the pain in my chest unbearable. It felt as if my entire world had crumbled into pieces, leaving nothing but devastation in its wake.

Every dream we had shared, every promise we had made to each other, now lay shattered at my feet.

I felt like I couldn't breathe, like the walls of the room were closing in on me. My life was slipping through my fingers like grains of sand. The thought of a life without Ari was too much to bear.

All I felt was emptiness.

I got up when I heard the garage door, rushing towards the sound.

"Goodbye, sunshine," he said when he saw me in the doorway, not pausing at all while he got into his car.

I watched as he backed out, and drove away...leaving me there, my heart in tatters.

———

I didn't know why I'd showed up to this shoot. Losing the love of your life was probably as good of an excuse as it got to skip work.

But here I was.

Going through the motions like I gave a fuck about this job, or this product, or anyone around me actually.

There were three of us on set today. And I was the only one sucking. We'd taken some shots with all of us, and now I was waiting on the sideline while the other two took a few pictures.

It was obvious that they were dating. There was an energy between them, a connection. Their bodies just fit together, like it was meant to be. I'd been in the middle of them, a square peg in a round hole with absolutely no chemistry.

And I didn't even want to try. Because *Ari* wasn't here.

People thought modeling was just staring into a lens... looking pretty. But it required emotion. It required a mood, a fierceness.

It required you to care.

And I just didn't.

The only emotion I was feeling at the moment...was numbness.

I aimlessly pulled up Instagram, scrolling through my feed. And like the universe was determined to fuck me up today...there were Ari and me in a Renage ad.

The two models in front of me had nothing compared to the two of us. The connection between us had been dazzling, tangible...they hadn't been able to take their eyes off us.

We were special.

Until we weren't.

A text came through and all I felt was dread.

Because it was Clark.

Not Ari.

Clark had still been trying, texting me constantly..but now

under the guise of *friends*. Most of the time I didn't answer. Because why would I?

Clark: Thinking of you. Has Mr. Hockey Stick done anything psycho lately? I'm always here for you. I want to help.

I grimaced, a flash of anger skittering through me. Ari wasn't a psycho. He was questionable...there was a difference. And the offer to "help" me was a joke. He wanted to help me alright...help me right back to New York. With the Shepfields. In high society. Stuck in a life I didn't want.

It made me think of all the times Ari had offered to help me—the times he actually had. And yeah, he'd wanted me to be his and obviously done everything to make that happen... but he'd also always wanted me to be, well...me.

We had an argument once. Actually, *I* had the argument. Ari had been perfectly calm and wonderful. I'd been stuck in my head, in a self hatred spiral before a shoot, feeling completely inadequate and insecure because of the number on the scale...

"What if I don't want to model?" I screamed. *"What if I want to be a barista? Or keep waiting tables. What will you think of me then?"*

"I think I'll just set up shop wherever you're working and get nice and fat ordering food and coffee all day so I can be with you," Ari said calmly. He gripped my chin. *"Sunshine, the only thing I want for you is happiness. In whatever form that takes. You don't have to be anything for me to love you. You just have to be you."*

"You just have to be you."

The words echoed through two more outfit changes.

Not for the first time, I wondered who I even really was.

The shoot finished, and I stepped outside of the warehouse, staring around the concrete jungle that was L.A. Most people thought of L.A. as Hollywood and palm trees and the ocean when they thought of this place.

But most of it was just...gray.

I walked down the sidewalk to head to my car, and I tripped, falling to the ground and scraping my knees and palms like an idiot.

"Fuck!" I winced, because my knee was definitely bleeding.

"Are you alright?" a voice asked, and I glanced over at a concerned looking man with bright green eyes.

They kind of reminded me of Ari's.

"I'm fine," I murmured, striding away quickly, not wanting to look at him anymore.

It was going to be like that forever, wasn't it? Always looking for Ari in every face that I passed. When someone had your soul, pieces of you would always search for them.

Forever.

I got in my car and stared down at my palms. They were red and irritated, and the skin was scuffed. They would heal soon, my body had always recovered easily from injuries.

It was the inside of me that I'd never been able to get better.

But why was that? Why hadn't I ever been able to figure my shit out?

I'd been a sad story since I was ten years old. And for the most part, I'd just been *content* with that. Or maybe not content...maybe just unwilling to do anything about it because I never felt like I could.

I drove down the street, thinking about all the things I hated about myself...that I wanted to change.

A light turned red in front of me, and I pulled to a stop, pulling down the visor and staring at myself in the mirror. Taking in my reflection. Trying to find something that I liked.

I shook my head and sighed, slamming the visor up as the light turned green.

Thirty minutes later, I pulled into Ari's garage. I guess, since it was a rental, it was going to be no one's garage since he was leaving.

A hitched sob burst out of my mouth and I leaned forward, trying to push down the pain. Because I couldn't handle it.

I froze then, realization sliding through me. That's what I was always doing. I was always "pushing down the pain." I'd always just told myself I couldn't handle it.

But I was *here*, wasn't I?

I mean, my father had killed my mother...and then himself, and I was still *here*. I'd lived in a group home and then been adopted by abusive, cold assholes. And I was still *here*. I'd cut and I'd purged and I'd wanted to die...and yet I was still...*here*.

I'd saved myself from a miserable life in New York. I'd done that. I'd come here and started a career. I'd been supporting myself. I'd let love in even when I was scared...

Cheater. Fat. Ugly. Stupid. Pathetic.

The words sprang from inside of me...but this time, instead of just pushing them back down where they would fester and rise up another day, I really looked at them.

I looked at each word as I got out of the car and walked into the empty, sad house. I looked until I was standing in front of the bathroom mirror, looking at...*myself.*

Cheater. Fat. Ugly. Stupid. Pathetic.

With trembling hands, I grabbed the lipstick tube I'd hastily used before running to the shoot. It was a hot, vibrant red, a coat of armor for the day, or so I'd thought.

Cheater. Fat. Ugly.

I etched each word into the mirror, every letter written out in fiery red.

Stupid. Pathetic.

I screamed.

Over and over, letting it all out, clawing at the ideas each of the words represented. I smeared the lipstick with my hands, my arms, until the words were nothing. Until they meant nothing.

No more. I wasn't going to do this. Not ever again.

"Let's get something perfectly fucking clear, sunshine. You didn't cheat on Clark. You were never supposed to be with him. He was a fucking imposter, holding you back from your destiny. Clark wasn't your soulmate. You weren't supposed to be with him. You were always supposed to be with me."

"I'm obsessed with you, crazy over you, in fact. I can't stand to be apart from you for any length of time. So when you tell me you hate this perfect fucking body that I worship with every part of my fucking soul...well, we can't have that, sunshine."

"You're perfect."

Ari's voice in my head clawed at the other words, drowning them out until all I could hear were his good ones.

I was gasping for breath as I stared at the aftermath of my fit, red smeared everywhere.

And then I laughed, the sound of it bubbling in the air around me, because I felt a little bit lighter. A little bit better...

I allowed myself to revel in the feeling for a few minutes...

And then I cleaned it all up, first the mirror, wiping away every red smear until it was sparkling and clean, not a mark of the words remaining.

Then I got undressed, stepping into the warm water of the shower. I cleaned myself, gently rubbing at the stains until they couldn't be seen, allowing my hands to trail all over my body, taking in my skin, and my bones, and my curves.

Taking in me.

After I was completely clean, I stepped out of the shower,

and stared into the mirror again at my now bare face. Water dropped in rivulets from my sopping wet hair, sliding down my body before they were caught in the towel I'd wrapped around myself.

"I'm perfect," I whispered, trying the words out on my tongue. I'd said them with Ari before, but never by myself. Never like this. "I'm perfect. I'm perfect. I'm perfect. I'm perfect!" I screamed. And I heard his voice in my head, cheering me on, because the only thing he'd ever wanted from me…was to be happy.

I sank to the ground, hugging myself, rocking back and forth as I chanted the words in my head.

I'd spent my whole life saying there was a reason I was like this. I cut to get rid of the pain. I purged to get rid of the self-loathing. I took pills to numb myself.

And even if I'd called myself the villain, I'd used all those things as excuses for why I was. *They'd* been the cause.

But really…*I* was the villian. I was the one *choosing* all of this. Choosing to stare into the mirror and hate myself. Over and over again.

I'd said I was tired of it. But what had I ever done to fix it?

Nothing. I hadn't done anything.

And that stopped today. I pulled myself off the floor and grabbed my makeup bag, sliding out the razors I kept in a small side pocket. Staring at them for a second, I threw them into the toilet.

And then I flushed.

My scale was on the floor. I grabbed it and strode outside, and I threw it onto the hard concrete so it shattered into a million pieces. I grabbed a broom and cleaned it all up, the remnants going in the trash.

The model agency actually had a mental health program. You could get free sessions of counseling. I didn't know if the therapists were good, but contacting them was a start. I filled out the form online and set up an appointment for two days from now.

I sat back on the couch, feeling a thrill of satisfaction. Because for the first time, I'd taken actual steps.

After getting dressed in some sweats, I ate. I cooked eggs and bacon and pancakes, and I ate every last bite. Until I was full.

Something I never did.

And it felt incredible.

I trailed my fork through the maple syrup Ari had gotten Miss Carlie to pick up since it was my favorite. And I thought about him.

Ari.

Everything he'd done. Everything that happened. Everything.

I knew what he'd done wasn't normal. It didn't fit into society's idea of right and wrong.

But...had it really been that bad?

It had been over the top, crazy possessive.

But had it been *bad*?

Would I have given Ari a chance–with Clark in my ear every second, hammering me with *I love you's*, and guilt, and the familiar?

I wasn't sure. Thinking about the scared ghost of a girl I'd been that day when Ari had walked into the restaurant, rear-ranging my entire life like a shooting star in the cosmos...I don't know that I would have ever been brave enough to be with him.

The only reason we'd ended up together was because he'd been the brave one. Because he'd taken the steps that I couldn't. Nothing he'd done had ever hurt me. It had just softened me, allowed me to accept what he was offering.

What was that saying, *all's well that ends well to end up with you.*

I shook my head, because what I was thinking sounded crazy...and yet.

A knock sounded on the door and I sighed, dragging myself off the barstool to open it. Solicitors couldn't get past the gates so guests were always at the door for an approved reason.

Through the glass I saw a professional-looking woman dressed in a sharp gray suit. I didn't recognize her at all.

I opened the door.

"Hi," she said warmly. "I'm Ashley Tenney, your divorce attorney. You hadn't called, so I thought I would stop by. Mr. Lancaster had indicated time was of the essence when we'd talked."

My mouth opened and closed, like a dying fish. Because I'd forgotten for a second just how far gone Ari and I had become, and now there was a divorce attorney standing at my door.

She cleared her throat, and I realized I'd been standing there, staring at her...

"Ms. Tenney," I said, my voice all of a sudden shaky from the tears. "Please, come in."

She nodded, entering my home with a briefcase in hand. Her gaze swept across the room, and I wondered if she could sense the shattered dreams hanging in the air.

I gestured toward the living room, where we both took a seat. The silence was palpable, broken only by the distant sounds of the city outside.

"Thank you for coming," I finally managed to say, my voice still trembling. Even though I wasn't thankful at all.

I wasn't ready for this.

Not even close.

The lawyer regarded me with a sympathetic expression. "I know this is an incredibly difficult time for you. Divorce is never easy."

I stared at her, my eyes welling up with fresh tears. Difficult was the understatement of the century, especially when... I didn't want it.

But I should want it, right?

She gave a gentle, understanding nod when I didn't say anything. "It's important to remember that you're not alone in this. I'm here to guide you through the process and ensure that your rights and interests are protected."

She pulled out a folder and began to arrange documents neatly on the coffee table in front of us.

"Mr. Lancaster has offered to give you whatever you want," Ashley began, her tone measured. "At the very least, he wants to provide you with ten million dollars as a settlement."

I felt like the air had been sucked out of the room, and I could hardly process what I was hearing. My voice came out in a shocked squeak. "Ten million dollars?"

Ashley nodded, her gaze steady on me. "That's correct."

My head was spinning. The idea of accepting any money felt disgusting. Money couldn't mend the broken pieces of my heart.

"I...I don't want any of it," I finally managed to say, my voice barely above a whisper.

Ashley nodded again, her professionalism unwavering. "Very well. We can proceed with the divorce without any financial settlement. Now, let me explain the legal process and the ins and outs of divorce."

As she delved into the complexities of what lay ahead, I tried to focus on her words, but my mind kept drifting back to Ari.

"Here are these documents to go through," she said, pointing out certain sections I was supposed to pay attention to.

I stared at the documents in shock, my eyes scanning the

unfamiliar name on the divorce papers. "This isn't the right name," I managed to choke out, my voice trembling. "My maiden name is Blake Shepfield."

She furrowed her brow, flipping through the paperwork before producing another set of documents. She showed me a legal declaration that the Shepfields' adoption had been declared null and void. "Mr. Lancaster said he took care of this?" she inquired, her tone laced with confusion.

I could hardly process what I was hearing. The realization hit me like a ton of bricks. Ari had somehow managed to undo my adoption by the Shepfields. It was an incredible legal feat, and my mind reeled at the implications of it all.

As the lawyer continued to speak, her words became a distant murmur in my ears. I couldn't help but tune her out, my thoughts consumed with memories of Ari and our relationship.

"Give me your pain."

"Tell me where it hurts."

"I love you."

"I see you, sunshine. I'll ace every test."

"I'll make you happy," he said. *"It might take a while, but someday I'll make you happy for the rest of your life."*

The pen clattered to the table.

What the fuck was I doing?

I'd always let life happen to me. I'd gone through the motions, accepting all the crap it threw at me.

And then it decided to gift me Ari Lancaster...my fucking soulmate. And I was going to fuck it all up.

Yeah, he was a stalker. And questionable. And he'd done terrible things to ensure he and I were together...

But he also possessed the most beautiful soul of anyone I'd ever met.

And he was offering me all of it.

What the fuck was I doing?

I needed to find him somehow, convince him he was my forever.

I wasn't going to *let* this divorce happen.

I was all in.

He could stalk me whenever. Just as long as I got him.

"I'm sorry. I won't be signing this today," I said, springing from my chair. I grabbed my phone and dialed Ari's number frantically, each ring feeling like an eternity.

It went straight to voicemail.

"Ari, we need to talk. Please call me as soon as you get this. I don't want to be over. I never want to be over."

I ran to my drawer to get my ring, needing the weight on my finger to reassure me everything could still be saved. But it wasn't there.

He must have taken it with him.

Panicking, I called three more times with the same result.

Okay, what should I do? I didn't know what time his flight was. He had left this morning. I pulled up the airline schedule for the day. There were flights leaving every thirty minutes. That wasn't helpful.

"Mr. Lancaster mentioned a flight at 8:45 tonight when I last spoke to him," the lawyer mentioned. She was standing at the front door, her briefcase packed up and in her hand.

I glanced at my phone. It was seven. I didn't know if I could make it in time.

But I had to try. Even if I missed the flight, I had to try.

I could get a flight to Dallas if I missed it.

I just couldn't let him go.

Ashley smiled at me. "I'll see myself out," she murmured, before opening the door and leaving.

I ran to the garage, jumping into the Maserati he'd bought me, turning the ignition.

It stuttered and whined…and wouldn't turn on.

What?

Please, please, please, I chanted to whatever god was in the heavens as I tried it over and over again. I didn't have the key for his truck..and I didn't know how to ride his motorcycle.

Fuck! I slammed my hand on the steering wheel, wincing at the bite of pain from my scraped palms.

Okay. Uber. Yes. That's what I'd do.

My hands were shaking as I pulled up the app and scheduled a ride.

Fifteen minutes?

This was L.A. There were Ubers everywhere. Why was it fifteen fucking minutes?

I took a deep breath and tried to call him again.

But he still didn't answer.

Had he taken an earlier flight? Was he already gone? Had he moved on for good?

I jumped out of the car and jogged out to the driveaway, checking the app every five seconds to see if the pickup time had improved.

Fuck, the driver had canceled. Fuck, fuck, fuck!

I scheduled another ride, whimpering when I saw it would be *another* fifteen minutes.

Frantic tears were sliding down my face, and I was contemplating fucking hitchhiking if something didn't go my way in the next minute.

I shouldn't have let him leave this morning. I should have figured my shit out sooner. Should've talked to him sooner.

I fucked up, but I wasn't going to give up.

I wasn't going to let *him* give up either.

I pulled out my phone.

> Me: We're not breaking. You said you wouldn't let us, and I'm saying it now. You're mine, Ari Lancaster. You'd better not get on that fucking plane.

And then...

There was a shift in the air, and I knew...without even seeing him.

My breath hitched and I lifted my gaze from my phone to the end of the driveaway. And there stood Ari, a windswept constellation I was desperate to see.

I wiped at my tears knowing I looked a mess as he walked towards me. No makeup, baggy sweats, wet hair in a bun...

"You're perfect," he murmured, as if he could read my mind.

"You're here," I sniffed, and his steps quickened.

Before he could take another step though, I was running, and he was scooping me up in his arms.

I was breathing him in. My tears all over him, peppering his face with kisses because I was so fucking relieved. My legs were wrapped around him, his hands on my ass, and my arms around his neck.

I was touching him. He was here. He hadn't gotten on that plane.

"Hi," he finally breathed, and I giggled, staring into his green eyes that I realized I never would have seen in anyone else–because no one else's compared.

"You didn't leave," I whispered.

"Nope."

"You blocked my ex."

"I did," he said, with absolutely no remorse in his voice.

"You planted drugs in his car to get rid of him."

"Yep."

"You got him on the no-fly list."

"Mmmhmm. And I'd do it again."

"You're crazy about me, aren't you, Ari Lancaster?"

He grinned, and the butterflies inside me, the one that looked like his tattoo...they went wild.

"Fucking insane for you, sunshine."

I was smiling crazily, but I didn't care. Because I hadn't known the human soul could feel this much relief and happiness at once.

And I was going to revel in it.

"Good. Because I figured out I'm crazy for you too."

"It's about time, baby," he murmured, stalking towards the house. "But I would have waited forever."

I continued to smile dreamily at him as he opened the front door and stepped inside.

"But thank fuck I didn't have to."

CHAPTER 26

BLAKE

We stood in the front foyer, still staring at each other with silly, insane grins.

And then…it was like a storm broke.

Ari's lips crashed against mine, his hand cradling my face. Staring at me soulfully, like I was his biggest dream come true.

I didn't feel like I deserved it after I had tried to break us. But I wasn't going to point that out.

He was giving me another chance. I'd spend the rest of my life showing him that wasn't a mistake.

Ari pulled back and I tried to chase his lips, but he held my head in place. "No more pushing me away. Because I can't take it. I need you. I've been *dying* without you."

I opened my mouth to say "yes," but he placed a finger on my lips. "I need you to really think about it before you agree. Because after this, you're never going to get another chance. *I will not let you go.* No matter what. No matter what happens. You will be mine and I will be yours. And that will be the end of our story."

He continued to hold me with one arm while he reached into his pocket.

"I think this belongs to you," he murmured, holding it up for me to look at.

"It does," I responded, no hesitation. Not anymore. And his face was giddy as he slipped it on my finger.

It felt like it belonged there now. It felt, well...perfect.

I stared up at him. And for the first time in weeks, there was no doubt. It was like it had washed away, disappeared like the lipstick stains down the drain. And somehow I knew, it was never going to come back.

He was it for me. Maybe he could be a hero and a villain at the same time, just like I could be.

And maybe it was what worked for us. Maybe it was the only thing that *would* work when you had someone with so much still to work through like I did.

But at least now I *was* finally working through it.

"I never want you to let me go," I told him, staring into those grass green eyes, and seeing my whole future in their depths. "I kept telling you I couldn't find anything wrong with you even as I fell apart over and over and you were there for me," I whispered. "And then when I found out everything...I immediately wasn't there for *you*. And it's taken me all this time to realize...there's still nothing wrong with you. I think you're perfect just as you are, Ari Lancaster. Perfect for *me*."

He closed his eyes, exquisite pain passing over his features. I knew what he was feeling. It hurt how much we loved each other. Your soul wasn't supposed to exist in another person, yet here we were. Ari had captured mine, and I finally had gotten to a place where I could truly let him have it without any reservations.

Ari lifted me up and my legs wrapped around him. After so many weeks, it felt like I had come home, like I was finally where I belonged. I could picture our souls intertwining, finally breathing again after so long.

"I'm crazy for you," I whispered, brushing my lips against his as he walked towards our bedroom.

"Right back at you, sunshine."

He laid me down on the bed, his fingers pushing into my leggings and panties and immediately gliding through my sensitive flesh.

I whimpered, because I'd been so empty without him. We'd been having sex multiple times a day before everything had happened, and living without his particular bit of "enlightenment"...that in itself had been misery.

Ari rubbed against my clit, pressing soft kisses on my lips and my cheeks and my neck until I was melting into the bed, everything inside me wanting him with everything I had.

"I've been dying without this," he whispered as he ripped off my clothes frantically until I was laying there, completely bare to his still fully clothed form.

"Fucking hell," he muttered as his eyes danced across my skin. "Can't get over how perfect you are. Can't believe I lived without this for weeks."

His fingers slid through my folds, tracing down my seam until he was circling my asshole, the tip of his finger sliding in.

I knew what I wanted then. I wanted to give him the one part of my body that no one else ever had.

"Take me there," I whispered, watching as understanding lit up his gaze. He did a sharp inhale and his gaze went wide.

"You want me to..."

I nodded and then moaned as his finger pressed in further.

"Yes. I want you to fuck my ass. Have every part of me. Always."

"Fucking hell, sunshine. You don't have to ask me twice," he growled. Ari abruptly flipped me over so I was on my hands and knees on the bed. My legs were shaking as his palm glided up my back before coming back down and massaging my cheeks with both hands.

"Drop down baby," he murmured as his thumbs spread my cheeks wide. I laid there with my face on the soft sheets, my breaths coming out in short gasps. Suddenly, he groaned and slapped my ass before gently massaging the spot that burned. The flat of his tongue licked through my folds, hot and wet, before sliding up to my ass and teasing the hole.

"You're going to fucking kill me, sunshine. Look at how sexy you are," he growled as he moved away. A second later, I heard the soft click of a bottle opening before his lubed finger returned to my hole, pushing inside and rubbing around. His tongue returned to my core, sliding in and out as his fingers stretched my puckered flesh. He continued to work my clit, and my body stayed relaxed even as he pushed another finger into my hole. It was an entirely different sensation than when he fucked my vagina. The sensations were ten times more intense.

My hips were arching back against his fingers, before he abruptly pulled them out. Warm wet lube dripped down my crack and he dragged his fingers through it, spreading it around.

"What a fucking good girl," he growled as he worked on stretching my tight ring of muscle.

The sensations he was giving me were driving me insane, and I was crying out with every pass. I glanced back, my eyes widening as I watched him spread the oil all over his cock. I wanted to watch him jerk off one day. The hotness of it might make me pass out.

Ari slid his dick through my crack and I shuddered, anticipating what was about to happen. I felt his thick head pressing against my opening, and then pushed.

You can't really imagine what it's going to feel like to have a huge pierced cock in your ass but...it was incredible.

I buried my face into the mattress, arching my hips back against him as he worked himself deeper, little by little as he gave me time to adjust.

"Look at you, you're taking my cock so good. What a perfect fucking ass. Take a little bit more, sunshine. Just a little more," he pleaded before he slid all the way in. A yelp burst out of me and he rubbed my spine, soothing away my nervous energy.

I thought I felt filled to the brim when his dick was in my other hole, but having it inside me like this? I couldn't think, I could barely breathe...fuck...all I could do was feel.

There was a reason that I'd never been able to do this with anyone else. The intimacy of it was completely overpowering. Having him deep inside of me was the most intense thing I'd ever experienced. He truly owned me.

"Tell me you're mine," he ordered as he fucked me gently, his long strokes slowly speeding up as I thrust my hips back against him. One arm went around my throat and he was lifting me back until my body was arched, my head cushioned against his shoulder, as I stared up at him.

"I'm yours. I'm yours. I'm yours," I chanted as his other hand moved from my hip to my clit and he played with it, gently circling and rubbing.

"Tell me you'll never leave me," he ordered as his thrusts sped up.

"Never. I promise," I gasped.

"Good girl," he purred as his fingers dipped into my core, fucking me with the same rhythm as the push and pull of his dick in my ass.

My vision was blurry, and I realized it was because there were tears streaming down my face, the euphoria of everything breaking me open. I felt closer to him in that moment than I'd ever thought possible. And what was building inside of me was a stronger sensation than I'd ever experienced, like lightning running through my veins.

"Fuck, your ass is choking me," he said through gritted teeth as he rutted into me. "Come for me, sunshine. Give me what I want, because I'm so close, and I'm not coming without you."

He fucked into me harder, and that little extra bite of pain sent me soaring, the edges of my vision darkening until there was just a pinprick of light visible as every single nerve ending in my body exploded with pleasure.

"I love you, I love you, I love you," were the last things I heard as the world faded around me.

I didn't realize I'd passed out until I woke up lying next to him under the cool sheets. He was propped up on one arm, his gaze grazing my skin, his finger trailing down my side. I moaned and moved, realizing how achy I felt. Which was expected when you let a nine inch rod up your ass.

"How long have I been out?" I murmured dreamily, stretching languidly. It had been so long since I'd felt any...peace.

And that was all I felt right then. That and overwhelming, starry eyed, obsessed love.

"Thirty minutes or so," he said. "Just enough for me to clean the both of us up."

I nodded, not feeling concerned about it at all. Everything inside of me knew that I was safe with him.

Plus, we were already married, so there wasn't much else he could do to surprise me.

"I'm fucking exhausted," he admitted. "But I'm scared to close my eyes. I'm scared this is all going to be a dream and I'm going to wake up with you still hating me."

"I'm sorry," I whispered. Because even after everything he had done, I had so much to apologize for too.

"I couldn't love you like you deserved when I hated

myself so much," I admitted. And it was the truth. Hating yourself was hard work. It was hard to find room for anything else.

"And how's that going?" he murmured, his finger moving to my cheek as he softly brushed against my skin.

"It's a work in progress. Maybe it will always be a work in progress. Maybe I'll always have some sort of sadness or self-loathing trying to suck me in. It's just…I'm not going to let it anymore. I deserve better than that. *You* deserve better than that."

"I stand by my opinion that I've always thought you were perfect, no matter what." He seemed fascinated by the answering tear that slid down my cheek.

"And I love you for that, but I'm ready to see what I—we can be like without me constantly getting in the way."

"I'm here for you no matter what. But I want you to know that I've fallen in love with every part of you. There's nothing you could do or say or be…that I wouldn't still want."

Was it possible to die from happiness? Because when he said those sorts of things, he meant them. He really saw something inside me that I never could.

He really was my soulmate.

Just then, my stomach growled, and he snorted before sitting up. My gaze got caught on those incredible abs of his, and I worked on controlling my drool.

That was my husband.

Crap. That was the first time I'd really said that in my head. I'd been too scared of it.

The feeling was great. Better than great. Magical.

Ari Lancaster was mine in every way possible and there was nothing anyone could do about it. It was like I had stumbled upon my own personal miracle.

Mrs. Lancaster.

I also liked the sound of that.

"What's in that pretty head of yours, baby?" Ari said as he slid off the bed. I was about to answer...but something gold caught my eye.

On his dick.

"What the—" I leaned forward, sure my eyes were playing tricks. Was that a ring attached to the tip of cock? And not just a ring...the smooth gold of it really resembled a...

"Like my wedding ring?" he said proudly, swinging his dick around like a fucking helicopter. "Got it on our wedding night. Seemed fitting, don't you think?" He thrusted his hips forward so I could get a better look.

"You have a wedding ring pierced through the tip of your cock," I said slowly, because really, it wasn't something you saw everyday. Or ever, actually.

"Yep. Now I've always got my ring with me. And judging by the way you were just screaming as I fucked your perfect little asshole...it feels good too. I got the "pleasure for her" ring, so I'll have to leave a good review."

I didn't know whether I wanted to laugh, or jump him. Something about it was weirdly hot, even when he swung it around like an elephant's trunk.

Still fascinated, and utterly bemused by what he'd done, I reached out and brushed my fingers across the smooth tip.

He groaned and thrust into my hand. "Fuck, baby. I need to feed you, and we aren't going anywhere if you keep staring and touching my dick like it's the fucking holy grail."

I leaned forward and dragged my tongue along the pierced shaft. "I think I've decided that I'm hungry for something else," I purred as I licked into his pierced slit. "I want to see if that ring feels as good down my throat."

His whole body shivered and a smooth, sly grin crossed his beautiful lips.

"I have a better idea, sunshine. I think we both should eat."

He flopped on the bed and within seconds had me straddling his face as his tongue fucked into me.

Well then, I thought, staring down at the pierced masterpiece in front of me, the gold of the wedding ring glinting in the sun streaming in from the window.

Time to feast.

———

Ari

She'd fallen asleep with me still inside her, and somehow she was still sleeping, even though I was fully hard...again. There was a blissed out expression on her face as I obsessively stared at her though, like she only felt complete like this too.

I was in heaven. This was how I always wanted it to be. Us together. Connected. Forever.

From the moment I'd laid eyes on Blake as a young boy, I'd known she was it. There was an unexplainable pull, an undeniable force that drew me to her. She was my very own kryptonite, and once I'd made that decision that I couldn't live without her, I'd also made her the only person that could actually destroy me.

I couldn't live without her.

And once I had that firmly established in my personal values, every step after that had been not only necessary...but the only step I could take.

I would have never let her go.

Leaving the Cobras midseason—yeah, that was never going to happen. When I made a commitment, I went all in.

Letting her divorce me? Also, never going to happen.

But I had needed a "come to Jesus" moment, where Blake

realized she was just as in this as I was. That she couldn't let go either.

And that...had required a little push.

So I'd hired an actress to pose as a divorce attorney, and I'd had a friend put together fake papers that had no legal validity. She could have signed those fucking things a million times and she still would have been married to me. If she had for some reason requested to take them to the courthouse herself...I had a plant in there too that would've pretended it was all real.

There'd been a million contingencies I'd had set up, but they all had one end goal...to get her back.

To help her to see that we were necessary to each other's existence.

I'd been waiting at a coffee shop around the corner until she left for her shoot. I'd followed her there, making sure she was alright, dying when she fell and I couldn't help her up. I'd followed her home, watching her on the house "security" cameras I'd installed for the rest of the day.

Watching as she'd destroyed her scale and actually eaten. I was sure there was more that happened in the bathroom that I couldn't see. But for once, it felt like maybe they were all good things.

Watching her with the fake lawyer.

Torture.

Even knowing it was fake, I'd had all the emotions watching the feed. Offering her money had even been a part of the plan, because I'd realized one of her hangups was all the money the Shepfields had—or pretended to have—and the way they'd shoved it down her throat, forcing her to be someone she wasn't. I'd known she would say no, even though I would literally give her all my earthly possessions to make her happy.

I saw when it finally clicked, when she realized that she couldn't live without me either. She had raced to her car...

But of course, I'd snuck in and removed one of its gaskets after her shoot...so she couldn't go anywhere.

Linc's idea, strangely enough.

Using the app I had reinstalled on her phone, I saw when she ordered an Uber. I'd logged into the account and canceled her ride so it didn't get there before I did.

I'd had a plan for everything. It may have sounded extreme. But I knew my girl. I knew she had to really feel it, she had to feel how much our relationship meant to her. She had to really let go of all the shit that had been holding her back, and come to the decision that she was all in. No matter what.

I was still struggling to believe she was really here though, that I was inside of her, my cock snuggled in her perfect warmth. I'd had moments of doubt, wondering if I really would have to kidnap her away to make her see reason.

Thank fuck it hadn't come to that.

I definitely would have done it. Linc had sent me the site for the cuffs...

"Ari," she murmured dreamily, and I brushed a kiss against her lips, because...why not. She was perfection.

I couldn't help but start to move, the ring making my tip so sensitive I could orgasm almost instantly if I let myself.

She stirred again, and I really wanted to see those gorgeous eyes of hers, even if she could use some more sleep.

"Baby, let me fuck you," I purred, and her eyes slowly blinked open as I lazily thrusted in and out of her. I'd never get enough. I knew that.

"Feels so good," she whispered as I rolled my body, expertly keeping us connected because I was an awesome sex god, until I was laying on my back and she was staring down at me. Her hair was kissing the skin on my chest as she bounced on top of me. I watched, fascinated, as my cock stretched her pink, wet pussy, sucking me in, swallowing every inch as I thrust into her, unable to stop myself from taking over.

"Touch yourself, sunshine," I murmured, groaning as she obediently slid her hands across her dusty pink nipples, tugging on them as she stared down at me like my darkest fantasy come to life. I played with her clit while she played with her glorious breasts, and I was so close to coming, it physically hurt.

"Please come for me, sweetheart," I begged as she fucked herself faster on my shaft, withdrawing all the way to the tip before slamming back down. It was so fucking good. Her breasts were bouncing up and down, the feel of her was outrageous. I was more convinced than ever that she was made just for me.

I was on the edge of dying when she started to come, a rosy blush spreading across her skin, soft gasps falling from her lush mouth.

Fuck.

I pulled myself out of her, flipping her to her back as I fucked my hand. In just a second I was coming, my cum coating her smooth skin. I stared at it for a second, admiring it as I took a mental picture, before I spread it all over her stomach and her breasts, softly licking at her nipple before I spread more cum on her chest.

There. All better.

I decide right then and there to coat her in my cum every day. I couldn't stitch us together, so this seemed like a good alternative.

"Ari, I love you," she whispered, another tear slipping down her skin.

I licked it up, wanting every part of her I could get.

The way she said it was different now, like she'd finally

found her peace with it—the fact that she'd found her soul-mate at ten, and that I'd made sure we were reunited. I'd do anything to keep us together forever.

"I love you so much it hurts," I told her, and it was the truth. Our love was a living, breathing, painful thing.

Because having someone else own your soul was always going to be a painful, *beautiful* experience.

One I wouldn't trade for anything.

One I would fight for with my very last breath.

And finally, I knew Blake was going to fight for it too.

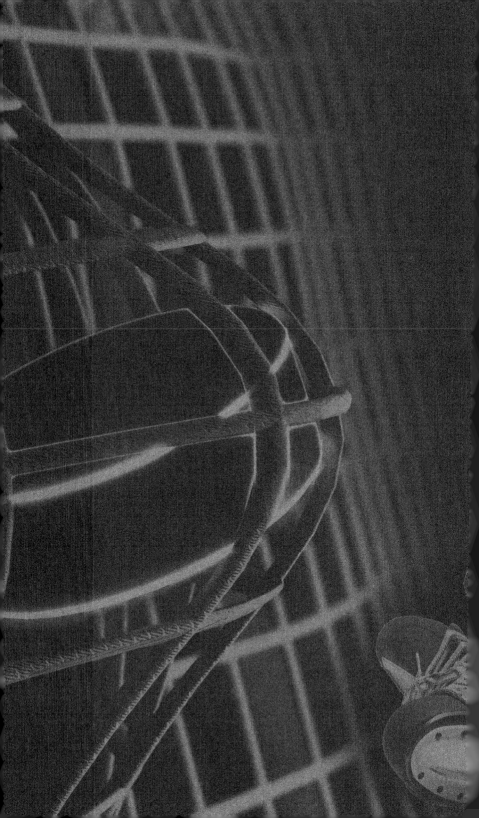

CHAPTER 27

ARI

Months Later...

T onight was the night, the game that would decide if
we made the playoffs. Or at least partially decide.
Thanks to some late season losses, we weren't
entirely in charge of our destiny. We had to beat Seattle, but
Dallas also had to beat Detroit for us to get in. Dallas, unfortunately, would be playing at the same time as us, so we
wouldn't know the outcome of their game until ours was
done.

I wasn't as worried about that second part though; Linc
had already promised he'd do whatever it took to get Dallas
the win. And my golden nugget of a best friend never let me
down.

The bigger concern was that *we* had to win—a tougher
hurdle for sure. Tommy had strained his quad muscle last
game and wasn't at 100%. Another of our defensemen,
Caffrey, had the flu this week, and Soto...well, Soto just
sucked.

I wanted to help my boys to the playoffs. We wouldn't be

winning the Cup—we weren't good enough—but I wanted the playoffs at least.

No matter what though, I'd stay on cloud nine, the same cloud I'd been living on since Blake had decided she absolutely wanted to be Mrs. Lancaster. Now I just lived in a constant state of happiness, like an eternal high.

It was AWESOME.

Blake Lancaster was the most amazing, beautiful, kind, perfect angel in existence, and getting to be with her was the best fucking thing in the world.

10/10 would recommend.

My phone buzzed next to me on the locker room bench where I was relaxing as I got in the zone.

"Hey there, golden boy," I drawled pulling him up on Facetime.

"Just making sure you showed up to the game and didn't get stuck again," Lincoln snorted, raking his hands through his golden god hair.

"That was one time!"

"It happened last week, buddy! And you somehow thought it would be a good idea to call *me* instead of 911... after you got your pierced dick stuck inside your wife! What the hell was I going to do? You were literally inside her as you were talking to me!"

"Pssh, your calming presence helped me to relax enough to get it out. You were very helpful."

Lincoln sighed, pretending to be annoyed with me. He was such a funny guy.

"Anyways..."

'Anyways...my gigantic pierced cock that you're wildly jealous over is not stuck in Blake," I said, right as Walker sat down next to me.

The weirdo fell off the bench at my comment. Even

though it was perfectly normal. A known risk for baller penises everywhere.

"Did Disney just pass out?" Lincoln snorted, raising an eyebrow, and I shook my head as Walker dragged himself off the floor, glaring at me the whole time, and sat back on the bench.

"Yes," I sighed with mock exasperation. "Definitely not 'circle of trust' behavior."

Walker huffed next to me and I gave him a little wink.

"Okay, focus, Lancaster. I'm going to go out there and score a million goals so we win, and you're going to hit a bunch of people and make sure Disney gets proper protection...deal?"

"Why does my job sound so much funner than yours?" I wondered aloud.

Lincoln snorted again and then hesitated. "Can you take me off Facetime?" he asked.

I frowned and nodded, making it a regular call and holding the phone up to my ear.

"What's up?"

"Year's almost up." There was a question in his voice, a question that was still an easy answer. Blake was completely on board even if it meant we'd have to fly back and forth to L.A. for her jobs sometimes.

"Yeah, what's your question?" I asked innocently, just because I wanted to hear him say it. Lincoln Daniels luvvvved Ari Lancaster.

"Are—are you still coming home?" He sounded so un-Daniels-like, a name usually synonymous with cocky badass. It was hil-ari-ous.

Hmmm, I never noticed, my name was in that word.

Fitting.

"Ari?"

"Sorry, what did you ask?"

"Fuck you," he growled, finally catching on to my little joke.

I glanced at Walker who was pretending not to be eavesdropping even though tension was threaded through his whole body. Poor Disney, he didn't know yet that I was going to make sure he came with me. With how well he'd done, and with Bender announcing his retirement from the Dallas net, it should be an easy sell.

"Yes, Linc. Your snookums is still planning on coming home."

There was a long silence, almost like my buddy was having trouble holding in his emotions.

"Snookums?" he finally said, sounding infinitely happier than he had before my answer.

"Not good? I'll keep workshopping."

I was smiling weirdly into the phone, but it was warranted. Lincoln Daniels was going to be my best friend forever.

"Make 'em cry out there tonight, Lancaster, and tell Disney good luck," Lincoln added as I heard someone in the background calling his name.

"You just score those goals," I answered before hanging up.

"Lincoln, um...did he say hi?" Walker asked, all cute and simp like. His usual M.O.

"He may have said good luck."

Walker perked up. "Wait...he said that? He said good luck?"

"I said he "may" have said good luck."

"Ari," Walker whined, looking so pathetic I had to give him what he wanted.

"Fine, he *did* wish you good luck."

Walker jumped up and did a shimmy. I scoffed indignantly. "I tell you good luck all the fucking time, and I give you an ass tap! What else could you want?"

Walker froze mid shake of his ass. "Right, it's totally the same."

"You're placating me! I don't like placaters, Walker Davis. No ass tap for you tonight!"

He pretended to be chastened even as his whole fucking body shook with laughter.

I stared around the room. The rest of my teammates were all tense and gloomy, like they were already confident in a loss before the game even started. Which was stupid. Yes, the team had issues, but we'd beaten Seattle this year...twice. This wasn't going to do at all.

I stood up off the bench. "Disney, give me a tune," I ordered, and Walker wasted no time in grabbing his phone. A few seconds later, "Shake It Off" hit the locker room speakers.

As usual, Tay Tay's music was instant magic. Our teammates, even the most stoic ones, couldn't resist the infectious beat.

Walker led the charge, attempting a moonwalk that resembled a drunken stumble. Eddy's moves were wild and unpredictable, like a toddler on too much sugar. He twirled, spun, and even attempted the worm—actually not that bad.

I let myself go, bringing out my "dad moves," even though the only people calling me "daddy" tonight were going to be the Seattle forwards. I really gave it my all, complete with finger guns and a sprinkler dance.

The last notes faded and I grinned, because as usual, our "Shake It Off" had done its job. The team was much more relaxed.

Coach's pre-game speech was a fucking masterpiece. He got in our faces, reminding us of the blood, sweat, and tears we'd poured into this shit. "You've trained your asses off, played your asses off, and sacrificed *everything* for this moment!" he bellowed. "That jersey ain't just cloth and colors, fellas. It's a fuckin' symbol of our legacy, When you step on that ice, you're not just playing for yourselves. You're playing for every Cobra who's ever bled for this team, for this city!"

The whole team roared, and with one last "Cobras" cheer, it was game time.

As I stepped onto the ice, it felt familiar.

It was a surreal realization.

I'd started this season feeling like an alien who'd landed on a foreign planet. I'd dreaded every practice, convinced myself everything sucked, that I couldn't wait to leave. I'd counted down the fucking days.

But now...I realized I was going to miss this place. Somewhere along the way, it had started to feel, well...nice.

I went to the glass to make googly eyes at Blake, pointing behind her. She shot me a quizzical look and turned around, only to see an employee holding a sign that said, "Mrs. Lancaster is my baby angel face. Do Not Touch."

"Nice," she groaned, her face turning a beautiful tomato color.

"You look hot in that jersey, Mrs. Lancaster," I yelled as I skated away.

The game kicked off, and Seattle wasn't taking any prisoners. They hit us hard and fast, like a bunch of crazed bulls charging at a matador. Walker was a fucking rockstar. He blocked shot after shot, making it look easy in the net.

"That's my goalie!" I yelled as Walker made his twentieth save...of the period. And it wasn't that I was sucking...I was kicking ass. Seattle was just killing our forwards with Tommy playing injured.

Seattle got called for high sticking and we found ourselves on a power play. Tommy somehow came up with a burst of speed despite his injured leg, skating like a man possessed. He maneuvered through their defense and fired the puck. It bounced off one of Seattle's own men and ricocheted into the net. We all went nuts.

In the second period, Seattle tied us with some flashy moves and slick passes after Soto decided to drop his gloves and engage in a bare-knuckle brawl with a Seattle guy. We watched, bewildered, but I guess it was…progress. He wasn't trying to beat up his own teammate for once.

Still fucking hated him though. And I still hoped he fell off a cliff or got hit by a car.

But progress was progress.

By the third period, victory was within our grasp. I blocked shots like a human wall, taking hits and deflecting pucks like the "James Norris Memorial Trophy" winner I was. And in the final minutes, with their goalie pulled, we knew we had it. I knocked the puck loose and sent it to Tommy, who made the easy goal.

The final buzzer sounded, and the whole team skated towards the bench to find out the Dallas score. Some of the staff had been tracking it while we played, and Dallas and Detroit were currently tied 1-1, with three minutes left. The arena was already in full celebration mode, obviously forgetting there was one important piece of the puzzle left…but we were glued to one of the assistant coach's iPhones. Every passing second was agony, our collective gaze locked on the screen as if we could *will* the result.

And then it came—Lincoln had a breakaway shot and slipped the goal right in between the goalie's legs. Because golden boy was my fucking hero, he pointed to the nearest camera and blew a kiss.

I snatched that shit up as the rest of the team started celebrating.

We were playoff-bound, baby!

I turned to look for Blake and saw her running through the aisle of seats. I slipped past some of the guys and awkwardly ran up the steps, my blades smacking against the flooring.

"You did it," she screamed, jumping into my arms. I spun her around, burying my face in her neck. Visualizing what it would have been like to have found her before last year's Stanley Cup win.

Then it really would have been perfect.

Next year, I vowed to myself. *Next year I'd make that happen.*

Right then, the bigger victory–the only victory that really mattered–was that Blake was in my arms.

And it's where she would stay.

Forever.

———

Blake

The night became a blur of laughter, music, and the clinking of glasses as we threw back shots. Cobras' ownership had thrown an epic party, turning one of the arena's specialty function rooms into a wild celebration that had spilled out into the hallways and everywhere else in the arena. Someone said that Walker was on the ice with some girl, with nothing but a sock over his cock.

It was that kind of night.

I was definitely feeling it, my cheeks flushed and my laughter easy and carefree. Ari was equally intoxicated and we were currently making a very unstealthy escape from the ruckus…so we could fuck. Holding hands, we navigated through the maze of tipsy players, staff, and fans, our laughter bubbling up as we tried to stay upright. The music from the party grew fainter with each step, and soon, we found ourselves in a quieter hallway.

Ari leaned against the wall, his trademark grin on full display. He'd lost his shirt somewhere along the way and I took him in, admiring for a second the Blake tattoo etched across his sculpted chest.

He looked so ridiculously hot. I could feel my body softening from just staring at him, my pussy getting wet and ready to be fucked. I wanted him any way I could have him.

"Is my baby feeling needy?" he purred as he pushed me against the wall.

I nodded as I slowly pulled up my jersey, but Ari grabbed my hand before I could get it off.

"I want to take you just in this," he whispered gruffly, and I nodded, shivering in anticipation. His hands reached under the hem of the jersey and pulled down my leggings, taking my thong with them. I held onto his shoulders as I stepped out of the clothes, the cool air making me well aware I was naked from the waist down. His gaze took me in and he pulled me towards him, grabbing my chin and angling my face as he pressed a hot, searing kiss on my lips.

My fingers dragged down his chest, and he bit down on my bottom lip as my nails sank into his skin. The hand that had been holding my jaw trailed down, holding onto my neck in a possessive, erotic grip while his other hand covered my breast through the jersey, gently squeezing and kneading at it. He leaned towards me, his hot tongue licking along the shell of my ear.

"All mine," he growled as his lips moved down my skin, stopping on my pulse point where he gently licked and sucked at my flesh.

"Ari," I whimpered.

"Shhh, sunshine. That's a good girl. I'm going to take such good care of you."

I heard something then, as Ari's tongue continued to slide across my skin, a slow, exquisite torture I never wanted to end.

Turning my head towards the direction of the sound, I

froze because one of the last people on earth I would've expected was standing at the end of the hall, staring at us.

It was Clark.

He'd still been texting me constantly, but I'd blocked his number—for real. I didn't want anything to do with the past. The therapist that I'd started going to had helped me work through the guilt I felt when it came to Clark. I didn't have to stay with someone out of guilt. I could understand that now thanks to weekly sessions. Clark may have been my past, but Ari was my past *and* my future.

Clark's gaze glittered in the darkness, and maybe it was the alcohol, or maybe it was just that I was tired of reminders from a past I'd finally let go.

But I didn't tell Ari he was there.

I suddenly wanted to make a point, just like Ari would have wanted.

That I didn't belong to my past or my guilt or anything else.

I belonged to Ari.

And I was all about that.

I didn't say anything as Ari turned me around and bent me forward so my ass was presented to him.

I didn't say anything as he lined our bodies up, slowly rolling his hard cock through my folds, getting the shaft nice and wet. His hand slid between my legs, massaging my clit with the perfect amount of pressure.

"Mine," he murmured as his other hand fucked into my core. "This cunt. It's ruined me."

I grabbed his dick. "Mine," I said back, my tone confident and possessive... His gaze lit up with amusement. I glanced at Clark over Ari's shoulder, so he would know that I meant it. His face was pale and shocked...and devastated.

I closed my eyes as Ari's fingers pressed and rubbed at

that spot inside me, and I came on his talented hands, arching and moving against him like we were fucking already.

"Most fucking gorgeous girl ever," he groaned.

I glanced down the hall, and Clark was *still* standing there for some reason. Obviously he hadn't gotten the memo yet.

Ari turned me around, his hands gripping my ass as he once again slid his pierced dick through my sopping wet folds. The friction sent another tiny orgasm fluttering through my insides. I was much louder than I would usually be because I wanted Clark to know that Ari made me feel things that he *never* could.

In the back of my mind, I was well aware that I'd lost it, that what I was doing was unnecessary. Cruel, actually.

But I wanted to give Ari what he always gave me. Complete and unrelenting devotion. I felt like this was my chance to prove I was all in, even if Ari was unaware of what I was doing.

His mouth claimed mine in a deep, hungry kiss, and I eagerly sucked on his tongue, whimpering with the need I had for his dick to be inside of me.

"Ari, please," I begged, loving the hot smile he gave me because he fucking loved when I begged for him.

"I've got you, baby," he promised. My eyes were heavy lidded as they ran over his flawless, muscled chest. Everything about him was designed to be my personal wet dream. I wanted to get on my knees to worship him. I glanced at Clark, frozen in place. I'd never had that desire with him.

Ari sucked on my neck, hard enough that he for sure was leaving a love spot. I loved when he marked me. I actually loved when he covered me with his cum too. Every day stoked the fires of both of our obsessions.

And it wasn't because I was drunk. Sober me felt like this as well. Like I couldn't get enough. Like I never would.

He rubbed his glistening head through my folds once

more and then he plunged into me, sucking my tongue greedily and capturing the relieved whimpers that were streaming out of my mouth.

"Yes, so fucking good," he groaned as he slammed in and out of me. That ring, that fucking wedding ring embedded into the head of his dick, hit the entrance to my womb every time, sending small spikes of pain and pleasure shooting through me. Ari expertly angled his hips, hitting different places and making me scream.

"So perfect. I'll never get enough of this cunt, Blake. Mine."

An orgasm was building inside of me. Again. And I bit down into his chest, trying to stave it off because it felt so intense.

"Do it for me, sunshine. Choke my cock with your sweet pussy."

His dirty words sent me over the edge and I was coming, setting him off too. His thrusts became erratic, and he groaned loudly as his warm seed spilled into me.

"Fuck," he said, burying his face in my neck, like he always did. We stayed there, connected like that for a long minute, before I remembered that we'd had a visitor.

When I peered down the hall though, Clark was gone.

Sick satisfaction slid through my veins, like a sinuous poison. It felt so good to have Ari claim me like that.

I had a feeling that Clark wouldn't be back, that the message had successfully been sent.

Ari Lancaster had ruined me.

There was no room for anyone else. I didn't want anyone else.

Ari pulled out and we both groaned, his fingers immediately going between my thighs, pushing the cum back in that had spilled out. He did that almost every time we had sex, like he couldn't bear for any of *him* to come out of me.

"I didn't know you were so into exhibitionism, sunshine," he murmured, and I froze, even as his fingers sank into me.

I stared up at him, afraid I'd see anger or maybe even disgust.

But all I saw was hot male satisfaction.

"I think you made the point quite nicely, Blake. And any time you want to fuck me to prove a point, I'm your man," he whispered.

I blushed and he growled as he bit down on my neck, before licking away the pain.

"Just as long as I'm your man all the other times too."

"Always," I murmured.

And I'd never meant something more.

CHAPTER 28

ARI

We lost in the first round. And even though I'd expected it, it still hurt like hell. I'd stressed for days, waiting to hear if Dallas was interested in getting me back. And when the call came from my agent, assuring me that the Knights were ready to do whatever it took to bring both Walker and me on board, it felt like a million pound bowling ball had been lifted off my chest. Now I just had to do the long wait until July to make it official when free agency kicked off.

I felt guilty that the Cobras would be losing us both, an unfamiliar feeling to be sure. They had been good to me, and I knew they wanted me to sign a contract to stay on—they'd been hounding Remi's phone every day.

My path was set though, just like it had been all those years ago when I'd met Blake. Some things were just meant to be.

And me playing with Linc in Dallas was one of them.

But there was a lot of time between now and July, and today, I only had one thing on my mind…proposing to Blake.

Yes, she was already my wife. And no, that was never going to change.

But I hadn't exactly proposed last time, so I'd planned something special tonight at the Griffith Observatory.

I didn't know why I was so fucking nervous. There was only one answer she could give me tonight.

I already had that girl locked down.

But I wanted to do this for her, and I wanted it to be perfect.

Blake

Ari was always surprising me, so when he mentioned he had something special planned for the night, I hadn't thought twice about it. Or at least he hadn't given me a chance to think twice about it. We'd been in bed all afternoon, and I'd had so many orgasms I was having trouble remembering my name.

We drove through the winding roads, finally heading up a steep hill before I realized where we were going.

"The Griffith Observatory?" I asked, sitting up in my seat to stare at the scene in front of us. It was one of those tourist things that I should have done already, but I hadn't ever set aside time. The observatory itself was a majestic sight, perched atop a hill, commanding a breathtaking view of the city below.

We parked the car and made our way up the steps to the entrance. The architecture was awe-inspiring, a blend of Art Deco and modern design that was both elegant and timeless.

Inside, we explored the fascinating exhibits, all about astronomy and the universe.

"You know a lot more about astronomy than I would expect," I mused as Ari pointed out pictures of various constellations and celestial objects as we strolled through the halls.

"Mmmh, for some reason, I caught the stargazing bug when I was young…and it never quite went away," he said with a wink.

I raised an eyebrow, but then a shot of a black hole caught my eye and I forgot what he'd said.

But the real surprise awaited us outside. As we reached the observatory's rooftop, the night sky stretched out above us, its velvet glory sprinkled with a million twinkling stars. Ari had arranged for someone to set up a cozy little spot with blankets and cushions, complete with a high-quality telescope pointed at the heavens.

I turned to him with a curious smile, my heart skipping a beat. "Are we going stargazing?"

Ari's eyes sparkled in the moonlight as he nodded. "We are," he said quietly.

As I settled down on the cushions, Ari adjusted the telescope, and I took everything in. The soft glow of city lights below us, the serenity of the night, and the promise of countless stars above painted a picture of sheer perfection.

He laid down beside me and we stared into the night sky, our fingers entangled together.

"I loved you from the moment I saw you," he murmured suddenly, and my breath skipped as I turned my head away from the sparkling heavens, and towards his face…where the view was even better.

"Really?"

He turned to gaze at me too, his hand coming up to stroke my cheek. "Twelve years old and I was done. Finished. I'd found what I wanted forever. It would seem silly if someone else told me that. But it happened to me."

I grabbed his hand to still it, and rubbed my cheek against his rough palm.

I'd always associated that group home with the start of everything bad that had happened to me. But I'd recently realized through therapy how much good there'd been too. I'd lost Ari there. But I'd also found him too. And that was how I was going to start thinking about that.

"I haven't gone stargazing since I left the group home," I murmured, frowning. "I think it hurt too much, because I associated it...with you."

"I was a cheesy fucker back then, wasn't I?" he grinned, and I snorted, bringing his hand from my face to my chest so I could snuggle against it.

"You're *still* a cheesy fucker. But I love it," I said, leaning forward to give him a kiss.

"Ari, do you think I'm going to be sad forever?"

Words from the past hit me hard.

"Blake, are you alright?" Ari asked, and I realized I'd been hovering above his lips...not saying anything.

"I'm not sad anymore," I whispered.

"What?"

"I'm not sad anymore. We were stargazing as little kids and I asked you if you thought it would last forever. And all this time...it has. But it's gone now." Tears slipped down my cheeks. "You did it."

He studied me, so much love in his gaze that it was hard to breathe.

"I don't think I can take all the credit, sunshine," he said gently.

And it was crazy that that was true.

Since that day where I'd started to take control of my life...I hadn't cut and I hadn't purged...I hadn't even weighed myself. I'd told myself "I was perfect" every single day in the mirror...whether Ari was inside me or not.

I'd gone to therapy every week faithfully, even when it sucked, or it hurt.

I had shown up for myself *every* day.

And of course, Ari had showed up for me too.

He was beaming as we stared at each other. There was no one more proud of me than him.

But it was even better that *I* was finally proud of myself too.

He pushed up from the cushions, his face paling a bit as he stared down at me. "Just to let you know, we're already married. And we're staying that way."

I gazed up at him, confused, before I sat up too, kneeling with him. "What? What's wrong?"

He pulled a violet colored, brocade box out of his pocket and opened it, revealing a diamond encrusted wedding band, one that would fit perfectly with the huge rock that hadn't left my finger since we'd reunited.

"Oh, Ari–"

"Blake, as you're well aware, you're already my wife. But I've had a speech planned since the moment I saw you on that billboard, how I was going to ask you to marry me. And I didn't get the chance to say it..."

He grinned, because he knew as well as I did, that was the understatement of the century for what had happened that night.

Ari went on unrepentantly, and I shook my head in amusement.

"So we're doing a redo tonight...if that's alright."

I nodded, already emotional, because I loved him so freaking much.

"Sunshine. I fucking love you. I'm obsessed with you. You're all I see. You're my past, my future...you're every-thing. I saw you at twelve years old, Blake, and my soul recognized you. Realized you belonged to me. In every circumstance, in every life...I would have found you. I know that, with every fiber in my being."

"Ari," I whispered, the world blurring from my tears–it was just so nice that they were actually happy ones for once.

"I made you a promise once, that I would spend the rest of my life making you happy. And even though you're doing a damn fine job of doing that yourself...it will still be my honor to ensure all your dreams come true. So, Mrs. Lancaster..."

I giggled, because it was a little odd to have a marriage proposal when you already had the groom. And his last name.

"And please remember, you only have one real option for your response," he reminded me as he pulled the band from the box and reached for my finger. "Will you do me the honor of letting me make you happy for the rest of our lives?"

He slipped the band on my finger so it fit against my other ring.

"Yes. A thousand, million times yes," I cried as I fell into his arms.

He made love to me after that, beneath a sky laced with glittering, hopeful stars...courtesy of paid off staff that knew the area was off limits while we had the place.

And I knew I was the luckiest girl in the world.

Nine months ago, I'd been in the wrong life with the wrong guy.

And I hadn't realized any of it.

Ari Lancaster was proof that miracles–and soulmates–existed. And I said a thank you to the heavens every night that he'd seen that billboard that day and moved heaven and earth to find me.

Every tear, every cut, every ache. It had somehow brought us here.

And as the great Taylor Swift said, *all's well that ends well to end up with...*

The pucking right guy.

A night out with the boys in D Town...only beat by a night out with my girl.

Walker had said he had something really important to say to the "circle of trust." So here we were—Lincoln and I checking our phones every few minutes to make sure our ladies were still together at my house.

"I have some exciting news!" Walker said as soon as we'd ordered our wings.

"Give it to us, Disney," I drawled as I stuffed some chips and queso in my mouth. This place was the bomb.

Lincoln went for a chip and I stabbed him with a fork. "I ordered all of this for myself. I've got months to make up for."

"Why didn't you tell me that?" he snarled, going to dip his chip again in my nectar of the gods.

"I will stab you again. And then you won't be able to hold your stick. Of any kind."

"Monroe will hold my stick," Lincoln said cockily, and I pretended to throw up.

"I'm going to be a daddy," Walker suddenly announced proudly.

I choked on my chip, hacking and coughing while Lincoln stared at the two of us like we were embarrassing him.

"Sorry. What was that? Are we talking about sex kinks right now? Because I need to prepare myself before I think about some puck bunny calling you "daddy."'" Lincoln scooped up some queso while I was trying to breathe.

"No, I mean a real dad," Walker grinned, neither of them seeming to care at all that I'd almost CHOKED TO DEATH!

"Okay…Walker. And are you adopting? Because I haven't seen any ladies around, and I know you were taught better than to not double wrap when it comes to those stage five clingers."

"It's a new thing. But you'll meet her soon," Walker said happily.

"So you got a one night stand pregnant?" I asked, still very confused.

"Naw. She's the love of my life."

Lincoln and I glanced at each other, twin grins on our faces. Because we were big fans of true love nowadays.

"What's her name? Is she excited about the baby?" Lincoln asked as he reached for one of my chips. I smacked his hand away. I did not share queso and chips. Not even with my bestie.

I forgot all about my monopoly of the chip tray though, with Walker's next words.

"She will be excited," he mused as he snagged one of my chips and started happily munching on it.

His chewing took fucking forever as Lincoln and I just stared at him incredulously. Finally, he was done.

He grinned at us both and said… "When she finds out…"

Read Walker's story in The Pucking Wrong Date here.

.

THE PUCKING WRONG GUY BONUS SCENE

Want more Ari and Blake? Come hang out in my Fated Realm for an exclusive BONUS scene!

https://www.facebook.com/groups/C.R.FatedRealm

THE PUCKING WRONG DATE

Want to read Walker's standalone story? Preorder The Pucking Wrong Date

http://books2read.com/thepuckingwrongdate

THE PUCKING WRONG NUMBER EXCERPT

Curious about Lincoln Daniel's red flags...keep reading for his story in The Pucking Wrong Number...

PROLOGUE
MONROE

"Monroe. My pretty little girl," Mama slurs from the couch. She's staring up at the ceiling, and even though she's saying my name, I know she's not talking to me. Or at least the me that's standing right here, scrubbing at the vomit stain she left on the floor. She's talking to the me from the past, or wherever it is her brain takes her when she's high as a kite.

There's a knock on the door, and I glance at it fearfully, dread churning through my insides. Because I know who it is. One of her "customers" as Mama calls them.

The door opens without either of us saying anything. I'm not sure Mama even heard the knock. In steps a sweaty, pale-faced man that I've seen once or twice before. He has rosy cheeks and a belly that protrudes over his jeans. Like a perverse Santa Claus. Not that I believe in that guy anymore. He's certainly never come to our place on Christmas Eve.

The man's eyes gleam as he stares at me, but then Mama groans in a weird way, and his attention goes to her.

"Roxanne," he says in a sing-song voice as he makes his way over there.

I want to say something. Anything. Tell him that Mama's in no shape for company, but I know it's no use. Besides,

Mama would be furious with me later on if she missed out on the money she needs to get her fix.

I leave the room and lock myself in the one bedroom we have in this place. Mama and I share the room, but more often than not, she can't make it any further than the couch.

The disgusting noises I've learned to hate start, so I turn on the radio, trying to drown them out. I fall into a fitful sleep, and my dreams are haunted by the image of a healthy mother that cares more about me than she does about escaping the life she created.

I wake with a start, panic blurring the edges of the room until I can convince my brain that everything's fine.

Except everything doesn't feel fine. It's so quiet. Way too quiet.

I creep towards the door, pressing my ear against it to see if I can hear anything.

But there's nothing.

I slowly open the door and peek out into the room. There's no sign of the man, or my mother. Thinking the coast is clear, I make my way out of my room, only to come to a screeching halt when I see my mother on the ground by the front door, a pile of green liquid by her face.

I sigh, thinking of the clean-up ahead. Again. I hate these men. Every time they come here, they take a piece of her, while leaving her with nothing. It's always like this after they're done with her.

When I walk over with a rag and bucket, I see Mama is shaking, tears streaming down her face. She's a scary gray color I don't think I've ever seen before.

"Mama," I whisper, reaching down to touch her face, only to flinch at how icy cold her skin is. Her eyes suddenly shoot open, causing me to jump. They're even more bloodshot than normal. Her bony hand claws at my shirt, and she frantically pulls me closer to her. Her lip is bruised and bloody. The bastard must've gotten rough.

"Don't let 'em taze your heart," she slurs, incomprehensibly.

"Mama?" I ask, worry thick in my voice.

"Don't...let a man...take your heart," she spits out. "Don't let him..." Her words fade away and her chest rises with one big inhale...before she goes perfectly still.

"Mama!" I whimper, shaking her over and over again.

But she never says another word. She's just gone, like a flame extinguished in a dark room.

And I'm all alone, with her last words forever ringing in my ears.

CHAPTER 1

MONROE

I sat on the edge of my bed, staring out the window into the dark, seemingly starless sky. Freedom was so close I could taste it.

18.

It felt like I'd been waiting my whole life for this moment. For this specific birthday. The thought of finally being able to leave this place, to start my life, on my own terms…it helped get me through each day.

I knew it would be difficult when I left. I only had my scrimpy savings from my after school job at the grocery store to start my life. But I'd do whatever it took to make something of myself.

Something more than the empty shell my mother had left me that day.

I'd been in the foster system since I was ten years old, the day after that fateful night where I'd lost her. Everyone wanted to adopt a baby, and a baby I had not been. I'd gone through what seemed like a hundred different homes at this point, but my current home was where I'd managed to stay the longest.

Unfortunately.

My foster parents, Mr. and Mrs. Detweiler, and their son Ripley, seemed like nice people at first, but over time, things had changed. They were different now.

Mrs. Detweiler, Marie, had come to think of me as her live-in maid. I was all for helping out around the house, but when they got up as a collective group after every meal and left everything to me to clean up–as well as every other chore around the house–it was too much.

Someday, hopefully in the near future, I would never clean someone else's toilet again.

While I could deal with manual labor for another month, it was Mr. Detweiler, Todd, who had become a major problem. His actions had grown increasingly creepy, his longing stares and lingering glances making me sick. Everything he said to me had an underlying meaning...was an innuendo. He'd started talking about my birthday more, like he wanted to remind me of it for reasons far different than the promise of freedom it represented to me. I'm not sure it had even occurred to any of them yet that I was actually allowed to leave after that day. Both my birthday and high school graduation were the same week. Perfect timing. I just hoped he could control himself and keep his hands off me long enough to get to that point. Some people might not think a high school graduation was anything special, but to me, it represented *everything*.

Ripley was fine, I guess. He was more like a potato than a person, which was better than other things he could be. His eyes skipped over me when we were in the same room, like I didn't actually exist. And maybe I didn't exist to him. As long as his bed was made every day, and he had food on the table, and toilet paper stocked to wipe his ass, he could care less. He was much too involved in his video games to care about the world around him.

I glanced at the clock. It was 4:55pm, time to get dinner

started before Mr. Detweiler got home from work. Sighing, I absentmindedly smoothed my faded quilt that Mrs. Detweiler had brought home from who knows where, and headed out to the hallway and down to the kitchen. The house was a three bedroom rambler in an okay part of town. It was nicer than other places I'd stayed, but I'd found that didn't matter all that much. The hearts beating inside the home held a much greater significance than how nice, or not nice, the house actually was.

I'm sure I could have been perfectly happy in the hovel I'd started life in with my mother…if only she'd been different.

I came to a screeching halt, and panic laced my insides, when I walked into the kitchen and saw Mr. Detweiler leaning against the laminate counter. How had I missed him coming into the house? I couldn't recall hearing the garage door opening.

He was nursing his favorite bottle of beer, which was actually the fanciest thing in the kitchen, costing far more than any of the other food they bought. Todd Detweiler was still dressed in the baggy suit he wore to the accounting office he worked at. He had a receding hairline that rivaled any I'd seen, so he brushed all the hair forward, carefully styling it to a point on his forehead right above his watery blue eyes.

He raised an eyebrow at the fact I was still frozen in place. But he usually didn't get home until 6:30, long enough for me to get dinner on the table and hide away until they were done.

"Well, hello there, Monroe," he drawled, my name sounding dirty coming from his lips.

I schooled my face and steeled my insides, taking methodical steps towards the fridge like his presence hadn't disarmed me.

"Hello," I answered pleasantly, hating the way I could feel

his gaze stroking across my skin. Like I was an object to be coveted rather than a person.

I knew I was pretty. The spitting image of my mother when she was young. But just like with her, my looks had only been a curse, forever designed to attract assholes whose only goal was to use and abuse me.

I reached into the fridge to grab the bowl of chicken I'd put in there earlier to defrost...when suddenly he was behind me. Close enough that if I moved, he'd be pressed against me.

"Is there something you need?" I asked, trying to keep the edge of hysteria out of my voice. His hand settled on my hip and I squeezed my eyes shut, cursing the universe.

He leaned close, his breath a whisper against my skin. "You've been thinking about it, haven't you?" Todd's breath stunk of beer, a smell that would prevent me from ever trying it, no matter how expensive and nice it was supposed to be.

"I—I'm not sure what you're talking about, sir." I grabbed the chicken and tried to stand , hoping he would back away. But the only thing he did was straighten up, so our bodies were against each other. I tried to move away, but his hand squeezed against my hip. Hard.

"I need to get this chicken on the stove," I said pleasantly, like I wasn't dying inside at the feel of his touch.

"Such a tease," he murmured with a small chuckle. "I love how you like to play games. Just going to make it so much better when we stop." There was a bulge growing harder against my lower back, and I bit down on my lip hard enough that the salty tang of blood flooded my taste buds.

My hands were shaking, the water sloshing around in the bowl. An idiot could figure out what he was talking about.

"Have you noticed how much I love to collect things?" he asked randomly, finally releasing my hip and stepping back.

I moved quickly towards the sink, setting the bowl inside

and going to grab the breadcrumbs I needed to coat the chicken breasts with for dinner.

"I have noticed that," I finally responded, after he'd taken a step towards me when I didn't answer fast enough.

How could anyone miss it? Todd collected...beer bottles. Both walls of the garage had various cans and bottles lined up neatly on shelves. There were so many of them that you could barely see the wall—not sure how social services never seemed concerned he might have a drinking problem with that amount of empties. But Todd was never worried about that. He added at least five to the wall every day.

"Virgins happen to be my favorite thing to collect."

I'd been holding a carton of eggs, and I dropped them, shocked that he'd outright said that, shells and yolk ricocheting everywhere.

Just then, Mrs. Detweiler ambled in, her gaze flicking between her husband and me suspiciously. "What's going on in here?" she asked, her eyes stopping on the ruined eggs all over the floor.

Marie had once been a pretty woman, but like her husband, her attempt to hold onto youth was a miserable failure. Right now, she was wearing a too tight flowered dress that resembled a couch from the eighties. It accented every roll, and there was a fine sheen of sweat across her heavily made up face, probably from the effort she'd had to make to get out of her armchair and storm in here. Her hair was a harsh, bottle-black color, and though she attempted to curl and keep it nice, it was thin and limp and I'm sure disappointing for her.

I usually didn't pay attention to looks; I knew better than most they could be deceiving, but Todd and Marie Detweiler's appearances were too in your face to ignore.

"Just an accident, honey," he drawled, walking towards her and pulling her into a soul sickening kiss that made me want to puke considering Marie most likely had no idea where else that mouth had been.

They walked out of the kitchen without a backward glance, leaving me a shaking, miserable mess as I cleaned up the eggs and tried to make dinner.

If that interaction hadn't sealed the deal that waiting for my birthday to leave wasn't an option...the next night would.

I was in bed, tossing and turning as I did every night. When your mind was as haunted as mine was, sleep was elusive, a fervent goal I would never successfully master. I'd never had a night where I could relax, where the memories of the past didn't creep in and plague my thoughts.

It was 3 am, and I was on the verge of giving up if I couldn't fall back asleep soon.

Light footsteps sounded down the hallway by my door. I frowned, as everyone had gone to bed long ago. I knew their habits like they were my own at this point.

Was someone in the house? Someone who didn't belong?

The footsteps stopped outside my door, and shivers crept up my spine.

"Hello?" I whisper squeaked, feeling like a fool for speaking at all when the doorknob tried to turn, getting caught on the lock I was lucky enough to have.

I felt like the would-be victim in a horror movie as I slid out of bed and yanked my lamp from the nightstand, prepared to use it as a weapon if need be.

The person outside fiddled with the lock and it clicked, signaling it had been disengaged.

There was a long pause as I stared breathlessly at the door, waiting for the inevitable.

The door creaked open and a hairy hand—that I recognized—appeared.

It was Mr. Detweiler's.

I didn't think, I just started screaming, knowing I had one chance to get him away from my room.

I needed to wake up his wife. With their bedroom right down the hall, I just needed to be loud enough.

Sure enough, a second after I started screaming, the door banged shut, and footsteps dashed away. A moment later, I heard the Detweilers' bedroom door fly open, and then a moment after that, my door cracked against the wall and Marie's harried form was there. Her chest was heaving, pushing against the two sizes too small negligee she was wearing–that made me want to burn my eyes–and her gaze was crazed as they dashed around the room, finally falling to me standing there in the middle of it, a lamp clutched to my chest.

A red mottled rash spread across her chest and up to her cheeks as anger flooded her features.

"What the fuck is wrong with you?"

"Someone was trying to get into my room. Someone unlocked the door."

I didn't say it was her husband, because that would give me even more problems.

A moment later, Todd was there, faking a yawn with a glass of water in his hand. "What's going on?" he asked casually. Our eyes locked, and in that moment, he knew I knew it was him. His features were taunting, daring me to say something, like his wife would ever believe anything that came out of my mouth when it came to him.

"The girl's saying someone was breaking into her room," Marie scoffed before pausing for a second and examining her husband. "Why were you up?"

The way her lips were pursed, the way her flush deepened—it told me a lot. Apparently, Marie wasn't so unaware of her husband's true nature after all.

Not that she would ever do anything about it.

"I was getting some water when I heard Monroe scream. But I didn't hear anyone else in the house." His gaze feigned concern. "Are you sure you didn't just have a nightmare?"

I stared at him for a long, tense moment before I took a breath. "Maybe that's all it was," I finally whispered, eliciting a loud huff from Marie.

"Get yourself under control, you brat. The rest of us need our sleep!" she snapped, whirling away and leaving, curses streaming from her mouth as she walked back to her room.

Todd lingered, a smug grin curling across his pathetic lips. "Sleep well, Monroe," he purred, a firm promise in his eyes that he would be back.

And that he would finish what he started.

I fell to my knees as soon as the door closed, sobs wracking through my body.

I'd never felt so alone.

He had ruined everything. A month away from a high school diploma, and he'd just torn it from my grasp.

If Todd got his hands on me, he would break me. And I wasn't talking about my body–I was talking about my soul.

The image of my mother's desolate, destroyed features flashed through my mind.

That couldn't be my story. It couldn't.

I had to leave. Tomorrow. I had no other option.

———

The Detweilers lived in a small town right outside Houston. I decided Dallas would be my destination, about four hours away. I'd never been there before, but the ticket price wasn't too bad, and it was big. Just what I needed to hopefully disappear. Surely the Detweilers wouldn't try and go that far, not with only a month left of state support on the line. I bet they wouldn't even tell anyone I was gone. They'd want that last check.

I didn't let myself think about what my virginity would be worth to Todd. Hopefully, "easy" was one of his requisites, and he would forget me as soon as I disappeared.

I went to school, my heart hurting the whole day. I'd never been one to make close friends—when you never knew when you'd be moving on, it was best not to make any close connections—but I found myself wishing I had longer with the acquaintances I did have. I walked the familiar hallways, wondering if it would have been hard to say goodbye at graduation, or if I was simply feeling the loss of my dream.

Mama had never graduated from high school. In her lucid moments, though, even when I was little, she would sometimes talk about her dreams for me. Dreams of walking across that stage.

I'd just have to walk across a college stage, I told myself firmly, promising myself I'd get a GED and make that possible.

After school, I went to the H.E.B. grocery store where I worked, putting even more hustle in than usual since I'd be a disappearing act after this shift. The timing worked out, because it was payday, and I was able to get one more check to take with me. Every penny would count.

After my shift, I bought a prepaid phone since I didn't want to take my Detweiler phone with me. Knowing them, they'd probably try and get the police to bring me back by saying I'd stolen their property. A part of me was a little afraid they could track me with it too. I knew I wasn't living in a spy thriller...but still, better to be safe than sorry.

Once I got home, I packed a small bag with some clothes, my new phone, and the cash I'd saved up. And then I sat on my bed, hands squeezing together with anxiety.

I didn't have a good plan. For as much as I'd been

dreaming of getting away, my plans were more fluid than concrete. And all of them had depended on me having a high school diploma so I could get a better job, as well as not having to look over my shoulder every second for fear the Detweilers were after me. The state also had a support system for kids coming out of foster care, and I'd been hopeful I'd have that to lean on.

But I could do this.

I cleaned up after dinner. Marie had ordered pizza, so it didn't take as much effort as usual. And then I sat in the corner of the living room, biding my time until I could say goodnight. It was a tricky thing. I had to escape tonight–late enough that they'd gone to bed, but not so late that Todd decided to give me another late night visit.

My departure was the definition of anticlimactic. My mind had conjured this image of the Detweilers running after me as I escaped with my bag out the window, the sound of a siren haunting the air as I ducked in and out of the bushes, trying to avoid the police.

But what really happened was that I slipped out the window, and everyone stayed asleep. I walked for an hour until I got to the Greyhound station, and no one came after me. The exhausted-looking attendant didn't even blink when I bought a ticket to Dallas.

It was nice for something to go my way every once in a blue moon.

The bus ride took twice as long as a car would have. And although I tried to catch a few hours of rest, I kept worrying I'd somehow miss my stop, so I never could slip into a deep sleep. My mind also couldn't help but race with thoughts of what my future held. Would I be able to make it on my own?

Despite my worries, a sense of relief flickered in my chest as the distance between Todd and me grew with each mile that passed.

At least I could cross keeping my virginity safe off my list of to-do's.

When we finally arrived in Dallas, the morning sun was just peeking over the horizon. Even with the dilapidated buildings that surrounded the Greyhound station, I couldn't help but feel excitement. I was here. I'd made it. I may have never been to Dallas before, and I may not have known a single soul here, but I was determined to make a new life for myself.

This was my new beginning.

———

It took about twelve hours for the afterglow of my arrival to fade and for me to find myself on a park bench, debating whether I could actually fall asleep if I were to try. Or if it was even safe to attempt such a thing.

I'd gotten off the bus and was in the process of calling for a cab to take me to the teen shelter I'd found online. And then I'd been fucking pick pocketed while I looked the address up. They'd taken all the cash in my pocket that I'd pulled out for the cab, and swiped my phone right out of my hand.

You can bet I ran after them like a madwoman. But with a backpack containing all my earthly possessions weighing me down, the group of boys easily outran me.

I hadn't dared to spend any of the rest of the cash I had left, except to get a bag of chips from a gas station that had seen better days.

I'd walked all over for the rest of the day, trying to find the shelter, scared to ask for directions in case anyone got suspicious and reported to the authorities that I looked like a runaway teen.

Obviously, I never found the place, because there I was, on the park bench. Cold, hungry, and pissed off.

And exhausted.

Apparently, when you hadn't slept for close to forty-eight hours, you could fall asleep anywhere, because eventually… that's exactly what I did.

———

I woke with a start, the feeling of someone watching me thick in my throat. Night had fallen, and a deep blue hue had settled over the park. The trees and bushes were indistinct shadows against the darkened sky. The street lamps had flickered to life, casting a warm glow on the path and the nearby benches. The light danced and swayed with the gentle breeze, casting long shadows on the ground. You could hear the rustling of leaves and the chirping of crickets.

I yelped when I saw a grizzled old man sitting next to me on the bench, a wildness in his gaze that matched the tattered clothing on his body. There was the scent of dirt and body odor wafting off him, and when he smiled at me, it was only with a few teeth.

"Oy. I've been a watchin'. Making sure you could sleep, my lady," he said in what was clearly an affected British accent.

I flinched at his words, even though they were perfectly friendly and kind, and scooted away from him.

"Oh, don't be afraid of Ole Bill. I'll watch out for ye."

I moved to jump off the bench and run away…but I also had a moment of hesitation. There was something so…wholesome about him. Once you got past his looks and his smell, obviously.

"This park's mine, but I can share. You go back to sleep, and I'll keep watch. Make sure the ruffians stay away," he continued. Even though I had yet to say anything to him.

I opened my mouth to reject his offer, but then he pulled a

clean, brand new blanket with tags out of his grocery sack. When he offered it to me...instead of talking...I found myself crying.

I sobbed and sobbed while he watched me frantically, throwing the blanket at me like it had the power to quell hysterical women's tears. When I still didn't stop crying, overwhelmed by the events of the past few days...and his kindness, he finally started to sing what I think was the worst rendition of "Eleanor Rigby" that I'd ever heard. Actually, it was the worst rendition of *any* song I'd ever heard.

But it worked, and I stopped crying.

"There, there, little duck. Go to sleep. Ole Bill will watch out for ya," he said soothingly after he'd finished the song—the last few lyrics definitely made up.

I was a smarter girl than that, I really was. But I was so freaking tired. And everything inside of me really wanted to trust him. After all, he had called me "little duck." Serial killers didn't have cute pet names for their victims, right?

"Just a couple of minutes," I murmured, and he nodded, smiling softly again with his crooked grin that I was quite fond of at that moment.

I drifted off into a fitful sleep, shivering from stress and exhaustion, and dreaming of better days.

When I woke up, it was far later than ten minutes. It was the rest of the night, actually.

Bill was still there, watching over me, and whistling softly to himself, like he hadn't just stayed up all night. My backpack was still under my head, the cash still in it, and at least I didn't *feel* like anyone had touched me.

Fuck, I'd gotten desperate, hadn't I?

"Do you have a place to stay, lassie?" he asked softly. I shook my head, biting down on my lip as I thought about spending another night on this bench.

"Ole Bill will take you to a good place. It's not as nice as my castle, but it will do," he said, gesturing to the park proudly as if it was in fact an English castle complete with a moat, and he was its ruler.

Despite the fact that he'd at least proven trustworthy enough not to do anything to me after a few hours, it was still pure desperation that had me following him to what I was hoping wasn't a trafficking ring, or something else equally heinous.

I relaxed a little as he took me to a slightly better part of town than where I'd been walking the day before. He chattered my ear off, all in that fake British accent, regaling me with stories about places I was sure he'd never visited.

Before I knew it, we were standing in front of the entrance to what appeared to be a fairly new shelter. The sign read that it was a women's shelter, and the sight made me want to cry once again.

"When you get in there, tell 'em Ole Bill sent you...they'll give you the royal treatment," he chortled, and tears filled my eyes for what seemed like the hundredth time—causing him to take a step away–probably fearing I would burst into hysterics again.

I hesitated for another moment before I finally ascended the steps that led to the shelter doors. Stopping halfway, I glanced back at Bill, who gave me another charmingly snaggletoothed grin. "I see great things for you, little duck," he called after me when I continued to walk.

I knew I'd never forget him. He may have been homeless and slightly crazy, but he was also one of the kindest people I had ever met. He'd watched over me, a stranger, and helped me when I needed it the most.

As I walked inside, exhaustion still stretched across my shoulders, I strangely felt at peace right then that everything was going to work out.

"Welcome to Haven," a kind woman murmured as I approached the front desk.

Haven indeed.

I could only hope.

Continue Monroe and Lincoln's store here.

Ari's Carne Asada Tacos

INGREDIENTS

FOR THE CARNE ASADA

1 1/2 TO 2 POUNDS FLANK STEAK
5 GARLIC CLOVES, MINCED
1 LIME, JUICED
1 ORANGE, JUICED
1 JALAPEÑO, CORED AND FINELY MINCED (OPTIONAL)
1/2 CUP FINELY-CHOPPED FRESH CILANTRO
1/4 CUP AVOCADO OIL (OR OLIVE OIL)
1 TEASPOON CHILI POWDER
1 TEASPOON GROUND CUMIN
1/2 TEASPOON DRIED OREGANO
COARSE SEA SALT AND BLACK PEPPER, TO TASTE

FOR THE TACOS

1 BATCH CARNE ASADA
12 TO 16 CORN TORTILLAS, HOMEMADE OR STORE-BOUGHT
1 BATCH GUACAMOLE (OR 2 AVOCADOS, SLICED)

TOPPINGS: CHOPPED WHITE ONION, CHOPPED FRESH CILANTRO,
SALSA (RED, GREEN OR PICO DE GALLO), CRUMBLED QUESO
FRESCO, SOUR CREAM, SLICED RADISHES, SLICED JALAPEÑOS

INSTRUCTIONS

MAKE THE CARNE ASADA.

1. MARINATE THE STEAK. PLACE THE FLANK STEAK IN A SHALLOW BAKING DISH, POUR THE MARINADE EVENLY OVER THE STEAK, AND TOSS THE STEAK UNTIL IT IS EVENLY COATED IN THE MARINADE. (ALTERNATELY, YOU CAN COMBINE THE STEAK AND MARINADE IN A LARGE ZIPLOCK AND TOSS TO COAT.) COVER AND REFRIGERATE FOR 2 TO 4 HOURS TO MARINATE.

2. BRING THE STEAK BACK TO ROOM TEMPERATURE. REMOVE THE DISH FROM THE REFRIGERATOR, LIFT THE STEAK OUT OF THE MARINADE AND TRANSFER IT TO A CLEAN PLATE. SEASON EACH SIDE WITH A FEW GENEROUS PINCHES OF SALT AND PEPPER, THEN LET THE STEAK REST FOR 30 MINUTES OR UNTIL IT REACHES ROOM TEMPERATURE.

3. COOK THE STEAK. HEAT AN OUTDOOR GRILL OR INDOOR GRILL PAN (OR CAST-IRON SKILLET OR GRIDDLE) TO HIGH HEAT. COOK THE STEAK FOR 5-7 MINUTES PER SIDE — RESISTING THE URGE TO MOVE THE STEAK AS IT COOKS SO THAT IT CAN SEAR PROPERLY — UNTIL IT REACHES YOUR DESIRED LEVEL OF DONENESS.

4. REST THE STEAK. TRANSFER THE STEAK TO A CLEAN PLATE AND LET IT REST FOR 10 MINUTES, WHICH WILL HELP TO SEAL IN THE JUICES.

5. SLICE/CUT AND SERVE. THEN SLICE THE STEAK AGAINST THE GRAIN AS THICKLY OR THINLY AS YOU PREFER. (OR YOU CAN DICE THE STEAK INTO SMALL PIECES.) THEN SERVE AND ENJOY!

PREPARE THE TOPPINGS. WHILE THE STEAK COOKS, GO AHEAD AND PREPARE THE GUACAMOLE AND WHATEVER OTHER TOPPINGS YOU WOULD LIKE. (IF YOU ARE MAKING HOMEMADE CORN TORTILLAS, YOU CAN ALSO MAKE THOSE WHILE THE STEAK IS MARINATING.)

ASSEMBLE THE TACOS. ONCE THE CARNE ASADA IS COOKED AND HAS RESTED FOR AT LEAST 10 MINUTES, SLICE OR DICE THE STEAK INTO BITE-SIZED PIECES. FILL EACH CORN TORTILLA WITH YOUR DESIRED AMOUNT OF STEAK AND TOPPINGS.

SERVE. THEN SERVE UP THE TACOS IMMEDIATELY AND ENJOY!

ACKNOWLEDGMENTS

I have never felt so deeply for a character. Blake is me. And maybe she's you, and the person next to you. She's the girl you pass in the street with a smile that's not real. She's the friend who doesn't tell you about her depression. She's you when you stare at yourself in the mirror and wish for a different reflection.

I wrote this book during a time of incredible personal turmoil. I cried with Blake every time she cried. And I celebrated Blake every time she healed.

I hope you are past your Blake phase. But I just want you to know that if you aren't...it's okay. The light will come. You can do this.

It's never too late to start again.

Or to heal.

You don't have to stay in the bed you've made.

I'm so thankful to the following people...

Raven Kennedy (aka "Bird"): This book would never have happened without you. Thanks for encouraging me, and challenging me, and offering your perfect insights. You're an angel, baby, pufferface, and I'm so grateful for our friendship. Love you.

Mila: You are always there when I need you and you shine so bright. I love you forever, bestie.

Jessa: Your encouragement and cheerleading was the

voice in my head this book. You are a dream of a bestie. My girl.

Alexis: Thanks for being the perfect voice of Monroe and Blake. Thanks for encouraging me, and uplifting me, and adding your insights. Thanks also for staying up super late to talk. Thanks for being my friend. ILY.

To Crystal: You're always there for me. Your encouragement lifts me up. I adore you.

To Jasmine, my editor, you always come through and you're patient and kind and encouraging. Thank you.

To Summer: I edit the way you do in my dreams just so you know haha. I love you.

To my PA and bff, Caitlin, you pushed me through this. You encourage me every day. The Ari to my Lincoln. ILY.

And to you, the readers who make all my dreams come true. It is a privilege to be able to write these words for you, and I will *never* take you for granted.

BOOKS BY C.R. JANE

www.crjanebooks.com

The Sounds of Us Contemporary Series (complete series)

Remember Us This Way

Remember You This Way

Remember Me This Way

Broken Hearts Academy Series: A Bully Romance (complete duet)

Heartbreak Prince

Heartbreak Lover

Ruining Dahlia (Contemporary Mafia Standalone)

Ruining Dahlia

The Pucking Wrong Series (Hockey Romance Standalones)

The Pucking Wrong Number

The Pucking Wrong Guy

The Pucking Wrong Date

The Fated Wings Series (Paranormal series)

First Impressions

Forgotten Specters

The Fallen One (a Fated Wings Novella)

Forbidden Queens

Frightful Beginnings (a Fated Wings Short Story)

Faded Realms

Faithless Dreams

Fabled Kingdoms

Forever Hearts

The Darkest Curse Series

Forget Me

Lost Passions

Hades Redemption Series

The Darkest Lover

The Darkest Kingdom

Monster & Me Duet Co-write with Mila Young

Monster's Temptation

Monster's Obsession

Academy of Souls Co-write with Mila Young (complete series)

School of Broken Souls

School of Broken Hearts

School of Broken Dreams

School of Broken Wings

Fallen World Series Co-write with Mila Young (complete series)

Bound

Broken

Betrayed

Belong

Thief of Hearts Co-write with Mila Young (complete series)

Darkest Destiny

Stolen Destiny

Broken Destiny

Sweet Destiny

Kingdom of Wolves Co-write with Mila Young

Wild Moon

Wild Heart

Wild Girl

Wild Love

Wild Soul

Wild Kiss

Stupid Boys Series Co-write with Rebecca Royce

Stupid Boys

Dumb Girl

Crazy Love

Breathe Me Duet Co-write with Ivy Fox (complete)

Breathe Me

Breathe You

Breathe Me Duet

Love & Hate Co-write with Ivy Fox

The Boy I Once Hated

The Girl I Once Loved

Rich Demons of Darkwood Series Co-write with May Dawson (complete series)

Make Me Lie

Make Me Beg

Make Me Wild

Make Me Burn

Make Me Queen

ABOUT C.R. JANE

A Texas girl living in Utah now, I'm a wife, mother, lawyer, and now author. My stories have been floating around in my head for years, and it has been a relief to finally get them down on paper. I'm a huge Dallas Cowboys fan and I primarily listen to Beyonce and Taylor Swift...don't lie and say you don't too.

My love of reading started probably when I was three and with a faster than normal ability to read, I've devoured hundreds of thousands of books in my life. It only made sense that I would start to create my own worlds since I was always getting lost in others'.

I like heroines who have to grow in order to become badasses, happy endings, and swoon-worthy, devoted, (and hot) male characters. If this sounds like you, I'm pretty sure we'll be friends.

I'm so glad to have you on my team...check out the links below for ways to hang out with me and more of my books you can read!

Visit my **Facebook** page to get updates.

Visit my **Amazon Author** page.

Visit my **Website**.

Sign up for my **newsletter** to stay updated on new releases, find out random facts about me, and get access to different points of view from my characters.

Printed in Great Britain
by Amazon

41227714R00228